EMBERS OF ETERNITY

BOOK II : HEIRS OF TENEBRIS TRILOGY

BY BRIANNA R. SHAFFERY

Cover and map design by Marcella Thaler

Headshot by Glamour Shots | Photographer: Marko Bulahan | Hair & Makeup: Tatiana Rosa

Publishing Services provided by Paper Raven Books LLC

Printed in the United States of America

First Printing, 2023

Hardcover ISBN: 979-8-9861732-3-8

Paperback ISBN: 979-8-9861732-4-5

*For my grandparents, for their unending support and love,
but more so for their stories and the sacrifices they made to
pave the way for the dreams of those who came after them.*

TABLE OF CONTENTS

MAP OF TENEBRIS
Eurland
Corvus
Sea of Harmony
Shelton Bay
Gossamer
Hart
Woodlane Manor
Covington
Glendale
Caselle
Huntington
Godberd Woods
Mageffery
Union River
Shadow Forest
Halberry
Barrier Plains
Amber Dunelands
Union River
Eurland
Capital
City
Corvus
Fortune Falls
Towns

Envy

Dinora surveyed the dust-filled cabin with disdain. The plain bed was left unmade, the kitchen bare and shabby, and the furniture too worn to be befitting of the woman—the queen—that was supposed to live here, however temporary. As her gaze slid over the unseemly cottage, Dinora could feel her lips curl into a snarl. Perhaps her dour mood was a result of the pain in her shoulder from where she'd had to pull that *girl's* knife from her back. Her eyes landed on the encumbered workbench. Or perhaps it was from her contempt for her new surroundings.

Dinora turned her nose up.

Messy. Pathetic. Useless.

She was better off with her only son dead. The gods knew he was never good for anything. Too intimidated to be of any use, and later too lovestruck by Astrid to be fully invested in their cause—in Corvus's cause. Cedric had fallen far below the expectations she'd set when she'd learned of her pregnancy. A prince. The Emperor's son. *Her* son.

He was to be the perfect son. He would keep her relevant in the eyes of the empire, and grant her power if her Emperor died tragically—an idea she'd admittedly considered. But as the years dragged on and Cedric's skills developed in art and kindness and compassion for even the lowest of courtiers—and servants—the shining light Dinora had crowned him with dimmed.

She'd hoped for a prince, who would grant her power and reverence, but she'd gotten a boy. A boy who grew into a weak man without ambition, without pride. A man who possessed only heart where there should've been grit or conviction. A man who possessed only compassion where there should've been power and loyalty.

Cedric had tried, even if his attempts had always fallen short. And this cottage was a representation of it all. Of her son, of the life he'd wasted, and of the potential he'd fallen short of.

There was no sentiment here.

But that girl—Astrid's heir—she had potential.

She'd *proven* it.

Nyla was young and untrained. But she had power—an immense amount of power, if Dinora were being honest. Thanks to Astrid's terrible cleverness, Nyla could pose a threat to all of her plans.

But fortune had granted Dinora the upper hand, even after Astrid's efforts.

Dinora had no intention of letting the power bestowed upon Nyla go to waste.

And she knew exactly where it would be when she needed it. The only thing she had to do now was make an army for herself. Dinora knew she needed more magic for her plans to come to fruition. The only matter left to settle was how. She didn't yet have the strength to gather it herself, but in time—Dinora had no doubts that she would not be so weak forever.

Perhaps her son had left some magic for her. After all, he'd taken so much of it for the potion that hadn't worked to break the curse between herself and that wretched manor. There *had* to be some left over.

After six centuries of trying and having every resource available to him in his freedom, Cedric had still failed to free her. It left Dinora wondering how hard he'd been trying. However hard he *did* try, it was never enough.

He had never been enough.

It was a good thing indeed that Astrid's heir had killed him. One less hindrance to foil her plans to bring about Tenebris's reckoning once and for all.

I. COMFORT OF THE SHADOWS

The soft flames of the fireplace crackled pleasantly, filling the silence with something other than Nyla's thoughts. Her mind was so far removed from the surrounding study that the room itself, and all its relics, ceased to even exist. The curious objects bathed in the dancing shadows of the fire's glow were long forgotten. Despite the flames that warmed the room with considerable eagerness, an icy chill had settled itself deep within Nyla. It left her shivering on the couch, staring unseeing into the shadows left untouched by the fire's lapping tongues.

The shivers had wracked her body for days. Her outstretched legs twitched in front of her with each breath of wind that ghosted the face of the Woodlane Manor. Thousands of unseen insects and webkers crawled beneath her skin, a phantom echo of the real ones crawling over the Woodlane Manor's domain. She fought the urge to scratch her arms, knowing it wouldn't alleviate the sensation in the slightest. Ever since Dinora had trapped her here, Nyla had known nothing but discomfort and resentment.

Sleep had become an old friend—or enemy, depending on how she looked at it. Even now as her dark and puffy eyes drooped, Nyla found herself wide awake every moment of the day. And though a sort of delirium, fatigue, and numbness had consumed her since she… Nyla swallowed and took a deep, shuddering breath.

"Anything but that. I don't want to think about it, just please, Corruptio," she begged as a single tear trailed down her cheek. "Please."

A few days had passed since the battle with Dinora and Cedric, but the fight still haunted Nyla to the point of insanity. She could still see the blood smeared down the wall behind the red-eyed man after she'd pushed him away from her. Dinora's snarled words echoed in her ears: *For centuries, I've wanted to spill your blood, but that's not good enough.*

The utter defeat that had clawed itself over her throat like a choking hand when she'd learned that Dinora had gotten away hadn't left her. If anything, it had only gotten worse. Stealing away her words and breath, the hand around her throat taunted her like a grim reminder. She was unable to do absolutely anything about the fact that Dinora had escaped. Thanks to the curse Dinora had transferred to her, Nyla couldn't leave the manor no matter how badly she wanted to. She *couldn't* simply walk out of the towering doors in the foyer and hunt Dinora down. Between the reminder of her previous failure to stop Dinora, and then whatever she'd done to Cedric, Nyla doubted she would ever know peace again.

Her mind still begged an answer to the question she'd come to hate. What *had* she done to Cedric, the man she couldn't seem to fully blame for all that'd gone wrong in her life since the fire?

Had she killed him?

She shuddered again, her prayer unheard. Instead of the comfort of sleep and sweet dreams, Nyla let the tears fall.

Sobs choked her and shook her whole body. The movement didn't help the memory of the now-healed injuries and bruising she'd sustained from her magical duel—of being slammed into the stone steps outside the manor—but there was no stopping the onslaught of emotions.

There never was.

And once it started, everything else came crashing down upon her memory, her insecurity, and her heart.

She couldn't break the curse that had bound her to this forsaken manor. A curse that Dinora and Cedric hadn't managed to break in over 600 years, that she, Xander, and Shamira were now tasked with hunting for a solution to—but it was no use.

In the handful of days since Nyla had been bound to the manor, they hadn't found a single book about how to break curses. Shamira, bless her pumpkie soul, couldn't use her magic to subvert it either. And nothing had come of the initial or subsequent plea for help Xander had sent his grandfather. Despite the constant reminder that they'd only been looking for a few days, Nyla couldn't help but feel that it was no use. No matter how hard they tried, she doubted she and her friends would succeed in finding a way to free her. Whether or not she was still a target to Dinora was uncertain, but the fact remained: she was stuck here, and her friends weren't.

Someone needed to stop Dinora. Not in a few more days, not a season from today, but now. Right this moment, someone needed to stop her before she could do anything to cause more pain than she and Cedric already had.

Nyla wiped at her eyes and reached over to the coffee table to grab the handkerchief she'd brought with her. It was no use feeling sorry for herself. She couldn't let their recent setbacks and her failures overwhelm her. There just *had* to be a way to set things right. Slowly, the sobs ceased, and she could breathe again. Her eyes closed for a moment, and she tilted her head back.

"Nyla?" She stiffened at the deep, sleepy hum of Xander's voice. Quiet footsteps padded over to stand next to her. "I thought I'd heard you get up."

Nyla didn't trust herself to speak. She couldn't even meet his concerned eyes, so instead, she sat up and went to make room for him on the couch. Xander stopped her by putting a gentle hand on her shoulder and instead told her just to scoot forward. She did as he asked, and soon, he'd maneuvered them so she was sitting between his legs on the couch, with her back pressed against his chest. He quickly unfolded a blanket he'd brought with him and cast it over them like a net. Gingerly, Xander wrapped his arms around her.

"You okay like this?" he asked as he leaned against the arm of the sofa just as she'd been doing before his arrival.

"Yeah." Her voice was a little hoarse, and she knew that he'd figure out that she'd been crying. She let out a long breath through her nose and tried to ease the beating of her heart. She leaned her head back against his shoulder, hoping the contact would ground her and show her that someone was here, that she wasn't alone. For the first time in the last three days, the chill that plagued her was gone.

"Remember the other day, before everything?" Nyla took another breath to steady herself, closing her eyes so she wouldn't have to see all that was and all that wasn't. "You promised to tell me how you learned to pick locks, but you never did."

A laugh vibrated in Xander's chest. "You're not gonna let that go, are you?"

"No." Nyla's lips cracked into a weak smile. "It's not like we don't have time. I'm stuck here forever."

"Don't say that." Xander's arms tightened around her for a heartbeat. Nyla's breath faltered, surprised by how badly she craved the contact, if only to know she wasn't alone in this moment. "We'll find a way to break the curse *and* stop Dinora. I promise."

Nyla hummed, opening her eyes and craning her neck to see if she could meet Xander's eyes. "Still though, we have time for a bedtime story."

"You're a difficult woman sometimes," Xander chuckled quietly. Nyla's lips twitched as if she were about to smile. Xander shifted, apparently getting in a more comfortable position, and at this point, the only thing that was stopping Nyla from scratching her arms and legs until she bled was the fact that he'd effectively caged her in.

"Once upon a hot, hazy day, the first of many during one particular Hugony, I was forced to remain inside to save myself from burning in the oppressive heat. I don't know if you've ever been to Huntington in the midst of a Hugony heatwave, but the buildings just trap the heat and make being outside unbearable. It was poor planning that led to poor air circulation, you see, so any breeze that *could* be is nearly nonexistent in the city. So, I roamed around the house. It was too hot to be in the kitchens, too boring to be in the library, and Issie was sick. So, what was I to do?"

Nyla listened as Xander led her through all the possibilities of what he couldn't do and how he'd exhausted every other means of entertainment until he'd set his eyes on the locked door at the end of the hallway. It was a storage room, he'd been told. But it was the only room neither he nor his sister Issie had ever seen inside, on account of a thick padlock. She listened as he went into detail about the lock and the theories that had run through his young mind at what could possibly be behind the locked door.

As Xander spun his tale, and Nyla relaxed for the first time since the battle, she'd nearly forgotten about the phantom touch of the webkers crawling over her skin as they skittered between the walls of the Woodlane Manor. She forgot about the tickle of the wind that blew against the face of the manor house. She even forgot about the pulsing heartbeat she'd come to understand was the manor's very essence and quite possibly the life force of the curse that'd made her hyperaware of the manor house she was bound to for the rest of her life.

Slowly lulled into a sense of safety for the first time in days, Nyla fully relaxed in Xander's embrace. Melting into the comfort she'd nearly forgotten existed since being cursed, her thoughts stopped scratching at her mind, and eventually, even Xander's steady voice was lost to her ears. As her eyes fluttered shut for the last time, Nyla felt a soft kiss pressed to the top of her head. It was so quick and barely there that she wondered briefly if she'd been mistaken. Perhaps she'd imagined it in the midst of the deep sleep that finally took her away for the first time since the battle in the manor's front courtyard.

***

The light brush of fingers on her forehead slowly pulled Nyla from her sleep as the bed dipped under the weight of something settling beside her.

"Nyla, you've got to get up," Xander whispered.

Nyla shook her head. All she wanted was five more minutes. Just five more minutes of that pure bliss of a good night's sleep. She didn't dare open her eyes and instead turned over, scooting away from Xander, mumbling her dissent.

"It's afternoon already," he added softly.

Her eyes cracked opened at that. Afternoon? Already? How had she slept so late? Nyla turned her head to look at him. It took her a moment to fully adjust to the dim light of the fire and the sunlight that fought against the curtains. It took her a few more seconds to realize she was in the bed in the room that she'd claimed for their time at the manor. Nyla knew she hadn't fallen asleep here, but she couldn't remember how she'd gotten back to this bed.

"Did you really carry me all the way up here last night?" she asked. As her sleepiness faded, her awareness of the bond between herself and the manor became more and more apparent. The unwelcomed tickle of wind creeping through the cracks of the manor ghosted over her skin, making her fingers twitch the more she regained her senses.

"I didn't want to disturb you and thought you'd be more comfortable in a bed." Xander offered her the breakfast tray he'd set on her nightstand.

Gratefully, Nyla took it and set it in her lap as Xander pulled the second plate toward himself, sitting back against the bed's footboard to keep her company. Glancing down at her own meal, her stomach clenched at the welcomed sight of seasoned potatoes and some meat that Xander had probably gotten from a hunting trip out in the woods around the manor. She took slow bites, all too aware of the fact that she hadn't eaten much over the course of the last few days.

"How are you feeling?" Xander asked as they ate.

Nyla shrugged, taking a bite of the potatoes. "The same, though maybe less irritated now that I've gotten some sleep."

The earthy and almost bittersweet taste of the seasoned potatoes sat on her tongue and warmed her senses.

Leaning back against the pillows, Nyla's mind wandered to the night before, to the kiss she'd vaguely remembered. Or had she only imagined it?

"Hey, Xander?" she started. He made a soft noise of acknowledgement. Hesitating, Nyla shook the question from her mind and instead asked, "Where's Shamira?"

"She's researching still," he replied, glancing up at her curiously. The arch of his brows eased with the slight shake of his head, as if he'd had to fight against his own reluctant question. "We figured we'd let you sleep, but I was starting to get worried maybe you were hungry or whatever." Nyla nodded and swung her legs over the side of the bed. Standing, she stretched and strolled over to the window, peeking outside. Bright, dazzling sunlight and fluffy clouds that sailed in the wind greeted her eyes. Even the Harvum-colored leaves of the Godberd Woods beyond the hedged garden paths of the Woodlane's estate seemed to laugh in the wind. Nyla watched the scarlet and plum leaves dance in the breeze, wishing for all the world that she could be amongst them, hidden by the honeyed-brown trees as she wove an imaginary path to the roads of Hart beyond.

"Well thank you then, for…letting me sleep," Nyla breathed out, letting the curtain fall closed again as she turned, quickly hiding her frown and replacing it with what she hoped was a more neutral expression. Xander was looking at her with pity in his eyes again, like he had been for the last few days now. Nyla hissed before she could stop herself. "Don't look at me like that."

Xander held his hands up in surrender. "We'll break this curse. And even if we can't do it ourselves, help is coming. They know about

Dinora and the curse now too. We're doing everything we can, and I won't be sorry for worrying about you in the meantime."

"Can you worry without looking at me like I'm under Corruptio's wing?" she whispered.

"You're not 'under Corruptio's wing.' You're just…" Xander paused, swallowing. "You're just not yourself right now. But we'll get through this."

Nyla bit her tongue, nodding. She watched as Xander stood from the bed and grabbed the tray she'd abandoned off of her bedside table. As he moved to leave, Nyla found herself wanting to reach out and stop him. It was like she was desperately grasping at something that kept slipping through her fingers, but she couldn't explain why or what it was that she was reaching for.

"Thank you—for everything," Nyla blurted. Swallowing her nerves, Nyla added more calmly, "You really didn't have to—"

"I do," Xander cut her off with a smile that twinkled in his dark eyes, "because if I don't, you won't. Remember?"

Nyla frowned, her brows furrowed. "Remember what?"

"In Caselle, when we decided to come here after you realized it might be the only place to get answers about your magic and the visions from Fortune Falls?" Nyla nodded for him to continue, even though she distinctly remembered the event in question differently than the way he was retelling it. He rearranged their plates on the breakfast tray. "Well, part of that was the fact that we both knew you wouldn't stop to take care of yourself, and that's why you let me come along. Sometimes you forget you aren't limitless."

Nyla let out a crackly laugh. It was as though her laugh was as broken as her heart felt. "You mean I'm not?"

Xander's smile widened into a lopsided grin as he reached for the door handle behind him and started to back out of the room. "Maybe you are."

Nyla blinked, nearly stunned. Before she could say another word, or ask how the story he'd been telling her last night had ended, Xander had slipped out the door and shut it softly behind him. Nyla stared after him, as if she could actually see him, and felt as his footsteps padded through the halls of the Woodlane Manor mapped out beneath the surface of her skin.

The sooner they broke the curse binding her here, to this wretched place, the better. Nyla dressed quickly, not wanting to spend the rest of her day burdened by the curse and overthinking what had happened, or how gentle Xander was toward her.

***

Xander strolled down the hall, knowing full well that Nyla was hyperaware of *everything* going on inside the manor house. Sometimes, he found himself wondering if Dinora's insanity was caused by being trapped in the manor for all those centuries, feeling every single thing that happened within the estate, from the drafts slipping into the manor house from the ill-fitted windows or down the chimneys to the *creak* of the floorboards, and even the rain against the stone pavers of the manor's courtyards.

But then he remembered that Dinora was the sorceress from the legends of the Shadow Forest people told around warm fires to entertain themselves. The legends recalled the forgotten war of over 600 years ago. Xander, like the rest of the kingdom, had assumed the war was an embellished legend—until recently. But now he knew the war was real and could truly explain why the Shadow Forest was haunted.

It was Tenebrese history shrouded in the secrecy of myths. Something that, when the fires died down and children were falling asleep beside their parents, the crowd could disperse and shake off as only that: a bedtime story meant to scare, to captivate, to pass the time.

But the legends were true, every last word of them. From the evil sorceress who'd stolen magic from the land to the trails of "smoke" that haunted the world hidden from the sun's light beneath the sapphire leaves.

Since Dinora's uncertain departure, and Nyla's miraculous recovery thanks to Shamira's healing abilities, Xander had managed to piece the forgotten history together. And what gaps his realizations had, Nyla or Shamira could fill in with what they'd learned. Between the three of them, he was certain they could learn the whole truth about what had happened some six and half centuries ago.

Xander shook his head. He'd recounted the history a million and one times over now, and he knew Nyla had done the same. Every time she had that faraway gaze in her eyes and she was still, he knew that's what she was thinking about. The battles of long ago, the curse, Astrid, how she was forced into whatever this ended up becoming, all of it. And there wasn't anything he or Shamira could do to bring Nyla back from the brink of destruction.

All Xander could do was make sure she ate and got plenty of rest. He knew nothing about magic or curses, so researching about how to break them was difficult. Shamira had tried to tell him it didn't matter, that all he had to do was read, but Xander wasn't so certain. What if he was reading the wrong things, looking for answers in the wrong places because he didn't understand how magic, how *this* magic, worked? Still, it was one of the few ways he might actually be helpful through all of this until Nyla could leave the Woodlane Manor again, a free woman.

He meant what he had told Nyla. She was nowhere near the realm of being corrupted, and definitely not on the brink of falling into darkness, or failing some test of Corruptio's.

A fickle god, yes, but Xander didn't believe Corruptio intentionally set tests for people to fail or fall from grace. People could freely make their choices based on what befell them, obstacle or no, and it was those choices that determined their character.

And if Nyla was worried about falling "under Corruptio's wing," then she'd only spiral further down into the mood she'd been in since the battle against Dinora and Cedric.

Xander pushed the door open to the kitchen and set the tray down on the island, bracing himself against the solid structure.

The image of blood-speckled lips and the rasping sound of wheezing breaths invaded his mind. His fingers curled. Closing his eyes, Xander took a deep breath through his nose, shoving aside the horrible nightmares of both his sister's death and Nyla's near-fatal battle from his mind. The eerie chill still rattled his spine, even as he tried to focus on something other than those two horrible memories. There wasn't a single thing he could've done, on either day. In a lot of ways, he supposed, there still wasn't a single thing he could do to actually help Nyla or Shamira find a way to break the curse and stop Dinora—if she'd even gotten away alive. Xander hadn't seen what had happened to her in the aftermath of her magic colliding with Nyla's, and neither had Shamira.

But Nyla was alive. Utterly exhausted, but alive. No matter how horribly the discovery of the curse had devastated her, Nyla was at least alive.

And she'd at least gotten a better night's sleep, so maybe their luck was changing for the better. Xander could only hope it was and that he wasn't putting too much faith in blind optimism. Shamira had tried tonics and sleeping spells, but none of it had worked. In confidence, the pumpkie had told him that Nyla's mind was too anxious for them to take effect. She had to feel safe, or believe that she could be.

It made Xander wonder about last night, whether it was yet another sleeping draft or if Nyla was just that exhausted and her body had finally given in to its need for sleep. Maybe it was both.

But if what Shamira had said about Nyla's mind were true, then what had changed? What had convinced Nyla's overactive subconscious that she was safe? The only real difference he could think of was that he'd stayed with her, but even so, it's not like he'd actually done anything to ease her burdens. He'd only been there with her, but maybe that was enough. Loneliness was a sort of devil against the mind in and of itself.

Shaking his head, Xander set about washing up the dishes and cleaning the kitchen. As soon as he was finished, he'd keep researching ways to break the curse. He'd search every book in that cursed library, every tapestry in this forsaken manor house, anywhere there might be an answer if it meant breaking the curse.

A small part of Xander couldn't help but blame Astrid for their current predicament. He could only assume it wasn't her intention for Dinora and Cedric to prolong their lives by more than 600 years and later turn her curse on her own descendant when she'd first created it. Though it certainly would've been easier for all of them now had Astrid killed Dinora.

But then he probably would've never met Nyla or Shamira, or gotten out of his own turn of dwelling in darkness.

He couldn't help but wonder what would've happened if only things had been a little different. If Cedric hadn't set the fire that killed Nyla's family, if he hadn't left Nyla alone at the manor that day, if Dinora hadn't managed to keep herself alive for centuries upon centuries, if Shamira hadn't been frozen by Dinora's magic, if…

Xander stopped himself. If he kept nitpicking at the different possibilities of the past, he really wouldn't be able to help Nyla now, and she really needed all the help and support they could muster.

He sent a silent prayer to anyone who would listen that they would find a way to break the curse—and soon, for all of their sakes.

2. A Study in Patience

Nyla stared numbly at the shelves upon shelves of books before her. The two-story library stretched endlessly. She used to revel in the sight, but now all she could see was a time-consuming obstacle that slowed her desire to break the curse.

"And she didn't say anything? No spell, no incantation, nothing?" Xander asked, as if she hadn't already told them both what had happened. Nyla's eyes cut to him. His arms were crossed over his chest as they all hovered in the doorway of the daunting room surrounded by floor-to-ceiling bookcases—and the loft of books on the second floor.

Nyla shrugged. She'd wished Dinora had said *something* when she'd cursed her. More than anything, Nyla desperately wished for some clue as to how Dinora had broken Astrid's curse on herself. Was it something to do with that dark potion Cedric had gotten on her, the one that her skin had absorbed?

Instead of drowning in more questions, Nyla answered Xander's. "No. Just that Astrid 'bound her here and put a blocker on her magic to prevent her from using the extent of it' and that she's wanted to 'spill my blood for centuries,' apparently."

The Elders can't be of much help until we can find out more about how the curse functions, Shamira stated matter-of-factly. The pumpkie's nonchalance grated against Nyla's nerves, an irritation she tried to contain before she lashed out and did something she'd come to regret.

"Well, I don't know what else to say other than there are things constantly crawling *all over me,* and if someone steps on the creaky floorboard outside of Astrid's bedroom one more time…" Nyla shut her eyes and tried to smooth the wrinkles in her mood. Still, none of them made to move from the doorway, and Nyla wondered if her friends were feeling the same sort of agitated hopelessness that she was. It didn't help that she'd lost control of her temper and had begun to take it out on them. All they wanted was to help her. Despite knowing that and even wanting their help, Nyla just couldn't leash her mood anymore, which only made things worse.

"Sorry, I just…" She trailed off, uncertain of how to explain that she didn't want to be this way, especially not toward them. So instead, she focused on trying to dredge up any new information that might help them. "When I try to go farther than the greenhouse or the fountain in the front courtyard, I start to get queasy and break out into a sweat like I have a fever or something. Then there's this pull that, if I go too far, 'drags' me back to the manor, and I…" Nyla took another ragged breath before she finished, "I can *feel* the manor, like it has its own heartbeat, and so does everything inside it."

At the unwelcomed reminder, Nyla fought the urge to scratch her arms, rubbing them instead as if that could get the things to stop crawling around the Woodlane Manor's nooks and crannies or to prevent the wind from dragging along the outside of the manor. It took all of her willpower to even force herself into clothes. The cloth, no matter how soft and comfortable it seemed, only further irritated the sensations. But her sheer willpower alone wasn't enough to prevent her from scratching at her arms. And in the two days that Xander and Shamira had been searching for an answer while she'd been healing, they hadn't come any closer to finding one.

I'll pass that along. Shamira blinked, her ruffled fur easing. Nyla swallowed the apology on her tongue, praying that her companions understood she didn't mean anything maliciously. Or not intentionally anyway. *So, do you think there's something worth searching for in here? Xander and I have been focusing on Astrid's workshop, as it seems the most likely place for an answer if Dinora hadn't found one in all her centuries of imprisonment.*

Nyla considered the library once more, this time with a critical eye. She'd never spent much time scouring through its shelves—that was more of her brother Derek's pastime. From what Derek had told her and Westley, these shelves held a forgotten history and preserved records the country or Legacy Committee would surely covet if they knew of their existence.

"No," she said slowly, wishing more than anything she could simply ask Astrid for the solution. "I don't think so."

"We'll keep searching as we planned, and if we don't find anything in the workshop, then we'll turn our efforts here," Xander replied.

Nyla smiled halfheartedly, exhaling a laugh filled with the same emptiness. "I hope it doesn't come to that."

"It won't," he assured her, turning toward her to catch her eyes. Nyla raised her eyebrows, wondering how he could be so confident.

I'm positive that if there's an answer within these walls, Astrid would've hidden it well. Shamira turned away from the library and started down the hallway toward the foyer. *And there was no more well-protected place in this manor than her workroom.*

"It'll be there." Xander nodded.

With companions as steadfast as these two were, a new hope began to bloom in Nyla's heart. She trailed after Shamira toward her ancestor's hidden workroom with Xander by her side. As they mounted the grand staircase, Nyla spared a rueful glance toward the stained-glass window. The dazzling sunlight streamed through the four coats of arms in the corner sections flanking the bloomed lilac in the steeple window. It was like the window—and lilacs in general—served only to mock her and her wounded heart. She turned her head away.

It wouldn't do anyone any good if she dwelled on things that bothered her. She'd already wasted enough time recovering from the battle in the front courtyard, even with the help of Shamira's healing magic and medicinal tonics to restore her strength. Though, if Nyla were being honest, she would've forgone the tonics if it were up to her. But Fate hadn't given her time to dawdle.

They *had* to break this curse.

By the time they'd reached Astrid's workroom, the budding hope in Nyla's chest had grown and taken root. Her resolve was growing more determined with every step she took. She only hoped that these measures could lead her to freedom.

Cresting the top of the narrow staircase into the attic room, Nyla's nose crinkled at the dust and cobwebs that covered Astrid's hidden study. The tiniest bit of uncertainty gnawed at Nyla as her eyes took inventory of Astrid's former belongings, lingering on the looking glass fixed on the wall across from her. Nyla shook the pests away, subconsciously scratching at her arm.

"Where should we start?"

Xander seemed to notice her scratching again and batted her hand away. "Your guess is as good as mine. Maybe we should split up and search every darkened corner here. Shamira and I have already been through that pile there," Xander said, indicating to a stack of books on the high worktable.

I'll work with the looking glass now that Nyla's recovered and my magic is restored to full strength. Maybe there's something in its memories that can help guide us in the right direction. Shamira stalked toward the magical artifact, her movements stiff as if she wasn't all that enthused about her idea.

"Do you want me to—"

No. I'm the most experienced magic user here, and I know how to handle looking glasses without tangling my essence with whatever lingering energy of Astrid's might still be imbued in it.

Nyla swallowed her retort and started toward a shelf burdened by dusty tomes. "Then I guess Xander and I will keep searching through the shelves and Astrid's journal."

"Perfect." Xander clapped his hands and cleared off a table and a pair of stools.

Taking the seat across from him, Nyla had never felt more disheartened in her life as she realized how many potential hours of research stretched before them.

3. THE BOND BETWEEN

Xander sighed heavily. Shoving aside the book he'd been searching through, he glanced over at Nyla and then toward Shamira. The pumpkie's body glowed with the faintest hint of sage, the physical embodiment of her green-colored magic as she did whatever it was she'd set out to do with Astrid's looking glass. Stretching, Xander stifled a groan as his stiff neck protested after hours of being hunched over the high worktable where he and Nyla sat.

"We should probably start thinking about dinner," he said hopefully.

"If you're hungry, eat," Nyla answered without looking up from the scroll spread out before her. "I'm going to keep looking."

"You need to eat, Nyla," Xander said. "If not because you feel hungry, then to keep your strength up so that, if something happens or we find a solution, you'll be able to handle it."

Nyla begrudgingly rolled up the scroll. "It's not like there was anything useful in this one anyway."

Xander grinned before he could stop himself. "See? It's like Fate wants you to eat."

She rolled her eyes in response. Her lips twitched as if she were about to laugh at his joke as she shifted in her stool, probably noticing for the first time how uncomfortable it was. "All right, maybe a break isn't such a bad idea after all."

"Do we…" Xander's gaze shifted back to Shamira again. She still stood on her hind legs with her front paws touching the surface of the looking glass, completely unaware of their decision. "Should we disturb her?"

Nyla paused. "I don't know."

Glancing at each other, Xander shrugged. Shamira should've really left them instructions about whether or not it was okay to disturb her in this state.

"Maybe we should just go on ahead without her."

Nyla bit her lip, but didn't disagree. As soundlessly as possible, they made their way toward the rickety staircase and down the uneven steps. Xander lingered near the bedroom doorway as Nyla hesitated by the workroom's entrance. He was about to ask if there was something wrong, but she flashed him a small smile and joined him, continuing out into the hallway. Whatever had gone through her mind just now, Xander hoped it wasn't something that weighed on her.

He couldn't tell what Nyla was going through. Even before the curse, he hadn't been adept at reading her. Every time he thought he knew her well enough to predict her next action, she proved him wrong. Regardless, he knew with an unshakeable certainty that this wasn't like her. Buried beneath the weight of the curse, she was a fraction of her former self. Xander worried there was more going on in her mind than she was willing to let him or Shamira in on. He wondered why. Why would she try to keep this all to herself? She didn't have to share, and maybe he *was* being invasive or selfish in thinking she should talk to him, or to Shamira.

Xander shook his head. He wouldn't force her, he wouldn't pry, and he wouldn't repeat mistakes he was guilty of or had resented others for. The only thing he would do was be there for her whenever she needed—just as he had been there last night. Whatever she needed, he promised himself, he'd be there when she was ready.

Reaching to push the kitchen door open, he turned toward her. "We still have some of that soup from yesterday if you'd like that, or I could make—"

"The soup's fine," she said, plopping down into one of the more comfortable wooden chairs the manor had to offer. "Do we still have some of that bread you made?"

"The loquette loaf?" he asked. Nyla nodded excitedly. "I have a whole loaf we can warm up."

For the first time since she'd been cursed, Nyla genuinely smiled. He'd even go so far as to say she beamed.

"Has anyone ever told you that you're amazing?"

He smiled back, laughing. "Maybe once or twice, but not over bread."

"Well, let me be the first then."

"Had I known loquette bread would make you this happy, I would've made it sooner." He turned away from her, making to grab the container of soup and the bread from his fresh bag on the counter. "Can you light the fire pit, please?"

Nyla offered him a nod and straightened in her chair. As he reached for the pot beside the sink basin, he saw her walk over to the countertop where the fire pit was carved out in and set the grate over the dancing flames.

"Thanks."

"No, thank *you*," she said earnestly. "It isn't much, but it makes me feel like I can still do things. It reminds me to remain hopeful, even though I'm slowly losing my mind."

"We'll find a way," he promised.

"I know," she said quietly, but this time Xander could've sworn there was a conviction in her words that hadn't been there before.

Xander nearly dropped the pot of soup as he realized she'd actually begun to believe that they *would* break the curse, she *would* be free again, they *would* defeat Dinora. He stopped himself from saying anything more about it and instead focused on settling the pot of soup over the eager flames. As he set the loaf of bread in the oven to warm, Xander wracked his brain for an easy topic of conversation. Before anything could come to mind, he noticed that Nyla's focus was set on the kitchen window even as her gaze confirmed that her mind was elsewhere. Staring into the depths of the saucepan, Xander's own mind wandered while he waited for the soup to heat up.

***

Nyla excused herself after dinner to take a walk. Xander didn't question it, knowing she preferred being alone right now. She'd been moodier than he'd ever known her to be—though he supposed he couldn't quite state that given how they'd barely known each other for a full season. Still, he felt he knew her well enough. And given the circumstances, he had to give her credit. He probably would've burned the manor down as soon as he'd realized he was cursed. Or maybe he wouldn't. He supposed it depended on what stage of life he was in at the time of being cursed. Even as recently as a year ago, he probably would've burned the manor down.

But now? Who he was today? If he were surrounded by the same sort of friends as he was now?

Maybe he would leave that as a last resort.

How is she? Shamira asked from behind him. Her gritty voice flitted over the forefront of Xander's mind like it always did, but this time he heard the same hopelessness he felt, an emotion he'd thought the self-assured cat-creature was incapable of.

"I wish you'd stop doing that to me," he grumbled, turning to face the ethereal eyes of the pumpkie's magical projection.

Life would be boring if I didn't, though, Shamira teased.

"Boring would be a change for the better, I think." Xander crossed his arms over his chest.

So not any better then?

He shook his head grimly. The pair was silent for a beat, and Xander's heart clenched. It seemed no matter how hard either of them tried, Nyla couldn't be helped, and any moment of happiness was just that: a fleeting moment. Rather than lament about it, Xander steered the conversation away from Nyla and the topic of her disposition or their fraying hopes.

"Sorry we left you up there. We weren't certain—"

I think I've found something. Xander blinked, unable to get another word in before Shamira continued. *But it's risky, and I'm not certain if it will work.*

"What is it?" Xander asked, lowering his voice conspiratorially.

It's a ritual, Shamira started. Her whiskers twitched in the way he'd come to know meant she was hesitant about something. *It's a tricky bit of magic, but if it works, it'll allow me to untangle the curse from Nyla's aura directly.*

"But it could work?" he managed to ask through the surge of hope pulsing in his throat.

I hope so, Shamira replied. She glanced around the kitchen. *How should we tell Nyla?*

"Well," Xander answered. "We have to tell her honestly, so we don't get her hopes up, only to shatter them again. I don't think that would be fair to her."

Shamira's lip curled into a smile. *Then I'll let you tell her. After I eat, I'll begin to gather the supplies we'll need.*

"When will you be ready?"

Tomorrow. I'll need the rest of today and part of the morning in order to gather everything we'll need.

Tomorrow. They could all be free from this place as soon as tomorrow.

"Perfect."

Without another word, Shamira's presence faded, presumably melding with wherever her physical body was. Her absence left Xander to battle between the mounting hope in his heart and the fear that the curse couldn't be broken. Somehow, he'd have to balance those two things when he told Nyla that there was finally something, a smidgen of tangible hope.

***

"Nyla?" Xander's voice sounded uncertain through the door. "Do you have a second?"

Turning away from the darkened window, Nyla let her arms fall to her sides. Any semblance of the troubles plaguing her mind receded, and she could only hope that any trace of them that might linger on her features had gone.

"Sure."

The door creaked open, grating against her ears until she was clenching her teeth. Xander sent her an apologetic smile, knowing full well that any movement within the manor was like a foot pressing down on her spine. Nyla quirked her brow as he lingered in the doorway, noticing how his hand tightly gripped the handle before loosening, feeling it as if he'd held her heart instead.

"Is everything all right?" she asked, facing him fully now.

Xander ran a hand through his hair. "Well…technically. Shamira thinks she found something." Nyla opened her mouth to interrupt him, but he kept going. "She's out gathering supplies now and says you should try to get some sleep so you two could perform the ritual tomorrow. She said something about your aura and maybe being able to 'untangle' the curse from it…though I really don't know what that means or what it'll actually entail."

The excitement brewing in Nyla's veins flattened at Xander's words, noticing the hesitation shadowing the hope in his eyes.

"Did she…" Nyla swallowed. "Did she seem hopeful?"

Xander glanced away. Absently, he reached a hand toward his chest, and Nyla found herself wondering just what was there that seemed to call to him when he was nervous. She'd caught glimpses of the thin chain around his neck, but had never dared to ask him about it. As if noticing her attention, he dropped his hand to hang awkwardly at his side.

"I think we're all just trying to be cautious about letting our hope give us wings," he said. Nyla nodded her head, glancing back toward the window and the starlit view of the Woodlane Manor's gardens. "Is the sleeping draft working?"

Shutting her eyes, Nyla shook her head grimly and turned her back to him as if that would hide her. "I don't think so. No more than the others, I guess."

It was the same one as the night before, so why wasn't it working? Her body was begging for sleep, to the point where she was on the verge of tears at any given moment.

"Do you want me to stay with you? Until you fall asleep?" Xander offered.

Nyla focused on his reflection in the window. His fingers fell from the doorknob as he shifted his weight from foot to foot like he was contemplating coming farther into the room. She couldn't quite name the open expression on his face, but her mind had taken her back to the night before, in the study.

"That's okay," she said, shoving aside the desperation reaching out from the far reaches of her mind. "At least one of us deserves to get some sleep while we're here."

"Okay." He nodded. Slowly, he turned and began to close the door behind him again when he stopped. Nyla forced herself to turn toward him again as he watched her with worried eyes. "You'll—you know you can come and get me if you can't sleep or don't want to be alone, right?"

Nyla's mouth ran dry. Her heart swelled until she was half afraid it might burst. "I know," she said quietly, forcing her hands to stay. "Thank you, Xander. I'm really glad that you're here."

He laughed a little, leaning against the doorframe. "I think you just need to face the fact that you're stuck with me."

"Am I?" she laughed, taking a step toward him, though the distance between them was too great for that step alone. "How do you know you're not stuck with me?"

"Then I guess we're stuck with each other." He flashed her a crooked grin that struck away the emptiness pressing down on her chest. "Goodnight, Nyla. Try and get some rest for tomorrow."

"No promises," she said. "Goodnight, Xander."

With the click of the door, Nyla stared at the wood panels. Her arms found their place wrapped around herself again, but she couldn't find it in herself to move—or even to return to her endless study of the gardens and the moonless sky. The only thing Nyla could do was wonder about the coming day and worry about whether she would finally be free.

4. TO BREAK A CURSE

Nyla followed Shamira's instructions as the pumpkie set about making a bubbling potion, lifting and measuring things with the help of her sage-colored magic. Shamira had gathered everything they'd needed between Xander's announcement last night and before Nyla had dragged herself out of bed this morning.

The sleeping draft hadn't helped in the slightest. Despite having used the same potion as the night before when she'd fallen asleep in the study, Nyla had had a fitful sleep. That meant that something had been different between the two nights. And the only difference she could think of between last night and the night before was Xander.

Nyla knew she had more pressing things that needed her attention than a phantom kiss to the top of her head, but the dreamlike memory made her wonder whether or not she'd imagined it. Shaking her head, Nyla dipped the paintbrush back into the clay bowl and drew the final saltwater sigil, completing the casting circle.

Nyla sat back on her heels and glanced over at the pumpkie. She was still working on the bubbling brew, so Nyla didn't dare interrupt the fierce concentration that gleamed in her sage-colored eyes.

Maybe it didn't matter whether or not she'd imagined the kiss to the top of her head the night before last. Maybe all that mattered was the fact that she'd finally gotten a good night's sleep, and the itching and the stubborn chill were temporarily forgotten—however briefly.

Ready? Shamira's voice skirted through Nyla's thoughts.

"As I'll ever be." Nyla's heartbeat quivered in her throat. "What do you need me to do?"

Stand in the center of the circle. Nyla watched as Shamira used her magic to ladle some of the brackish potion into a goblet. Nyla crinkled her nose, hoping she wouldn't have to drink the sludgy mixture. Moving to stand in the center of the circle, Nyla half poked at the bond between herself and the manor, seeking out where Xander had gone off to for the time being. She told herself that she was just checking up on him, but part of her wished he were up here with them. After all, he *was* with her when she'd discovered her magic at Fortune Falls and had kept her calm. Using the manor's bond to trace him, Nyla had just found him lingering in the kitchen when the goblet floated over to her, breaking her concentration.

And you'll need to drink this.

"How much?" Nyla turned her nose up at the floating goblet. With a stern look from Shamira, Nyla grasped it and stared into the cooled liquid.

All of it.

With a grimace and hardened eyes, Nyla gulped as much of the drink down in one swallow as she could. The thick, gritty sludge slowly made its way over her tongue and down her throat, simmering in her stomach. She eyed the goblet warily.

"Why does it taste like hopples?"

I enchanted it to taste better than it looks. Now focus. Shamira carefully joined Nyla in the center of the protective circle, standing across from her. *Gather your magic. Show me your aura.*

Nyla finished the potion and gently set the goblet down beside her, avoiding the sigils she'd painstakingly drawn. Closing her eyes, Nyla steeled herself. A prickle of static traveled down her bones, raising the fine hairs on her arms and the back of her neck. Warmth radiated outward from her core in time with the steady pulse of her heartbeat. Her aura shone around her like a wavering halo.

Shamira had briefly explained that auras were always there and how everyone had one, even beings without magic. Auras could be sensed, and sometimes seen by others, but when a magic user displayed their aura, it showed more than just who they were as a person. It showed their magical signature and all the energies or external forces interacting with them.

That's what made this ritual so versatile. By having a magic user expose their aura in full for all to view, it made dissecting the outside forces interacting with it easier to identify—and possibly separate. With this spell, Shamira could metaphysically sever the curse binding Nyla to the Woodlane Manor from her aura.

That was—*if* Astrid's curse allowed it.

Shamira had explained that some curses were stubborn. She'd warned that severing the bond from Nyla's aura might be painful, maybe even dangerous. Nyla hadn't known how to respond and instead contemplated the words even as Xander had gone stock still when Shamira had told them. She'd promised to stop if it inflicted more damage and injury than was necessary. But even as Nyla had objected to this, both Xander and Shamira had persuaded her otherwise. Breaking the curse meant nothing if it ended up killing her.

They were right; she knew that, but her desire to be free had utterly consumed her. She yearned to be free. She wanted to be able to hunt Dinora down to the ends of the earth and settle this once and for all before the vile woman could hurt anyone else.

Exhaling, Nyla slowly opened her eyes. Her aura outlined her body completely. It pulsed in time with her heartbeat. The hazy cloud was a mixture of colors, but the core of it was lilac, like the color of her magic. There was some scarlet near the fringes, perhaps an interaction from when Dinora and Cedric had transferred the curse to her, or perhaps something else. There were some shadowy spots mixed in with the area that spoke of Nyla's person, but that was to be expected. She'd known grief and bitterness and loneliness like old friends. She didn't doubt that the shadows were only a manifestation of those, and of how she'd let them fester in her for two long years.

It was also possible that some of the shadowy spots were a result of wishing someone dead—and to be the reason that they were.

Shamira had said nothing about the shadowy spots, but Nyla had seen the slight narrowing of her eyes when she'd first beheld her aura. At least now, the pumpkie's features were entirely blank. If it weren't for the grave concentration evident on her face, Shamira would've been almost a picture of serenity.

Nyla's breath hitched. She screwed her eyes shut as Shamira began to speak in a lyrical tongue she didn't know. Heat kissed her skin, and Nyla found herself leaning into the warmth. Beads of sweat broke out along her drawn brows.

A sharp throb stabbed through her gut. Nyla cried out, gasping. Something tugged at the outskirts of her aura, and even though she knew it was only Shamira trying to sever the curse's connection to her, Nyla panicked. Magic thrummed through her blood, sparking at her fingertips. She sucked in a breath and exhaled slowly. The pain eased, and Shamira's voice grew louder inside her head as the pumpkie continued to pull the curse away from Nyla's aura.

Nyla gasped. Ice flooded her lungs. Something inside of her seemed to burst under the pressure as Shamira worked at a spot on her aura's outer edge.

Shamira's measured chant cut off with Nyla's scream. The curse crackled on the outskirts of Nyla's aura, sending a violent spark straight into the core of Nyla's essence. Nyla doubled over, crashing to her knees with a jolt at the impact. Wood cracked. Dull thumps and broken glass sounded as Shamira was sent flying backwards into a bookcase.

Nyla panted, her arms wrapped around her middle as rolling cramps quaked through her gut. She thought she was going to be sick. Breathing in through her nose and out through her mouth, Nyla fought against the nausea churning in her gut. The sensation passed a little more with each breath. The only remnant of their attempt that remained was an unsteadiness that shook Nyla down to her very bone, her limbs trembling like she hadn't eaten for days.

"Shamira?" Nyla called out weakly, blinking away the dazed stars before her eyes.

The pumpkie got to her paws, swaying. *I don't know what went wrong. It was working!*

"Are you okay?"

Shamira blinked. *Yes, thank you. What about yourself?*

"Fine." Nyla coaxed her numb limbs into standing. Regret instantly wove its way through Nyla's blood as she pitched to the side, barely managing to hold herself upright. "Ooh…"

Footsteps pounded up the narrow staircase. Bursting into the room, Xander came to a grinding halt at the top of the staircase and looked from Shamira to Nyla and back again. His desperate eyes raked over the broken bookcase and the pieces of old knickknacks scattered across the floor surrounding the splintered shelves.

He panted. "What happened? Are you okay? I heard you scream and—"

Nyla held up a hand; a steady throb jarred her temples. "We're fine. I'm still cursed, though."

Her eyes fluttered. She really needed to sit down.

"You should both get some rest. Come on." Xander took Nyla by the arm and gently guided her to the stairs. Shamira followed close behind.

"Don't get cursed," she slurred, leaning on Xander for support even though they could barely stand side by side on the narrow staircase. "It really sucks."

"We'll find a way to break it. It's just a matter of time."

Nyla sat herself on Astrid's bed and watched as Shamira curled up by the dead fireplace.

"I hope so."

5. MAGICAL ENGINEERING

Shamira silently made her way back up the uneven staircase into Astrid's workroom. It was good to see Nyla resting, but it would be better to see the girl looking young again and smiling. But Shamira knew that wouldn't happen until they broke the curse.

There was still Dinora to deal with and the uncertainty surrounding Cedric's condition. A shadow draped itself over Shamira's thoughts. She'd inspected every inch of where Nyla had struck him down and subsequently investigated the manor on both the physical and astral plane. There was no sign of his certain death. The only evidence she could find was that of the immense power exchanged in the battle on that day. But the musty scent of death mixed with Cedric's essence had not been amongst all those traces. Based on what she'd found, and the sheer amount of blood smeared down the hallway wall, Shamira could only assume that wherever Cedric had gone, he'd died there.

She was almost too afraid to go looking. It was the fear of what she might find that stopped her from pursuing the matter further, even if the knowledge of his certain death could bring Nyla some peace. Shamira didn't want to know that truth—whichever way it might fall—until all of their spirits were lightened.

As she crested the staircase, Shamira's eyes swept over the disarray of the workroom. Xander was already up there, searching through more of Astrid's haphazard scrolls.

Find anything? Shamira asked.

"Not a thing," he sighed, leaning back on his stool and stretching. "Nyla's still asleep?"

Shamira nodded. The pinched tension that plagued Xander's demeanor eased somewhat with the slight slump of his shoulders.

"Good, she really needs the rest." Xander glanced back toward the ancient tome on the high table before him with downturned lips.

She waited for him to say something more, but he didn't. Shamira knew that he was worried about Nyla—they both were—but there was something about the level of attention Xander regarded the girl with that made facing this situation harder for him. She knew it, but she couldn't explain it herself. It was like Xander was in pain, too, but he was completely unharmed. All she knew was that the soft emotion wafted off of him and seemed to wrap around her senses. But it wasn't suffocating. Unlike any other emotion Shamira had been forced to sense thanks to her empathetic talent, whatever it was that Xander felt toward Nyla was something that made her heart ache but didn't weigh her down.

Determinedly, Shamira approached Astrid's looking glass again, praying her renewed efforts would reward them with a solution. She'd followed so many paths along the astral plane that the enchanted object had recorded, but thus far, she'd had no luck in finding what she was looking for. If she could only find the memory of Astrid devising the curse, they could break it.

Cautiously hopeful, Shamira stood on her hind legs and rested her front paws on the cool surface of the smooth glass. Her fur rippled as she bid the looking glass to life. The glass clouded over with the faintest tint of sage, the color of her magic. Her magic cleared, and before Shamira's eyes was the astral plane of the Woodlane Manor, as recorded by the looking glass's all-seeing eyes.

Without Astrid's magic to fuel it, the looking glass would've been an ordinary mirror. That was the only true difference between a useless mirror and a looking glass. Once imbued with the owner's magic, a looking glass was able to record nearly every aspect of the owner's life from an omnipresent, unbiased viewpoint. The user could also store their own memories as seen through their eyes within the looking glass, and that's what made them so dangerous. If Shamira were to try and use the looking glass to record her own life, her magic would tangle with what lingered of Astrid's and cause her great harm. But there wasn't any harm in looking through the enchanted object's archive. Between both the looking glass's memory and Astrid's, Shamira was confident that she would find *something* to help them in their quest to break Nyla's curse.

Diligently, Shamira sorted through the astral plane, searching for any thread that would lead her to the memory of Astrid designing or casting the curse.

Her ears twitched and swiveled in the direction of Xander's stool legs scuffing against the worn floorboards of Astrid's attic workroom. Even as he murmured that he was going to check on Nyla, Shamira persisted, glancing briefly at each strand of magic.

She saw a lot of Astrid and Cedric. Mostly happy memories, some tender, but others seemed tense and stark in comparison. The happy memories were shrouded in bitterness, as if Astrid no longer viewed them with such compassionate care. The later memories, the ones that would've seemed out of place had Shamira not known any better, were shrouded in hatred, and maybe even a twinge of anguish.

Astrid had loved him, and Shamira was certain that the red-eyed man she had loved was in part responsible for her murder and so many more crimes now.

From murdering Nyla's family to aiding Dinora these last six centuries, Cedric had a part in it all. It would be better if he were dead. One less problem for them to have to sort out later, his death would have been a blessing.

Drawing her attention back to her mission, Shamira set her sights on the memory she had originally seen in the looking glass a few days before. Even though she wanted to see it from Astrid's perspective, to see if she could get a better view of whose magic had played a part in killing her, Shamira knew that wasn't what was important right now.

Right now, that memory was her best link to when Astrid had designed and cast the curse. Based on the memories Nyla had witnessed when she'd found Astrid's journal, Astrid had probably cast the curse shortly before that final, fatal confrontation with Cedric and Dinora. If Shamira could locate that memory again and then work backwards to find the memory of Astrid designing the curse, she might just be able to figure out how to break it.

Shamira dug further down into herself, focusing the last of her waning energy into running along the astral plane of the manor's magical essences. Once Shamira had made it to the center of the puzzling plane, she studied each strand that came close to the focal point, the one she had so feverishly sought out just days ago.

Her heart sank, her stomach knotting.

There was a gap in Astrid's memory, as well as the looking glass's.

Astrid had destroyed those memories. Shamira's lips pulled back into a snarl.

She'd probably done so as a final precaution should Dinora figure a way into her warded workroom. Shamira could admire her foresight, but not her commitment issues. If she'd only killed Dinora and Cedric, then none of this would be happening now. Nyla wouldn't be cursed, Dinora wouldn't have prolonged her life by six long centuries, and all of magic wouldn't be hanging in the balance.

Shamira nearly howled in frustration. Racing back along the astral plane, her mind spun. What was she going to tell Nyla and Xander? How was she to explain that Astrid had truly left them nothing to work with, that even all of these books might be useless in giving them a clue on how to break the curse? How could she face them with such devastating news? There just had to be something. There had to be a way…

There was a way to retrieve the destroyed memories…but it was costly. Much too costly.

Her fur rippled as her soul body merged with her physical body. Growling, Shamira's eyes snapped open as she pushed away from the glorified mirror. Her front paws *thumped* against the wood planking of the attic as she let gravity pull her weight down in her frustration.

How were they ever going to break this curse?

Shamira eyed the doorway on the far wall. She dreaded the walk down the staircase and into Astrid's bedroom. She'd have to tell them that she'd found nothing—again—and Shamira wasn't sure how many more setbacks Nyla would be able to face before becoming embittered. She and Xander knew full well that the girl's mental state was fragile.

Shamira hadn't expected to see so much shadow in Nyla's aura. A little, yes, but what she'd seen while examining Nyla's aura shocked her. She'd known that Nyla had experienced untold loss and had expected to see some shadowy spotting along the outskirts of her aura, but Shamira would've never been able to predict that there would be pockets of shadow *within* her aura, encroaching on her core.

She wondered just what it all meant. She didn't believe Nyla to be capable of evil or becoming spiteful, more so than anyone else in her position, but the shadows worried her. Shamira wasn't certain if she should tell Nyla or if the reminder would only allow it to fester more. It was strange what worry and anxiety could do. Nyla was on a precipice, and if something didn't change for the better soon, there was no telling which way she would fall.

Fate was a fickle thing. It could be unkind or harsh, but it could be fair or full of blessings too. But in all of her years, Shamira had never learned how Fate decided its whims.

She doubted if anyone would ever unravel that great mystery.

Shamira shook her head. There was no use in delaying the inevitable. She had to walk down those creaky old stairs and deliver what news she had before she lost all of her nerve.

As Shamira stepped out into the well-lit bedroom, her eyes landed on Nyla and Xander. Sat beside each other on the bed, their backs against the headboard and Nyla still bundled up under the covers, Shamira paused a moment to study them, wishing for all the universe she had better news to interrupt them with. They were speaking quietly. Nyla was telling Xander about their attempt to sever the curse from her aura. Astrid's journal sat forgotten on Nyla's lap. A plate of snacks Xander must've made while he'd waited for them to finish the ritual and during their rest after the failed attempt sat between them.

Nyla looked over at her with hopeful eyes. "Did you find anything?"

The memories I was hoping to find were… Shamira trailed off, searching for the right word. *They were missing. I suspect that Astrid must've removed them from the looking glass's records in case Dinora ever found a way into her workroom.*

"Is there…can they be retrieved somehow?" Xander asked, glancing tentatively over at Nyla.

Nyla's gaze intensified. Her lilac eyes did not waver even as Shamira noticed she was holding her breath as if that would shield her from the worst of possibilities. Shamira swallowed unsteadily. She always thought of herself as an honest creature…but for Nyla's safety… *Not that I know of.*

"But there could be?" Nyla pressed.

I don't think so. Looking glasses require powerful magic, and powerful magic is… Shamira struggled to find the word that would deter Nyla. *Powerful magic is deadly if you interact with it and you aren't wanted. If Astrid is as cautious as I think she is, those memories aren't meant to be restored, if it's even possible to do so.*

Nyla scowled like a petulant child. "Then we're right back where we started: with nothing."

"We'll—"

"Please don't say it." Nyla's face screwed up as if she was physically pained by the idea of what Xander was about to say. She gathered up the journal in her lap and made to throw the covers back. Xander barely managed to move the plate of cookies to the nightstand before she tossed the covers aside and swung her legs over the side of the bed, tucking Astrid's journal against her chest. "I know we'll break the curse, and I know we'll figure something out…I just," she sighed, closing her eyes for a moment, "I want it to be now."

Xander leaned over the bed and caught her wrist before she could walk away. He grinned, his eyes flashing teasingly.

"Then you won't be mad at me if I say it again?"

Nyla's lips quirked. Shamira breathed a sigh of relief as a smile tugged at Nyla's face, an actual smile.

"I absolutely will be. Completely livid, I swear it."

"But I made cookies." Xander released Nyla's wrist and straightened himself up, apparently intent on reaching for the plate of cookies. Nyla only rolled her eyes and continued on her path around the bed.

Shamira barked out a laugh at that. *And do cookies make everything better?*

Both humans froze, wide-eyed in disbelief as they turned to face her. Their answer came in unison. "Yes!"

Shamira's whiskers twitched. How could a food, a mere *morsel*, make a situation better?

Xander must've sensed her confusion because he ran his free hand through his hair, the other still holding the plate of cookies safely aloft.

"Butter chips are a comfort food. It's like…I don't know. It's more of a feeling than something that actually makes a situation better or fixes a problem."

Ah. And butter chips are?

"They have a warm brown sugar and butter flavor, but every now and again, you hit a bit of chocolate, and it's just…" Nyla sighed fondly. "They're best when they're still kind of warm from the oven because then the chocolate is still gooey, and the whole thing just melts in your mouth." Nyla's expression turned wistful for a moment before her eyes flicked toward the plate in Xander's hand.

"There's one left…" Xander tempted, taking a step toward her near the foot of the bed.

Shamira watched as Nyla tensed, her eyes going from the plate in Xander's hand to him. Even the air seemed to stop as the pair of humans held a silent exchange.

"Mine!" Nyla burst. She half lunged forward, but let her magic do the rest as she bid it to steal the cookie from the plate. Xander snatched it in midair.

He took a bite, winking. "Don't worry, Nyla. There's more in the kitchen."

She smacked his arm with the journal playfully. "That was the cruelest thing you've ever done to me!"

Shamira rolled her eyes as they started to tease each other and pressed past them both. If they overcame this test of will with their sanity intact, it would be a miracle.

6. AN OLD FRIEND

Nyla stared blankly out the window above the sink basin. She dried the same dish as Xander stood beside her and washed them in the stoppered basin.

To say she'd been disappointed, as well as physically exhausted and slightly ill, after their failed attempt at the ritual was a gross understatement. It was working—it would've worked. She was sure of it. Maybe if they had tried just a little longer, if Shamira hadn't been afraid of hurting her, if…Nyla swallowed the torrent of useless speculations. Somewhere deep down inside of her, she knew any further attempt at severing the bond from her aura would've killed her. Shamira had been right to stop.

But when Shamira had come back and told them that the looking glass was virtually useless, any hope Nyla had reserved in her heart had waned.

She was never going to leave this manor house again. The Woodlane Manor would be her home until the day she died. Shamira would have to go on and stop Dinora alone. Xander would have to leave. He had a life of his own to live. Why should he stay too? He wasn't cursed, they weren't family, they weren't anything to each other.

Angry tears choked her throat. Nyla could feel her face tighten as she fought against the tide, pursing her lips.

"You're thinking about the curse again, aren't you?" Xander murmured, his voice pulling her from her spiraling thoughts.

"No, I was actually thinking about the weather," she snapped. She forced the tension from her mood and attempted to sound more relaxed than she was. "Does it look like it might storm to you?"

The tightness in her voice prevailed. Beside her, Xander passed off the newly clean dish to her and grabbed another, completely unbothered by the shortness of her words. His features were pensive as he plunged the dish into the soapy water and scrubbed at it.

Lightly, he said, "I don't know. I suppose it's a bit gloomy and feeling sorry for itself…"

Nyla risked a glance at him. "I thought we were talking about the weather."

"And I thought the weather was a metaphor for your mood." Xander handed her another dish to dry.

With a little *rattle*, Nyla set the plate she'd been drying on the counter and accepted the dripping pan from Xander. "I suppose it is."

"Well then, why are there storm clouds?" he asked earnestly.

Nyla bit her lip. When the seconds dragged on and she didn't answer, Xander gently bumped into her shoulder.

The shoulder with the faint scar that became more pronounced as it led to her collarbone. The scar that Cedric had given her when he'd attempted to stab her in the ballroom during one of her only two—and completely unintended—astral travels.

"I don't want to be forced to stay here until I die," she ground out, "alone."

The words were slow and difficult, but once she'd said them, it was like her fear of them became tangible. Her lip wobbled. She held her breath before slowly releasing it.

"It's a good thing you're not alone then," Xander laughed, turning his head to give her a broad smile.

Nyla roughly set the dish towel and damp dish in her hands aside. "I'm serious, Xander. I don't want to die here alone!"

Xander turned to face her, pulling his hands from the water and reaching for a towel to dry them. His eyes sobered.

"And I'm serious too. You aren't going to die here, and you aren't going to be alone. Consider it part of that curse: you're stuck with me until we find a way to break it."

"But what if we can't?" Nyla whispered. Her hands trembled by her side. She didn't know if she could bear the weight of holding his gaze any longer for the fear that she might crack under the exposure of her words.

"There's no way we aren't, so don't even think like that," Xander said. Nyla nodded. He raised an eyebrow at her, tossing the towel down on the countertop beside him. "You don't think so, do you?"

"I don't know, and that's what bothers me."

Xander remained quiet, glancing down at the floor. Nyla didn't think he was taking any of this seriously at all. How could he determine that they'd find a way to break the curse in a timely manner, or at all? How could he assure her that she wouldn't die here, or that she wouldn't be alone? He couldn't know that, and he had no right to promise her that he wouldn't leave her alone either.

Her indignation flared up inside of her again. At Dinora for cursing her and getting away, at Cedric for even having lived in the first place, at Shamira for not trying harder to sever the curse from her aura, at Xander for being so selflessly optimistic, at Astrid for designing the curse instead of killing Dinora, at the curse itself for immersing her into the very heartbeat of the Woodlane Manor.

But most of all, she was angry at herself for being angry. She didn't want to be. She didn't want to be difficult or constantly snapping from one emotion to the next in the blink of an eye. All Nyla wanted was a chance to breathe, to feel like herself again. She'd even accepted how she'd felt about her magic upon its emergence and everything that had happened before the manor, how she'd felt helpless and afraid. Helpless because of how small she was in comparison to the mountain of her mind's insecurities and questions, and afraid because she didn't know where to find the answers or what to do at all.

Even though she had feared the potential damage she could do as an untrained Caster, she'd still felt in control of herself, of her emotions, of her body.

But now?

It was like she was merely a presence in her own body. Everything, from the beat of her heart to her emotions, seemed like it was controlled by someone she didn't know—and who definitely didn't know her.

"How can you just stand there and promise to throw your life away?" she burst. Xander opened his mouth to reply, but Nyla didn't give him the chance as the words came flooding through the gates she'd tried to keep sealed. "We don't know how long this is going to take, if we even do—"

Xander gripped her by the shoulders and angled his head so they were about eye level. Nyla's breath caught in her throat as they were mere inches apart. "Staying here wouldn't be throwing my life away. Throwing my life away would be leaving you here all alone and trying to move on but living with the guilt of having left you here all alone." He paused, shifting slightly as he studied her. His hands slipped gently from her shoulders, but even as he just barely pulled away, his hands didn't fall. "I don't care how long it takes. We're breaking this curse, and until then, I'm not leaving you alone here. There might be times when I need to leave to get things to make life here a little more livable, but I will never leave you here. I would never be able to forgive myself if I did."

Nyla opened and closed her mouth. There weren't any words she could possibly say in response to his statement. It was more of a vow than a statement. Xander's words had wholly overwhelmed her.

But they'd confirmed something for her, and she didn't know what to make of it. The kiss to the top of her head the other night hadn't been her imagination or a desperate wish for home or a sense of belonging in someone else's heart.

"I'm gonna," she started, licking her lips, "I'm gonna go sit on the veranda, maybe try and get through more of Astrid's journal. Maybe there's something there that could change both our futures, for the better."

"I'll finish up here," Xander replied.

Neither pulled away for a long minute. It was strange how openly she'd stared at him, and Xander at her. For the first time, Nyla noticed the light dusting of freckles on Xander's cheeks and wondered briefly if there was anything about herself that he was only just now seeing. She found herself wanting to ask about the kiss, to hear what he would say, but she couldn't find the words to do so. She couldn't tell if there was something he'd wanted to say to her or not, but realizing the vulnerability in their hesitation, Nyla slowly leaned away from his warm touch and gestured vaguely toward the door.

"I should," she started, "I should probably go and read that journal so we can leave."

Xander nodded but said nothing as his hands slid from her arms. Nyla didn't say anything more as she hesitantly turned and dragged herself out of the kitchen. Once she'd stepped over the threshold, Nyla inhaled a deep breath and loosened the tension around her heart. It wasn't that she'd felt trapped or even angry at him anymore. It was more concern or…something else. She wasn't certain what. But whatever it was, she was startled by it and left utterly breathless and whole at the same time. She ran down the hallway once she was certain Xander wouldn't see her and didn't stop, rounding the grand staircase and continuing her brisk pace down the lengthy hallway that ran the breadth of the manor until she came to the door of the veranda. It wasn't until she'd plopped herself down on the porch's steps that she realized she didn't even have Astrid's journal.

Cursing, Nyla wrapped her arms around herself and waited for her heartbeat to calm. The air was crisp and calming. The warm yet sweet scent of Harvum's approach soothed her soul, even though the manor's miniscule inhabitants were active thanks to the damp chill in the evening air. Light goosebumps erupted along her arms as she rubbed her skin, though she didn't feel the coolness of the evening air. Restlessness and a flutter of adrenaline gave Nyla a gentle flood of energy. She wanted to run, to pace, to do *something* to shift through the simmering emotions in her chest instead of sitting here to let them stew.

Nyla pushed herself to her feet. Even though she couldn't go far, she wanted to walk around the grounds. Maybe the fresh air and the change of scenery would help bring her back to herself.

As she followed the path that ran along the back of the manor, her thoughts plunged deeper into their current circumstances between the curse and whatever end Dinora sought. There was still a reckless part of Nyla that wanted to look into Astrid's looking glass. She wanted to restore the memories and get her life back once and for all, no matter the cost she might pay for it. She'd seen the tilted look on Shamira's face when the pumpkie had spoken of the dangers involved with looking glasses. Shamira wasn't one that seemed to scare easily, but Nyla had seen the restraint and glow of fear in her eyes. Nyla shoved aside the tempting whispers from the far corners of her mind. In regard to the looking glass, running toward the cerbertes was out of the question. Nyla shuddered at the image the old adage brought to mind. The dark soulless eyes of the creature more commonly known as a hellhound was almost as terrifying as the prospect of being bound to the manor for the rest of her life.

Even if she *did* ignore Shamanna's warnings and try to use the looking glass herself, there was the fact that they didn't know *when* Astrid had cast the curse.

Was it just before her death? Was it after she'd sent everyone else in the manor away? Did those memories Nyla had experienced when she'd first touched Astrid's journal mean anything at all? Or had Astrid cast the curse on a rainy day during the course of the Corvid Uprising when she'd felt like it?

As usual, Nyla didn't have the answer to that mystery. The memories she'd seen when she'd first discovered Astrid's journal were only so detailed. Not even the memory Shamira had found in the looking glass of Astrid's death had provided much in the way of an explanation.

If anything, both instances had left them all with more questions and even fewer answers than they'd had previously.

Maybe if she were braver, she could ask Astrid herself. But Nyla didn't feel very brave anymore. With each day that escaped her in her captive state, it was like she'd lost a piece of herself too. There wasn't any safe way she could ask Astrid, and even if there was, Nyla didn't know how to. And even if she did, she doubted she would. She'd had enough of astral traveling for one lifetime.

Nyla kicked a stone across the hedge-lined path and buried her hands in her pockets. She glanced around, coming out of her thoughts just long enough to realize she'd crossed into the front of the manor and was on the path to the stone-pillared porch and front entryway.

Her mouth turned to sand.

If only she'd aimed for Dinora's heart, this all would've been easier.

She still remembered the panic and absolute hatred that had called her magic to hand when she'd seen Dinora round on Xander after freezing Shamira with her foul scarlet-colored magic. For the briefest of seconds, Nyla had thought that Dinora was going to kill him, and there was nothing she could do to stop her.

Thankfully, that hadn't been entirely true.

She'd been so proud of herself when she'd launched her knife at Dinora, enhancing her aim and strength with what little magic she could muster in her weakened state.

But Nyla knew now that she should've aimed for the wicked woman's heart. The evil sorceress named in the legends of the Shadow Forest didn't deserve mercy. She hadn't deserved it over 600 years ago, and she certainly didn't deserve it now.

So why had Nyla let her live and get away? Why hadn't she aimed to kill Dinora?

Xander's words from a lifetime ago came to her: she wasn't that sort of person.

Nyla swallowed. Some small part of her wondered if that were true, given how much she wanted to kill Dinora and Cedric. She'd even made her peace with the prospect of having murdered Cedric—if he'd truly gotten away only to die elsewhere. Was it so damning to hate someone like Dinora or Cedric? Hating them to the point of wanting them to die? Or to be the hand that brought about their death?

She didn't know what to make of it. Nyla didn't know if she were truly becoming the sort of person to be feared like Cedric or Dinora, but she'd held onto one truth and one truth only: she'd had multiple opportunities to kill both Cedric and Dinora that day, and she hadn't.

She very well could've, but she hadn't, and perhaps that was answer enough.

With a little less misery and confusion in her heart, Nyla mounted the stone steps. A rusty crimson still faintly speckled the gray stone. At the sight, her spine shuddered with a phantom pain, one that reminded her of the way the breath in her lungs had escaped her parted lips, lips that could not cry out. With a grimace, Nyla let herself back into the manor house.

***

Xander hummed quietly to himself after Nyla left, intently washing up the dishes so he wouldn't focus on anything else. Yet as he worked, his mind wandered.

Nyla had confided in him that she didn't want to die alone. And while that was a blunt statement, it gave him a grave insight into her mental wellbeing. Nyla was free-falling. He didn't know how to tell her that he wasn't leaving her here alone, curse or no curse. Or how to convince her that it wouldn't be throwing his life away if he did stay. The way she'd looked—no, *stared*—up at him before she'd gone had nearly killed him. The depth of vulnerability he'd felt had almost made him confess to Nyla that there wasn't much of a life waiting for him anyway.

But even if there was, that look and the way it had filled his heart would always make him choose to stay. And this time, he wouldn't break that promise. No matter how hard Xander tried to tamp down his guilt, that snide voice in the back of his head taunted the possibility of what might've been had he stayed with Nyla and Shamira instead of going alone to Gossamer.

Whenever he'd brought it up with Shamira, the pumpkie would curl her lip and tell him it didn't matter what either of them *thought* would have made a difference that day. And he'd had to tell her something similar when she'd expressed her own regrets and "should haves."

Lost in thought, Xander mindlessly continued to wash their dishes. He jumped at the sound of a knock.

Grabbing the first knife he could get his hands on in the pile of dishes beside the sink, Xander whirled around to face the unexpected visitor.

"After all these years and you pull a knife on me?" the tall man said, leaning against the doorframe.

"*Edwin?* What in Balmae's name are you doing here?" Xander sputtered in disbelief—or maybe it was something more like relief.

"Your grandfather sent me," Edwin answered, as if that explained everything.

Xander dried his hands off and closed the gap between them. "And after all these years, you're still not very talkative."

Edwin shrugged and extended a note out to Xander bearing his grandfather's seal. Hesitantly, Xander accepted it and thumbed the dark blue wax. Resolutely, he broke it and glanced over the note, his brows arching the further on he read and the words sank into his mind.

Yes, his grandfather had sent Edwin to aid them in breaking the curse. Yes, his grandfather would offer his assistance. And yes, his grandfather wanted them to come to Huntington "posthaste."

Xander swallowed. He inhaled sharply and let the note curl up on itself, his now free hand rubbing the back of his neck.

"So, you're here to help then?"

"However I can." Edwin nodded. "I excelled at curses at the university."

Xander's eyes snapped to Edwin. "You were accepted into the program?"

His friend's eyes flashed proudly. "I *graduated* from the program."

"That's amazing, congratulations!" Xander shook Edwin's hand vigorously. Granted, Xander knew next to nothing about the University of Magic, other than the fact that it was Edwin's dream to attend it since they were kids.

"Thank you." Edwin glanced away, a small smile on his face that couldn't quite hide his self-satisfaction. For as reserved as he was, Xander knew how much Edwin prided himself on his skills and accomplishment as a Caster.

Xander hesitated. Edwin was, and always had been, a man of few words. But the fact didn't mean he was any less of a troublemaker than Xander. It's probably why they were such good friends growing up. That, and Edwin's unwavering loyalty.

"Well, I'm sure Nyla would like to meet you, but I'm not really sure where she is right now, so how about a tour?"

Edwin bobbed his head. "Sure."

As Xander led the way out of the kitchen and started toward the library, he tried to get more answers out of Edwin about what home was like, the things he'd missed out on after he'd left, and what university was like. Edwin wasn't forthcoming with answers or news of Pemberly Hall. The less Edwin answered him, the more anxiety wormed its way into Xander's gut. He shoved those concerns aside, reminding himself of the crumpled note burning like acid in his hand. His grandfather had agreed to help them—to help Nyla. He'd even sent them help in the form of a familiar face, and if his request for them to come to Pemberly was any indication, his grandfather intended to help them in more ways than just sending Edwin to break the curse on Nyla.

Xander showed Edwin into the library. "And this is where we met the source of all our problems. Dinora tried to claim that she was the keeper of this manor, before she and Cedric attacked us."

Edwin's eyes danced over both floors of the library as if he could see its secrets lying bare before him. He hummed. "And Dinora is still alive somewhere?"

"Unfortunately," Xander sighed. Irritation seeped into his veins. And what, exactly, had Edwin meant by asking that? Was he implying that they'd failed? That they were to blame for Dinora getting away?

"She'll be found. Your grandfather reached out to the Caradels, I think." Edwin turned on his heel and looked over the shelves along the same wall as the library doors before his sharp eyes met Xander's. "To be honest, no one's really interacted with your grandfather since he received your letters. He's been…busy, I suppose."

Xander's eyebrows twitched, his eyes narrowing. Why would his grandfather reach out to the royal family and not the Chamber of Commons? Or the military? And to isolate himself completely…Xander swallowed, forcing himself to ask the question he feared to have answered.

"What do you mean?"

Edwin hesitated before speaking again. His gaze dropped to the floor, the way it always did when he felt like he shouldn't say something he was about to. When he next met Xander's eyes, he noticed the cold calculating look had faded from his friend's eyes, revealing the honesty that Xander remembered as the basis of their friendship. "I don't know—I mean, it's not really my place, but…Lord Huntington's been shut inside his office more often than not lately. Barely anyone's seen him or spoken with him. He's even taken to eating his meals there.

Your aunt Marilynn has been running the house and handling business matters 'as per the lord's instructions,' if you want to believe that."

"Why?"

"I don't know." Edwin shrugged. "It was quite a shock to receive your notes. I was actually responsible for delivering the first one to his lordship when it arrived in Huntington…I didn't know it was from you until I saw the look on your grandfather's face when he'd opened it and realized his regret before he'd dismissed me. That's when he began withdrawing himself from Pemberly Hall's daily routine."

Clicking his tongue, Edwin shook his head, as if there wasn't anything more he could say about the matter. Xander studied his longtime friend as Edwin turned away from him and began to look over the shelves of books with a renewed interest.

Xander steeled himself. His thoughts whirled in a flurry of concern for his grandfather and for how this all would fall on Nyla. After all, he'd hardly expected a response from his grandfather when he'd resolved to send him that first note, let alone for him to send help *and* insist they come to Huntington for what promised to be more help…

…and maybe a confrontation Xander wasn't ready to have, for better or for worse, yet.

Xander locked the thought away. *That* was a problem for another day—if that day ever came. Instead, Xander focused on urging Edwin out of the library and finding him a place to settle for his time here.

***

Once Edwin had retired, Xander knocked lightly on Nyla's half-open door. When there was no answer, he knocked again and waited. Hoping she'd fallen asleep, he peeked inside.

"Nyla?"

Her slumped figure didn't answer from where she sat in the winged chair by the fireplace. A pot of tea and mismatched teacup sat abandoned on the round end table beside her. As he approached, Xander smiled, relieved that she'd managed to fall asleep after all. He debated whether or not to place her in bed, but what if he accidentally woke her up?

Hesitating for just a moment, he decided to leave her. Xander knew how difficult it was for her to fall asleep lately, and he wouldn't want to be the reason she didn't get any sleep tonight.

Xander blew out the remaining candles in her room and silently made his way back toward the bedroom door. With the room cast in glowing shadows from the endless fire Nyla must've lit with her magic, Xander let himself out and shut the door quietly behind him.

He'd have to tell her about their unexpected company in the morning, preferably *before* Nyla ran into Edwin first. He dreaded how the two might get along. Nyla's patience was short enough already, yet Edwin had a near endless supply of the virtue, and the thoughtful consideration of his words to go with it. He wondered if it would be like trying to mix water and oil together.

And then there was Shamira to consider. How would they get along? Xander's lips pressed into a thin line. They might be okay, given how Edwin could be quite fixated on whatever task he felt he needed to see through. It was probably why he was so short now. He doubted that fact had changed. When Edwin's mind was occupied by something, it was all he could think about until he'd resolved it. Until he did, Edwin wouldn't quite be himself, too consumed by his objective to notice or do much of anything else. At least Edwin and Shamira had that in common. Analytical to a fault, Xander could see them working well together. Or so he could hope. Maybe they'd be irritated by each other's respective processes.

Xander shook his head, letting himself into the room he'd claimed for himself across the hall from Nyla's. He couldn't worry about that, though. What mattered now was that there was one more person working to free Nyla from the curse.

7. AS THE RAVERIN CROWS

Soft morning light flooded through the large windows of the library. Nyla found herself in the midst of an interrogation conducted by Xander's friend Edwin, the alleged help sent by Xander's grandfather. Gripping the arms of the plush chair in the library's central sitting area, Nyla's patience waned as Edwin opened his mouth to undoubtedly ask another rephrased question.

"So, can you help me or not?" she interrupted, disgruntled after having answered yet another question about the potion that had seeped into her skin after Cedric had gotten it on her. Nyla didn't know what to make of it, or of Edwin. She didn't know why Xander's grandfather had sent him to help them, or how his incessant questions were going to lead them to an answer. All he'd done thus far was ask her the same questions in as many ways as the raverin crows. They weren't even new or original questions, but rather the same ones she, Xander, and Shamira had been trialing over these last few days. She tried to tamp down her irritation, but she was tired of his lack of communication—and his lack of answers.

Edwin paused, glancing over at Xander, who leaned against the end table across from Nyla with his arms folded over his chest.

"Well…it might be difficult, but I think so."

"Difficult *how*?" she insisted.

Xander smirked at her with laughter in his eyes, as if to say the pale-eyed man's vague and roundabout mannerisms were typical.

"Difficult in that there are limited options," Edwin replied, obviously meaning not to say anything more than that. At her sharp stare and arched eyebrow, Edwin continued, "I'd like to skim that journal and see the looking glass you mentioned before I say definitively what I suspect."

"Don't want to give me false hope?" Nyla asked shortly, forcing a bitter smile to her face.

Edwin blinked before smiling in what might've been the first hint of genuine emotion she'd seen from him. "Exactly."

Nyla's eyes gravitated toward Xander's. He shrugged, offering little more in the way of communication than his childhood friend. Nyla's gaze flicked back to Edwin, and she nodded.

"Be my guest. I think Shamira's up in Astrid's workroom right now and can show you the looking glass. I'll meet you two up there with the journal."

Nyla decided it was best to take a slight reprieve from Edwin. If she had to stand his questioning on top of the irritable itching beneath her skin, she was going to snap. As if he could sense the thoughts buzzing angrily in her head, Xander pushed himself away from the end table and motioned for Edwin to follow him.

"I'll show you the way to Astrid's workroom and introduce you to Shamira," he offered, already making his way toward the door.

Edwin offered her a polite nod as he went to follow after Xander. "I suppose if there's anything more to ask, it's not at your expense anyway."

Nyla nearly laughed. Allowing herself a small smile, she stood and stretched her stiff limbs.

Edwin paused, glancing back at her from the doorway where Xander still hovered, waiting. He seemed to hesitate before he said, "I have no doubt we'll find something. No curse can remain unbroken, not even one seemingly as powerful as this."

Nyla blinked, stunned. Maybe it was Edwin's naïveté of the war and Dinora and Cedric's full history, or maybe it was the foolish hope of someone new to a problem, but still, Nyla found herself accepting his words as truth.

"We'll see, then," she managed to say. "It's not just the curse we're working against, but time itself."

Edwin nodded slowly. "Unfortunately, I know nothing about fighting against time, but curses…" He paused, his eyes flaring with something Nyla couldn't say wasn't wicked or vengeful. "I happen to know a lot about curses."

Nyla tilted her head. Edwin didn't offer her any more of an explanation, only a lingering curiosity. He turned back to Xander. "So, the workroom?"

Xander's eyes briefly caught hers over Edwin's shoulders. Her silent question was reflected there before he turned away to lead Edwin upstairs. Nyla shook her head. If Edwin had ever been cursed himself, it must've been during the last few years when he and Xander hadn't spoken, as he'd seemed just as perplexed by his statement as she had. Maybe Edwin hadn't meant anything by it other than to assure her they'd find a solution to her current predicament.

Nyla wondered just what he'd meant, and the depth she thought hid behind his words. Clearing her head, Nyla made to grab Astrid's journal from her bedroom before meeting everyone in the workroom.

Climbing the spiral staircase up into the library's loft, Nyla weaved her way through the bookcases until she reached the tapestry hung on the wall off to the loft's side. Despite the invisible insects crawling along her skin and the footsteps pressing down on her ribcage at all hours of the day and the near-impenetrable chill of the curse, Nyla found that she preferred using the Woodlane's hidden passages whenever she could in order to avoid the stained-glass window of the foyer.

Besides, Nyla told herself as she brushed away new cobwebs that the webkers must've recreated in the night, the passage was a more direct route to the bedrooms she and Xander had claimed for their time here.

Pushing the spring-release button at the end of the passage, ancient gears rumbled. The wall panel receded into the passage. The tracks shuddered as the panel moved aside to let Nyla pass. She would've never known about this passage if it weren't for the curse. Though she was perfectly content with the things she'd already discovered about the manor during her time spent visiting and playing here with her brothers growing up, learning all of the Woodlane's hidden passages was one thing about the curse she dared to say she might actually enjoy.

Walking down the hall and into her bedroom, Nyla's eyes swept the room. She couldn't remember where she'd left the journal, only that she'd been reading it late last night. Nyla spotted it carelessly left on the end table beside the chair where she'd fallen asleep. She didn't know when she'd fallen asleep or when she'd even stopped reading. All she remembered was watching her eternal fire.

Learning how to forge magical fires that required no wood was the best thing Shamira had ever taught her. Magical fires didn't give off the same smoky scent or use licking flames, but they allowed her to keep warm through the whole night without having to stoke it or put another log on.

Staring into those lilac-and-plum flames, Nyla had experienced a contentedness she couldn't remember. Or perhaps it was part of the drain from fueling the magical flames for so long. Shamira had encouraged her to find more ways to use magic throughout her day so as to improve her stamina and lessen the magical drain—the negative effects of wielding her magic. Magical drain explained all the fainting and fatigue she'd experienced since discovering her magic and using it more.

Not wanting to keep everyone waiting, Nyla plucked the journal up and set off for Astrid's workroom. By the time she'd gotten there, Edwin had begun to investigate the contents of her ancestor's hidden room. Nyla leaned against the high-top table beside Xander. Grasping Astrid's journal like her life depended on it, she listened as Edwin and Shamira discussed the looking glass.

Biting her lip, Nyla wondered just what Edwin could propose that they hadn't already considered or tried. She shoved aside her worries as she listened to Shamira's explanation of what she'd seen in the looking glass.

Out of all of them, Shamira seemed the most welcoming of Edwin—a fact that struck Nyla. She would've assumed that Xander would be the warmest of them all, but he didn't seem too excited to see a familiar face. Nyla supposed he was just as anxious as she was, though for different reasons. Perhaps Xander was second-guessing reaching out to his grandfather. Maybe it was something he never intended to do, or wasn't ready for. But yet he had, for her—*because* of her.

Nyla would never be able to repay him for all he'd done for her since they'd met. Or the fact that he was willing to spend the rest of his life here if the curse couldn't be lifted. She didn't know what to make of it, just as she didn't know what to make of Edwin or Xander's grandfather. Xander hadn't told her much of anything about him either, but with Edwin's arrival and alleged bid for help, Nyla had to keep herself from prying into things that Xander obviously wasn't ready to talk about. So instead, she'd have to make do with listening to Shamira's explanation of Astrid's death at the hands of Dinora and Cedric and the missing memories in the looking glass's archive again.

Edwin glanced toward Nyla at the pumpkie's words as if noticing her presence for the first time. As Shamira's attention shifted to her and Xander leaning against the table, Edwin gestured to the book in Nyla's hands.

"Is that the journal you mentioned?"

"Huh?" Nyla glanced down at the lilac book she held. "Oh, yeah."

"May I?" Edwin waited for her to pass him the journal. Nyla swallowed her apprehension and nodded her assent as she relinquished the journal to him. "Thank you."

Nyla's eyes slid to Xander beside her as he laid a light hand on her shoulder, as if he knew the difficulty of allowing a complete stranger to glimpse into the life of her long-dead ancestor. Edwin quickly began flipping through its pages, a pinched look of concentration on his face.

"Do the dates mean anything to you?" he asked no one in particular.

"No," Xander said, "we've just begun to assume that it's somehow connected to the myths of the Shadow Forest and around the same time."

Nyla nodded her head, adding, "Yeah. Dinora had told us a story about the 'Great Tenebris War,' though I don't think there's much truth in what she said, but…"

Edwin arched his brow in question. Nyla glanced between her companions, lingering on Shamira's steadfast gaze. Shamira trusted Edwin. Xander trusted Edwin. So why couldn't she? What reservations did she have against his help?

"…some of the things," Nyla continued, her voice beginning to strain, "make sense when we compare them to the myths of the Forest."

"You think she was the sorceress and that this 'Great Tenebris War' actually happened? That the myths are somehow true?" Edwin sputtered in disbelief.

They are, Shamira said. Edwin blinked, stunned into still silence. The fur on Shamira's neck bristled and settled within a single breath, like she was steeling herself. Nyla swallowed, fearing Shamira knew more than she and Xander could've possibly pieced together themselves. Shamira's eyes misted, staring over all of their heads as she wove her tale.

The myths humans tell of the Shadow Forest are a history my kin have never forgotten. And in this way, by perpetuating these legends, neither has Tenebris.

Shamira's weighted gaze landed on Nyla, pained and nearly pleading for a forgiveness Nyla wasn't certain she had to ask for.

The few records that survive are scattered across the clans for safekeeping, and all of those who could remember and tell us of that war and that sorceress are gone. We too, only have our shared memories and legends to remember this history by.

But from what I'd gathered before meeting you and now with what we've all pieced together from across these sources, I know it in my blood that Dinora led the Corvids in what most of us know as the Corvid Uprising.

Nyla's mouth ran dry. Everything Dinora had said that day in the library was a version of the truth—twisted but wholly true. If she replaced some of what Dinora had said, about King Harrison and the Royal Mage, and in its place added what she knew of Astrid and what she'd gleaned from that journal, it all made sense.

Dinora had led a war against Tenebris, though Nyla didn't know for certain why. Astrid had become a prominent opponent and had died protecting Tenebris. She gave her life to imprison Dinora, yet Dinora and Cedric had both somehow managed to prolong their lives, and now Dinora was free—all because of Nyla.

Nyla's chest squeezed and closed in against the shallow breaths of air she could manage.

"What else do you know?" Xander asked, rubbing the tension away from her shoulder as her mind began to spiral.

Not much, unfortunately. Many of our ancestors were slain in the war, and the few who did survive are no longer with us to tell their tales, Shamira said solemnly, her eyes downcast. *There are pumpkies old enough to have known the survivors of the war, though contact with them has been difficult. They listen, but they will not speak with me.*

"But they're aware of what's going on?" Edwin asked. He tucked Astrid's journal against his chest and tapped his fingers against it thoughtfully.

Yes. I assume they are discussing it privately. Shamira bowed her head, dejected. Nyla didn't know much about pumpkies or the clans, but she knew Shamira had disobeyed the Elders by coming to find her. She assumed that even with these developments, Shamira was being shunned as punishment for breaking the laws of her clan and venturing into Tenebris without the Elders' blessing.

"Then all we can hope for is breaking the curse on Nyla and getting to Huntington as soon as possible," Edwin said decisively. It was as if he believed it to be that easy, and with the way he spoke so assertively, Nyla found herself believing maybe it *could* be as easy as that. "I'll read through this as quickly as possible to see if there's anything that might be of use to us in terms of the curse, and then perhaps," he said, turning toward Shamira, "we could devise a plan to break the curse from there?"

Of course.

"Then if there's not much else to do, I'll start getting something together for dinner," Xander sighed, pushing away from the table.

Nyla inhaled slowly through her nose. "I'll be…I'll be in the greenhouse if you have any more questions."

Maybe being amongst the plants would help ground her and bring her a sense of home. After all, she'd grown up in the fields of her family's farm and the woods surrounding their property—surrounding *this* property. Maybe the greenhouse could offer her some kind of solace, and working to help maintain the plants would keep her busy enough to feel like she was doing something other than waiting idly for answers she may never be blessed with.

"I'll walk with you," Xander offered with a soft grin.

"Sure," Nyla said distractedly. She chewed on the inside of her cheek, playing over everything they knew as she moved toward the crooked staircase leading down into Astrid's bedroom.

The stairs creaked behind her, the only sign of Xander's presence trailing after her. They'd just barely made it out into the hallway before he matched her pace, and she couldn't help it anymore. A chuckle that turned into a wild laugh fell from her lips. She knew she sounded like a madwoman, and maybe she was, but she didn't care. Xander faltered beside her, eyeing her curiously, which only made her laugh—truly laugh—harder until she couldn't walk any longer. Once she'd calmed, she wiped the imaginary tears from her eyes.

"I'm sorry. It's just that everything leads to more confusion and more questions and fewer answers, and, Helpet, we should've never left Caselle. I miss Nan and George…and Nan's banana cake."

Xander chuckled. "Since when do you call Gerri 'Nan?'"

"Since just now, and I was thinking about how much simpler things would be now if we never came here."

Xander paused, hesitating for a heartbeat. Nyla studied him with a slight downturn to her lips but not quite a frown. She almost added on to what she'd said, to help clarify what she'd meant, but found there weren't any words to do so. Instead, it was Xander who found the words Nyla hadn't realized she'd overlooked.

Quietly, he said, "It's not all so bad, though."

Nyla considered him briefly, wondering what had led him to draw that conclusion. As the possibilities flashed through her mind—memories of their travel here, the day spent at the beach, the phantom kiss, homecooked meals—she found herself inclined to agree.

Nodding slowly, she said, "I guess not, no."

Xander hummed, but said nothing in reply. Their gazes didn't falter from one another, though Nyla wasn't all that certain they were actually seeing each other. She was lost in a world of her own.

Nyla shifted and forced herself to carry on down the hall again. If she hadn't known any better, she would've thought that she was looking for something in Xander's gaze, or maybe he in hers. She tilted her head slightly, thinking once more about the kiss to the top of her head that'd felt like a dream until Xander's voice broke her away from her thoughts.

"We did promise to visit them again." Xander matched her idle pace. "Maybe we could even stay a while. Nan wouldn't mind."

"I'd like that." Nyla smiled.

Pride

She remembered it like it was yesterday. Not much had marred Dinora's memory over her six centuries of imprisonment. Even six centuries more wouldn't have been able to gray the memory of the day she'd killed that wretched woman.

The flow and hum of the magic she'd harnessed from the land thrumming throughout her body and crackling through her veins—pure power and strength. And it was all hers. The magic sparked around her, a full display of her power to anyone foolish enough to tangle with her. Dinora had known nothing like it before.

It had all culminated into that one moment. The long years of suffering. The years she'd spent hiding like a peasant for a petty crime—the crime of wanting to uphold her empire. But in that one glorious moment, it had all been worth it. From vying for the Emperor's hand in marriage and being cursed with an inept son, the moment she'd killed Astrid had more than made up for it all.

She'd had to take matters into her own hands, as she always did. Cedric, the fool that he was, had allowed her to gain the advantage. He'd cowered to her attacks. Even if he'd had the magical talent to see his only task through, Dinora knew he didn't have the strength to defeat his dearest love.

But she had.

As Astrid fell, Dinora beheld that wisp of power. Her husband and her country were avenged. For a few precious moments, she was triumphant. She'd never known a taste so sweet than the bright flavor of absolute victory on her tongue. The promise of it had settled in her bones.

All too soon, it had turned sour. Only moments later, she had realized what Astrid had done. With it, her victory had dulled. That anger boiled in her blood for six long centuries. The sly wench had enchanted herself, had used herself as a talisman to cast the curse *and* will her magic away.

No matter how many days, weeks, decades, she'd spent analyzing how Astrid had managed that parlor trick, she wasn't able to figure it out. She'd hoped that her son, her guileless son who had spent all his time with *her*, would have at least learned a few things from the Royal Mage, but even he hadn't been able to reverse-engineer Astrid's spell work.

During those long years of her imprisonment, Dinora had done nothing but plan for Tenebris's demise. The need to avenge Corvus and her Emperor consumed her until it became the very breath she drew. It whittled away at the bitter defeat and anguish of Astrid's curse until they were only a simmering memory in the far reaches of her mind. Instead, she'd come to focus on the victory of surviving each day, season, decade that had passed. It made the waiting worthwhile.

And she'd wait six more centuries if it meant killing Astrid's heir would be just as sweet.

Once she'd killed Nyla, Tenebris would fall, and Corvus could be rebuilt and made whole again, just as she'd always wanted. Now, she need only to plan to take what she wanted.

8. TURNING IN CIRCLES

Xander looked from Edwin to Shamira. Any semblance of his fatigue and the warmth he'd savored at the manor had fled as they'd dragged him out to the far reaches of the manor's boundary. All Shamira had told him was that she and Edwin had a theory. She wouldn't risk saying anything more until they were on the outskirts of the manor's estate, for fear of Nyla overhearing them and getting her hopes up.

It didn't stop the irritation that had flooded his veins as the pumpkie's astral form had stared at him as he'd sat up in bed. Naturally, she'd startled him awake—a trick Shamira seemed to enjoy.

But now Xander understood.

It wasn't a solution they'd gotten him out of bed for, but a test.

A test that could lead them to breaking the curse.

"So, just to make sure I understand what you two are proposing," he said, bringing his hands up as if he could push back on their bursting eagerness, "you want to use a version of that ritual you and Nyla tried, but on the manor while I monitor her for any adverse reactions?"

Yes, Shamira said. *If we can examine the manor's aura, maybe we could sever the curse that way.*

"And if not," Edwin added, "then we'll at least have a better idea of how Nyla and the manor are related, and how the curse is interacting with the both of them."

Xander shook himself, still trying to wrap his head around their plan. At best, their plan sounded half-formed to him. Eyeing his companions skeptically, he realized that these two might be the most thorough magic users he knew. He needed to trust in them, if not because they were his friends, but because of their skill.

"All right," he said at last. Almost threateningly, he pointed at Edwin, adding, "But you're helping me set up my distraction."

Edwin groaned, covering his face with a hand. "Don't tell me you're scheming again. I swear, it's like nothing's changed!"

"Nothing, except the year," Xander joked. "Come on, the night isn't getting any younger, and I don't want Nyla to catch us."

While you two are doing…whatever it is you're planning, Shamira said, *I'll begin the preparations for the ritual.*

"Perfect." Xander nodded his head toward the manor they'd all left behind. Edwin rolled his eyes, setting his jaw as if he realized there was no use in trying to derail what Xander had in mind. "We'd better get going."

"If we must," Edwin sighed. As they started up the path again, he asked, "So what is it you have planned *this* time, Xander?"

Xander grinned, surveying the darkness. "Something I think Nyla will really like."

Without even looking, Xander could feel the prickle of resignation wafting off his friend. If Xander could be certain of anything, he knew Edwin was recounting all the times they'd gotten into trouble as kids as a result of one of his or Issie's "schemes." Even Xander's own mother used to chastise them for being so devious—a trait he was certain ran in the family as evidenced by the stories his father used to tell of her when she was younger.

But unlike their youth, there wasn't anyone at the Woodlane Manor who could wag their finger and tell them to behave.

Mounting the back steps of the manor house, Xander nearly laughed at the thought.

It wasn't like his plan was anything worthy of being scolded over anyway. In truth, he hadn't really had much of an idea on how to distract Nyla while he, Shamira, and Edwin had been standing in the dark, cold night, but the walk here had helped him solidify the vague notion he'd gotten in his head.

Silently, he led Edwin to the season room. Nyla had spent a great deal of time in the glass-paneled room the two days it'd rained earlier in the week, just staring endlessly out over the downtrodden garden beyond its clear panes. As soon as Edwin had mentioned that Xander was to help distract Nyla, the season room immediately came to his mind. In the morning, the sunlight streamed in through the large windows, bathing the room in a soft golden light. The beams danced and haloed the loose canopy of Harvum leaves outside, beyond the garden, making the estate look as if it was surrounded by a rippling sea of plum and scarlet.

Xander couldn't imagine anything more peaceful than that. But now that he'd had time to think, he realized it wasn't a quiet peace Nyla needed. He knew what silence could do to the mind, especially when one was already tormented in some way.

No, what Nyla needed—what he needed for this distraction to work—was something engaging, that killed the silence, and gave both of their minds something to latch onto and ground them.

"Do you think the Woodlane's hiding any instruments?" he asked Edwin, leading him into the season room at last.

"Why?" Edwin hovered in the doorway, even as Xander walked toward the center of the room, stopped only by the couch facing the windows overlooking the garden.

"Because," Xander started, turning in a full circle and gesturing widely to the room around him, "we're going to turn this into a ballroom, for dancing."

Edwin let out a chuckle of disbelief. "Isn't there a simpler distraction, one that doesn't require us to move dusty old furniture? Or go searching through the manor in the middle of the night for instruments we may or may not find?"

"Hey, you and Shamira are the ones who roused me from my sleep and dragged me from my warm, comfortable bed only to tell me you had a theory that *might* lead to a solution," Xander pointed out. "Besides, couldn't magic help us track down some instruments?"

"Only if they exist here in the first place," Edwin muttered, finally stepping forward. Waving his hand in an arc, light flooded the room, banishing the dim moonlight. "Where do you want to start?"

Xander rolled up his sleeves. Walking around to one side of the couch, he braced himself, getting ready to move it. "First we'll clear the space. Then we'll worry about the instruments…You can enchant them right? Because if you can't, then there's no sense in finding them."

"Of course I can," Edwin said in mock offense. He took his position at the opposite end of the couch. "What would you have them play, maestro?"

Xander paused, tilting his head a little. After a moment, he asked, "What about a waltz?"

"Whatever you want." Edwin gestured to the couch. "Let's get this over with so we can get some sleep tonight. Shamira and I have a busy day ahead of us, and I still have to make the signal potion."

Xander's brow arched. "Signal potion?"

"Yeah, in case our investigation of the manor's aura starts to negatively impact Nyla," Edwin explained. "All you'll have to do is break the bottle, and the magic will do the rest."

Xander nodded. Bracing himself, he shoved at the couch as Edwin began to do the same. Once they'd gotten it against the far wall, Xander straightened, wiping his hands. Eyeing Edwin from the corners of his eyes, Xander asked, "And do you think it will? That whatever you two are going to do will hurt Nyla?"

Edwin considered this for a moment before replying. "It shouldn't, but I've never seen a curse quite like this one before."

"But you've seen many?"

His friend didn't respond immediately. In the spanning silence, Xander glanced over at him just in time to see him shake the haunted expression from his face. "I think that's a story best fit for another day."

Xander swallowed. "All right then." Tucking away the fact that there *was* a story to be told that Edwin seemed reluctant to share for some other time, he glanced toward the old rug adorning the floor. "Ready to tackle the carpet?"

"If we must. I hope it's not terribly dusty," Edwin nearly whined.

Xander laughed a little. "I can't promise that it won't be."

"It can't be dustier in here than the hidden passages at Pemberly, though."

"I wouldn't be so sure," Xander teased. "I haven't seen any ghostly staff members here over the last week, and I really don't think Dinora knows the best practices for keeping up an estate such as this."

"You know," Edwin said, glaring at the carpet, "I don't typically condone frivolous use of magic, but this might be the exception. What else do you want done to the room besides rolling up the carpet?"

"What do you mean?" Xander questioned.

"I need a clear picture of it in my head so my magic knows what to do."

"Ah," Xander said, still not entirely certain what Edwin was going to do. Even so, he explained how he wanted to roll up the carpet and move the buffet closer to the back wall so that the entire center of the room was clear for dancing without the risk of bumping into anything.

Edwin closed his eyes and rubbed his hands together. Xander rolled his eyes, imagining that his friend was mainly doing this all for show. A silvery glow emanated from Edwin's hands as he raised them and moved them outwards toward either side. Xander's eyes widened as the carpet rolled itself up and the buffet slid noiselessly across the floor into the corner.

"There," Edwin said proudly. "Anything else?"

Xander shook his head, still baffled at the display. "Since when are you so casual with your magic?"

"Since it's the wee hours of the morning and we're in an old abandoned manor that is most certainly haunted and I'd rather be in bed," he yawned, taking lazy strides toward the door and leaving Xander standing in the corner just as confused as ever. "Let's go find those instruments, and then I'm going to sleep."

"Yeah," Xander said, glancing back at the room. "Let's do that."

***

Nyla watched Edwin out of the corner of her eye as the three of them ate breakfast together at the kitchen island. Shamira was off somewhere speaking with the Elders again, no doubt reporting their lack of progress to the mystical and utterly unhelpful beings. She brought another forkful to her mouth and savored the delicious bite.

He hadn't said much of anything at all. Not about the journal or if he'd finished reading it through, not late yesterday afternoon when they were all researching in the library, not at dinner, and not even when Nyla told him to avoid stepping on the loose floorboard outside of Astrid's bedroom because it made her teeth hurt. Edwin had only assured her that he'd be more careful and that he should have a solution soon. Dumbfounded, she hadn't answered him. Instead, she'd only latched onto the hope that that single word instilled in her.

Soon.

It was the most definite answer they'd ever gotten about anything, and it was still obscenely vague.

Nyla tapped her foot against the empty air. Patience might've run in her family, but it certainly wasn't a trait that had passed to her. Her parents were patient. Her older brother Derek was patient in most things, and so was her twin Westley. She couldn't say either way about Lydia because the youngest of them all never had to wait long for anything. With so much available to her through passed-down relics her older siblings had outgrown, Lydia wanted for nothing—except to do what her older siblings were doing at all times.

Nyla herself knew the feeling all too well. Things always seemed more interesting when you couldn't do them.

And right now, Nyla wanted to walk the length of the manor's driveway. She wanted to walk up and down it a million times just because she couldn't. She wanted to walk down the dirt roads that made her heart wrench and long for something that wasn't possible anymore, if only to acknowledge her freedom.

But instead, she was trapped, and Dinora's newfound freedom was her doing, her fault. If they'd never come here, if they'd turned back at the crossroads to Hart like Nyla's insecurities had wanted to, Dinora would've never been freed, and Nyla wouldn't have to be responsible for her friends' decisions to stay here with her.

The clinking of their dishes and the scraping of utensils faded as they each finished their meal. Nyla reluctantly prepared herself for whatever might come next. She slid off of her stool and walked over to the sink. Even though she'd grown up without plugic—the system of pipes and water reservoirs that brought water to taps on demand via magic—she sorely missed it. Caselle didn't seem like such a bad place to linger if they ever managed to set her free of the curse.

Once she defeated Dinora, of course.

"Shamira and I will be working on a theory of mine this morning if you two want to continue researching possibilities." Edwin's smooth voice sliced through the kitchen. Nyla turned around, leaning against the sink basin. He didn't offer any more of an explanation. Her eyes shot to Xander.

"Okay, sure," Xander said lightly. He seemed to avoid her gaze, focusing on collecting the remaining dishes spread over the table. Her eyes narrowed, noticing Xander's struggle to school his features and the depths of the concern showing on his face clear as the day outside. "We'll see what we can find then."

Without another word, Edwin left Nyla in stunned silence. Xander still hadn't met her questioning eyes. Exasperated by the pair of them, Nyla turned back to the sink and studied the view outside the kitchen window.

A theory? A theory of Edwin's?

Nyla's lips drew into a thin line as she silently ranted about how it would've been nice of him to share his theory, but she supposed he wanted to spare her hopes if it didn't work. Still, she'd like to know what was going on or feel like she was a part of something that wasn't stewing in the limitations drawn by the curse on her being.

She brushed aside her dislike and forced a smile to her face as Xander brought the collection of dishes over to the sink.

"So…dishes and research?"

"I actually have plans this morning," Xander said, much to Nyla's surprise. He grabbed the bucket they used to bring water in from the well pump outside. "Meet me upstairs by the bedrooms in about half an hour."

Nyla placed a hand on the counter, watching as he fiddled absently with the bucket's rope handle.

"Why?"

"It's a surprise." He grinned.

"A surprise?" Nyla raised an eyebrow, partly in question, partly in suspicion. "Are you and Edwin related by any chance? Because you're doing the same thing and withholding details, and it bothers me."

"I haven't the slightest idea what you mean," Xander half-sang as he left her standing by the basin and started out the back door. Hovering in the doorway for just a moment, he flashed her a grin. "Just promise me you'll be there?"

Nyla huffed in annoyance. "It's not like I'm going anywhere."

He pretended not to hear her as he disappeared outside, and Nyla clenched her hand at her side and glanced out the window. First, Shamira kept things from her, and then Edwin showed up, also withholding information, and now Xander was trying to be mysterious too. It was like they all wanted to try her patience or drive her into madness.

She almost found herself being empathetic toward Dinora. She was alone here for over 600 years, growing rotten thanks to her own bitterness. Nyla was cursed for barely a week, and she was already insane, slipping slowly into a dark abyss.

And she wasn't even alone!

As she stalked out of the kitchen, Nyla found herself huffing again. She hoped that was a habit she could break herself out of once she was in better spirits. Well, if she only had thirty minutes until Xander's grand surprise, then there was no sense in getting bogged down in research. But with nothing else to do, Nyla ended up in the library all the same, exhausted by the idea of searching through Astrid's workroom again to no avail.

***

Xander knew Nyla was annoyed with him, but it couldn't be helped. Right now, Shamira and Edwin were getting ready to poke around the aura of the Woodlane Manor from a distance—a distance at which Nyla hopefully couldn't feel their presence. While Shamira and Edwin were doing the magic part, Xander turned his attention to his distraction. It was a miracle that they'd found a few string instruments in the attic. Now all that was left to do was get ready—and hope that he wouldn't have any use of the glass vial sitting in his pocket. Edwin had discreetly handed the signal potion to him while Nyla had had her back turned to them as they'd all been preparing breakfast.

He nearly laughed at how changed his friend was. Stealthy but not sneaky, quiet but not reserved. He wondered what changes Edwin might have noted in himself, what changes his grandfather might see, and if they were for the better.

There would be time to think about that later. For now, Xander wove his way toward Nyla's bedroom. Almost stiff with alertness, he fought the urge to tiptoe. There was no telling if Nyla was spying on him right now thanks to the bond between herself and the Woodlane Manor.

He knocked thrice on her bedroom door.

Nothing.

Cautiously, he opened it with a *creak*. He poked his head into the room and glanced around. A smile spread across his face.

Nyla wasn't anywhere in sight.

Xander smirked victoriously and darted across the hallway into his room. Carefully grabbing the gown he'd found, Xander quickly ran back into Nyla's room. He set the gown on the bed with care and moved to the wardrobe. Frowning at its emptiness, Xander turned on his heels. He supposed that it was a good sign that Nyla hadn't wholly moved into the prospect of spending an indefinite amount of time in the manor. There was no time to relish in the thought, though. Nyla would probably come early to see what this was all about, and he needed to find her backpack to hide it so she'd be forced to wear the ballgown, if only for this one scheme. His heart pounding, Xander desperately looked around the room in search of her backpack. He sagged with relief when he saw it beside the armchair near the fireplace. Snatching it up, Xander shoved it inside the armoire before he went for the bedroom door.

Xander poked his head out into the hallway. Just because he didn't see Nyla didn't mean she couldn't 'see' him, but he still glanced each way before sprinting across the hall and into his room.

Breathless, he took out the suit he'd managed to find. He hadn't thought anything of it until last night when Shamira and Edwin had approached him with their plan. It'd taken them just as long to locate the suit as it had for him to devise this plan to help distract Nyla. But once he'd figured out how to distract her, the rest was easy. He knew what Shamira and Edwin were doing was important, but Xander couldn't help but think about that day on the beach. It was a break Nyla had needed, even if she hadn't wanted to admit it when they'd first gotten to the lake, and he suspected today would be much the same.

What was the harm in a bit of fun, especially in the wake of everything that had happened since Nyla discovered her magic at Fortune Falls? Xander continued to muse, probably more excited than he should've been given the circumstances, but he couldn't help himself. He changed as quickly as he could. Nyla's patience could wear thin at any moment now, and he would be ready.

***

The minutes dragged on like molasses. Nyla heard each tick of every clock in the manor like a symphony. They rattled her patience until she couldn't take it anymore.

What was Xander up to?

She turned down another hallway, searching for Shamira, for Edwin, to see if maybe she could help them, but she couldn't find them, not even through her bond with the Woodlane Manor.

It wasn't that she'd gotten used to feeling every movement within the manor—or stalking her friends with it—but it was strange to not be able to find anyone when she wanted to. Nyla poked at the bond, vaguely sensing Xander moving about excitedly upstairs. She didn't dare focus on the sensation enough to pinpoint the exact floorboard he stood on, not wanting to spoil his surprise for her, but the temptation was there.

Nyla took in a pinched breath and let her feet carry her aimlessly through the hallways until she found herself climbing down the side wing of the foyer's grand staircase. She paused on the landing and stared up at the stained-glass window. The eternal purple lilac glowed and pulsed in time with the heartbeat of the manor. Until she'd discovered the auras of everything in the manor, she had loved this window, the way the light hit the crests of old in the four corners of the steeple window and haloed the lilac in the center. But now?

Now it looked fiery, and not in an awe-inspiring way. The image sent shivers down her spine. The window gave her a sense of impending doom with its aura ebbing around it.

Maybe if all else failed, shattering the window could be their last attempt to break the curse.

Nyla smiled at the idea. She would love nothing more than to destroy a symbol of all that had gone wrong in her life recently. The impulse to shatter the window this very moment crested until she had to force herself to move up the other wing of the staircase toward the portion of the Woodlane Manor they'd chosen to call "home."

It would be a shame to shatter such a beautiful window for no purpose at all, Nyla supposed. The fondness she'd once had for it in the past didn't stop her from envisioning its demise as she ambled down the hallway toward their chosen bedrooms.

As she rounded the corner, a faint smile pulled at the corner of her lips. Nyla's eyes landed on Xander. He was waiting for her outside of her bedroom, fingering a…cufflink?

"What are you doing?" she gasped. Nyla's eyes widened as she took in the ill-fitting suit and the way Xander had jumped at the sound of her voice echoing down the hall.

Xander glanced up and held her eyes with a grin. "*We* are having fun today."

"And that requires…formal wear?" She shifted nervously.

She should've known that the moment he'd found that dress in Astrid's armoire when they were searching the manor for answers about her magic, she'd end up in it one day.

Normally, Nyla probably wouldn't have minded the distraction, but today? Today, she did mind. They didn't have time for this.

"Yes, and before you argue, we have all the time in the world, so why not?" Xander opened her bedroom door and gestured inside. Nyla leaned forward, peering inside.

Waiting patiently for someone—for her—the emerald lace dress was laid out with care on the bed.

"We really don't have time for this, though. There're so many other things we could be doing with—"

"Do you remember that day at the beach?" Xander interrupted. "You said we didn't have time for that either, but we had a great time anyway."

Nyla rolled her eyes. He was right, she supposed. "An hour, no more than that."

"Deal." Xander held out his hand to shake on it, and Nyla took it skeptically.

Today was shaping up to be a strange day. As if she were walking to her doom, Nyla hesitantly stepped into her bedroom and shut the door behind her. Eyeing the green dress, she swallowed thickly and willed herself to move toward it.

As she changed out of her clothes, Nyla's mind wandered back to a couple of nights ago when she'd fallen asleep in Xander's arms in the study. She nibbled her lips, eyeing the buttons that ran down the spine of the dress. She wasn't worried about doing them up, as that's what magic was for, but she'd be lying if she said she wasn't wondering about what was happening between her and Xander—if she was overthinking everything as a side effect of being cursed.

Was she imagining it all? The kiss to the top of her head as she'd fallen asleep? The way the idea of it had given her comfort? Or that maybe, a small part of her, craved companionship so much so that she'd imagine something like that? Was it familiar or romantic?

Nyla sighed. She didn't have any answers, and up until last season, she'd been used to her loneliness—or rather resigned to it. She knew she definitely didn't want to turn the matter around in her head for a moment longer. Instead, she pulled the smooth dress up and over her hips. Wiggling into it, she pushed her arms through the straps and pulled it the rest of the way up.

Nyla found herself missing that day on the beach outside of Huntington. It was much less treacherous than today. Maybe *treacherous* was the wrong word, but she couldn't think of it any other way. Since meeting Xander all those weeks ago, she'd been forced to face how lonely she was, and that she wasn't merely on her own but actually deprived of interaction with someone that mattered to her. And all too quickly, she'd come to find that she did care for Xander. Just how deeply she couldn't say, and she certainly didn't feel comfortable in exploring the mystery right at this moment. Not if it made her seem crazy for falling so quickly. And definitely not if it led her to discovering a different deep truth about herself or her friendship with Xander.

Slowly, Nyla turned toward the armoire. She might as well try and do something with her hair before joining Xander for whatever he had planned. The armoire opened with a creak as she sought out its mirror. She sucked in a breath. Emerald was definitely her color. The skirt flowed and rippled with each movement, perfect for twirling.

If only she had found this dress when she used to come here with her brothers! She would've never taken it off.

The dress surely would have gotten ruined, but it would've been worth every second.

Nyla snapped out of her daze and held the straps in place on the slope of her shoulders. Turning to the side, Nyla watched as her magic slid the buttons through their buttonholes and the gown came to sit perfectly on her frame. Eyeing herself in the mirror, Nyla ran her hands down the front of the delicate material, smoothing the years of abandonment from it.

A faint smile ghosted her lips. She'd never worn a dress like this before. It was fancy and beautiful, and everything she didn't need or want in her day-to-day life, but it seemed like a promise of what could be if her wildest imaginings came true. Wiggling her toes, Nyla's heart leaped. Xander had better be asking her to dance if he was making her put this on. The flowy skirt was meant for twirling and swishing, though Nyla doubted that the ballgown was suited for the Harvum Feasts she'd danced through over two years ago.

Those nights were filled with dirt and bare feet and lively music, laughter, and clapping in time to the music. Nyla started to sway as she remembered the jaunty jig-type music that the band would strike up once the feasting was done. It accompanied the traditional Harvum Dance—a dance she'd mastered. Once the couples had relinquished their hold on the night's music, the fun started. The whole party would join in, young or old, single or not, and they'd dance until there was only one left leaping and turning, their chest heaving.

A small smile pulled at Nyla's lips. Her eyes shone with a heavy sort of happiness as she longed to go back to those days of laughter and taunting her oldest brother over the Harvum Dance. For many years, Derek had been the last one dancing when the band played the final note of the Harvum Dance—that was until the Harvum Feast when Nyla had usurped him. For four years, including her last Harvum Feast before the fire, Nyla and Derek had exchanged friendly taunts to each other each Harvum, but she'd kept winning. Annabeth, the girl Derek had fallen in love with, was probably in part to blame, but Nyla knew it was because she'd spent hours that first year practicing the dance, wanting nothing more than to be the last one dancing.

As the mist of her most precious memories faded, Nyla held her own gaze in the mirror. There was no possible way that this dress could perform such a feat as mastering the Harvum Dance. This dress was meant for something gentler, just like its delicate lace. Her stomach twisted. Xander had to ask her to dance. It was the only thing this dress was meant for, but the only problem was Nyla's heart was too consumed by the weight of this last week. From Dinora's escape to her overwhelming desire to be a free woman again and rid herself of the curse, not even the happy promise of this dress seemed like it could save her from drowning.

Squaring her shoulders, Nyla's lips pressed into a grim line. She wouldn't do this to herself. Not today, not when she knew Xander was right. She needed a distraction, and whatever he'd planned for them was nothing more than that.

Nodding to herself, Nyla turned on her heel and strode toward the door. She nibbled her bottom lip. Her hand hesitated over the door handle as her stomach fluttered.

Why was Xander like this? Why did he *insist* on surprising her with distractions, even if she actually needed them and didn't want to admit it?

Taking a breath, Nyla turned the handle. As the door swung open, she was met with Xander pushing himself to stand straight from where he'd previously been leaning against the opposite wall.

His eyes widened as he stared at her. "Wow."

Nyla laughed, even as heat bloomed along her cheekbones. She brushed a piece of hair behind her ear. "Thanks. The dress is like it was made for me."

"I wish I could say the same about this suit." The suit he'd found was a bit big for him, but she didn't dare tell him he still looked dashing. It's not like she could between the nerves buzzing in her bloodstream or the dryness of her throat at the way his eyes had glimmered when she'd come out. Xander offered her his arm. "So, are you ready?"

Nyla forced herself to focus on what was happening around her, smiling.

Taking his arm and letting him lead her away from their bedrooms, she said, "You better be taking me to dance."

"If I told you, it would ruin the surprise." He led her down the hall and toward the main staircase.

"So you *are* taking me to dance?" she asked eagerly. Nyla took hold of the dress's skirt and lifted it ever so slightly so the hem wouldn't be in her way as they descended the stairs.

Xander only hummed and patted her hand teasingly. "You'll see."

As they reached the bottom of the main staircase, Xander gracefully led her around and into the Woodlane Manor's back hallway, the opposite direction of the ballroom. Both relieved and slightly confused by his change of course, a crease formed between her brows. No matter how badly she hoped she would get to dance in this dress, she hadn't realized in her excitement that it would mean being in the ballroom where so much had gone wrong for her after she'd discovered her powers. Rather than mention her confusion to Xander only to get some snarky tease in reply, she let him lead her to whatever destination he had in mind.

Her stomach twisted, but Nyla paid her nerves no mind. Too swept up in trying to figure out what Xander had planned, Nyla didn't care about the pull of static on her bones or the simmering fizzle in her blood that briefly made her think of the ritual they'd used to try and sever the curse from her aura.

They didn't travel very far down the hall before Xander slipped his arm from hers to open a door, and he bowed at the waist, inviting her into the season room with a sweeping gesture.

"After you, my lady."

"Oh, why thank you," Nyla giggled.

This whole thing was absurd. A small part of her could admit that, but this was the most excited she'd been in a long time. Even the thrum of the manor's heartbeat had subsided, its creeping creatures still for the moment—probably subdued by the nerves buzzing in her veins… *was* she that nervous? Nyla wasn't certain anymore.

Her eyes roved over the space as she stepped into the bright season room. Panes of thick glass stood for the walls above the hip-high wainscoting. The furniture had previously been pushed aside, making a small square where an area rug had once lain. Nyla spotted it in the corner, rolled up against the wall.

Instruments hovered in the air off to one side. At a glance, she couldn't see an active magical aura around them like when she used her magic to lift, move, or manipulate things, but if she focused just a fraction harder, she could see the magical signature around them.

It was a pale silver, quiet, though she didn't quite recognize it. She assumed it must be Edwin's.

Standing in the center of the room, Nyla turned to look at Xander. He stood in the doorway, watching her with anxious eyes.

"Edwin said all you'd have to do is touch them with your magic. The rest is already taken care of."

"Are you asking me to dance?" she asked teasingly.

"No," Xander replied with a smirk. He took measured steps to close the gap between them, the dazzling sun catching his hair. Bowing ever so slightly again, Xander offered her his hand. "But I am now."

Nyla made a show of thinking about it, quirking her lips. "I don't know if you'll be able to keep up with the dancing I'm used to."

"Good thing you're in a ballgown then."

Nyla laughed heartily and took his hand with a clumsy curtsy. Straightening, she summoned a bit of her magic and let it reach out to the enchanted instruments. They came to life as if an imaginary conductor had tapped their baton against their stand. The bow struck the first note of the violin.

Letting Xander position her free hand on his shoulder, Nyla found her eyes trailing toward the instruments.

Sheepishly, she admitted, "I don't think I know how to waltz."

"Just follow my lead," Xander smiled reassuringly, resting his other hand on her waist.

As the other instruments joined in, Xander led her through the basic steps, directing her through it until they were able to move in time with the music.

As the steps started to come automatically to her, she lifted her eyes to Xander's. He seemed to be in a world of his own, though his eyes were focused on her. Maybe the music had whisked him away, and he didn't realize he was staring. In a sense, Nyla's mind had gone utterly silent. Captivated by the music and carried away by the memories of past Harvum Feasts, Nyla was blissfully losing sight of reality, but not enough to forget who was leading her through this dance and why they were dancing in the first place.

With each square they completed, the space between them diminished. The pair lazily floated across the small space Xander and Edwin must have cleared earlier, wholeheartedly living in this single moment. It was almost as if time had frozen, and they were suspended in a perfect world, one which they owned. The song seemed to repeat itself at times, as if it were passing the notes between two or three instrumentalists, while other parts bounced in a way that remained fluid at the same time. It was beautiful and tranquil and yet so powerful. It simultaneously made Nyla's heart ache and soar. It managed to quell the mournfulness inside to make her swell with happy contentedness.

Her skirts swished and swayed around her legs like the ebb and flow of the waves on the sand. The season room spun around her before she faced Xander again. Nyla hadn't realized he'd twirled her until it was over, dizzy from how sudden the move was. The motion was so quick and fluid, she must've been floating on a cloud. It was the only thing that made sense.

The song, the dance, and the fragile nature of the present moment seemed to steal her breath away. She dropped her gaze in an effort to gather her thoughts and drive the cloudiness from her mind. This was the most content she'd felt in days. Even the bond between herself and the Woodlane Manor had gone quiet, like it too was content for the time being. All that seemed to be left was her pounding heartbeat and the breathlessness in her chest. A quiet realization slowly sank into her mind, still more a question than a sure conviction or notion.

Startled by her own mind, Nyla's eyes sparked as they met Xander's again, still reeling from the question posed by her heart. So many things she hadn't noticed as the dance washed away the fear and the world around them came to her awareness. But now she saw how soft Xander's dark eyes were, how *soft* he was. They stared at each other for a long time, just dancing in the golden light of the season room as if nothing really mattered. And maybe nothing did. He twirled her again.

They were so close. It was as if they were supposed to be like this, and Nyla thought it was only natural. A tiny smile tugged at her lips. She glanced down and fought the urge to rest her head on Xander's shoulder. It was the perfect height for her too, and maybe she would have if Xander hadn't gently brushed away the stray strands of fine silver hair from her face just then. The gesture sent a ripple through the emotions that had begun to rise in her, and she couldn't meet his gaze. Instead of pulling away, he cupped her face, as if it were a silent plea for her to look at him.

Nyla bit her bottom lip, lost in wading through the nameless jumble of emotions that slowly blossomed out to every fiber of her being. They began to hum when he swiped his thumb across her cheek, and that's what finally made her tilt her head up so she could meet his gold-flecked eyes. She only hoped that what she saw in them was a reflection of the complicated tangle of emotion inside of her.

At some point or another, they'd stopped dancing. Xander's hand had returned to her waist, resting comfortably there, and it wasn't like Nyla was in any rush at all to pull her hand away from where he'd set it on his shoulder or from the hand he still grasped.

"Xander?" she whispered softly. It was a miracle she could speak at all with the bubbling emotions that had finally crested her soul.

"Yeah, Nyla?" Xander sounded as if he drowned in the same way she did.

"Nothing, really. It just got really quiet is all."

Xander hummed in agreement, but that was all. Slowly, he started to move again. The way they moved now was even more graceful and made their pace before seem rushed. And all too soon, Xander twirled her again, and their eyes broke contact. That was soon rectified, though, as he dipped her, and they froze. Staring at each other again, Nyla believed they were entranced. She was almost afraid to blink for the fear of shattering this moment. Neither one seemed to want to break whatever trance had befallen them.

Xander licked his lips, and Nyla wasn't sure if the hitch in her breath was from being dipped, or if the dress was suddenly a smidgen too tight, or if it was because they were so close they could almost—

I hope I'm not interrupting, but I think we've found something.

Faster even than a bolt of lightning, the pair was upright and had sprung away from each other to face the pumpkie lingering in the open doorway. An emptiness flooded Nyla's chest that she didn't quite understand. She had a sneaking suspicion it had to do with the lingering breathlessness and the fresh memory of how it felt to hold Xander's hand.

"What is it?" Xander cleared his throat and seemed to struggle with composing himself to address Shamira.

Edwin's waiting for us in the library—you'll want to hear it for your-selves. She hesitated a moment and begrudgingly added, *I want to warn you that while it's something, you shouldn't allow your hope to overwhelm you.*

"Well, if it's something, it's worth it." Xander turned to Nyla, his eyebrow raised.

Nyla blinked, not quite sure where to look or who to address. "Right. I'll…meet you both there. I…uh…I think I'll change first."

"Do you need help up the stairs?" Xander asked, offering his hand again. Nyla hated herself in the next moment for stepping away, but she couldn't accept his help, not if she wanted to regain her composure.

"I'll be all right, thank you, though!" The forced words had barely left her mouth before she hurried out of the season room. She hiked up the hem of the dress in what was probably a very unladylike manner, but the hallway had started to close in on her like tunnel vision. Nyla gripped the banister of the main staircase and hurled herself onto the first step, running up the flight of stairs as quickly as she could. If anyone had asked her, she wouldn't have been able to tell them how she took the stairs two at a time in the ballgown. Or what exactly she was trying to escape.

The relief hit her instantly when she closed the bedroom door behind her. She slumped against it for a moment and touched the tips of her fingers to her lips. What would have happened if Shamira hadn't interrupted them?

"More importantly, would I have liked it?" she questioned the empty room. Her eyes fell closed for a moment as she drank in a deep, grounding breath.

9. BLURRING THE LINES

Xander didn't know what had happened. One second, he and Nyla were waltzing, and the next they'd sprung away from each other as if they'd each been burned.

Though it was more like he didn't know what *would've* happened had Shamira not interrupted them. Would he have kissed Nyla? Would she have kissed him? What would've happened then, if they'd kissed? Would things change between them? Was he reading too much into them and their friendship? Had Nyla left so abruptly because she *didn't* want things to change between them?

Xander shook himself out of his own head, shoving away the memory of the soft way Nyla had stared back at him, and followed after Shamira's brisk pace down the winding halls of the Woodlane Manor. Upon their entering the magically lit library, Edwin straightened and let his arms fall to his sides. Even without crossing the room, Xander could see the downward twitch of his friend's lips when his gaze had gone past them only to see that Nyla wasn't with them. The brief wrinkle of confusion that'd passed over his friend's face was gone in a flash as he came to meet them halfway.

"How'd your distraction go? Was Nyla okay while we were pushing the curse's boundaries?" he asked.

"Yeah, fine, I guess? I don't know." Xander ran a hand through his hair, trying and failing to gather his thoughts. "She didn't seem like there was something happening to her or that the curse was particularly bad or anything."

Edwin shot him a wry smile. "And your waltzing feet? I hope you haven't forgotten how while you've been away."

Xander stiffened at the reference to his past…relationships—if they could even be considered as such. The girls he'd known growing up had either liked him for his family name, because they were supposed to, or the appearance of who he was rather than who *he* was. All anyone had wanted from him was the association of being a friend or someone more to a Huntington. It was never about him, or a genuine interest in cultivating meaningful connections. Because of these deceptions, Xander had few examples of true friendship and even less in regards of what a true relationship was like. He glared at him.

"Nyla's not like them."

Not like who? Shamira asked at the same time as Edwin offered his defense.

"I didn't say that. I asked about you." Edwin brought his hands up in pacification.

"It was implied. Nyla and I are friends, and we both just needed a break from all of this. You weren't here—"

She's coming! Shamira hissed. The pumpkie still glanced between them with suspicion in her eyes, and if the twitch of her whiskers was any indication, Xander knew she was going to ask for an explanation of what Edwin had meant by the remark.

Xander blinked and tried to settle the anger in his blood. Maybe he should've never reached out to his grandfather. It just wasn't worth dredging up the past.

"What'd you find?" Nyla asked as she barreled into the room like a force of nature, haphazard and clearly distracted by something.

"You," Edwin said without hesitation.

Nyla stopped short. Her mouth opened and closed, but ultimately remained silent. Her eyes flashed with confusion. His brows furrowed at Edwin's lack of an explanation. He wished someone would just tell them what they'd found.

While you and Xander were dancing, Edwin and I were outside the manor's boundaries. We tested the curse from outside and realized that it's not you that's cursed, but the manor itself, Shamira explained.

Edwin picked up where the pumpkie left off. "That's probably why you can feel the manor like it's a part of you because you aren't bound to the manor—the manor is bound to you."

Xander glanced between the two of them. What did this all mean in terms of breaking the curse?

"Then how did Dinora curse me if the spell is on the manor?" Nyla asked before he could get a word in.

"She transferred the bond from herself to you," Edwin clarified.

The only curse on Dinora was a power-dampening spell.

Xander's head spun as he tried to keep up with all the magical talk. Neither Shamira nor Edwin seemed as if they wanted to say what needed to be said. Based on the fleeting look they shared, Xander didn't think he wanted to know what they knew.

But Nyla evidently did.

"So…if I'm not 'cursed,' how do we break the bond?" Her voice was timid, uncertain. "Burn down the manor?"

"Well, no, that might kill you too. You need to transfer the bond," Edwin answered quietly, unable to hold Nyla's gaze.

"Transfer the bond?" she echoed. Xander frowned as the words twisted over in his mind. If Dinora transferred the bond to another person—to Nyla—then all Nyla had to do was the same thing. If it worked once, surely it could work again. Nyla *had* to transfer the bond.

At the realization, he went stock still at the same moment Nyla squared her shoulders. Taking a quick glance at her, he saw the moment her own confusion melted from her features. Annoyance crossed her face. Her nostrils flared, and Xander couldn't help but see the way she'd looked when she'd forced herself to standing that day on the Woodlane Manor's stone stairs.

He'd called her an avenging angel as she'd stood there with her magic crackling all around her, outlining her like a halo. He hadn't been able to see her face then, not from the distance between them, but the glint in her eyes now seemed just as powerful as the impression that image had left on him—and hopefully on Dinora too.

With a deadly voice, Nyla ordered, "Shamira, tell me everything, or so help me I *will* burn down this manor."

Shamira shifted on her paws. *You have to transfer the bond to someone else in order to be free of it yourself. Severing it from your aura can't be done because it's like an echo of the curse, not the curse itself. The only way to stop an echo is to stop the maker or the curse's vessel—in this case, the manor—and we can't do that in a timely manner. The spellwork is too complicated and powerful for the three of us to work through if we ever want to catch Dinora and stop her.*

As it was, Edwin and I had a difficult time summoning the manor's aura to examine it. We tried to sever the curse from it, but it couldn't be done. There was too much interference, and we were afraid of hurting you.

Silence fell as Shamira looked away, with a dazed shake of her head, as if she felt ashamed of their efforts or that they'd failed in some way.

Xander tried to digest and sift through all that Shamira had said, and what Edwin had said in his own way. It seemed as though there was only one option, and that was to transfer the bond. He couldn't imagine transferring it to Edwin, seeing as it might take every magic wielder—human or not—to stop whatever Dinora's plans were. It couldn't be passed to Shamira because she was the only one who could rally support from the pumpkies, and she was also a powerful magic user.

"Transfer it to me." He turned to plead with Nyla. "I'm the only one here who isn't necessary to stopping Dinora."

Edwin coughed in the background, a sign Xander recognized as his discomfort.

"No," Nyla hissed, "I'm not transferring this infernal curse to you so you'll be bound here."

"Nyla—"

"I said *no*, Xander."

Nyla didn't give him, or any of them, a chance to say something more before she turned and stalked out of the library's double doors. He watched her go, exasperation in his heart. Maybe springing that declaration on everyone—on her—wasn't his brightest idea, but what else were they supposed to do?

If the bond between Nyla and the Woodlane Manor had to be transferred, then it had to be transferred to someone who was…

Expendable.

Xander made his excuses to Edwin and Shamira and followed after Nyla as quickly as he could. He made it out of the library just in time to see her hurry around the corner into the foyer. She was probably heading outside, like she always did when she was angry or overwhelmed and trying to ground herself.

Desperately, Xander swerved into the kitchen, stripping off his suit jacket and tossing it away as he darted out the back door. He took off down the cobblestone path in an attempt to catch Nyla before she got too far.

Hardly a second later, he saw Nyla pounding down the steps of the veranda in the distance. Xander picked up his pace.

"Nyla!" he called out once he got a little closer.

She stopped in her tracks and whipped around. Xander braced himself for anything, but when he took in the look on her face, it was as though he'd been punched in the gut. It wasn't anger or irritation that plagued her features, but rather a grave mournfulness and a sad gleam in her eye that made his chest tighten. He briefly registered the contemplative look before a grim expression took over Nyla's features right down to her pursed lips and the slight narrowing of her eyes.

"You're not talking me into transferring the bond to you. So don't even try, Mr. Silver Tongue." She wagged her finger at him.

"I wasn't—" Xander stopped as Nyla fixed him with a glare before she started walking again. "Okay, so maybe I was, but I can put that off for now if you've got something else you wanna talk about."

"Such a gentleman," Nyla muttered as he trailed next to her.

For a while, they walked in silence, occasionally crunching the fallen leaves when one came across their path. Xander started humming absently. After a few measures, he realized it was the song from before, from the distraction he'd planned for Nyla.

"I'm not transferring the curse to you," Nyla said quietly, wrapping her arms loosely around herself.

"I'm not asking you to," he replied, "Well, not right now anyway…"

Nyla bumped into him jestingly. "You better not ask me ever again because it'll always be 'no.'"

"Well, then I guess I won't be asking again." He bumped into her in return. "So then, what are we going to do? You need to transfer the bond *and* go after Dinora."

"I was thinking about trying to astral project, but actually being conscious of it this time," Nyla said uncertainly.

Xander froze, and Nyla followed suit, staring at him expectantly.

The first two times Nyla had astral projected, she hadn't been aware of what she was doing and had essentially been comatose for two days. The only good that had seemingly come of that was the fact that they'd gotten to see Nan and George.

"Okay…" he started, matching her tone. "One question, though, do you know how to astral project on demand?"

"No…but if I can collapse a ceiling in, then astral projection should be just as easy, right?"

"And you have enough energy to do that?"

"I mean, I don't *think* my magic is limited like Dinora's was, though I haven't really tried anything big since…well, you know."

Nyla got an excited gleam in her eye and started to bounce on her heels.

"No, whatever you're about to suggest, no. Talk to Shamira first."

"And here I was thinking you were fun," Nyla pouted. She started to turn toward the path ahead and looped her arm through his. "Next Harvum, hopefully when this is all over and we can both leave, we'll have to go to a Harvum Feast so I can teach you how to *really* dance."

Xander laughed as he let her lead the way around the fountain and up the front courtyard to the stone steps.

"And astral projecting is going to get us there?"

"Yes and no," Nyla laughed. "I was hoping to speak with Astrid again. Now that I have control over my magic and actually *know* about magic, it'll probably be easier to get some answers out of her."

Xander didn't respond, bobbing his head in thought.

Nyla turned to him as they approached the front doors of the Manor. "I should go find Shamira."

"I should probably get out of this suit."

She reached up and fixed his bowtie, her hands lingering just a fraction of a second.

"Probably."

Nyla didn't make to move away. Xander couldn't find the will to glance away or move from this spot either.

"We're not going to change, are we?" Nyla asked quietly. Her lilac eyes searched his face for something Xander wasn't certain of.

"Not if we don't want to." It was all Xander could think to say. Change could mean a lot of things, and like everything right now, he wasn't certain in which way Nyla meant.

"Good, because I like how things are. Just you and me." Nyla beamed up at him, half laughing. "Well, and Shamira too, I guess."

Xander rolled his eyes. "Yeah, and Shamira too."

Nyla poked him playfully as she stepped away and approached the door, reaching a hand to open it. "I thought you two were getting along better."

"We are," Xander said, stepping in after her and shutting the huge door firmly behind them, not that it kept the cool air from wafting through the drafty manor house. "Sometimes it's hard, though, not because of Shamira, just…in general."

Nyla nodded sympathetically. "I get that. Maybe one day, it won't come between you two."

Xander didn't answer, choosing to ignore the subject like always. He didn't want to think about his sister's murder at the clutches of a cerbertes—a hellhound—or the impact witnessing that gruesome scene had had on his heart. He parted ways with Nyla in the foyer, telling her that he'd meet her after she spoke with Shamira about her astral projection idea.

Right now, he needed to find Edwin and see if there was maybe another loophole to help them break or transfer the bond. The more options they had, the better their chances—the better Nyla's chances— of being able to leave this place and stop Dinora.

***

As she watched Xander's retreating back, Nyla found herself frowning. There had to be another way; there just *had* to be. Even though Shamira and Edwin seemed convinced it was too time-consuming to sever the bond from the manor's aura, Nyla needed to believe there was another way to free herself—a way that didn't come at a cost to someone else. Maybe if the three of them tried, they could manage such a feat.

But she knew they wouldn't risk it, and she didn't want to die. There was too much to live for still.

Instead, Nyla shifted her focus to her astral projection idea. If she could find Astrid on the astral plane, then Nyla could ask her everything she'd ever wanted to know.

She could ask about why her family had been murdered in that fire two years ago, about her newfound magic or if she'd always had magic like Shamira had claimed, about Dinora, and then about Cedric. Nyla could ask Astrid about how to break the bond.

And once she had those answers, they could all leave. Then she could go after Dinora, and Xander could…

Nyla didn't know what Xander would do, or what she wanted to hope he'd do. She knew he'd asked his grandfather for help on her behalf, but she didn't want to force Xander into a situation he wasn't ready for or didn't want to be in. By all means, Xander had no obligation toward her—and never truly did, just as she had no obligation to him aside from their new and steadfast friendship.

Stowing her hopes away for later, Nyla closed her eyes in concentration. Opening her mind up to the bond between herself and the manor, Nyla sought out Shamira's whereabouts. She supposed that one day she'd have to use her own magic to sense others' signatures, but right now, she had a highly accurate means of finding whoever it was she could possibly look for—so long as they were within the boundary of the Woodlane Manor.

As Nyla paced around the foyer, she focused on finding Shamira. The pumpkie was nowhere within the manor. Nyla frowned, not too keen on waiting for Shamira to return. She could always ask Edwin, but she'd rather work with Shamira. After all, everything she'd learned about magic thus far, Shamira had taught her.

But Shamira wasn't within the manor's bounds. Standing in the middle of the foyer, Nyla let her magic flood her veins. Invisibly, she let it flow through the manor, stretching beyond its foundations, seeking out her friend. She was able to pick up a faint trace of Shamira to the northeast, but there was a stronger, fresher trail of Shamira's signature directly to the north. That was the trail Nyla focused her magic on.

As her magic followed the trail of Shamira's essence, Nyla sensed the pumpkie in the woods, completely still. Nyla's brow furrowed. Still or…

She didn't let herself finish that concern. Instead, she did the only thing she could think of. She urged her silent words to reach Shamira. *Can you hear me?*

Nyla? What are you doing? came Shamira's distant reply.

Nyla's lips quirked into a smile. *Looking for you.*

Is everything all right?

Fine! I just have to ask you something, but it can wait until you're back. I'll be there in a minute.

Nyla let the connection fade. Her magic receded back to her and faded, waiting to be called upon again. Nyla could feel her lips stretch into a wide grin. It seemed that every day she was doing something new with her magic, things she never would've thought possible. Proudly, she stared up at the stained-glass window as if she were goading it. She wouldn't shatter it, not yet. She wanted to make certain it survived long enough to witness her triumphs. Then, and only then, would Nyla return to see it—and maybe the whole of the Woodlane Manor—destroyed.

You had something to ask me? Shamira stalked into the foyer from around the grand staircase.

Nyla blinked away her visions of grandeur. "Yeah. I want to astral project."

Shamira's eyes crinkled like a human would furrow their brow. Her whiskers twitched, and Nyla wondered if this was the pumpkie's way of frowning. *You want to astral project?*

"Well, astral travel, if there's a difference. I was hoping to find Astrid again on the astral plane and ask her how to fix this," Nyla explained, wringing her hands.

That's a great idea. I can't imagine why we didn't think of that sooner. Shamira's praise made Nyla's pride swell despite her reservations about astral projecting again. *Have you ever astral projected before?*

"Well…" Nyla bit her lip and gathered up her courage to recall what had happened in Caselle. "I have, but not *consciously*."

Shamira narrowed her eyes. *What do you mean, 'not consciously?'*

Nyla took a breath and quickly explained how she believed her magic was reactionary and sometimes acted on the behalf of her subconscious. In the case of her astral travels, Nyla reasoned that her magic acted on her need to find clarification for the visions Fortune Falls had shown her. Or maybe she was pulled onto the astral plane because Astrid seemed to be waiting for her when she'd first come to the astral copy of the Woodlane Manor.

But that didn't explain how she'd ended up astral projecting into the ballroom, or why Cedric had been waiting for her. Would he have pulled her onto the astral plane too? Nyla didn't know what to make of the ballroom fight with the red-eyed man who'd not only tried to kill her, but had killed her family. She still had a scar on her collarbone and the faint trail of it on her shoulder from his attempt on her life.

When Nyla had finished recounting the tales of her astral travels, Shamira was silent for a moment. After a heartbeat, Shamira said, *That must have taken a lot of magic, and an even greater toll on you. Did you see a Healer?*

Nyla shook her head. "Xander knew a doctor, and she gave me some tonics to help restore my energy and alleviate the pain."

Sounds like a competent doctor then. I know you humans have a hard enough time seeing eye to eye on science versus magic, so to find a doctor that acknowledges the strides of Healing and where it intersects with your 'conventional' medicine is quite an accomplishment.

"Nan's rational like that."

Nan? Shamira bobbed her head, her tail flicking. *I didn't realize you were in contact with your extended family.*

Nyla laughed. "No, they're all in Eurland, and I haven't seen them since…well, since I was a baby, probably. Some of them came over to see Lydia when she was born, but I don't really remember that all too well either." Nyla paused for a second, contemplating what her distant relatives had come to think of her in her two-year absence and if they ever made it to Hart to pay their respects. She shoved her curiosity aside and shrugged. "Nan is Xander's…I don't know how they're related, but Xander calls Gerri 'Nan,' so I call her 'Nan' too."

Shamira seemed to arch her brow, but didn't remark on that.

Then I suppose you should get comfortable, Shamira stated, already turning to lead the way up the grand staircase. *Astral travel can be demanding, and sometimes difficult to achieve. I have no doubt you'll manage, though.*

Nyla uttered a hesitant "thank you" and begrudgingly followed the pumpkie upstairs. Her fingers trembled. Nyla shook her hands out to steady them, shoving aside the hum of fear beating in her heart. It might not be Nyla's favorite plan, but it was far better than the alternative. Transferring the bond to someone else wasn't even an option she was willing to consider. She would never do to someone what was done to her. If she did, it would only make her as bad as Dinora and Cedric.

Nyla was exhausted by the unending riddle of her life. She wanted to take back control, as quickly as possible, and find that place to settle down, lay her roots again for good. No more running from the past, *her* past. Rather than hiding in the shadows, Nyla wanted to bask in the sunlight and declare herself as alive and happy and content. No more finding refuge in places like the perilous Shadow Forest or self-destructive adventures to wretched manors with evil sorceresses hiding within.

Nyla was done searching for answers that only caused more pain and distress than they were worth.

When Dinora was dead, Nyla would rest and live for her own happiness, as she'd promised her family when she'd returned to Hart only a week ago after two long years of running away from her life, from her grief.

10. Against All Odds

Shamira gave a lengthy lecture on astral traveling. She explained the best practices, the dangers—though Nyla was all too aware of those—and the energy it took to travel for an extended period of time, especially on the astral plane.

What Nyla found truly interesting, though, was Shamira's explanation about the astral plane itself. The plane was a state of suspension. It was neither the world of the living nor the afterlife. Neither was it the state between the two. The astral plane was like a mirror world of sorts: it was the past, the present, and the realm of being. Everything that existed in this world first existed on the astral plane, and an astral representation remained on the plane. According to Shamira, that was the astral body and the one Nyla would assume while she traveled. An exact copy of her, the astral body was quite literally the representation of her soul on the astral plane.

And if something happened to either her physical body or her astral body…Nyla swallowed at Shamira's reminder. If something were to happen to either body, and the connection between the two was severed, Nyla would die.

Once Shamira was done with her lesson, she eyed Nyla grimly. *And you're sure you have enough energy to travel for an extended period of time? You don't want a tonic now?*

"I'm sure," Nyla replied shortly. Guiltily, she added, "Maybe afterwards…if the tonic could be made into something more desirable?"

Like a cookie? Shamira offered.

She nodded, laughing. "Yes, like a cookie."

Shamira barked a laugh. Wishing Nyla luck, she took up her position in the window seat of the bedroom and watched as Nyla reclined back on the bed. Shifting around, Nyla tried to get comfortable and clear her mind. Finally satisfied that she was comfortable with the pillow arrangements, Nyla closed her eyes.

Her skin prickled. Nyla forced her muscles to loosen, for her mind to go quiet. Her face twisted into a pinched frown. Her nose wrinkled. Her lips twisted in mock discomfort. Nyla opened her eyes and craned her head to glare at Shamira.

"Maybe you could refrain from staring at me while I do this?"

And what would you have me do? The pumpkie bristled.

"Anything but stare at me."

With a scowl, Shamira stood and walked in a circle atop the cushion of the window seat. Nyla watched as she turned her back to the room and settled to look out of the window. *Happy now?*

"Very," Nyla breathed, easing back against the pillows.

Once again closing her eyes, Nyla focused her breathing. Her power awakened and spread through every fiber of her being. She brought Astrid to the forefront of her mind. In doing so, Nyla hoped it would allow her to astral travel and easily find her ancestor. There wasn't any guarantee that even if she managed to astral project, she'd be able to contact Astrid.

Her limbs turned to nothing. The weight of her body fell away completely. Wind rippled over her. Goosebumps erupted on her skin. A phantom chill tingled down her limbs, down her spine. When Nyla opened her eyes, she was staring down at her own body.

To say she was perturbed was an understatement, but Nyla was much too proud of herself to linger on the disturbance. She turned excitedly to Shamira. The pumpkie glanced over at her body, her eyes focused slightly to the left of where Nyla stood.

"Can you see me? Or hear me?" Nyla asked.

Shamira's whiskers twitched. She sniffed the air.

When no reply came, Nyla shrugged and started for the bedroom door. "Well, in any case, I have a long-dead relative of mine to find."

Nyla yanked open the door and staggered backward. Wind swept by and caressed her body as it blew through the door. A few leaves swirled inside on the light breeze, furthering Nyla's astonishment. Her eyes followed the colored flagstone path up to the front steps of the Woodlane Manor. The success of her astral projection sank in as she swallowed the bundle of nerves sitting in her throat. Much like the night when they'd arrived at the manor, magic leapt and danced in the bowls hanging from the metal claws of the gleaming raverin statues that lined the driveway. The flameless torches spread throughout the front courtyard, bathing the Woodlane Manor and its entrance in a soft whimsical light. This was the manor in its prime, Nyla realized.

With wonder in her eye, she stepped onto the stone pathway. The doorknob disappeared from beneath her fingertips. She tossed a glance over her shoulder, but the Woodlane Manor she'd been bound to and had known since childhood had faded away. In its place was the Woodlane Manor of the astral plane. Nyla tried to blink away the haze that seemed to cling to everything before she realized it wasn't her vision causing it. Everything seemed too crisp, too sharp, but the more she stared, the more that sharpness gave away to a hazy outline. The soft glow of everything around her and the near-pristine condition of the manor were the only indications that Nyla had succeeded in her aim to astral project…well, that and the fact that her bedroom door had led here rather than out into the hallway.

Nyla prayed to whatever power that would listen to her that she'd find Astrid here.

Like the night of their arrival, Nyla slowly made her way up the mosaic cobblestone driveway, but this time she was alone. There was no archer at her back or a warrior pumpkie to lead the way. There was only herself and her magic.

Nyla knew she'd be okay. She'd made it through so much already, and now she knew how to use her magic. Let Dinora find her—or Cedric if he were still alive. She was ready for whatever might lie ahead.

The water fountain babbled happily, a stark contrast to the trepidation its presence had instilled in her upon their arrival.

Nyla hurried up the stone steps, not wanting to linger on the front entryway for too long. Although Shamira had healed her bruises from the recoil of Dinora's magic and her own magic colliding with each other, sometimes she could still feel them. The backlash had slammed her into the stone steps, a scene that replayed only as a feeling in her nightmares. It was strange how her body remembered every minute sensation of the battle's final moments, but her mind could only recall fragmented pieces after their magics had fought against each other. Nyla supposed it was better that way. She wasn't certain she wanted to be able to remember those harrowing moments. It was bad enough to feel the impact, the gasp of her lost breath, and the jolt of her body against the stone in her nightmares during her seldom moments of rest.

Nyla shook the vague awareness from her mind and reached for the sparkling handle of the tall steeple door. As she did, the door opened. Reeling back, Nyla rallied her magic, only to let it fizzle out as the figure in the door's shadow stepped into the light.

Astrid stood in the opening, her silver hair shining in the afternoon sunlight. Resolutely, Nyla stared back at the lilac eyes that had become her own. One breath, two breaths, silence. Nyla clenched and unclenched her hands.

"You wanted to speak with me?" Astrid stepped aside and motioned for Nyla to enter.

"I was hoping to ask about the curse—and the war?" Nyla stepped inside and watched as Astrid shut the door and ushered her further into the foyer. Coming to a stop at the base of the stairs, she glanced up at the stained-glass window with a rueful smile. Even now she couldn't find it in herself to see its beauty despite the happy sunlight spilling through it.

"I'm sorry," Astrid said, completely still beside her. "I never knew it would come to this."

Nyla turned to her, shrugging. "Did anyone?"

Astrid frowned, her eyes downcast. "I suppose not, but I should've considered it. I should've never left this up to Fate."

Nyla turned from the window and squared her shoulders. "Why couldn't you end it?"

The lilac eyes that had since become her own snapped up to look at her. Astrid's features sharpened before they lost all tension. Sitting heavily upon a stair, Astrid didn't hold Nyla's stare.

"I don't know," she said dejectedly.

Nyla said nothing as she sat beside her ancestor on the grand steps. Briefly, Nyla wondered who else was here, if anyone. How did the astral plane work? Did it manifest around your will and intention, or was it preexisting and you were only a visitor to its being?

"War is a difficult, terrible thing," Astrid said at last, her voice withdrawn. She wrapped her arms around her middle and took a deep shuddering breath. Nyla studied her intently and tried to rein in the anger simmering in her blood. She knew, rationally, that Astrid had done the best she could at the time and couldn't say what she would've done had their roles been reversed.

"I wasn't much older than you are…well, maybe I was, but I was still fairly young when the war broke out," Astrid explained. "At the time, the Royal Mage had just stepped down, and I was newly appointed. Cedric and I…we'd parted ways bitterly because I had recently learned that Dinora was loyal to the old Corvus, from before the war for Tenebrese independence. I didn't know until well after the Corvids had invaded that she was the lost queen, and he the lost prince. People had said that they'd died in the previous war, the Ten Years' War, but that had not been true.

"Sometimes I still wonder how they'd managed it, how she'd managed to conceal themselves within our own court. I suppose it was with magic and a good deal of luck. But there was no denying it when the Corvids came and she joined their ranks as their leader, and Cedric had gone with her. By then, it was too late for so many things." Astrid paused, glancing at her lap. Nyla studied her face, the one she'd initially thought had seemed so much like hers. But in truth, beyond the eyes and hair that they shared through the magic Astrid had bequeathed to her, they were nothing alike. Astrid had lines etched into her gaunt face and a dullness that dampened the image of the bright young girl in the portrait Nyla had seen in the Woodlane Manor. "You asked me why I couldn't end it, but in truth, I don't have an answer."

"You truly loved him, didn't you?" Nyla asked quietly.

Astrid swallowed, drawing her arms tighter around herself as if she could hold herself together under Nyla's scrutiny. "I did, and no matter how much I try, there's still a part of me that foolishly loves him. Love is…unkind that way. Sometimes it makes us hold onto people longer than we should because of the fondness we have for them, and no matter how much you think you've moved on…there are days when you haven't. I hate him, but part of me betrays my rational mind, and I despise it too."

The words sank in slowly. Staring out across the foyer, the image of Cedric strolling into the Woodlane Manor after Xander had left came to Nyla's mind. Slow and sure of himself, he'd stalked into the manor without a care for the terror his presence had brought her. And now, he was probably dead in the aftermath of all that had transpired. He might've survived the ceiling Nyla had caved in, but she still wondered whether that magically enforced shove had injured him gravely enough to kill him.

"I…We believe Cedric might be dead," Nyla said quietly.

"Cedric is dead?" Astrid said in a hollow voice. After a heartbeat, she shook her head. The dazed expression Nyla's words had brought faded into a sharp focus. The furrow of her brows angled in determination rather than shock or worry. "It's for the better perhaps."

Nyla silently agreed, watching Astrid straighten beside her and compose herself with the clearing of her throat. Astrid had a darker gleam in her eye than she did, a pessimism that seemed all too bitter for the life Nyla wanted to live.

Curiously, Nyla asked, "He hasn't shown up in the afterlife yet, or to you?"

Astrid shook her head. "No, but you didn't really come all this way to talk about Cedric, did you?"

"I suppose not," Nyla sighed. "Dinora transferred the bond to me, and I need to break it as soon as possible because she's free and more than likely alive."

Astrid let out a long sigh and scrubbed her face with her palms, standing. Nyla followed her with her eyes as she began to pace up and down the wine-colored carpet runner. Astrid's head bowed as she mulled over Nyla's predicament, or at least that's what Nyla assumed the woman was doing. After a moment, Astrid threw her hands up and crossed the long runner one last time before she stopped a few paces away from Nyla.

"There are so many things I wish I could do differently," Astrid started, "but lamenting about my own failures won't help you now, and it won't bring your family back. I am truly sorry for what happened to them."

Nyla stood, her voice pleading. "Then help me now. Tell me everything, and no more riddles, no more vague heroic prophecies, please. I don't have time for mysteries."

"No, you really don't," Astrid snorted. "I'm sorry if you feel I've only given you 'vague heroic prophecies' instead of the bald truth, but the truth is I am still afraid of Dinora and the lengths she will go to in order to win. She has a means of spying everywhere, and I feared she would have her ways here too. I don't believe she does, not anymore at least. But meeting here in the Woodlane Manor of the astral plane, with her bound to it, I was skeptical. Even though I designed the curse on the manor, I didn't know if the bond between it and Dinora would allow her to sense its astral plane too."

"So, you *knew* the bond would make whoever was bound to the manor aware of *everything* within the manor's borders?!" Nyla interrupted.

Astrid's laugh was almost gleeful. "I wanted to make sure Dinora would suffer. In doing so, I only punished whoever she transferred the bond to, but after 647 years, I would have thought she'd never figure it out. Tell me how this all happened."

"It's a long story," Nyla admitted with a sigh. "I'm afraid we don't have time for it all, but the facts are this: Cedric had this potion that weakened me, and I think it helped break the dampener on Dinora's power because he was stealing magic from the land, so I'm assuming he gathered it for her or to help her break the curse—I mean the binding. And then Dinora bound me to the manor before she got away."

"Sounds like quite the plot." Astrid clicked her tongued against her teeth. Her eyes flashed to Nyla, warmed with concern. "Are you all right?"

"I am now. Shamira—she's a pumpkie—managed to heal me, but according to her, I was nearly dead." Nyla's eyes fell. The words lingered between them for a heartbeat before Nyla added, "I collapsed the ceiling. Well, two ceilings, but Dinora and Cedric fixed them to get through."

"Bold, impressive, though if I might suggest a more direct attack next time?" Astrid offered with a smile.

"Noted." Nyla returned the woman's smile, a warm nostalgia filling her chest. She missed this sort of familial connection. Even if she'd initially harbored a resentment against Astrid, it was easy to fall into this kind of banter with the woman. Even though they were generations apart, they weren't so different. And though they hardly knew each other as family or even as individuals, there was that connection that Nyla longed for, a familiarity that transcended generations, the very fabric of her roots.

"I need to break the bond, now," she nearly pleaded. "Could I, Shamira, and another Caster break the bond? My magic isn't limited… that we know of."

Astrid shook her head. "Even if you had all the magic in the world, you couldn't break the curse. I designed it that way, as a precaution. I didn't know what side of the war, or of the living, Cedric would end up on, so it was the only way I could ensure Dinora would die here."

Nyla shrank, crestfallen. If they couldn't break the bond, then what was she supposed to do?

"I'm truly sorry, Nyla." Astrid wrapped her in a strong hug. "You have to transfer it. Any living thing should work, but if not, sacrifices have to be made if you want to stop Dinora."

"Any living thing?" The flicker of hope inside of Nyla brightened once again as they pulled away. "I could transfer it to a plant then?"

"In theory, though I'm not positive. The bond might recoil, but you will live…" Astrid trailed off. "Maybe it's best to transfer it to a person who wouldn't mind aiding in the effort to save the world, and that's not a 'vague heroic prophecy' or hyperbole. Dinora will tear apart the very fabric of the universe to achieve her ends."

"And what end is that?"

"She rallied an extreme sect of Corvids by manipulating their anger and grief in the aftermath of the Ten Years' War to exact revenge on Tenebris and Eurland for the atrocities committed when we seceded from the Empire of Corvus."

"What atrocities?"

"They broke Corvid Law," Astrid explained simply. "The Ten Years' War was a bitter war, no matter what side you fought for or stood with. I was only a child at the time, but I remember the hardship, the air of betrayal and mistrust. It was stifling, like…like smoke. We were all Corvid at one time, but in the end, there was Eurland and Tenebris alongside a weakened Corvus. Some people, especially Dinora as the dethroned queen of the empire, never forgave the underhanded methods of the rebels, but Dinora has arguably broken more Corvid Laws and lines of morality than any one before her."

"You're Corvid?" Nyla asked curiously.

"By blood only. I am proud to be Tenebrese and to have served my country. I only wish I had served it more faithfully and hadn't allowed its enemies so close to its defenses."

"Cedric?"

"He was my right hand." Astrid's eyes glazed over with memories. Nyla searched for a sign of emotion, for fondness or hatred or regret, but Astrid's features had gone completely blank, withdrawn. "I loved him, and that is my biggest regret of all."

Nyla was quiet for a moment. "You shouldn't. If you loved him, then there was probably a reason, and I trust you believed it was a good one. All love has to teach us something. Don't let it embitter you because then you go through life as someone no one wants to be around, and then you will never know love at all."

Astrid blinked. "I can't forgive him."

"You don't have to, but you should forgive yourself." Nyla shrugged. "After all, you died for Tenebris. You sacrificed yourself to try and save everyone, and in a sense, you did."

Astrid stood and put a hand on Nyla's scarred shoulder, holding her gaze firmly. "Do better than me. *Live* for your country. Survive."

Nyla clasped her hand over Astrid's. Determination crested in her heart. "I intend to."

"Good." Astrid nodded firmly, sliding her hand from under Nyla's. "I'm glad you came to see me. You seem less anxious and altogether lighter, less lonely than you had when we met last."

Nyla tilted her head to the side. She didn't see how Astrid could be right in assuming so. If anything, she felt worse. After all, there was an evil sorceress seeking revenge against Tenebris over a centuries-old conflict, and as of right now, Nyla and her friends were the only people working to stop her.

"I'll have to take your word for it then," Nyla responded. With downcast eyes, she added, "I should probably get back and let them know what our options are."

Astrid stopped her from turning, her eyes flashing urgently. "Did you find it? My wand?"

"Yeah," Nyla started, her brows drawing together in confusion. "But why did you want me to find it? What good is it to me?"

Astrid smiled almost wickedly. "Wands are powerful tools if you use them well," she explained. "With my wand you could practice precise magic, or you could absorb energy without taxing yourself. It's a safe means of magic absorption, and my wand is one of the strongest ever made, a fact I'm sure still holds true."

"How?" Nyla asked, dumbfounded.

"The crystals, and the gold. Gold is a strong conductor of magic, and crystals make the perfect body for the storage of magic. When used in tandem," she started proudly, "the magic it can store is exponential."

"But how does that help me now?" Nyla insisted.

Astrid shrugged. "It may not help you now, but it may be of use later. I just didn't want Dinora to find it. I never imagined she'd transfer the bond, or live this long, and though I trusted my wards, the longer she remained alive, the more anxious I became that she would break them and find that wand. Promise me, no matter what happens, you'll keep it on you?"

Nyla nodded. "I will."

Silently, they strolled back up the foyer and toward the front doors of the Woodlane Manor. As they reached the doors, Astrid explained, "To reenter your body, picture it. Picture sitting up, not looking down at your body, and you should return to your plane of existence already reconnected with your physical form."

"Okay." Nyla nodded nervously.

As she pulled the oak door open and took a step through, Astrid called after her. "Take care, Nyla."

Nyla didn't look back. Focusing her mind on sitting up in the bed she'd left behind on the physical plane, she took a breath and held it. With another step, gravity took hold of her. Nyla shut her eyes tightly as the weight of the world pressed down on her. A softness that she could sink into seemed to mold itself around her. She wiggled around some, her limbs too heavy to move.

Nyla? Shamira's voice flitted across her consciousness.

At the gritty sound of the pumpkie's voice, Nyla cracked her eyes open. "By Helpet," she marveled, nearly whining at the effort it took to lift her hand from the bedspread, "I'm back. I'm in my body. I'm back!"

Xander laughed off to the side, and Nyla shifted to see him sitting by the fireplace. He'd angled her favorite chair so he could keep an eye on her as well as watch the wood-burning fire he must've started.

"Laugh all you want, I'm genuinely *shocked* this went as smoothly as it did."

"Well, I'm glad astral travel can be added to your list of successful accomplishments," Xander teased, standing from his chair, "but I'm afraid energy tonic cookies can't be added to mine."

Nyla groaned. "So, I have to *drink* the tonic?"

I enchanted it, Shamira said in an attempt to comfort her.

"Can you enchant the texture?" Nyla's face pinched into a look of disgust.

It'll probably make it worse.

"Fine." Nyla struggled to sit up. Once she had, Xander offered her a slimy-looking drink. While it tasted like butter chip cookies, it was anything but. "Shamira, I consider you a friend, so I say this from a place of love, but you need new tonic recipes."

Shamira let out a gruff laugh. *Sorry my clan's heritage doesn't suit your human tongue.*

Nyla finished the rest of the tonic off with a grimace that wracked down her spine. With a hiss, she handed the glass back to Xander. "I have to transfer the curse, but Astrid says it can be to any living thing, not necessarily a person."

"And that's safe?" Xander asked skeptically.

"We'll find out, I guess."

I don't know if that's such a good idea, Nyla. The bond might not take to any living thing, Shamira warned.

"I have to try. I am *not* transferring this curse to another person or creature, especially not without trying another means of ridding myself of it," Nyla spat. Taking a deep breath to calm herself, she added, "I'm trying this whether you two support me or not."

Shamira and Xander shared a look, something she'd noticed they'd taken to doing often now. Nyla waited patiently for either of them to say something more to dissuade her, but neither of them did.

"So, what are you going to transfer the bond to?"

Nyla glanced toward the window beside the armoire. In her mind's eye she saw the large tree with its sprawling branches that stood proudly in the center of the back courtyard's maze.

"I have an idea."

***

Having spent the better part of the afternoon recuperating from her astral travels, Nyla led her friends through the courtyard until they reached the very center. Edwin joined them to help Shamira with a magical shield in case the attempt to transfer the bond recoiled on them. While she appreciated his contribution to Shamira's safety precautions, Nyla wasn't so certain she wanted Edwin there. Despite how hard he'd tried to help them—to help her—she still couldn't say how she felt about him. His presence was a strange mix of cool professionalism and familiarity. When she'd asked Xander about it, he'd only laughed and assured her that Edwin was a good friend, a friend who sometimes became so focused on his objective that he forgot himself entirely. She supposed that was all there was to it. Edwin wasn't consciously standoffish or rude; he was just focused on his task, as she was now.

She greeted the towering tree with its lingering scarlet leaves like the old friend it was. She used to climb to the top of its branches when she was younger. To this day, she still swore that from the topmost branches of the massive tree, you could see all of Hart and beyond the horizon.

Now, Nyla wore a somber expression. It was one that told those around her that she was swept away in fond memories, reminiscing while on the precipice of something bittersweet. Even though she knew that the tree had been here for a long time and would be here for much longer, the task before her still gave her pause.

With a soft smile, Nyla reached out her hand and laid her palm on the rough, golden-brown bark.

"You're sure you're ready for this?" Xander asked from behind her.

"As I'll ever be." She tried to sound confident, but even she could hear the hesitation in her voice.

We'll be right here if you need us. Shamira assured her.

Nyla took a deep breath to steady herself. Shifting her feet shoulder-width apart, she squared her shoulders and braced herself for any kind of backlash. Closing her eyes for a moment to clear her mind, Nyla gathered her magic and bared her aura. When her eyes opened, she could just see the edges of her body's mystical outline. Planting her feet firmly on the soft dirt beneath her boots, she focused on the tree until its shimmering, iridescent aura glowed around it. The ebbing energy cast her in shadow, but Nyla was undeterred. She focused on shifting the deep lilac, nearly plum energy that she knew to be the bond's manifestation on her aura to the tree's.

Slowly, a thin wisp of plum detached from her aura. A single tendril reached out and seemed to latch onto the tree's aura. Nyla watched in quiet wonder as the tendril melted into the tree's aura, leaving her just a little less aware of the unseen insects crawling between the manor's walls. When another tendril reached out and met the tree's aura, Nyla started to feel hopeful.

A bead of sweat rolled down her spine. Nyla persisted. Heartbeats turned into minutes, and those minutes turned into several more. With each tendril that pulled itself from her aura and sought out the tree's, the itching in her blood stopped, the tingle in her mind faded, and the unwanted weight on her joints vanished.

Almost there... Shamira's voice faintly skirted through her consciousness.

Nyla furrowed her brow in concentration. The last thing she needed was to lose sight of the task at hand. She didn't want to know what would happen to her if she did, or to the tree for that matter.

Her aura exhaled as the last tendril of the bond seeped into the tree's aura. Nyla removed her palm from the trunk and took a step back, peering up into the tree's stretching branches. Plum blended into the outskirts of the tree's aura. As Nyla withdrew her magic, a gust of wind blew her hair back. The remaining Harvum-kissed leaves overhead rustled in the breeze.

It was done. She did it. And she hadn't been hurt.

"I think..." Nyla panted, "I think that went well."

She turned around, staggering a few steps toward her companions. Shamira and Edwin's shield of combined magics dropped, no longer needed to protect themselves and Xander if this experiment had gone wrong.

Yes, I think it did too. Shamira bared her teeth in a grin. *Your aura is clear of the bond.*

Nyla breathed a sigh of relief as Xander wrapped his arm around her shoulders. She wrapped her arm around his waist, more for stability than anything else.

"Congratulations, Nyla," Edwin offered her a glowing smile, "you're free!"

"When are we leaving?" she asked excitedly, glancing between him and Xander.

"As soon as you rest up a bit. Tomorrow," Xander said, leading her back up the path.

"I don't want to wait another second," Nyla groaned.

As your attending Healer, I have to agree with Xander. We'll leave tomorrow.

"Fine," Nyla relented, pulling away from Xander to plop herself down on the top stair of the veranda.

Edwin laughed, "I'll go on ahead to Gossamer and write back to Pemberly."

"When?" Xander asked.

"Right now," Edwin responded matter-of-factly. "I'll make sure our travel arrangements and accommodations are ready in the meantime, and then you three can meet me there tomorrow, or later tonight."

Nyla nodded. "I like that idea."

Xander glanced at her, but she only stared out over the world beyond the manor's courtyard.

The world before her seemed brighter, but not in the way that the bond had heightened her awareness of the manor.

Nyla felt a smile tug at her lips.

It really was the little things in life that were best savored, she realized. The warm hug of sunshine on your skin after a week of rain, the first breath of air against your skin when the humidity broke, cookies that melted in your mouth, but most of all, the flutters in your heart when you're excited about something for the first time in a long time. Nyla closed her eyes, savoring this moment as the stair creaked beside her. Cracking her eyes open against the setting sun, Nyla smiled as she saw that Xander and Shamira had joined her. Edwin offered them a final word of goodbye as he passed them by, congratulating her once more as he did, and made his way inside the manor house to gather his things.

Tomorrow. They were all leaving this place, tomorrow, with the sunrise if she had any say in the matter at all.

Anything was possible, and no one was going to take that from her again. Especially not Dinora.

11. FREEDOM'S COST

Morning came quickly. Xander hadn't heard Nyla get up in the night, a first since she'd been bound to the manor. The hollowness of her eyes seemed to have faded as they sat across from each other in the three-season room last night, talking over their plans to stop Dinora and how they were getting to Huntington. He'd moved the furniture back into place yesterday with the help of Edwin while Nyla and Shamira were going about the whole astral travel plan.

He'd needed something to fill the time rather than worrying about what would happen to Nyla if she managed to successfully astral project. They still didn't know for certain whether or not Cedric was dead, or where Dinora was, or what she was doing, and Xander didn't know if they could find Nyla on the astral plane like Cedric had before. But he didn't dare tell Nyla he thought her idea was unnecessarily risky. She'd made it quite clear that she wasn't leaving any option unexplored if it meant giving them a better means to break the bond—one that didn't leave someone bound to the manor in her place.

And she'd been absolutely right.

Xander finished packing up his clothes. His eyes roved over the bedroom for anything he might've left behind. Then he searched the drawers for the fifth time, along with the armoire. Frowning, he fingered the ring he wore on a chain around his neck. If he *had* mistakenly left anything behind, he'd know where to find it. He supposed it wouldn't matter so long as he had his mother's wedding band.

The plain band was delicately thin, with only a small chip of black onyx in the center. The matching band made for his father was the same, only wider in size. He had no idea where that ring was now. His parents had left it to his sister, Issie, upon their passing, and Xander had fought to have her buried with it when she'd died at the jaws of the hellhound three Serenmaes ago. It was a minor thing, looking back on it now, but at the time, he and his grandfather had exchanged terrible words over the matter, words that devolved into a torrent of things neither of them had since forgiven. All he knew for certain was the fact that the ring had been on her finger during the wake, but anything could've happened afterwards. His grandfather could've easily ordered the ring returned to him before Issie was laid to rest, and Xander would never be the wiser. Allowing the ring to decorate Issie's finger could've been a placating gesture to avoid a scuffle in public and nothing more.

Xander swallowed. Even after these three years, he still wasn't ready to face his grandfather. He didn't even want to think about what might happen when they were in the same city as each other, let alone the same house, or even the same room.

Edwin's news from home wasn't all that comforting either. If anything, it only added to Xander's distress about returning to the place he'd sworn he would never return to as he walked down that mile-long driveway, still yelling angrily at his grandfather—anger that his grandfather returned.

If his grandfather really had shut himself in his study, one of two things was going on: the business was in trouble, and he was taking the sole brunt of the matter on his heart, or it was a family affair. Given the nature of what was going on, Xander assumed it was the latter, and his grandfather was having as hard of a time with their impending reckoning as he was.

"Almost ready? We're losing light," Nyla called eagerly from the door.

Xander turned and hauled his pack up on his shoulders. Nyla was basically bouncing on her heels.

"Ready as I'll ever be."

"Don't sound so grim." She beamed, strolling into the hallway as he faltered. "We don't have to accept your grandfather's help. I think we could do this on our own if we really wanted to," she assured him as they strode down the hall. Well, he walked down the hall, Nyla basically floated. He feared she'd burst from excitement.

"That's okay. I think this is right," Xander explained, starting down the grand staircase for what he hoped was the last time. He was only glad that this time, Nyla and Shamira were leaving with him. Although he didn't know where the pumpkie was now. "He has connections that neither of us have, so he may know more about the Ten Years' War and the Corvid Uprising plus their relation to each other. And a little help from the military might not be a bad option, or the Caster Corps."

"Your grandfather has connections to the military and the Caster Corps?" Nyla asked.

Xander's blood froze. Nearly sputtering, he composed himself enough to explain, "He knows a lot of people, and is, uh, entrenched in the political sphere…"

Nyla bounded down the last of the steps beside him, but said nothing. Xander peeked at her from the corners of his eyes, catching her facial features change from pensive to a look he knew meant something devious. Without a word, Nyla rushed toward the front door.

"Race you to the second gate!"

She threw open the tall oak door and bolted outside. Xander wondered if she was using magic to run faster or make her pack lighter. Cursing, Xander pounded down the rest of the stairs and out the door, slamming it shut behind him.

By the time he made it down the front steps, Nyla had already made it across the courtyard and was stepping onto the drive. There was no hope of winning this race, cheating or no.

He did gain some ground once he reached the flat stretch of the courtyard, but still not enough to make up for Nyla's surprise lead. She passed through the first gate, and a moment or two later, he did too. A blur sped by him, and Xander nearly fell on his face.

Why are we running? Shamira cast a look over her shoulder at him, slowing to keep pace with him.

"Nyla thought it would be fun to race," he puffed. "Second gate's the finish line."

Oh. Shamira's lips curved into a smirk. *See you at the second gate then.*

And she was off, easily closing Nyla's strong lead. Xander cursed, loudly.

"Shamira, don't you dare!" Nyla yelled up ahead, swerving into the pumpkie's path to stop her from taking the lead.

Shamira countered Nyla's attempt to keep the lead and crossed behind her. Xander watched as the pumpkie surged forward as the second and final gate of the Woodlane Manor loomed before them.

At least he'd managed to somewhat catch up to Nyla. He was just at her elbow when she passed through the second gate and slowed to a jog and then a walk.

"I almost had it!" she hissed, panting.

Shamira only snickered.

"If you hadn't cheated, it would've been more of a competition," he pouted.

Nyla bumped into him playfully. "You cheated when we were at the lake."

"So did you!" He laughed.

"I did?" she giggled, breathing deeply. Nyla shook her head, glancing between him and Shamira as the pumpkie led the way up the dirt path of the Godberd Woods. Xander met her gaze. He watched as the beginnings of a bright smile faded from Nyla's lips. Instead, a bittersweet look overtook her for a moment as she faced the road ahead. Xander glanced around, looking for any signs that might've caused the sudden change in Nyla's demeanor. He found nothing but the peaceful sway of the leaves in a gentle breeze and the soft dirt of the wooded path. Nothing obvious presented itself as being responsible for stealing Nyla's happiness, though he supposed it could be a great many things weighing on her mind in her newfound freedom. Maybe it was just the fact that this was her home, the place where she'd lost her family and had spent so long running away from that seeing it now reminded her of all of that—or it could be the cost of her freedom, the knowledge that Dinora had been freed from the Woodlane Manor and she blamed herself for that.

A grave look painted her face as she took another step down the long-forgotten pathway and turned to face the tree-lined path. Her soft-spoken words squashed any contentedness he had, reminding him of the threat Dinora posed to them, and to all of Tenebris. "To freedom—and wherever this road may lead…"

***

The walk to Gossamer was pleasant, even though her concerns about Dinora and Cedric hovered in the background of her mind. With the bond between herself and the Woodlane Manor severed, there was no other distraction. Even her freedom was shortly celebrated as the weight of Dinora's escape poked at the forefront of her thoughts. Still, though, Nyla was happy to see that many of the trees still retained most of their scarlet leaves. Shamira had started to explain to her the properties of the land's magic and why it was detrimental when it was stolen.

The leaves stored magic, helping to rejuvenate the land's magic by catching the sunlight and harnessing the light's energy. When the leaves turned in Harvum, it was a sign that enough energy had been stored to get through Serenmae, when the majority of the magic able to be harnessed was obstructed by clouds and earlier sunsets. Places like the Amber Dunelands and the outer edges of the Barrier Plains didn't have as much magic as the forests. There were fewer ways for the land to absorb energy from the light and replenish its reservoir of magic. The cycle of magic helped the flora thrive and balanced the energies of the species who lived there, humans included. When the cycle was disrupted…it could decimate an ecosystem, which had Nyla pondering over the battlefield she'd seen courtesy of the visions shown to her by Fortune Falls. It also brought to mind the patches of land she and Xander had stumbled upon during their journey to the Woodlane Manor from Caselle.

Was Dinora that desperate to break the bond that she had her son harvest magic from the land, even though she'd experienced the repercussions of stealing too much magic from the land firsthand? Why hadn't Cedric freed her years, if not centuries ago? What had stopped them? Why hadn't Dinora transferred the bond sooner?

Nyla bit her lip as the question lingered. Noticing the pinch of her face and her furrowed brows, Nyla shook the concerns away. There was time—they'd transferred the bond, and now they could hunt Dinora to whatever reckoning would come of it. And with any luck, Dinora wouldn't know she was free, that Xander's grandfather was offering to help them stop her, or that there was *any* kind of opposition forming to thwart her.

For right now, though, she chose to relish the weightlessness that carried her body with each step she took from the Woodlane Manor and through the gentle slopes of the Godberd Woods.

Her soul savored the warmth of the sunlight filtering through the arching and loosely woven limbs of the honey-colored trees and scarlet-blotched plum leaves of her home. She'd never expected such a sight would bring her such a comforting joy, but it did now. So unlike when they'd first arrived in the Godberd Woods, Nyla's heart welcomed and seemed to sing at the familiar surroundings, of the farmlands, and the whinnying or *clops* and *cheeps* of the small livestock kept by the few farmsteads they'd passed on the roads.

Even as she led Xander and Shamira down the dusty roads of her childhood, she didn't dare stray too close to where her home had once stood, or to where her neighbors might spot them—if her neighbors still remained in Hart to recognize her.

All Nyla knew for certain was that she was finally free of the Woodlane Manor. Even with all that they'd learned of Astrid, of Dinora and Cedric, and the forgotten wars of Tenebris's distant history, Nyla refused to dwell on the bleak clouds blotting out her future. For once, she chose to focus on the now, rather than worrying about her future. That would come in time, and until then she wouldn't worry about what had happened that had led to this path or where it would lead her. Instead, she took another deep breath, savoring the spicy scent with a hint of sweetness of Harvum's approach.

She was home, in a manner of speaking. Even with the dangers looming over her heart, she wouldn't let the future—especially not when Fate seemed to be on her side for the first time in two years—dampen the swelling of her heart. Her hand brushed her pocket, taking solace in the wand and broken necklace tucked away safely there.

***

About an hour outside of Gossamer, the trio stopped and ate a quick lunch. It was nothing like the lunches Xander had made while they were staying at the Woodlane Manor. They were back to camping food, and Nyla sorely missed having a full kitchen at their disposal, even if it had only been a few hours since they'd ate a fine breakfast at the manor.

In the silence of their waning lunch, Shamira made a noise that sounded like an attempt to clear her throat.

Nyla looked up at the pumpkie anxiously. Shamira wasn't one to hold her tongue, and if she was making a nervous gesture like a human would, then she had something to say that either herself, Nyla, or Xander wouldn't like.

I have been called back to the clan, Shamira started, eyes fixed on the ground between them. *This is where I leave you two…for now.*

Beside her, Nyla saw Xander freeze mid-chew, his utensils still in place to cut and spear. Nyla swallowed around the lump in her throat, her plate utterly forgotten in her lap.

"You're leaving us?"

For now, Shamira nodded, *until I can rejoin your company again. I didn't expect the Elders to order me back, though I suppose it's for the better. I know how humans perceive my kind, and you two are heading into denser populations now.*

Xander set his utensils down on his plate and sat up straight. "Will… will you be easy to contact?"

"Yeah, how will we…oh right," Nyla started. "You and I could just visit each other astrally. Or talk telepathically, I guess?"

Xander blinked, shaking his head as if overcome by dizziness. "Wait, you can speak telepathically like Shamira now?"

Nyla smiled mischievously and pointedly took another bite. *Hi, Xander.*

"No," he exclaimed, dramatically swiping his hands diagonally in front of him. "My own voice in my head is enough. A pumpkie's is unsettling, but yours too? No." He shook his head and folded his arms over his chest. His eyes narrowed as he addressed Shamira. "I can't believe you're leaving just when we started to be friendly."

Friendly? Shamira questioned with a playful growl. *I think you mean cordial and cooperative at best.*

Nyla laughed, even as her chest began to constrict.

"Exactly! Whatever will I do without you to keep me in check and keep me on my toes?"

Your mocking is duly noted, human, Shamira sassed. *But yes, this is where I leave you two. We'll be in touch. I'm hoping this means that the Elders are open to joining the cause against Dinora and stopping her, once and for all.*

Nyla set aside her plate and flung herself at Shamira, wrapping her arms around the pumpkie's neck loosely. "I'm gonna miss you."

I'll miss you too, Nyla. Shamira nosed her cheek. Shamira backed away a little, looking over at Xander with sincerity in her eyes. *Both of you. I'll miss both of you.*

"The only thing I won't miss is you sneaking up on me," Xander replied almost sarcastically despite his soft smile. "I will miss you otherwise, though."

The trio was somber as they cleaned up their lunch things and said a final goodbye to Shamira. Nyla watched her go, but all too soon the wild woods shielded Shamira from view. The pumpkie melted into the Godberd Woods around them. Xander stepped up to stand beside her, lightly laying a hand on her shoulder.

"Just so you know, you're stuck with me for a while, maybe longer." Xander smirked.

"I was just thinking it's a pity you're stuck with me for a while too," Nyla laughed. "We should probably get back on the road too."

"Probably," Xander said. His hand slipped from her shoulder as he turned to face the road beyond the trees.

"We could still run," Nyla offered, settling her backpack on her shoulders as she watched his rise with a breath and then still for a second before the tension eased.

Xander chuckled and hauled his pack up onto his shoulders. "We could, but where would we go?"

"The Plains?" she offered with a smile, weaving a path back to the dirt road.

"I've never been to the Plains," he mused, following after her and falling into step beside her once they'd reached the road. Nyla only hummed in response, and together they continued on their way in quiet companionship.

***

Once they reached the port town's limits, Xander took the lead, guiding her around and down back alleys until they reached a brick building. Xander hesitated as he reached for the door.

As she stepped over the threshold, Nyla blinked against the bright lights of the magic bulbs. She didn't know magicity was available in Gossamer. Then again, she didn't know how magicity actually worked, only that the magic gave light to homes, businesses, and cities without the use of flames or oil or wood.

Unlike the inn they'd stayed in while visiting Caselle after their adventure to Fortune Falls, whatever this building was, it did not have a single candle or oil lamp. Everywhere she looked, around the boxes stacked along one wall to the bins lining the shelves, there was not a single means of conventional light. Even the lanterns hung from the ceiling that illuminated the narrow aisles were magicitric.

Was this the store room of a shop? Was it another one of George's shops? After their visit with George and Nan in Caselle, Xander had told her that George and his grandfather were in the merchant and trading business. They co-owned the business, though they had both taken a step back now that they were older and more inclined to retire, with his grandfather naming Xander's parents as his successors.

But then Xander's parents had passed in an accident—though he'd never said anything more than that—and his grandfather had taken hold of the business again.

Nyla had her suspicions about which business this might be, as very few private businesses operated out of Gossamer, especially one with the reach she'd gathered that his grandfather's business had. No matter how much she tried to squander her curiosity, it didn't stop her from wondering who Xander was—who his family was—now that there wasn't anything else to occupy her mind. She didn't know why Xander wouldn't tell her, but she didn't want to pry either. Nyla knew enough, and her best guesses to fill the gaps satisfied her curiosity for the time being.

When Xander was ready to tell her that he was essentially the heir to the H&R Trading Company, he would. And for now, she'd play along supportively, even if she was slightly bothered by the fact that Xander didn't tell her himself. She'd come to the conclusion that he was ashamed of something, whether it was his family, the circumstances that had caused him to abandon his home, or where he'd come from that ultimately made it hard for him to tell her. It wasn't a question of if she believed he didn't trust her with this information, so much as she couldn't imagine how difficult it was for him to come home, and especially to be doing so because of her and not his own volition.

Was he even ready to face his grandfather? Did he *want* to? Nyla didn't know, but she knew she wasn't ready to face her extended family in Eurland or her former neighbors in Hart. She had no idea what she would tell them or how she would explain all that had happened to her and all that was currently happening to her.

And what if it put them in danger?

Nyla shook the worries from her head. She didn't have time to downward spiral into her anxieties. She needed to stop Dinora. Then she could face the rest of her life, wherever it might lead her.

At the sight of a door, Nyla stopped and shot a glance behind her at Xander. He motioned to the side, and Nyla turned the corner of the aisle to find a flight of stairs along the side wall of the storage room.

As she approached, a door creaked open, and footsteps hurried down the wooden stairs. Edwin came into view shortly thereafter and met them on the landing without so much as a "hello."

"Everyone's gone home for the day, and the apartment's ours for the night. I think La—" Edwin broke off with a cough. Nyla arched her eyebrow, knowing he'd done so on purpose but couldn't explain why. What was it that he was going to say that he'd thought better of it? Was it something she wasn't supposed to know? Nyla glanced at Xander to see if he'd caught Edwin's mistake too, only to see him glaring at the other man. Nyla pressed her lips together, wondering if it was this look that had made Edwin reconsider his words. "Excuse me. I just wanted to let you both know that Marilynn is supposed to arrive tomorrow, and will probably want to stay in the apartment."

"Great," Xander sighed. Nyla eyed him suspiciously. "We'll leave first thing in the morning then." As if remembering her, his eyes met hers, startled. "I mean, if you're up for it?"

"I'll leave right now if you want to," she said determinedly.

"I think a nice meal and a good night's sleep are worth waiting until the morning. No one's been able to track down Dinora, and there haven't been any obvious signs of her either," Edwin offered.

"And Cedric?"

Edwin shook his head.

Nyla shared a look with Xander. At least Dinora wasn't actively destroying all of Tenebris or stealing swaths of magic from the land while Nyla was imprisoned in the Woodlane Manor.

"Okay…then we'll leave tomorrow morning," Nyla agreed. She took a step toward the stairs, but a question that had come to mind made her pause. "How *are* we getting to your grandfather's?"

Xander paused, tilting his head. "That's a great question."

"Oh, did I forget to mention?" Edwin asked with a slight quirk of his lips. "Your grandfather sent me with a carriage and sagittarii. From here, we'll ride to Covington, and then we could take the train into Huntington. And no debates. Your grandfather gave me explicit instructions."

Nyla opened her mouth to protest, or ask about why Mr. Huntington would be so specific about their travel, but realized his means of getting them to Huntington would be the fastest route there. They'd never make it in a timely fashion if they had to trek through the Godberd Woods from its northwestern-most point back toward the Shadow Forest.

"I've never taken the train before," she said instead. "Sounds like this will be an adventure and less of a death march after all."

Xander laughed and started leading the way up to the apartment. "I thought you enjoyed walking?"

"I hate it," Nyla groaned dramatically as she followed after him. "I mean, don't get me wrong. I've had some good adventures, but if I walk across the country one more time, my feet are gonna fall off right where I stand in protest."

"And have you? Crossed the country?" Edwin asked from behind her.

Nyla paused on the stair and glanced down at him. "In full? Maybe once. But probably thrice over by now in terms of how long I've been traveling by foot."

"Interesting," he marveled, climbing a step closer. Taking his cue, Nyla resumed her ascent. She didn't make it two steps before Edwin's voice came again. "What was your favorite place you've visited?"

Ahead of her, Xander came to the apartment's landing and opened the door, glancing at her over his shoulder with a frown. "Yeah, you know, you've never said what your favorite place is."

Nyla stepped into the apartment after him, her lips pursed thoughtfully. "I've never thought about it. In a strange way, I like the Shadow Forest, but…" She bit her lip. The Shadow Forest wasn't anyone's favorite place except for maybe the storytellers who had never traversed it. "I guess here—well, Hart, but you get the gist."

Setting his pack down beside the door, Xander's lips quirked as he stared at her. "Of all the places you must've seen, Hart is your favorite?"

"It's the most beautiful place I have ever laid eyes on. And that includes Milton Bay."

There was nothing like the gentle, rolling hills and peaceful valleys she loved so much. Hart was the most picturesque place Nyla had ever seen. Her love of Hart didn't just stem from the fact that she'd grown up there or had spread her roots in its soil, but because there truly was no other place like it.

"I don't know," Xander said, making his way into the living room. "I hear Milton Bay is amazing."

The overwhelming glare of the sun glistening off of the rippling waters and the *squawks* of the galulls riding the sea breeze overhead came to Nyla's mind. No matter how much the salty breeze had kissed her skin, all she remembered of Milton Bay and its harbor was a haziness that clung to her, to the sandy earth, and now to her memory of it.

"Maybe, but I didn't think it was so impressive while I was there. Must have been the lack of magic getting to me then, and I just didn't know it." Her eyes roved over the apartment as she found herself frozen near the entryway. In some ways, it was exactly like Nan and George's, but in all the ways that mattered when it came to making a house a home like Nan and George had done with their apartment, it was distinctly different.

The apartment was huge, easily the full size of the shop below if she had to guess. From the entry, Nyla could see a cozy kitchen, a spacious living room, and an opening to the dining room. Off to the right was a hallway that must have led to a couple of bedrooms and a washroom. She set her bag down next to Xander's, dazed by the rich furnishings. Taking a couple of steps into the apartment, Nyla gravitated toward the hallway, wanting to see more of the place before dinner. From what she could tell, no expense had been spared for the comfort of those using the apartment for whatever time they were in Gossamer.

Warm wood tones graced the ornate furniture and exposed rafters overhead. The brick was tied in nicely by the neutral paint of the interior walls. Paintings and portraits hung on the wall thoughtfully. By all means, the apartment was both full of life and sparse. Nothing seemed too personal, as if no one from Xander's family had decorated it themselves. If anything, the apartment seemed like their own private inn, and it probably was.

At least the couch and matching armchairs looked like something you could melt into after a long day. That wasn't something Nyla could say about most of the furniture in the Woodlane Manor. Some of the straight-backed chairs were stiff and hard. The couches and chaise loungers were worn. It was rare to find a comfortable seat, thanks to the countless centuries that had passed since their making, and often-times, they were as hard and awkward as a gravel road.

"I'm gonna wash up before dinner…" Nyla trailed off, motioning vaguely to the hallway as Xander rifled through the cabinets, apparently taking stock of the apartment's kitchen.

"Okay, I have to run out and grab a couple of things," he replied distractedly.

Edwin rolled his eyes from the spot he'd claimed on the couch with his book. "He means, 'second door on the left.'"

"Got it." Nyla retraced her steps and grabbed her bag by the front door before heading into the hallway.

From the opening, she could see that she could go left or right. Heatless magicitric sconces were placed every few feet. Nyla went left and passed an open door. Peering inside as she passed, she saw that it was another, smaller sitting room. Shelves of books lined the walls. She wondered how small of a fraction this library was in terms of how many books the Huntington family had.

Much to her curious mind's dismay, she'd reached the washroom before she'd had any time to take stock of the rest of the apartment.

As Nyla's eyes took in the spacious room with the swing of the door, she found herself stopping short. Not only was there a tub, but a standing cubby to rinse off in. When her father had come back from his travels, he'd told them of plugic, and how the cities were using magic and spells to bring water on demand into their homes and businesses. He'd explained how chamber pots emptied themselves with the pull of a cord, a toilet. And then he'd told his mystified audience about showers.

It was like standing under a gentle rain, he'd said.

As tempted as Nyla was to try this new invention, her feet were aching, and the desire to soak her body in warm water for the first time in weeks ultimately won.

Gluttony

Heaving a breath, Dinora braced herself against the shabby kitchen cupboard. Her blood pounded in her temples. Stars floated in front of her hazy vision. Her hands clutched at the firm countertop. Dinora swayed on her feet.

She needed more magic.

How was she ever going to be able to steal Nyla's magic if she couldn't even conjure a distraction long enough to weaken the girl and distract her companions?

With another deep breath, her swimming vision settled. Dinora sagged against the cupboard and folded her arms against her chest. Her jaw clenched. At least she had time. She had time to build up her strength now that she had access to her full wealth of power—and she'd need every drop if she were to succeed.

If only her son had left her something of use here. Not even that damn raverin had come to her when she'd called it. Had the beast abandoned her too?

It was no matter. Dinora shook her head. The bursts of light returned to her vision.

She was used to doing everything on her own. After all, she was the only reason Corvus had tried to keep Eurland and Tenebris from dividing the great Corvid Empire with their thoughtless bid for independence all those centuries ago. The Emperor was a gentle soul and, more often than not, a foolish man. He hadn't wanted to see a war through. It wasn't until she reminded him of Corvus's need for the two countries and the privileges their people would lose should they succeed in gaining their independence that he'd conceded to the mounting calls for action.

But then they'd killed him.

His own people had slaughtered him—had tried to slaughter *her*.

Never would she have thought the threat would come from within their homeland. Corvids were loyal. Corvids were faithful.

But then she remembered the generations of Corvids who didn't know their homeland. *They* were responsible for the collapse of her empire, for stealing the powers she would've had all to herself.

If only things had gone according to her plan…

Even then the Thornraven family had thwarted her. But this time, she smirked, this time they would not.

Dinora's eyes flicked to the crystal ball. Smiling to herself, Dinora knew exactly how to solve both of her current problems. Not only would she gain more magic, but she could eliminate the threat Astrid's descendant posed to her in a single instant, just as she had ended Astrid in one gloriously splendid moment.

But first, she would rest. She would bide her time and gather her strength.

This time, she would be better prepared to face that girl. And she would be crowned triumphant once the dust of the girl's demise finally cleared.

12. THE HOME OF THE PUMPKIES

Shamira trod through the Godberd Woods at a brisk pace. The sooner she reached the Brewardt Clan—her home—the better. The Elders had sounded cordial when they'd requested her to return, but she still wasn't certain what to expect upon her arrival.

She'd broken nearly every vow her clan had by leaving under the cover of darkness as she had. Interaction with the human world was to be limited, if at all. Leaving without the permission of the Elders on matters that could entangle the clan was punishable by death. Forsaking her duties within the clan could mean banishment.

Pumpkies were pack animals, dependent on community for their survival. Clans had always existed, Shamira knew that, but after their species was nearly decimated during the Corvid Uprising, the clans became reclusive.

Or rather, what survived of the three clans went into isolation to rebuild their strength.

Born a few centuries after that, Shamira knew that only a fraction had survived the war. As it was, the last surviving Brewardt from before the war had passed shortly before her birth. All that remained was the generation who had known the survivors and all those that had come after them.

Now, they relied on whatever knowledge had been passed down and what few records survived the war and the centuries since.

That was why the clans remained in isolation. Her species had nearly faced extinction. The balance of magic had nearly unraveled. And all for what? What did their past victory mean if it were all happening again anyway, if Dinora had survived all these years and was once again free to do as she pleased?

The pumpkie slowed her pace.

Whatever in the world had she gotten herself into? What had she brought upon her clan? The Reyharts? The Zeldhers?

But if she hadn't…

If she hadn't gone in search of the source—of Nyla—that had disrupted the balance of magic, what would happen then, to this world, to magic, to the future?

Shamira didn't regret it, not when she thought of her actions in that context.

She'd achieved her objective and found Nyla. The girl she had since proven was the Royal Mage's heir, a prospect noted by the surviving pumpkie archives. In the time Shamira had spent researching the Corvid Uprising to explain the shifts in the world of magic she'd felt, she had grown close with her clan's Seer, Kasand. He'd often offered her information passed down to him in the records of the former Seer, Rhigul, who had unfortunately died in the war.

But even with all that she had learned from both the archives and Kasand, Shamira was unable to illuminate a full history. Kasand had not known everything, as Rhigul had passed before even naming Kasand as his successor, let alone training him—and the surviving records were scattered across the clans for safekeeping.

Shamira didn't see how that was safekeeping, but what did she know?

Apparently, more than all of the Elders combined.

The Brewardt Clan's Elders had not wanted to listen to her, or to Kasand when he'd bade them to. None of them had lived during the war, but every pumpkie born into this world had heard the stories, had been told about the atrocities committed by those involved, and just how decimated their species was by the end of it.

There was no denying it now that the future of this world rested in a precarious balance. Nyla couldn't do it alone, and neither could whatever humans she or Xander could inspire to stand against Dinora.

No matter how much Shamira had tried, and still tried, she couldn't find Dinora. She couldn't confirm Cedric's state of being either, a detail that troubled her. Why couldn't she find them? Why hadn't she been able to sense his body in the aftermath? If he were alive, she should be able to track him—and Dinora as well.

Unless they were using a means of cloaking. The pumpkies had used magic to shield themselves and their whereabouts from the world for centuries. Any well-adept magic wielder could use a cloaking spell to mask their whereabouts from anyone who might want to find them.

If all went well and the Elders weren't looking to punish her for her crimes, then Shamira would convince them to join the cause against Dinora. She'd convince them to send the best trackers amongst them to seek the pair out. Finding them before they could wreak havoc would avoid an unnecessary war and maintain the clans' centuries of preservation.

With renewed hope in her heart, Shamira regained her speed, sprinting through the changing landscape of the Godberd Woods. The farther northeast she traveled, the harsher the land became. Nyla had always spoken fondly of her home, but Shamira knew Nyla had never been to the extremes of the Godberd Woods, untouched by humans.

Here, the trees grew thinner, and the rolling hills morphed into sharp, rocky inclines where stone and gravel were more common than the soft soil Nyla's family would've cultivated all the way down in Hart. It was amongst these mountainous peaks and slopes that the pumpkies had carved out their own little domain between Tenebris and the countries across the sea. Always the guardians of Tenebris,

Shamira thought it strange that even after the near genocide of their species the surviving Elders of old had chosen to make their sanctuary so close to those who would have destroyed them.

Now, Shamira supposed, it wasn't necessarily the Corvid Empire that had tried to eliminate Tenebris and their pumpkie allies. It was an extreme faction manipulated by a vengeful woman who'd sought only her own power and, subsequently, the destruction of those who'd "wronged" her.

With the waning sun, Shamira diverted off course and sought out a meal. She'd missed traveling at her pace while she'd been with Nyla and Xander, but now she missed them more.

Well, mostly Nyla.

But the fact was, she'd grown fond of the pair and had gotten used to their presence. She only hoped their mission was as successful as she prayed hers would be.

If they managed to gain support from the Tenebrese government to fight Dinora and Shamira managed to bring the pumpkies as an ally, Dinora would be stopped once and for all. She had full confidence that between herself and Nyla, they had learned the mistakes of the past. One way or another, Dinora would not burden this land again.

And neither would Cedric—if he still lived and breathed.

***

With the sunrise, Shamira started for home again. She didn't waste any time in dawdling. The sooner she returned to the clan, the sooner she would know her future—and that of all of magic and the humans' country.

The air grew brisk the higher Shamira climbed. The trees had stopped growing. Up ahead, Shamira could see the veil meant to cloak the pumpkies' domain from the human world. The magic rippled in the morning sunlight, something only those gifted with the acute sense as she had would be able to see outright. Others would have to concentrate and focus their senses in order to see the shimmering magic, but why would they think to do so in a place like this?

Shamira came to a halt at the border. Panting, she cast a single glance over her shoulder. She drank in the way the sun shone on the mountain below, how the scarlet leaves in the valley glowed in its warm light. She committed the sight to memory, as if she expected to never see such a peaceful sight again.

Resolutely, Shamira faced the veil. With a single step, Shamira crossed the boundary. Once her eyes adjusted to the bright sunlight again, Shamira saw that the Elders had been waiting for her to step through.

Shamira took in their grim faces and the gravity wafting through the air like an electric current—the only emotion she could sense— and swallowed. Bowing her head, she couldn't help but wonder if she should've ignored the request and continued on to Gossamer with Nyla and Xander. Perhaps, if not for their protection but her own, she should've traveled with them and stayed true to their journey.

In the simmering silence of the morning, Shamira wondered if there was anything here for her after all. It was her home, and these were her kin, but what if her place was among the humans? What if destiny—or Fate—had called her elsewhere, and she'd ignored its whispers?

But now that she had come, there was no turning back. She would face this. She would stand before the judgement of the Brewardt Elders and her kin, but she would not yield. She would not forsake her sacred duty as a guardian of Tenebris, even if it meant losing everything she held dear.

13. THE ROAD TO COVINGTON

Nyla watched the world outside roll by through the carriage's window. Xander sat beside her, his nose in a book he'd picked from the apartment's library this morning. Edwin also had his nose in a book across from her.

Absently, she bounced her leg. She swore she could walk faster than the team of sagittarii were pulling the carriage, but she didn't dare complain. They were, at least, moving.

She only prayed that the train would be faster and that would make up for the time she feared they were losing.

"Something wrong, Nyla?" Xander asked without looking at her. Instead, he turned the page of his book.

Across from them, Edwin let out a stifled laugh that was more of a snort than anything else.

He sent her an apologetic look over the top of his book. "Sorry."

"It's fine. I'm just…sitting…waiting…completely bored out of my mind!" Nyla burst, twisting to face Xander full on, crooking her leg flat against the seat between them. "How do you people travel like this? It's so *boring*!"

"'You people?'" Xander asked. He set his book down on his lap, marking his page with a piece of scrap paper. Even though his voice held the hint of confusion, his eyes still bore a teasing gleam that she'd normally find amusing, but right now she was too irritated by her boredom to play along.

"Yes! 'You people,' as in people who have grandfathers that send them and their friend in need a carriage with a team of sagittarii and let them use their family's apartment overnight and seemingly have other apartments across the country because of the nature of their family business," Nyla said in mock exasperation.

Edwin arched an eyebrow, lowering his book to say something, but Xander interjected before he could get a single word in.

"We could play a travel game?" Xander offered almost desperately. Across from them, Edwin shook his head and returned to his book.

"What kind of travel game?" Nyla asked, choosing to be merciful today. She wondered how long he believed he could keep his family's status from her.

"Anything." Xander tucked his book into the overhead storage cabinet before bringing his legs up on to the seat and stretching them out as much as the bench seat allowed him. His leg bumped into hers as he did, and she found a part of herself wondering if he'd done so on purpose, not that she minded either way.

Nyla mirrored him and stretched her own legs out alongside his. She was just short enough that her bootless feet were tucked up against the side of his hip, but able to lie flat across the bench. Leaning her side against the back of the seat, Nyla rested her head against the padded wall of the carriage, holding Xander's gaze as though she was enchanted by the soft look.

"Let's see…" Nyla trailed off as she considered what she might ask him that she didn't already know the answer to. "What's somewhere you'd like to visit, but haven't been yet?"

And so, the game began. Like their former travels from Caselle to the Woodlane Manor, the pair spent the rest of the carriage ride asking each other countless questions about the things they had seen and done in their travels. Xander hadn't traveled as much as she had, but he'd been overseas because of the trading business and was able to tell her about Eurland and what Corvus was like now.

According to Xander, Corvus was a country of short grasses, like the outskirts of the Barrier Plains closest to the Amber Dunelands. The once-mighty empire had since rebuilt, and Nyla knew from her own schooling that after much turmoil and a few different royal families, Corvus was once again stable in both country and commerce. But that was all she remembered. Having been out of school for so long and dependent on herself for her own survival, any ancillary facts she'd once had memorized had vacated her mind.

She didn't even remember her own trip to Eurland, as she and Westley were hardly three years of age when her parents had brought them to visit her mother's country. Nyla vaguely remembered when a few of her mother's relatives visited after Lydia's birth, but it was more of a faded sentiment than a true memory of faces or instances.

So, she listened with rapt attention to Xander talk of his former travels, especially his journey to the western continents. It was a long, agonizing journey apparently, not one he desired to make again. The novelty of sea life, he said, had worn off very quickly as there wasn't much for him to do on the ship, being as young and inexperienced as he was at the time.

Reflectively, Xander added, "Though I was seasick for most of the way there because we crossed some pretty horrible weather."

Across from them, Edwin *tutted*. Nyla glanced over at him in time to see him set his book down irritably and roll his eyes.

"Everything all right, Eddie?" Xander snickered, failing to hide his smirk. Nyla twisted herself to look out the window behind her in an effort to hide her own laughter.

"Fine," he drawled, stretching his legs out in the empty space of the carriage floor between their benches. "Why do you ask?"

"No reason," Xander said.

Nyla glanced over at him, biting her lip to stop the snicker she could feel twisting her lips into a smirk.

Edwin's eyes slid to her. Pinned under his gaze, Nyla didn't know what to expect. She hadn't realized that their conversation had been of any interest to him, or had broken any attempt at concentration he'd had. By all means, she'd wholly forgotten he was even there. Her lips pursed when his question settled in the still air of the carriage.

"What do you know about magic?"

Nyla swallowed. There was no sense in lying. The only way Edwin could possibly be of any help would be if she were completely honest with not only him but also with Xander's grandfather once they'd met. They all deserved to know the truth, however disheartening it might be.

"I don't know much about magic," she started. Her eyes strayed from Edwin's and fixated on a point between time and space, unseeing as she laid the truth bare between the air of the carriage. "It seems super reactive to my emotions and subconscious urgings. Shamira did teach me some things, a good foundation of magic maybe, but she said that human and pumpkie magics were different. But time slipped away from us, so there was only so much she could teach me. I know the basics, though, like the elements and how all magic is essentially energy and completely dependent on your intentions."

"That's a good foundation. Most people don't ever grasp that," Edwin said as the carriage rolled to a stop. He leaned over his seat and glanced out the window. "I think we're stopping for lunch and to water the sagittarii."

"Finally!" Nyla burst, essentially climbing over Xander as she sprang from her seat and lunged for the carriage door. She swung the door open wildly, the sound of Xander or Edwin snickering behind her not even grating on her mood as she leapt from the carriage. The footman, Quentin, hadn't even been able to bring the footstool over for her to step down onto, instead giving her a slightly bemused stare as he lingered at the rear of the carriage. Stretching and basking in the glorious sunshine of the plum-and-scarlet-ringed meadow, Nyla spread her arms toward the sky as her companions slowly caught up to her.

"I have never in my life done so much sitting all at once!"

She inhaled deeply as if the carriage ride were stuffy. In truth, the carriage ride had been fine—aside from her initial boredom and the overall restlessness buzzing in her bones. Feeling as though she wasn't making any progress toward stopping Dinora had pounded in her bloodstream to the point of torture.

It was a sort of torture she could only avoid while in motion. When she was still, the voice in the back of her mind that weaponized her fears and anxieties was stronger, especially coupled with the urgency in her blood. She didn't know what to do—with any of it. But breathing in the bright scent of the late Hugony air soothed her mind. Smiling at the tapestry of plum and scarlet leaves of the trees circling the brookside grove, Nyla wondered if her companions would be opposed to leaving the carriage behind and saddling the team of sagittarii to ride the remainder of the way to Covington.

Wiggling her toes, Nyla considered if she could even ride a sagittarii of this stature. Her family had had an old archette—a strong and stout breed of sagittarii she knew were primarily used to aid in agricultural work or hauling goods between destinations via wagons—but he hadn't taken to being saddled well and had passed shortly after Lydia was born.

As she watched their driver, Huey, lead a couple of the sagittarii over to the trickling waters with Quentin close behind with the remaining sagittarii, Xander came to stand beside her, her boots in hand.

"I don't suppose you'll be wanting these then?"

Nyla shrugged. "Do I need them?"

"Not if you don't want them." Xander placed them back in the carriage. Nyla bent and slipped out of her socks before she completely ruined them, placing them inside her boots, and followed the team of sagittarii down to the stream to refill her canteen.

The stiff whisper of guarded propriety met her on the gentle breeze as she fanned her magic over their surroundings, reaching out to sense what she couldn't see or hear with human senses. A shadow loomed over her a heartbeat later. She hadn't heard him coming over the soft grass, but based on the energy she sensed, she knew it was Edwin without ever turning around.

"Issie would have liked you," he said as he knelt next to her.

"Were you two close?" she asked without glancing over at him. Xander didn't really talk about Issie much, but he'd told her about how Issie had died. Nyla supposed he still blamed himself for the attack, and his guilt clouded his remembrance of her.

"Not really." Edwin offered her a hesitant smile as she finally dragged her eyes up to meet his. Rather than the apathy she'd grown accustomed to while they were attempting to break the bond, there was a sprig of warmth, of Edwin's hidden soul there, as if he had a fondness for Issie. Or perhaps, and much more likely, Nyla thought, a fondness for his bygone youth and simpler times. "Issie didn't really like me much. Too stuffy, she'd say."

Nyla snorted, tightening the cap on her canteen. "Well, you are, so…"

"You and Xander seem to get along really well," he observed as she trailed off. Nyla dreaded the guarded inquisition in his voice. "How long have you two known each other?"

Nyla hesitated, considering her answer carefully. She knew they hadn't known each other all that long by any means, but the way in which they'd met and all that they'd been through together made it seem as though they'd known each other for years now, or maybe a lifetime. "A while."

"That could mean a lot of things, Nyla."

"It means 'a while,' Edwin." She sat back on her heels and glared at him. "A long time, but not forever."

"There's a lot of people who would want to take advantage of him," he shot back, matching her glare.

Nyla burst to her feet. "Then maybe you should go and find them."

She didn't wait for a response. Her lips twisted in a slight frown. She just didn't know what to make of Edwin. He could be short and almost mechanical, or personable and even a little snarky, but now he was questioning her integrity, and that wasn't something Nyla took lightly. He hardly knew her, and she doubted meeting someone while cursed counted toward a first impression, though perhaps that was all Edwin knew of her.

But he was Xander's oldest friend. By all means, he was only here now because Xander's grandfather had sent him to help them break the bond between herself and the Woodlane Manor and then deliver them safely to Huntington. That was all.

Edwin didn't have to be her friend, and she didn't have to be his. But they were Xander's friends. That was all that mattered. The least they could do was be civil toward each other, but Nyla could wait a little longer before she worked at that. Right now, she wanted to push him into the stream for insinuating that she was only friends with Xander to take advantage of his family's wealth.

She didn't even know he was the heir apparent to the biggest trading company in the country until he'd left her at the Woodlane Manor to send his grandfather a note from Gossamer. And then Dinora and Cedric had attacked her, so she hadn't brought it up in the days that followed, and neither had Xander. Never once had Xander come out and told her who he was—or who his family was.

She'd never ask either, not until he was ready to tell her. She didn't know the circumstances that had led him to sever ties with his family, with his grandfather, but she imagined it was something heart-wrenching. What else would lead someone to sever a bond as sacred as family?

Nyla pushed her interaction with Edwin from her mind as best as she could and turned her attention to the rest of her companions. Huey, Quentin, and Xander had built a fire and assembled a loose circle of wooden folding chairs made for camping.

"Hope you don't mind pollies for lunch." Xander glanced up as she approached his cooking fire, blissfully unaware of the conversation that had just taken place between her and Edwin.

She forced herself to smile, taking the seat beside him. "Not at all, though I will miss the fancy cooking and cookies from having a full kitchen at your disposal."

"I won't." He sprinkled more herbs over the pan. "If I ever start to miss the Woodlane Manor, I've been possessed."

"Duly noted," Nyla laughed, a true smile on her face now. Her brow creased with the turn of her thoughts. "How much farther is Covington?"

"We should reach it by nightfall, Miss," Huey answered.

She groaned, letting out a pitiful whine at the prospect of spending hours more in the carriage. "That's so far away!"

Xander snickered, "Would you rather be hiking there?"

"At this rate? Yes! Anything but sitting in that carriage for another eternity."

Huey glanced between them before walking away, a look that Nyla read as uncertain skepticism, but not the malicious sort. She wondered if he'd ever met someone who hated being a passenger in a carriage as much as she had. The novelty of it had worn off in less than an hour thanks to the unchanged landscape of the Godberd Woods she still knew by heart.

Maybe if there were more people passing by or if she were unfamiliar with her surroundings, it wouldn't be so bad.

"Wait…" she said aloud. Everyone stopped what they were doing to look at her. "What day is it?"

"It's the 72nd of Hugony, miss," Huey answered with a question in his voice.

Nyla furrowed her brows. "We should've passed more people on the road. Either coming or going to the markets."

She glanced at her companions in turn, but none of them seemed to be following her line of thought. "It's just that, this far north in Tenebris, our harvests are a little later, so the end of Hugony and early Harvum see the best bounty. There should be tens of farmers on the road going to the market or returning home, so why haven't we seen any?"

Nyla presumably knew these roads better than anyone around her. And if it was only the 72nd, then there would definitely be more people on the road. The Harvum Feast surely wouldn't have happened yet. She wracked her memory for a time when the seasons were warmer and the harvest boom was earlier, but she couldn't recall a single Hugony like that recently, even if she hadn't been in the Godberd Woods for two harvests.

"I don't know. Maybe I've just been cooped up too long in the manor or away from Hart for so long that I'm misremembering."

"No…you're right, Miss." Quentin began to pace nervously off to the side. "I grew up in Glendale, and it's much the same as you describe. The later growing season compared to the Plains or even the Shadow Forest would make this time of year a very busy time to be on the roads. We should have passed more people on our way here, especially coming out of Gossamer this morning. I don't recall seeing the market as busy as it should have been."

"Then why?" Nyla asked no one in particular.

Silence blanketed their camp. Nyla strained her ears to hear anything. There was only the breeze that dragged the scarlet-blotched leaves of the trees around the glade. Every now and again, she heard a *twitter* or *chitter* of some small creature in the golden-brown trees beyond the stream, but there was a distinct void around them, as if the Godberd Woods was holding its breath.

By the time their lunch was cleaned up and Nyla forced herself to get back into the carriage, she'd wholly convinced herself that something was disastrously wrong.

As if they'd sensed her distress, Edwin and Xander had offered to leave the windows open, and she'd somehow ended up in the seat Xander had held closest to the door before they'd stopped for lunch.

The longer the afternoon drew on and their carriage ambled on in near silence with not a thing to occupy herself, the antsier Nyla became. She breathed a long, slow exhale in the hopes of cleansing the grim anxieties from her head. Choosing to focus on the passing Godberd Woods outside her window, Nyla attempted to loosen the tension coiling in her muscles. In an effort to put herself truly at ease, Nyla reached out to the world around her with her magic like Shamira had taught her, only a gentle breeze that caressed and traveled over the landscape around her.

In doing so, she was able to sense her surroundings and beyond at a more microscopic level. The grit of the dirt beneath the carriage wheels, the pressure as they turned over the fine dirt road, the sunlight dancing over the canopy of the trees and the warmth of the magical energy held within its beams, and the way the air vibrated between nearly nonexistent vapor particles thanks to the mild humidity washed over her. She even noticed the scamper of clawed paws or the flutter of feathered wings as birds flew through the air. The corners of her lips turned up softly. Nothing was amiss, not for miles around.

Lust

Magic thrummed in her bloodstream. Ebbing and flowing through her, Dinora turned her face to the sky. She relished the tremble of power beneath her veins. The earth beneath her feet rumbled. Waves of amber emanated from the ground as color drained from its surface, leaving behind nothing but a dull sand. Greens and barely there hues of blue joined the parade of color washing over her with the magic she consumed.

Dinora had forgotten what it was to feel this sated. What she wouldn't do to bottle this feeling and have it forever. She smiled, supposing she wouldn't have to now that all was finally going according to plan.

The discovery that Nyla and her companions had severed the curse had been tragic news indeed, but then Dinora had realized it was an opportunity. With that demon cat gone and the addition of more bystanders to protect, her own magic would be the least of Nyla's concerns once Dinora had weakened her enough to take it.

Then Dinora would have enough magic to raise the army that had sat in waiting for 647 years.

Dinora sighed, reluctantly slowing her consumption of magic. She should've taken more than enough to raise a few of the worthless souls who'd failed her during the Great Tenebris War. At least their sacrifice would prove useful. It was the only thing those cowards had been good for. Granted, she hadn't expected the traitors who called themselves Tenebrese to gather the strength necessary to combat them, let alone nearly take the tide of war into their favor, but she had never doubted their ultimate victory. Corvus always won. It's why they had an empire worth fighting for to begin with. If it hadn't been for the blood, sacrifice, and unwavering devotion to the empire and in their heritage as Corvids, there wouldn't have been anything for Dinora to defend in the first place.

At the very least, she mused, the cowards who had abandoned her and their cause, who had petitioned for peace, or who had reluctantly died for their cause would actually prove their value to the Empire of Corvus, and to their rightful queen.

Her gaze landed on a small grouping of the onyx-colored rocks nearest her. They'd taken root where once an army had stood against their enemies. She studied them and was pleased to find that the faded signature of their souls remained.

Setting her jaw, Dinora drew upon the buzzing power thrumming beneath her skin. The unrelenting light of the cloudless sky dimmed. Eclipsed by the sheer force of her will, the light of day fled. And in its place was the searing energy of Dinora's magic. So bright the scarlet was nearly white, but thanks to the plentiful magic she'd mined from the land, the glare didn't bother her, just as it hadn't bothered her 647 years ago.

The earth beneath her feet resumed its grumbling, shifting, and quaking. Haloed by her magic, the rocks began to morph. The jut of their points smoothed, taking on the appearance of a human head, but not quite, as the jagged edges remained. The base of the three rocks split, each forming a pair of legs on which her creatures could stand, though they were bowed at an awkward angle which forced them to double over and crawl.

Watching with satisfaction as her creatures grew arms with long, sharp claws that would surely spill the blood of Corvus's enemies, Dinora's wicked smirk only grew more sinister. Falling to stand on all fours, the creatures let out a piercing wail as Dinora continued to infuse them with her power.

They would be indestructible, unstoppable, invincible.

Nyla would either die at their hands or at Dinora's own when she came to collect what was owed to her. Dinora would make certain of it.

"Go," she ordered, stopping the flow of magic and letting what was left buzz in her chest. The power crested within her, flooding her with strength. "Kill them all, but leave enough of the girl for me to deal with. I need her magic."

The creatures shrieked.

Dinora's eyes sparkled darkly as they turned about and sprinted away, thundering over the still landscape. Soon, her creatures disappeared into the thick foliage of the great forest beyond the now-barren landscape she had drained.

Soon, Dinora promised herself. Soon she would have all she ever desired, and it would be thanks to Nyla and the woman who'd failed to stop her all those years ago.

14. THE SHADOW FOREST MOVES

They were all too young to bear the burdens they were facing. He didn't know exactly why the thought came to mind now, but it did. Maybe it was the fact that his return to Pemberly was all too imminent or that Shamira was off to face the judgement of her clan all alone.

He wasn't sure which of them had the worst of all their tribulations. Shamira or Nyla with her inherited magic and a war for the world.

His mind begged the question: if they managed to find Dinora, would it really be up to Nyla to stop her?

Surely, there were other people more equipped to fight and defeat Dinora. Just because Nyla had inherited Astrid's magic didn't mean her future was written. It was a precaution, one he doubted even Astrid had the foresight to see transcend generations.

Staring absently at the pages of his book, the words blurred together. A lifetime was inconceivable—a natural lifespan, an average life was enough to boggle his mind. How could a single person fathom eighty years? Ninety?

Even when you look back and reflect on all those long years, how could one quantify them? How could you recognize them as your own and reconcile all you'd lived through, experienced, *survived?*

Then he imagined extending that life to six centuries as Dinora and Cedric had done.

Xander's breath sputtered at the thought. He couldn't. He couldn't imagine what he'd see in six long centuries. But Dinora and Cedric had done just that. They'd lived long after their natural lifespan, though he didn't know the cost of those years. Perhaps it was the cause of their insanity.

How could they ever think that after 600 years, their cause, their fight, their relevancy had impact on today? Corvus and Tenebris had healed. Eurland and Corvus had healed. Corvus was stable once more, though reduced from the mighty empire it had once been. By all means, their presence here, in this century, was meaningless.

If they'd been discovered in a different time, a time that still remembered them and the Corvid Uprising, then maybe it wouldn't have fallen to Astrid's descendant to defeat them. But today?

Xander didn't see why it was necessary for Nyla to face them, or to bear the burden of her ancestor and the kingdom's history.

Closing his book, Xander turned toward the window. The cover was firm and comforting in his grasp. The feeling grounded him as his mind wandered and the world outside their carriage passed by in a watercolor of plum and scarlet leaves, rich soil, and honey golden trees.

His eyes fell shut. Slumping against the back of his seat, Xander was inclined to get some rest of his own. At least Nyla was managing to get some rest now. He didn't know if she would survive the remainder of their journey, wishing he'd picked out a book for her too even though she'd declined his offer to borrow one. Maybe he'd offer her his, as he'd read this one a few other times and had found it was a good book to read while traveling. There was no use in watching the countryside roll by or pretending like he was going to read when he was utterly exhausted, tired down to the very bone.

"What in Corruptio's name?" Quentin shouted, his voice cutting through the carriage.

Xander's eyes burst open. He glanced at Nyla. She'd somehow remained undisturbed by the shout, a fact time didn't allow him to ponder. The carriage swayed uncharacteristically as Huey must've swerved to avoid an obstacle in the road. Nyla jerked awake as the carriage lurched, bolting upright and pulling her legs from his lap as she straightened, wide-eyed and gaping. Their eyes met briefly in their confusion, though Xander's attention quickly turned to the front of the carriage as Huey's and Quentin's shouting could be heard from the driver's box. Edwin twisted around and opened the little window behind his head that was meant to aid passengers in communicating with the driver.

Xander's eyes flicked back to Nyla, meaning to ask if she was all right, but the look on her face stopped him mid-thought. Her stare was withdrawn, her brows furrowed in concentration. A moment later, her eyes cleared. He didn't have the heart to ask what it was that made her lips twist and her chest heave.

"Is everything all right?" Edwin called over their escorts' panic.

It was Quentin's wide, fearful eyes that glanced inside the carriage, the glint of his long gun just out of view but not quite. Xander's blood ran cold.

"Just a bit of a situation, sir. Remain seated—we'll handle this."

Edwin didn't get a chance to ask him what "this" was before Quentin had turned back around and shifted out of view, presumably glancing around the carriage to assess something they couldn't see from inside. A single shot rang out, breaking the seconds-long silence that had befallen their driver and footman.

From Edwin to Nyla and back again, the three of them shared a look. Neither Caster said a word, and Xander didn't know what to say or do. It could be bandits, but…why couldn't they hear others? Why hadn't they simply stopped the carriage?

No, Xander realized. This wasn't the work of bandits. They were being pursued.

As the fact sank into the pit of Xander's stomach, he lost sight of the world around them. It could be anything. Man, monster, anything.

And given their circumstances, he doubted very much the bow and quiver of arrows packed away and stowed on the luggage rack on the back of the carriage would be of any use against their attackers anyway.

***

Nyla dared to peek outside. Her magic continued to poke and prod at the magical energy roiling off of their unidentified attackers. It was strange writhing energy that was familiar to her in a way she couldn't place. Full of sorrow and tortured by anger and guilt, it was like—

Grief.

The energy she sensed was shrouded by grief like a shadow upon the earth.

Without sticking her head outside the window, she couldn't see anything. The swaying of the carriage didn't bode well for them. From the driver's box, she could still hear Huey and Quentin yelling at each other and the *bang* of another shot ringing out, but their words were lost on her. Twisting back in her seat, Nyla pushed her magic to touch the shadows' essence. She gasped, startling Xander out of his trance beside her. She put her hand on his shoulder, squeezing it as she attempted to steady herself, bracing another hand on the carriage wall beside her. Still, she pushed her magic to identify the auras but to no avail.

Nyla's mouth went dry as her magic recoiled away from the beasts that were trying to overtake the carriage.

Edwin caught her eye. "Do you know what's attacking us?"

"Please say 'bandits.'" Xander pinched the bridge of his nose with a resigned sigh.

"I don't think it's bandits," she said, turning in her seat once more and grabbing hold of the window's edge. Poking her head outside, the carriage lurched as her weight shifted. As she looked behind their carriage, her blood ran cold at the creatures gaining on them.

They were human in shape only. Gnarled and twisted, the onyx-colored creatures were relatively short and doubled over into an awkward position on their front limbs, but their jagged edges and facelessness sent a shock down her spine.

They were natural—to a point—but whatever magic had crafted them was vile and hateful and old.

Dinora.

Nyla clamored out the open window, stepping on the edge of the window frame to reach for the rail fixed to the roof of the carriage to haul herself up. She ignored Xander's panicked reprimands and situated herself on the roof of the pitching carriage. Crouching low to keep her balance, Nyla surveyed the scene behind them with a white-knuckled grip on the luggage rails.

The beasts were wild and hellish, essentially rabid. Instinctually, Nyla knew these creatures would stop at nothing. She also knew that these monsters weren't native to the Godberd Woods. Confidence told her they weren't even native to the Shadow Forest, having traveled through its depths herself and having never seen a beast like this. By all means, they weren't of this world, and yet...Nyla watched them for a second longer, recognition tugging on the edges of her mind.

Their clawed hands kicked up dirt, scattering the rare rock or twig in the road as they sprinted along behind the carriage on all fours. They didn't seem to breathe or pant, so definitely not alive in the sense that she or Xander were. Nyla could see that they had sharp, jagged teeth and a cavernous mouth, but aside from that, she couldn't make out eyes or a nose. They were without a face, but still with the means to tear their throats out if they got a hold of them. The realization sent shivers down her spine as the closest one to their carriage was nearly upon them.

"I thought we told you to remain seated!" Quentin's voice sounded over the snorts and whinnies from the team of sagittarii and the grating movement of the beasts drawing nearer.

"I didn't listen," she called over her shoulder in time to see Quentin shove the ramrod down the barrel of his rifle. She watched him carefully, her body tensing as he brought it up and took aim at the creatures once again. "Just focus on staying on the road and keeping the sagittarii calm!"

"How are we supposed to do that exactly?" Huey shouted.

Quentin fired another round at the creatures. Nyla flinched at the harsh *bang*, so much louder than it had sounded from inside the carriage. Glancing at the creatures gaining ground on their carriage, her heart plummeted. In spite of the obvious chunk missing from one's side, the creatures hadn't even faltered.

"I don't know! You just have to figure it out yourselves!" There wasn't any time for trivial questions. Clearly, they were all going to die a horrible, bloody death if the creatures caught them.

Based on the wild rocking, she guessed that an axle was broken— and the creatures were probably to blame for it.

The three onyx-colored beasts were mere paces behind them now. Nyla had to do *something*, anything. At the sight of her atop their target, the three creatures let out a wail that pierced Nyla's eardrums. One of the beasts—one of the three that wasn't missing a chunk of its side—seemed to sprint faster, gaining on the carriage until it started to pass alongside it, screeching at her as it did.

"Okay, that's enough of that," she hissed.

Using her magic, she took aim at the beast making to ram itself into the side of the carriage. At the contact of her lilac-colored magic, the creature yelped in pain, falling to the side. The other two stepped over their disoriented comrade without a moment's hesitation, growling and snarling.

They both lunged at her.

Nyla conjured a shield and shoved. The shield crackled upon impact with the creatures, but held as she willed it. The two monsters fell to the ground below with a harsh *clatter* rather than a *thump*. Dust and chunks of a dark material scattered in all directions at the impact, but Nyla didn't have time to consider that. None of them were necessarily defeated. Her body faltered as the sway of the carriage tilted violently to one side. She quickly fought to restore her balance, irked by the sudden movement and worried that maybe she'd missed a creature. Maybe there was one beneath the carriage or the one she'd shot first had recovered.

Edwin's boney hand grabbed at the rail as he pulled himself up onto the roof. Nyla scowled at him, or rather at the realization that he and Xander had caused the carriage to tilt. Knowing Xander, he was trying to make his way up here too, but she had to stop him. It was too dangerous for all three of them up there.

"Xander, don't come up here! You have to balance the carriage!" she yelled with the fraying hope he'd listen to her.

"NYLA!" Xander shouted from below. "So help me if you think—"

"XANDER, PLEASE!" she shouted desperately, "Listen to me just this once!"

Silence. The carriage balanced out, though it bobbed with every inch of road they careened down with the creatures close on their heels. Nyla shot another creature to keep them at bay as Edwin settled himself beside her.

"What are those things?" Edwin breathed, his face pale.

"A gift from Dinora, I'd bet," she answered grimly, eyeing another creature as it pushed off the ground on powerful limbs, leaping through the air in a great bound. Without a second thought, Nyla unleashed a bolt of power at it, shooting it down in midair. The beast fell, skittering across the road in a cloud of dirt, leaving a long scar across the dust before finally coming to a stop. The beast lay curled on its side, a mound of dirt curved around its arched back. The other creatures didn't pause in their pursuit of the carriage.

"Energy doesn't work on them!"

Fire erupted from Edwin's hands. He threw the eager flames at the two beasts trailing behind the carriage.

"What the—?!"

Nyla and Edwin watched in horror as the flames licked at the beasts, but to no avail. The flames soon flickered out in the harsh wind created by the creatures' unyielding pace. They still trailed after the carriage, alive and smoldering from the extinguished flames. In the distance, the third beast rose and raced toward them, with a gaping crescent in its jagged side. Nyla pursed her lips at the sight. Edwin rained down his silver magic upon the two creatures, shards flying in all directions, but of what she couldn't tell. The third beast joined its compatriots, the gnarly gap in its side unnoticed.

She let out a frustrated cry. Magic crackled from her fingertips. Nyla stood and grounded her feet. Mercilessly, she set her magic loose on the nearest beast. Her magic ripped and slashed at the beast. It yowled in pain. Nyla gritted her teeth as the sound made her heart cry. They weren't alive in the sense that she was, or the way that an animal was. The reminder didn't soothe the ache in her chest or the tight twist of her frown. Forcing her ears to block the screeches from her mind, Nyla channeled more magic into her attack, hooking her magic into the hard exterior of the beast's aura and ripping tendrils of it away like she was tearing into paper. Turning the beast's aura into nothing but vapor with each tendril that wafted away from the core of its essence, Nyla focused her magic on tunneling though the creature's sapphire and scarlet signature, mercilessly dissecting the humanoid figure. Hunks and pieces and chips flew in every direction as Nyla urged her magic to break the beast from the inside out. Dark, jagged pieces of what she realized to be rock—not blood, not flesh, but *rock*—flew through the air, raining down upon the earth in a flurry as Nyla hacked at the beast with her magic until there was nothing left to tear into.

Her vicious attack made her stomach turn, but the thing finally stopped. There was nothing left for Dinora's magic to puppeteer. The beast, reduced to hundreds if not thousands of pieces at Nyla's behest, couldn't be manipulated. There wasn't enough of it left in one piece to make it worthwhile if Nyla's hunch about Dinora controlling them was correct.

Her chest heaved. Lightheaded, Nyla blinked and willed her eyes to focus on the two creatures still racing behind their carriage, unbothered by their fallen companion. Forcing her heartbeat to even out, Nyla scraped together the magic simmering in her bloodstream. She set her magic on the second beast. Edwin watched, silent and still beside her. As if snapping out of a daze, his cool silver magic joined hers in tearing the rock-creature apart piece by piece. Just as it was nearly destroyed, Nyla panted, almost tumbling off of the carriage. He caught her just in time.

"Don't use any more magic!" Edwin ordered her. She nodded weakly, sitting back down on the roof of the carriage. Through a haze, Nyla watched as Edwin's silvery magic clawed at the final beast, tearing it limb from limb until it was no more.

Nyla surveyed the road behind the carriage. Where she expected to see evidence of the creatures strewn down their path, there was nothing. The carnage left no bodies in its wake. Wavering wisps of smoke took the place where the onyx-colored shards had once lain. After several yards, the carriage finally rattled to a stop. Immediately after, the carriage tilted with the shift of people disembarking.

All at once, Huey, Quentin, and Xander started asking questions. The sagittarii quieted. Every now and then, Nyla could hear their hooves stomp in place, accompanied by a whinny.

"Are you all right?" Xander appeared in front of her, standing on the foothold meant to help load luggage onto the roof of the carriage. He was disheveled, as if he'd tried to tear his own hair out as a result of his concern or fear, maybe even both.

"So much magic," she replied tiredly, her chest heaving and temples pounding from lightheadedness.

"Too much magic," Edwin muttered, sounding just as fatigued as Nyla felt.

"What were those things?"

"I don't know, but I bet Dinora sent them." Nyla scooted closer to Xander.

"You might be right," Edwin said, lying back on the roof, his chest heaving. "Just leave me here. I'm not moving."

"We have to," Xander countered, taking Nyla by the waist and helping her down from the roof. Once on the ground, she leaned into him, her weight too much for her own legs to bear. Xander shifted, keeping a welcome arm around her waist and helping her stay on her feet as though it was second nature to him. "If Nyla's right and Dinora's behind this attack, we have to keep moving."

"Fine," Edwin grumbled, "but you're helping me down too."

"Get your own Xander!" Nyla whined hotly as Xander half led her, half carried her away from the carriage. "This one's mine!"

"I'll help Mr. Maffis, sir," Huey offered, though Nyla wasn't sure if Xander heard him over his fit of laughter.

"Yours, huh?" She could almost feel the smirk he was surely wearing in her soul.

"Mm, my head is pounding," Nyla whispered, her eyes half closed against the afternoon sun as she leaned further into Xander. Her footsteps faltered. "Pity we can't collect some of the rock. It's all gone up in smoke."

"I'm sure whatever the rock's energy could tell us isn't anything more than we could guess ourselves," Edwin said, leaning against Huey for support.

Xander steered her away from the road and led her to sit under a tree.

Quentin came over with a blanket and set it down for her and Edwin to sit on.

"Are you all right, Quentin?" she asked.

"I'll be all right, Miss." The quake in his voice said otherwise, but she didn't get to say anything more before he'd walked away and began to survey the carriage.

Huey led Edwin over, and he sat down beside her with a groan. "Let's never do that again."

"I don't think we'll have a say in the matter," she replied flatly. She glanced up at Xander. "You okay?"

"I'm more concerned about you two." He eyed them both in a way Nyla was all too familiar with, a way that analyzed them from head to toe for any injuries they might have. "Let's just hope we make it to Covington safely."

She only groaned in response as she curled in on herself. That was doubtful, but she didn't dare tell Xander that.

***

Once Quentin had the carriage fixed, it was a long and thankfully uneventful trip to Covington. Nyla and Edwin slept much of the way there. Their lack of companionship left Xander alone to his thoughts.

If Nyla was right about Dinora conjuring and controlling those creatures, then there was no telling what else might happen during their journey to Huntington. Or if it came to fighting an all-out war against her.

And if war *did* come, what would be expected of Nyla then? Would she have to fight against Dinora's threat all because of Astrid, and her connection to the Corvid Uprising? Would she have a choice?

Would she *choose* to fight?

He glanced at her, sleeping peacefully beside him. There was no way Nyla would choose *not* to fight Dinora. He didn't know how he knew it with such conviction, but he did.

Xander's mind begged the question: what did *he* choose? He hadn't given it much thought, too consumed by his impending homecoming, but now it was all he could focus on.

The carriage jostled. Xander readjusted Nyla's legs from where they'd nearly slipped off his lap, making sure she was undisturbed, and fixed

169

the blanket he'd draped over her with a soft smile. At least they were safe, and at least his worried mind could find comfort in the fact that Nyla was capable of protecting herself—and those around her.

Shifting his eyes, he found Edwin's weary eyes watching them. How long had he been awake?

"It's not really like you to listen to anyone, especially in a situation like that," Edwin murmured, sitting up with a twisted expression on his face as if he'd pulled a muscle. "What made you?"

Xander tilted his head. "What do you mean?"

"Well, for one," Edwin started, running a hand through his messy hair, "you're a stubborn jerk when you want to be; and two, when has the great Alexander Huntington the Third ever listened to anyone when his heart bids him to act?"

Xander scoffed, glaring at Edwin.

"No, really." Edwin straightened, letting the blanket he'd been wrapped up in fall to his lap as he set his feet on the floor of the carriage. "You've never backed down from a fight before, or a challenge, so why did you?"

"She's never yelled like that before…" Xander said quietly, glancing away.

Edwin arched an eyebrow, his lip quirking. "Plenty of people have yelled at you in your life, and you've *never* minded them."

"Nyla's never yelled before, ever," Xander said, scrubbing his face with his hands. Why couldn't Edwin sleep as long if not longer than Nyla? "And besides, I'm a different man, a better man than when I left Pemberly."

"Because of her?"

Xander thought for a moment, reflecting on the seasons that had passed since he'd left home. Spending a few weeks here, several weeks there, meandering from small town to small town and working for his keep and drinking…

"Maybe." His hand found the ring beneath his shirt. His fingers ached to curl around the smooth metal and clutch it along with the memories it brought to his mind before he ultimately dropped his hand. "But I think it has more to do with time—and being away from the expectations of my status."

Xander's answer hung in the air between them before Edwin averted his gaze to the drawn curtains of the carriage window.

"Perhaps," Edwin said distractedly. "You've definitely matured."

Xander chuckled. "And you haven't changed."

"Let's hope it stays that way," Edwin breathed. His eyes shone with worry for the first time since he'd come to their aid. "Do you think your grandfather will help you, against Dinora?"

"Do you think he won't?" Xander tilted his head. "I thought by sending you and asking for us to come to Huntington that he was inclined to help?"

"I couldn't say," Edwin admitted. "These were the only instructions he gave me, but he didn't give any indication about what would happen once we reached Huntington. But knowing your grandfather, he wouldn't have called you home under these circumstances without reason."

"We'll worry about it when we get to Huntington. For now, let's just…keep this between us," Xander said at last.

"As you wish, my lord," Edwin smirked, lying back down.

Xander rolled his eyes. "Please don't. We've been over this, Sir Maffis of the Caster Corps."

Edwin made a face of pure disgust. "You never do get used to it, do you?"

"Imagine being born into it," Xander grumbled, glancing over at Nyla again with the fear their discussion might've disturbed her. To his relief, she was still peacefully asleep, and probably would be by the time they reached Covington. "Being branded by your title through your entire life."

"I'd rather not—it sounds dreadful."

"It wasn't all bad, I guess." Xander smiled to himself, though Edwin didn't reply. He only settled further into his seat and drew the blanket up around his shoulders.

Left to his own devices once more, Xander's mind wandered. He contemplated what he'd told Edwin, about growing up with a title, and in one of the more established houses of Tenebris no less.

In many ways his upbringing wasn't bad, even if his parents were always busy and his grandfather steadfast in his expectations of the family, but they'd been together at least.

But reflecting upon it all now, and where he'd ended up in life, he wondered where he would be now if he hadn't been born a lord.

Would he have fought with his grandfather? Would his parents and Issie still be alive? Would he have set off for Fortune Falls? Would he have met Nyla? How would Nyla's path have been different if they hadn't met? Would she have made it to Fortune Falls?

"You're overthinking something." Nyla startled him from his thoughts.

"No, I'm not."

"Yes, you are. You've got that crease between your brows." She propped herself up on her elbow and looked toward the curtained window beside him. "How much farther?"

He considered that for a moment, glancing briefly out the window. His hand subconsciously rubbed her calf as he contemplated her question before he realized what he was doing and stopped. "About an hour, maybe."

"And where are we staying? Are we camping?" Nyla asked, her lips turned up in a lazy smile as if she already knew the answer.

"No more camping for us, not so long as we're accepting my grandfather's help."

Nyla made a face that wasn't entirely a frown and definitely couldn't hide her excitement. "I *guess* I can live with that if it means a proper bed."

Xander chuckled quietly, not wanting to disturb Edwin. "Is that your only condition for accepting his help?"

"At the moment, yes. You spoiled me in Caselle."

"If I hadn't, we would've been camping outside the city when you astral projected, and I would've had to leave you alone to get Nan to come and help."

"Fate really is a funny thing." She sat up, drawing her knees to her chest, and rubbed her arms. The cool late-Hugony air filled the vacancy where her legs had rested over his lap. "Tell me about him, your grandfather, so I know what to expect."

He sucked in a long breath. He supposed he did owe her some kind of explanation about his grandfather, and Nyla had waited much longer than he'd ever given her the courtesy of.

He didn't want to describe his grandfather as an unforgiving man, even if he could be uncompromising, but he also didn't want Nyla to be surprised by his blunt nature.

"He's…particular and sometimes difficult."

Nyla nodded, encouraging him to go on. The two, nearly three, years away from home and all the miles between his grandfather and himself made forming a coherent thought difficult. But Xander pressed on, telling Nyla some of his favorite memories and some of the things other people had said about his grandfather, leaving out the very important aspect that they were Huntingtons. For whatever reason, Xander just couldn't bring himself to tell her. He didn't think it would matter to Nyla, but he'd been wrong before, and his name had ruined many of the potential connections he'd hoped to make with people in the past—actual connections unrelated to status and personal gain or favor.

And with Nyla, it had all been forgotten. For once in his life, he was only Xander, a fact he savored the farther into the country he traveled and put Pemberly farther behind him, where his face was unknown and his name didn't matter.

But the closer they drew to Pemberly, and the more Nyla saw of his life and what his grandfather had in store for them, the closer his illusion of freedom and individuality came to shattering completely.

Of all the things Xander was unprepared to face, this—that thread that could snap in half and fray their friendship—was something he wasn't yet ready to face.

Sloth

Dinora sagged against the workbench. Her chest heaved. Sweat beaded along her brow, dripping down her temples and onto her cheeks like tears. They might as well have been as frustration buzzed in her chest. Dragging another long breath into her lungs and then another, Dinora closed her eyes. It had taken nearly every ounce of strength she'd had to resurrect the souls of the wretches who'd failed her before, only for them to fail again as stone.

Dinora shook her head bitterly. She was weak. There was no denying it. Compared to the fresh blood that coursed through Astrid's heir and the magics combined in her, she was weak after centuries of surviving on her bound magic.

And unlike Astrid's foresight, her worthless son hadn't even granted her her rightful inheritance. His magic had already been stolen by the land, absorbed for its own renewal. For his methodical approach to practicing magic, he hadn't thought to bequeath his magic to her should something happen to him. Useless. Pathetic. Guileless.

She pushed away from the workbench, idly stalking across the cottage with furrowed brows. Pacing up and down the length of the homely cottage, Dinora's mind whirled bitterly.

Cedric had learned nothing from her, from her sacrifices, from her loss. He was a disgrace to the royal bloodline. He never would've been fit to be Corvus's heir.

Utterly useless. His potion hadn't done a bloody thing for her. It was merely happenstance that she'd thought of transferring the curse to Nyla after watching her kill Cedric. And what little magic that potion had possessed had been just enough to get the job done and shatter the constraint on her magic.

What had he done with all that magic? What was the purpose of collecting the land's magic, only for a potion that hadn't worked at all?

If only she'd thought of transferring the curse to *him*. If she'd done that—Dinora clenched her jaw. It was no use. She knew, for all of his failures, her son was a competent magic user. She needed him to keep her alive all this time as she plotted her revenge. If she'd turned the curse on him, she would've lost him for good as Astrid had nearly stolen him from her with her pretense of love and affection for him.

Dinora cursed and whirled on the overburdened workbench. Her mind scattered, searching over the remnants her son had thought to keep over the centuries. Scrolls he probably never glanced at, books he clearly never dusted, magic he never used.

Her eyes fixated on the glowing quartz, the last drop of potent magic Cedric had gathered from the land.

Dinora had always had to do everything for herself. From vying for the Emperor's hand to securing her marriage to waging war for the sake of Corvus and all that her husband had built. She would do it all again, better this time. But right now, the only thing she could possibly do was grow stronger.

That was the only way. She would have to build her strength if she could ever hope to restore the former glory of the Corvid Empire.

Though, she wondered curiously, after 647 long years, who would remember? Who would join her cause?

Dinora's nostrils flared.

They'd murdered her husband, her *Emperor* in their petty rebellion against Corvus, and now they'd finally be brought to justice for their crimes. And then her people would pay for forsaking their crown, for allowing their enemies to extinguish their country, their sovereignty.

She would make certain of it.

She would build an army of the souls trapped within the stone points of the sapphire forest. They might not have been the indestructible soldiers she'd sought to make, but they had proven to be useful, if only as a distraction. And with this scrap of magic from the land, she'd make them stronger—she'd make herself stronger, just as she'd intended 647 years ago.

If it was one thing she knew, it was that Corvids always remembered, and if she were the last of the great ones, then so be it. She would avenge Corvus for the whole of the empire, even if those who'd remember its greatness and the power they once wielded weren't around any longer. And when they realized her cause, they would remember their history and just who had fought to preserve them.

Corvids *always* remembered.

15. THE THREE PUMPKIE CLANS OF TENEBRIS

Shamira bowed her head respectfully. The seven Elders, Kasand among them for once, remained silent. The void in her mind from the lack of external emotion that usually assaulted her frightened her. She had no indication of the Elders' moods, of their intent. She had only that overwhelming sensation of impending doom pressing down on her. Were they masking their emotions from her? She risked a glance up at them through her lashes, not daring to move an inch. At their unflinching gaze, Shamira swallowed.

Now she understood what Xander had meant when he'd proclaimed his hatred for silence but not quiet. Now she understood the difference, the one he'd tried in vain to explain to her during the long, strenuous day they'd spent by Nyla's bedside. Shamira hadn't understood his meaning then, perhaps still recovering from healing Nyla after their confrontation with Dinora, but now she understood. And she found that she wholly agreed with the boy.

Silence and quiet were not synonymous. Silence was rigid and static. Quiet had a hum that caressed and soothed the soul, and what Shamira wouldn't trade for something to ease her soul right now.

Instead, the palatable tension prickled the fur on the back of her neck.

Shamira. Kasand greeted her at last.

High Seer, Shamira returned, matching the neutrality in his tone.

His lips quirked into a wry smile, an expression he rarely gave. *We didn't believe you would return. Many who desert the clan never look back.*

When the Elders summon, it is my duty to answer them, she replied carefully, raising her head to look at them each in turn. *I have always had the clan's best interest in mind, even if it required me to break my sacred vows.*

We are glad to hear that, the High Elder spoke. Her voice was crackled and weathered, but didn't hold the vaguest hint of her intent. Shamira bobbed her head once again at the address. *And have you acted in the clan's best interest?*

Shamira imagined that if she were human, she would've licked her lips like Nyla and Xander had when they were nervous about giving an honest reply. *I should like to believe that I have, but it is not for me to judge.*

The High Elder glanced at the Elders on either side of her. They communicated with each other for a long minute that dragged into an eternity, all while Shamira was forced to exercise a patience she didn't have the nerve for, not with the way her stomach quaked as she forced herself to remain composed. Her tail longed to twitch and flick with the churning of her thoughts and the worry harbored in the deepest parts of her mind. Flickers of emotion passed quickly over their faces, but aside from those brief glimpses, Shamira could garner nothing of their mood or any indication of what their plans may be for her. She nearly drowned in the void her own emotions were left to fill within her. It was rare for her to realize her own emotions, and rarer still for her to find anxiety such as this pooling in her gut.

Was Kasand shielding them, knowing she had no choice but to acknowledge them thanks to her gifts? More importantly, was he doing so of his own accord, or by order of the Elder Council?

Either way, the answer didn't bear well for her.

Then we have much to discuss, Elder Hecates, a pumpkie with tawny fur and wizened green eyes, spoke at last. Shamira knew he regarded her as nothing more than a member of the clan, though his neutral tone was warmer than she remembered it being. She nearly felt her eyes narrow in suspicion before she stopped herself. Just what were the Elders planning to do? *Come.*

Shamira blinked as the Elders turned tail and filed up the path that led into their village. Kasand lingered a moment, looking back at her.

I thought you obeyed the Elders? Was that a lie? the crystal-blue-eyed pumpkie asked. His snowy tail flicked with the slightest bit of amusement.

No, High Seer. Shamira started after them with Kasand keeping close to her side.

I don't believe they're looking to punish you, not with all that has happened under their noses. Their ignorance is your blessing.

Shamira glanced at him sharply. How could he be so certain of her safety?

A secret between Seers, my friend.

I am not a Seer.

Perhaps, but you could be, Kasand mused. *I have yet to pick my successor.*

Do you feel you need to? Shamira knew Kasand was old, but not nearly old enough to be expecting death. She'd heard of pumpkies who would live to be a thousand years old, or close to it, prior to the Corvid Uprising. Now, it was as though they—as a species—were beginning anew. The oldest Elder, the High Elder Florence, was said to be 668. Only two Elders had managed to survive the war from the Brewardt Clan, her clan. Of the Reyhart Clan Elders, three had survived the war, and the last Zeldher Elder succumbed to the void of magic shortly after the supposed end of the war. Only a third of all pumpkies that had fought in the war survived, and it was with those numbers that they now struggled to maintain their heritage and numbers in the aftermath.

Not yet, but I would like to train my successor as my predecessor could not.

Shamira hummed in response. *That would be most advantageous to your successor.*

Kasand remained silent, instead leading her up the steep incline that would allow her to catch the first glimpse of her home in two years. Shamira's stomach clenched tightly at the thought of all she'd left behind in her search for Nyla.

As they crested the final step cut into the rocky mountainside, Shamira took in the sight of her village in the valley below. Everything looked the same as it always had. Shelters crafted from rock and mud were scattered throughout the valley. Built by the aid of magic, seldom were shelters carved out from the mountain itself, but now as their numbers grew, it became necessary to harvest stone from the mountain to build their homes. Simple domes in shape, the shelters were only meant to house a couple and their litter. But once the cubs could walk and hunt on their own, it was time for a new shelter. From here, Shamira couldn't tell if any shelters had been built in her time away, but she wouldn't be surprised if there had. Not bothering to count the simple shelters she could see from here, her eyes roved over what humans would consider to be the 'town square.' The center of their village boasted their meeting hall. The hall was now barely big enough to accommodate the few hundred pumpkies that the Brewardt Clan had grown to over the last six centuries.

It was this building that Kasand and the Elders led her to. As she and Kasand passed through the village, familiar faces peeked out of their shelters or stopped in their tracks as Shamira was forced to walk by. Most expressions were unreadable. Others were apprehensive, as if rumors of her mission and whereabouts had already spread. A few were openly hateful. Those accusatory eyes seared themselves into Shamira's memory.

Here we are, Kasand said lightly.

His teal-colored magic peeled back the woven leaves that curtained the doorway. Shamira paused in the entry. Not only were her clan's Elders seated on the high dais, but the High Elders of the Zeldher and Reyhart Clans were also present.

The High Elders rarely left their respective clans. Whatever their reason for being here, Shamira knew it didn't bode well. Kasand joined the Elders on the dais, leaving her to stand alone in the center of the hall.

At least this meeting wasn't public. Shamira didn't think she could bear such open judgement on her being.

Shamira, High Elder Florence spoke, *you stand before us as a deserter and potential threat to the clans, though you claim you have always had the clans' best interest in mind. Do you agree with that charge?*

Shamira bowed her head. *I do.*

About two decades prior to your leaving, you and High Seer Kasand forewarned us about a disturbance in the balance of magic involving the human country. You left two years ago to investigate that disturbance?

I did.

And you have found the source?

Speak your piece, Shamira, Kasand interjected with a pointed glance at Florence.

The pure night-colored cat bristled. Her whiskers twitched in the slightest hint of irritation. Her eyes sent a withering gaze toward the unperturbed High Seer. *Perhaps it is best for you to tell your tale in full, as the High Seer has suggested, so the whole of the matter can be judged fairly.*

Shamira nodded, stealing a grateful glance at Kasand. *As you have stated, High Elder, around two decades ago, both High Seer Kasand and I felt a shift in the world's balance of magic. While our records here were helpful, I was unable to determine what the cause of the disturbance could be and sought out the High Seer for guidance.*

It was upon bringing the matter to him that we discovered that we had sensed the same disturbance, and so we began searching more fervently for any record that described the same manner of magical signature we sensed then.

In our search, High Seer Kasand and I discovered some records from the Corvid Uprising. Based on these records, we were able to confirm the manner of disturbance was the same or similar essence as was recorded then.

Shamira paused, studying the collective before her. A few of the Elders had shifted where they sat at the mention of the Corvid Uprising, but still, Shamira was unable to gauge their emotions. The eyes of the Zeldher High Elder nearly seared into her soul, though she didn't know if the intensity of his gaze was a result of his character, or his condemnation. She forced herself to persevere, even as the prospect of her impending punishment loomed over her. *High Seer Kasand and I brought our findings to the Brewardt Elder Council, though nothing came of them at the time.*

At the mention of their inaction, the Reyhart and Zeldher High Elders glanced to High Elder Florence between them with a matched indignation. Shamira noted their surprise and pressed on, hoping the High Elder wouldn't reprimand her for mentioning the Elder Council's decision to ignore her reports of these magical disturbances over the years. The warning in High Elder Florence's eyes rang clear, though Shamira didn't heed it.

It was interesting that the Elders hadn't at least notified their kindred clans. Shamira didn't have the time at present to consider why, not as she pressed on in her narrative, watching for any other indicators that could help her guess what might be in store for her future.

Years later, I sensed a stronger disturbance, a different one than the initial shift in magic the High Seer and I had previously discussed. This was two years ago, and with a third disturbance more similar to the first, I knew in my heart that someone needed to investigate the matter further, even if it meant forsaking sacred clan vows. I felt it was my duty as a protector of Tenebris to act, as that is the first and foremost vow each pumpkie has taken since we made peace with the humans of Tenebris upon their independence from Corvus.

I searched far and wide until I finally traced the source of the first and third shifts in the balance. My search led me to find a human girl named Nyla. Two years ago, her family was murdered by the source of the second disturbance, Cedric and Dinora Kashar, as named in our records.

Through my search and companionship with Nyla, we have learned that she inherited magic from Tenebris's Royal Mage, which would explain why the disturbances Kasand and I sensed bore similar, if not the same, signatures as those recorded in our surviving archives and history.

Nyla is a strong Caster and, with a little more discipline, a strong warrior as well. But she is young. Shamira hesitated, concerned that what she had to say next would be her undoing. *Dinora Kashar has been freed from her imprisonment, and the status of her son is uncertain. Nyla believes she gravely injured him in a magical battle at the Woodlane Manor, though we have been unable to trace either of them since Dinora freed herself from her imprisonment.*

When Shamira had finished, she was met with more silence. Each of the Elders glanced at the Elder beside them and then over each other's shoulders. Shamira's heart thudded against her chest. The silence pounded in her ears as she waited for any sort of response. She wasn't sure if the Elders were murmuring telepathically amongst themselves or if she'd stunned them into silence. All but one.

Elder Hecates's hard gaze was fixed on her. She nearly shrank under the force of his gaze, but no matter how she tried to read the pumpkie's expression, the less certain she was of his motive for doing so. Was he casting judgement on her? Was his silence a testament to his displeasure at their lack of punishment for her transgressions?

Was it a warning?

Before she could draw her conclusion, the sharp eyes of her clan's High Elder landed on her, further rooting her to the spot. *Thank you, Shamira. You may go now. We will summon you before the gathering tonight.*

Shamira blinked. Her stomach seemed hollow for the time being, emptied of the nerves that had roiled in her gut during her ascent into her homelands. The fact left Shamira feeling altogether vacant.

That was all? They were allowing her to…to what, exactly?

Welcome home, Kasand added, though his words provided no comfort.

Shamira bowed her head. Gathering her wits, she managed to express her gratitude. *Thank you.*

She left promptly before the Elders had time to reconsider, or finish their deliberations, as surely that was the cause for delaying her punishment. As she stalked through the village, her head spun. Why were the Zeldher and Reyhart Clan High Elders here? Was she to be punished later? Why was there to be a gathering?

Shamira swallowed. A long time had passed since a pumpkie of the Brewardt Clan was publicly punished, but the spectacle had left an impression on her young mind. She imagined that was why the Zeldher High Elder was here. The Zeldher Clan was known for their strict conduct and swift punishment. But even that inference didn't make sense. High Elder Florence could've easily communicated with him privately about the matter if she'd wanted his guidance. So why were the other two clans' High Elders here?

Was it because of the gravity of her transgressions? Or the impending involvement in external matters of the clans her reports indicated?

Shamira didn't know, and at this rate was too afraid to guess.

Pumpkies eyed her curiously as she passed. She could sense their confusion, their awe, their resentment. She didn't dare meet their eyes, knowing only uncertainty and apprehension shone in hers.

With nowhere else to go, but unwilling to seek out her own home or even those who might be happy to see her—if anyone possibly could be—Shamira left the village behind her and stopped in the field of the hillside, as far away from the village center as she dared to. Shock numbed her mind into utter silence as she replayed her meeting with the Elders.

How severely was she to be punished for leaving the clan and exposing the Brewardt Council's reluctance to heed her and Kasand's prior warnings?

Shamira found no answers in the surrounding mountains and valleys, nor did she find any solace in them as her mind whirled with fear.

Through her own emotional tumult, her inner balance seemed to shift. Shamira pitched to the side as though she were about to fall over, but managed to catch herself just in time. Her nose burned as though plagued by a sneeze that would not come. As her mind frantically sought the source of the shift in magic assaulting her, her thoughts turned to her friends.

Panting, Shamira's eyes darted to the interior of Tenebris hiding beneath the haze of her mountaintop home. Vainly wishing she could see across the miles between them and make certain that Nyla and Xander were all right, her heart pounded in her chest. She wished she could go to them, certain that the only reason there would be a shift in magic this substantial was because of Dinora.

But alas, Shamira knew that leaving now would brand her a traitor not just of her clan, but of her kin, and that was something she knew Tenebris couldn't afford if they all were to survive the coming war against Dinora.

16. COVINGTON

Covington afforded them another private apartment above yet another of the H&R Trading empire's shops, a fact that Xander had never been grateful for until today. It wasn't that he hadn't benefited from them before, only that he'd always taken these comforts for granted until recently.

Xander sighed, dragging a hand down his face. It wasn't even the longest of the *long* days in his life, and yet somehow this was the worst bout of exhaustion he'd ever felt. He set his bag down on the chair beside the bedroom door and kicked his boots off. How they'd survived the carriage ride here, he didn't know. Between the attack of those creatures and his own trepidation, it was a miracle that he'd made it this far and could finally collapse into bed for the night.

Not even bothering to change out of his travel clothes, Xander yanked back the covers and slipped beneath the heavy pile of blankets, pulling them up and over his head.

They'd survived the journey from Gossamer to Covington, a journey that had never seemed dangerous before today.

A part of him wondered what their train ride into Huntington would have in store for them tomorrow, but a smaller part was still fixed on the sight of Nyla's and Edwin's magic tearing into the apparent stone beasts. Utterly helpless, he could only watch from behind the swaying curtains of the carriage's small rear window.

The sheer amount of magic the two had used to tear apart the beasts would be forever imprinted on his mind. He doubted he would ever recover from the sight of Nyla's magic ripping into that first beast. It was too easy for him to imagine what that same magic could do to a human, or an animal. And with that thought had come the realization of what Dinora was capable of and how, at the moment, there was only a single person ready to take up the fight against her.

A single person—woman—against an evil sorceress vile enough to live on in the legends of the haunted forest.

A single teenager with silver hair and lilac-colored eyes, a girl with no family and a broken heart who hadn't known she'd had magic until recently. A girl who was willing to sacrifice everything, nonetheless.

Xander couldn't fathom it, the odds or Fate if that's what it was. He understood the personal vendetta Nyla harbored, but what he couldn't quite wrap his head around was the fact that this was happening at all. Dinora and Cedric had been forgotten for centuries. The Corvid Uprising was all but erased from memory.

So why was it all happening now? If it were truly Fate, then he wanted nothing to do with the concept. It shouldn't be happening now, it shouldn't be Nyla's burden, and she shouldn't have to choose this battle—if she even had a choice at all. The image of her on the stone steps of the Woodlane Manor came to him. His mind's eye saw the pile of ash that the ogre had been reduced to. Then came the destruction of the manor's ballroom, the aftermath of Nyla's fight against Cedric while she'd astral projected. Through all of these horrible circumstances, Nyla had fought and survived. Yet his mind persisted.

Dinora was wicked and zealous. She knew no boundaries, a fact solidified in the myths of the Shadow Forest.

They'd barely survived today, so how was Nyla supposed to survive a war against Dinora?

Did his grandfather understand that, what they were up against? Or had he only sent Edwin to help them break the curse, and calling them all back to Pemberly was just a way to exercise some form of control over Xander, his wayward grandson?

Xander shook his head to clear his mind. It was only the day's mental exhaustion that gave these anxieties life, nothing more. Edwin had said it best: Alexander Huntington wasn't a man to waste resources on something he wasn't willing to see through. And even if his grandfather decided not to aid them in finding Dinora and defeating her, Xander had to have faith in Shamira and her goal to inspire the pumpkies into action.

Flipping onto his other side, Xander forced his mind to stop but to no avail. As his thoughts swirled and fixated on that fateful day in the courtyard, the nightmare that had plagued him for well over a season now came back to him. It'd started weeks before he'd even met Nyla—long before the battle in the Woodlane Manor's front courtyard.

While he hadn't experienced it since that battle, the nightmare still haunted his conscious mind. If anything, it'd only gotten worse in the wake of the courtyard battle. Watching Nyla and Dinora fight, he'd thought in that moment that his nightmare had come true. But since he'd had time to analyze it, he'd realized a few differences.

First, it was impossible for him to see things that hadn't happened yet, as he hadn't a drop of magic in his blood.

Second, in his dream he'd never managed to see either of the figures' faces. All he'd ever been able to make of them was their general stature and, of course, the colors of their magic. Lilac and scarlet, colliding, exploding. Of course he knew now that the lilac energy belonged to both Nyla and Astrid, and that the scarlet energy likely belonged to Dinora. But it didn't solve the mystery of which two figures he actually saw in his nightmare, even if he'd begun to believe the one wielding the now familiar lilac-colored magic was Nyla.

And finally, his dream had always taken place in a field, not the manor's courtyard. He knew that dreams and reality differed, but he'd had this nightmare for weeks before he'd even met Nyla. So how could he dream of her, of Dinora, or of anything that was happening to them now before he'd even known about any of it?

Xander tossed and turned. Questions and thoughts like these would be his undoing if he couldn't get any sleep before having to face his grandfather tomorrow. There wasn't any way he could abandon Nyla now and head back to anywhere that wasn't Huntington.

He would face his grandfather tomorrow. As surely as the sun set in the west, he would face his grandfather, for Nyla—no matter the cost.

***

"How'd you sleep last night?" Nyla asked, nearly laughing as she sipped on her tea, leaning against the detailed cabinets and stone countertop of the apartment's kitchen.

Xander squinted against the harsh glare of the sunlight and magic-itric lights of the kitchen. He did *not* get enough sleep for the amount of energy she had today.

Or rather, he hadn't gotten enough sleep for today at all.

"Fine," he muttered, rubbing the sleep from his eyes.

She smirked over the top of her mug. "Liar."

He couldn't bring himself to laugh. It would only serve to encourage Nyla, and based on the sparkling excitement brimming in her eyes, he knew she didn't need any help squaring off with today.

Instead, he buried his head in a cabinet and searched for something easy to make for breakfast, mumbling as such while he did.

"If you want, I could make ponanchkas?" she offered. "I mean, it's been a while, and I'm not nearly as good at cooking as…well most anyone else, but ponanchkas are pretty easy."

Xander turned to her with a half-quirked eyebrow and closed the cabinet door blocking her from his view. "What are ponanchkas?"

Nyla's eyes widened. In her dramatic shock, she set her teacup down on the pale countertop with a gasp.

"You've *never* had ponanchkas? How?! You've actually been to Eurland!"

She pulled her hair up and tied it back in a ponytail. Xander started to back out of the kitchen, uncertain of what was about to happen. He watched in apprehensive silence as Nyla started to move about the kitchen in a flurry, rifling through the cabinets and drawers for whatever cooking instruments she'd need, not giving him a moment to answer her question—or answer his.

"It's a good thing Edwin's a morning person and that I already sent him out to get the ingredients we didn't have here." Nyla shot him an apologetic smile. "Yeah, I was going to make ponanchkas whether or not anyone else wanted them. I'm not entirely sorry."

Xander plopped down in one of the sitting room's winged-back chairs so he could still see the kitchen but was safely out of her way. "Are you a morning person?"

Nyla stopped dead in her tracks, kneeling halfway into a cabinet as if she expected to climb inside it and shut the door. She backed away and frowned at him over her shoulder. "I think they might be growing on me. What about you: morning or night?"

"Afternoon?"

She laughed, resuming her search, though he didn't know for what exactly she was looking for. "Doesn't count."

"What doesn't count?" Edwin asked, coming in the front door of the apartment with a bag full of groceries in his arms.

"All I said was that I was an afternoon person." Xander crossed his arms and leaned his head back against the stiff cushion of the chair, stretching his legs out.

"I don't think you can do that. You're either a morning person or a night person. There is no in between."

"There is, and it's called 'the afternoon,' as in the best time of day. It's not too early and not too late. It's when the sun is highest and most people are awake and you can do anything you want and avoid what you can put off until tomorrow."

All was quiet for a moment. He didn't even hear Nyla rummaging around in the kitchen anymore. He cracked an eye open in time to see Nyla and Edwin sharing a look of mutual agreement. Who knew something as simple as being a morning or night person would see them both on the same side?

"You make a good point, but…most people are either a morning or night person." Nyla unloaded the bag of groceries Edwin had so generously picked up for them and spread the ingredients out on the kitchen island. Xander wearily eyed each new ingredient as she unveiled it. There was nothing too exotic from what he could see. Eggs, flour, milk, et cetera, but he didn't know what the berries were for. Or the sugar.

But as Nyla began measuring out ingredients and dumping them in a bowl or pulling out another bowl and adding other ingredients to that one, Xander's gut began to simmer.

He'd never seen Nyla cook. But if it was like nearly everything else she did, he wondered if he should be a little bit afraid. Nyla was one of the greatest people he knew but sometimes overzealous and, at times, reckless. His worries were only confirmed when a cloud of flour burst from Nyla's fingers as she plopped the powder into a bowl.

"You look worried," Edwin whispered over the top of his book.

"I am."

"Should I be too?"

"I can hear you both!" Nyla glared at them from the kitchen. The whisk clinked against the inside walls of the bowl in her arms as she stood angrily at the threshold between the kitchen and seating area. "I'll have you know that ponanchkas are my signature dish…I mean, they're my only dish, but I'm good at them."

"Was that supposed to make us feel better?" Xander asked on behalf of both himself and Edwin, who looked as if Nyla had struck him across the face.

She paused, tilting her head—and the bowl at a dangerous angle. "Yes?"

As if his worried fixation on the bowl reminded her of its presence, Nyla straightened and turned back to the kitchen. "I just need a little while longer because I have to make the syrup still…and, well…you know, cook."

"Take all the time you need!" Xander's eyes roved over the flour streaked across the door of the upper cabinets and the egg dripping down a drawer.

No matter how good these ponanchkas turned out to be, he dreaded the cleanup in their future. It might take all three of them the better part of the morning, he realized as Nyla grabbed a pot from a drawer and filled it with water. She added sugar and some kind of something that he couldn't see because she'd blocked his view as she set the whole thing on the stove to simmer.

He stole a glance at Edwin. As if sensing his concerned gaze, his friend lowered his book just a fraction to shake his head before returning to whatever it was that he was reading.

With a sigh, Xander closed his eyes. The least he could do was get a bit more sleep as Nyla made breakfast.

Something bubbled from the kitchen, presumably the syrup she was making. Its sweetness tickled his nose. He inhaled deeply. Was that twiberry syrup? Xander couldn't answer that, so he only snuggled further into his chair. On one hand, he wanted the chair to swallow him whole so he wouldn't ever have to leave this apartment. But on the other hand, he at least wanted to eat breakfast first and find out what ponanchkas were.

All he'd been able to gather was that they were a Eurish breakfast dish that Nyla's mother had probably taught her how to make. That was all he had to go on. Well, that, and the fact that they were fairly easy to make if Nyla, a self-professed novice, considered them to be her signature dish.

More dishes *clanked* from the kitchen. He forced his weary eyes to open, finding Nyla standing on her tiptoes to pull a set of plates down from the cupboard. With that accomplished, she hurried back over to the stove, where only a skillet and the pot sat over the low flames of the burners.

He watched in wonder as three place settings floated over to the dining room table and set themselves down accordingly. His eyes darted back to the kitchen as Nyla flipped one ponanchka while she used magic to pour batter into a second pan. She already had a few of the fluffy, circular ponanchkas heaped on another plate, and Xander found his mouth watering as he registered for the first time the warm, savory aroma that had engulfed the apartment.

"Almost set!" she called without looking over at them, intent on the ponanchkas still over the flames.

Xander shared a look with Edwin. Hesitantly, Xander peeled himself away from the embrace of the armchair and stood on stiff legs with a groan.

"Yeah, definitely not a morning person," Edwin laughed as he sauntered into the dining room. He sat with his back to the kitchen and gazed wistfully out the bright window.

Xander wisely put his back to the window, perking up when he noticed that Nyla was flicking off the burners. She quickly drained the contents of the pot into a cloth strainer spread over a pitcher in the sink and pressed the syrup from it. Taking the pitcher and the plate of ponanchkas in her hands, Nyla made her way into the dining area.

She set the towering plate of ponanchkas in the center of the table and took the seat beside him. "All right, dig in!"

Xander hummed happily, reaching for a few of the wonderfully aromatic ponanchkas. The comforting baked scent gave him high hopes that these were in fact edible and that the mess in the kitchen would be entirely worth the cleanup. Xander supposed that the cleanup would be worthwhile no matter what—if only because it delayed the inevitable confrontation with his grandfather until much later today.

He really ought to thank Nyla, especially as the ponanchka all but melted in his mouth. His soul sighed in contention.

"These are delicious," Edwin said between bites, reaching for the pitcher of twiberry syrup.

"Thank you!" Nyla paused to swallow. "It's a family recipe."

"So…there's no sense in asking for the recipe then?" Xander asked, glancing hopefully at her with a pleading smile.

She shook her head. "Ma always said that recipes were meant to be shared, even if they are a family recipe. Besides, who else am I going to pass it along to?"

"I don't know," he said, forcing himself to swallow. The lingering taste of the sweet and savory ponanchkas turned to sand in his mouth. "We have a lot of life to live yet."

"Yeah, but…" She trailed off, biting her lip and dropping her gaze entirely.

Any attempt at small talk was squandered. Nyla's words hung in the air like static. Xander stared at the pool of ruby-colored syrup on his plate. It brought to mind the blood that had speckled Nyla's lips as she lay sprawled against the stone steps of the Woodlane Manor, nearly dead but alive enough for Shamira to heal.

Xander forced himself to at least finish his plate, even though the weight of what Nyla hadn't said knocked the wind from him. She didn't see a future for herself. She didn't seem to expect that she'd survive whatever was to come, whatever that may actually be.

For all any of them knew, none of them would have any part in subverting the doom and destruction Dinora would enact. Someone more capable than them would ensure the kingdom's safety, and the three of them, Nyla specifically, could go about their lives and wait out the coming storm.

Nyla's chair scratched against the hardwood floor as she pushed away from the table. "Is everyone done?"

Edwin nodded. "You should get ready for the day. We'll clean this up."

"I can…I made this mess," Nyla said, beginning to take the pitcher and plate of ponanchkas from the table.

"It's only fair," Xander said, forcing himself to smile through the clouds swirling around his thoughts. Standing from his chair, he stopped Nyla's busy hands in their tracks and took the plate and pitcher from her. "Go get ready. We'll take care of this."

Nyla's lilac eyes stared so intently, he feared she'd see into his very soul if they didn't break eye contact. She bobbed her head once in a shallow nod.

"Okay. I'll be back to help soon." She glanced over at the kitchen and cringed. "It's a pretty big mess, isn't it?"

"I've seen worse," Edwin drawled. "The communal kitchen in the boarding hall at university was horrific during exam week. Coffee splattered everywhere and dishes overflowing from the sink…I have nightmares about it sometimes."

Nyla laughed, finally relenting and starting towards the hallway. "Well, if you're both certain, thank you."

Barely a second had passed after Nyla had disappeared down the hall and they'd shifted into the kitchen when Edwin turned to him.

"You've got that look again, that concerned frown and crease between your brows."

"Edwin, don't start with me. Let's just get this cleaned up." He reached for a towel and was about to dampen it at the sink when Edwin *tsked*.

With a wave of his hand, the kitchen was magically restored to its pristine glory. "All right, now the cleanup's done."

"You can't—" Xander pinched the bridge of his nose and squeezed his eyes shut, crossing his arms over his chest like a shield. "All right fine, *fine*. What do you want, Edwin?"

"Knock it off, Alexander." Edwin leaned against the counter and stuffed his hands in his pockets. "What bothered you at breakfast? That Nyla's a better cook than you?"

"What is this, an inquisition?" Xander glared half-heartedly. "And that remains to be seen, because this is the first time Nyla's done any cooking since we met."

"Something *did* bother you, though." Edwin wasn't going to let the matter fade away.

Xander drew a deep breath through his nose. He forced the tension from his shoulders, letting them drop and the overall stiffness from his body loosen. What was the harm in telling Edwin? Xander couldn't think of a reason not to, especially since Edwin was probably the only person who could come close to understanding. A few years older than both him and Nyla, Edwin had the unique position of being both a trained Caster but also young enough to share the same regard for all the years yet to come in their lives.

"I'm worried about Nyla and what she might face against Dinora if my grandfather decides not to help us," Xander finally admitted. "It doesn't sound like Nyla expects to survive whatever it is that will happen."

"And you're worried she'll do something altogether daring that results in…her not surviving it this time?"

Xander nodded.

Edwin's eyes withdrew thoughtfully. Long seconds stretched by, and no response came. Xander gave up on waiting for one and turned to walk away.

"His lordship will make sure Nyla's in a position to survive." Xander meant to ask how he could be so certain of that, if his grandfather hadn't given any indication of his stance before Edwin left, when his friend added, as if by an afterthought, "He's changed, since you left. I don't know how to describe it…but your grandfather has changed somewhat over these last few years. He's still a force to be reckoned with in business, though."

Xander hesitated in the threshold between the kitchen and the seating area. He fingered the sculpted molding of the opening as if the pristine paint were flaking.

"There's not a force on this earth that'll stop Nyla when she sets her mind to something, trust me. She might be just as strong-willed as he is. This is a match my grandfather may not win."

Edwin snorted. "That'll be a first. I think I might be looking forward to our impending doom now."

Xander rolled his eyes. The best he could plan for, it seemed, was to be there for Nyla if she needed him, just as he had been since she discovered her magic back at Fortune Falls. Until then, he'd just have to survive Huntington society again—and make peace with his grandfather.

17. REVELATIONS

Nyla tapped her foot against the platform, staring out at the tracks. She chewed on her bottom lip, oblivious to the people bustling around Xander, Edwin, and herself. The train station was much busier than she'd anticipated it would be, but that wasn't the problem that worried her gut.

It was the anticipation of what to expect. What to expect on the train, what to expect when they got to Huntington, what to expect of Xander's grandfather, what to expect of the near future and the days to come. That final expectation on an endless list of things she was anticipating was enough to make her pulse quicken.

She honestly didn't expect to survive until the end of this, especially not when Dinora specifically sought to kill her. Nyla tried to tell herself that she was insignificant compared to the war Dinora promised to wage against Tenebris, but then the mousy voice inside her head reminded her that Astrid had willed her magic to someone in her bloodline—*their* bloodline—for a purpose.

And now that purpose had come. Astrid's magic and whatever spell she'd designed had known now was the time it would be needed as an added strength. Nyla only wished she knew why it had chosen her, but she supposed she never would.

Having read Astrid's journal during her brief imprisonment and in the quiet moments afforded to her by their travel, Nyla had learned more about the wars of Tenebris's past than she ever imagined. She'd learned more about her distant ancestor and of her—their—magic than she ever thought possible.

The war, whatever you wanted to call it—the "Great Tenebris War" or the "Corvid Uprising"—hadn't started in the way that Nyla imagined most wars did. There was no tension between the two countries at the time. Certainly, times had been difficult, and a faction of Corvids remained bitter about the previous war that had granted Tenebris and Eurland their independence from the empire, but the countries had rebuilt in the two decades following the revolution. Eurland had isolated itself, and it did not offer aid to Tenebris after Lord and Lady Hart's assassination—more distant relatives of Nyla's, if she'd understood Astrid's journal entry. Corvus hadn't offered aid either, too embroiled in their efforts to battle the furious force Dinora had manipulated in her quest for vengeance within their own country.

And so Tenebris had to face the faction of Corvid rebels alone. Or at least until the pumpkies had joined the cause several weeks after the initial battle had caught Tenebris unprepared.

Nyla had started when she'd read that. Dinora's newfound freedom and the centuries that had passed between the Corvid Uprising had taken its toll on the kingdom's ability to foresee such a war. She was in part to blame for this coming surprise. If they'd never gone to the Woodlane Manor, Dinora wouldn't be free. But Nyla knew if she kept fixating on that, she'd never be able to overcome her guilt and aid whatever chances Tenebris had to stand against her and defeat her once and for all.

If not for the sake of her country, then for her own sake. Nyla chose to focus her attention on warning anyone who'd listen to her about Dinora's wrath. She'd focus on stopping Dinora—by any means necessary.

Even if she fought alone.

No matter how many rock creatures Dinora conjured or how much magic she stole from the land, Nyla would stop her. Whatever the cost of defeating Dinora, Nyla would pay it. She'd known that the moment she'd managed to send her knife flying toward that wretched woman in the courtyard. Even when her body had wanted nothing more than to collapse, when her very heart had threatened to give up, Nyla had vowed to stop Dinora, to save her friends, to save Xander.

It devastated her to break the promises she'd made to her family and Astrid, to live and to make a good life for herself. It devastated her to forsake the happiness she hoped would come in her future, and whatever might have come of her friendship with Xander. But Nyla couldn't deny the path Fate had presented her—if not wholly chosen *for* her.

The anticipation of all that she would face was nothing compared to the fear of disappointing her family. She knew, rationally, that no matter what she'd done, they would never be disappointed in her. It didn't stop her from wondering what they would think of her decision or her acceptance of this burden, of the weight she'd placed upon her own shoulders.

Her parents had wanted the world for her—for her siblings.

Nyla had promised them only so many nights ago that she would make that world for herself and live. She'd promised Astrid only days ago that she intended to live and live well rather than sacrifice herself as she had done. But standing on this platform and waiting for the train, traveling from Gossamer to here, and having seen what Dinora was capable of thanks to the visions Fortune Falls had shown her, Nyla knew there was no possible way she could carve a happy life for herself when it would be threatened anyway if no one defeated Dinora.

Nyla knew the world was hers, but she couldn't let herself take hold of it for the fear of being pulled away from it and those she'd come to hold dear.

She jumped out of her skin at the burst of the train's whistle. It was more of a battle cry from the heavens than a train whistle to her ears.

"Ready?" Xander asked, stooping to shoulder his pack again.

"As I'll ever be," she breathed. "The real question is: are *you* ready?"

"Yeah, why wouldn't I be?" Edwin teased. "Oh, I'm sorry, you were asking Xander again, weren't you?"

Nyla rolled her eyes and hoisted her backpack onto her shoulder. "Well, I'm glad to hear at least one of us isn't dreading this foray into Huntington."

Xander laughed. By some way or another, their hands found each other, though Nyla wasn't entirely certain if she or Xander had initiated the contact, only that Xander's hand was warm against her own. Pulling her to the edge of the platform as the train pulled to a stop, he said, "At least the trip won't be boring."

"Let's just hope this is as interesting as it gets," she said, eyeing the steam-powered behemoth in front of her. "Am I going to like this, or is it going to be as boring as the carriage ride *before* Dinora attacked it?"

"Time will tell," Edwin answered.

"By the grace of Balmae, you'll hate it because you're bored," Xander added.

Nyla opened her mouth to respond when the thin wooden door of the train slid open by magic. Edwin stepped onto the train without so much as a backward glance. Xander took a step toward the train, ready to board, but Nyla found that she couldn't follow him.

As her hand slipped from his, Nyla turned on her heel and drank in the sight of the Godberd Woods of Covington. She'd never liked Covington much. It was dusty and busy and full of people who never seemed to take in the world around them.

She was one of those people now, but as she stood there, jostled by the few people walking by or pushing their way toward a train car, she found that she didn't want to leave again. She didn't want to leave the scarlet leaves that would return to their rich plum in Agergy or the first sense of home she'd had in a very long time.

"Nyla?" Xander stepped up beside her.

"If I survive this, I never want to leave these woods again." Tears welled in her eyes. If, if, if. It was all she could think about. Not "when" or "where" or "with whom," but "if."

"*When* you get through this, you'll never have to."

She blinked away the tears, not ready to shed them yet. It was no use crying over uncertainties and things that hadn't happened yet or may never happen.

"Then we'd better board that train before I change my mind."

"I think I'm more at risk of changing my mind than you are."

"We could run," she offered with a reserved smile, angling herself toward him.

"Think that would work?" His smile was crooked slightly, but earnest and soft. She couldn't help but be reminded of the day they'd stood at the manor's kitchen sink, watching the storm, and they'd jokingly considered running away from everything, from Dinora, the manor, and even Shamira.

Nyla's lips quirked into a lopsided smirk as she made a show of mulling it over. "Probably not, but I'll run if you want to."

"Just promise me that whatever happens, you won't hold it against me?" Xander glanced away, toying with a button on his jacket nervously.

"Why would I hold anything against you? You're only trying to help." She reached for his hand. The train whistle blew a short *clap*, a signal that it was time to board or else they'd miss it. "We don't have to do anything we don't want to, and we most certainly don't have to accept your grandfather's method of help just because we asked for it. We aren't bound by anything here."

Xander nodded, squeezing her hand once. "Then we'd better get on that train."

"It's the only way I'll ever get to come back here," she sighed dramatically. "I have to leave it first if I expect to never leave it again."

Xander laughed nervously, leading her onto the train and down the corridor. "No more trekking across the country for you then?"

"No carriages, but also no more trekking. I'm thinking of learning to ride a sagittarii." She studied the compartments along one side as they passed. The two compartments they passed already had their wood-paneled doors shut and shades pulled down for privacy. The mahogany wood of the train's interior glowed in the midmorning sunlight streaming in through the windows on the one side.

She lurched as the train began to move accompanied by a final blast of the whistle. Stumbling, Nyla put her free hand against the wall under the windows of the one side and used it to steady herself as they continued down the aisle.

"I mean, I used to, but our archette was old and more of a work sagittarii than anything else."

"Well then, if you don't like the train ride, I'm sure we could find some sagittarii to ride back to Hart or wherever in the Godberd Woods you want to go." Xander smiled over his shoulder at her.

"So now you're coming with me?" she teased.

He shrugged, not answering. Nyla bit back a laugh and shook her head. Something told her that they were never getting rid of each other, and she was just fine with that—more than fine with the prospect, she realized. Her heart fluttered as the dance they'd shared at the Woodlane Manor came to her mind and, with it, the moment she'd thought she was going to kiss him.

Nyla shoved the memory from her mind, forcing herself to focus on the present moment, knowing the promise of what could've been would only make her decision to fight Dinora that much harder on her already weary heart.

Xander led her to the train car's very last compartment. Inside, Edwin waited for them, already with his nose in a book.

"For a second, I thought you two weren't coming," he said by way of greeting.

"We almost didn't." She sat with a sigh and shucked off her backpack, depositing it at her feet.

Xander stuffed his bag in the overhead compartment and latched the door shut. "Here's hoping that holds. I forgot how small the luggage storage is on the train."

"You *were* the one who didn't want to use all the money your grandfather sent with me for the private car," Edwin pointed out as Xander took the seat beside her.

Out of the corner of her eye, she saw Xander stiffen. The hand that had meant to rest on his knee clenched. She bit her lip to stop the laugh that bubbled up in her chest at the sight of Xander's off-balance expression. It was like he was caught between a glare and abject embarrassment, Nyla couldn't help herself.

"Don't be so hard on him, *my lord*," she giggled, turning her face toward the window to watch as the countryside passed them by in a dazed kind of motion picture.

"I—you!" Xander sputtered. "THIS WHOLE TIME?!"

"Not this *whole* time." Nyla turned to him and offered an assuring smile. "Just recently, since Gossamer. I mean, I started to suspect at the Woodlane Manor, because who would you know in Gossamer that could help us in a situation that's been brewing for centuries? Between the notes you left me when you left for Gossamer that day, about how your grandfather often has business there and how your letter would get to him sooner than the regular couriers, as well as the vague hints to your family's business and then the apartment over H&R's building in Gossamer, I'd pretty much figured it out. And then I remembered you grew up in the Huntington area, and it all sort of came together then. You're a very open person, Xander Huntington."

Edwin gave her a wry smirk, closing his book. "You might be the first person ever to leave his lordship here dumbfounded. Were you really going to let him think you didn't know?"

"It's the little things in life that you have to enjoy, Eddie."

"Ah, not my full name? I'm growing on you," he teased.

"Like fire blight."

"It's great that you two are getting along now, but can we just," Xander interrupted, "can we just go back for a second? When were you going to say something about knowing who I was?"

"I wanted to see how long you planned to avoid telling me. Consider it a test in my patience, and I lost."

"So you're telling me that I should consider this a win, Nyla…?" Xander shook his head, puzzled by something as suggested by the crease of his brow. "You've never told me your last name."

"And you've never *technically* told me yours." She turned to look out the window and watch the patchwork of scarlet and plum leaves. "It's Delhart, by the way."

Edwin turned thoughtful. "Nyla Delhart…"

"Delhart, as in 'Hart,' the town?" Xander asked.

"Same spelling, yeah, just add D-E-L, why?"

Shifting her eyes to study Xander's reflection in the window, she saw him shake his head.

"No reason, just wondering."

Nyla rolled her eyes. It's not like either of them had asked for more than a first name. They hadn't even known where the other was from until recently. For as close as they were, Nyla knew there was still so much they didn't know about each other. It wasn't intentional—Xander's omission of his surname aside—but getting to know each other as friends did was something they simply hadn't had time for between meeting in that cave and figuring out if they could trust each other on their trek to Fortune Falls. Then she'd discovered her magic, and from that moment on, there hadn't been time for anything but the series of questions and lack of answers that had led them to this very moment.

By the time they'd left Caselle, it didn't matter to Nyla what they should or shouldn't know about each other as friends because she knew that she could depend on Xander and that she *did* depend on his companionship.

"I'm sure," she grumbled, nudging Xander's foot with her own. "Not everyone who shares a name or a similar name with a town is basically royalty. It's just my family name."

"Whoa," Xander started in mock defense, shifting beside her and twisting to face her squarely. "My family is definitely *not* royalty."

Nyla laughed, "I know, but you might as well be. H&R is a household name, *my lord*."

Edwin made a choked noise that called Nyla's attention to him. Tears dotted his eyes as he tried desperately to keep himself composed.

"And *this* is why it's difficult to tell people," Xander said, turning serious. Nyla's eyes flicked back to him, her lips going slack. But he wasn't looking at her. Instead, his gaze was fixed on his hands resting limply in his lap. "People generally try to take advantage of the fact that I'm…who I am, and it was nice, not having that burden for a while."

Her heart nearly broke at the forlorn look on his face and the faraway glaze over his eyes. Nyla shifted in her seat, reaching over and taking one of his hands in hers. "If it helps, you'll always be 'just' Xander to me, even if I know who your family is now."

At the sound of her voice, Xander seemed to come back to himself. "I know that," he said softly, smiling at her in a way that assured her worried heart, "and I'm grateful for that, for you."

Silence descended upon the carriage as Nyla found herself at a loss for how to respond. If Edwin had any reaction to the interaction, he kept it to himself. Nyla squeezed Xander's hand in the hope that it could convey how much his words had meant to her as her mind turned over their adventures thus far.

"Do you ever wonder where Shamira went?" she asked quietly.

Xander didn't hesitate to reply. "I'm sure she'll be all right. She can take care of herself."

"I know, but still," Nyla sighed, "I wish we knew."

Edwin cleared his throat. "I read somewhere that the pumpkie clans lived in the northern extreme of the Godberd Woods, along the Sea of Harmony's border."

Nyla shook her head. "That's impossible. It's too mountainous to inhabit. There wouldn't be anything for them to hunt."

"They're pumpkies." Edwin said it like that would explain everything, and Nyla had to admit that it could if only she knew more about the Godberd Woods' northern mountain range. It was the only place in the whole country that she hadn't gone, other than the Dunes in the far east of Tenebris.

If they were anything like the Dunelands of the south, she had no desire to see them.

Nyla brought her legs up on the seat between herself and Xander, half curling against the seat as she stared out at the moving landscape. She knew they still had several miles to go before they would be in the Shadow Forest proper again.

A soft smile danced on her lips when she realized the premise filled her with dread. It wasn't all that long ago that the idea of leaving the Shadow Forest had done just that. Now, here she was, in agreement with the rest of most sensible Tenebrese in finding the Shadow Forest a place lacking in comfort and refuge. It was strange to her, and slightly foreign, that only a few weeks ago, she'd found an odd sense of security in the haunted forest—and perhaps it was thanks to her newfound knowledge of the country's long-ago history that proved there were hidden truths in the legends of the Shadow Forest.

As her traveling companions fell into silence, Nyla replayed the attack of the stone creatures on their carriage ride in her mind's eye. They were strange, but more than that, they felt familiar to her in a way she couldn't place.

Her mind began to turn over what she knew of Dinora and the wars for Tenebris's sovereignty. People told stories about the haunted forest, and Nyla knew these legends well. She knew of the sorceress who had stolen magic from the land, and had subsequently lost control of it. She knew that the magic had been unleashed upon the land in a horrible fury—and on the army that had stood with the evil sorceress. And since hearing these legends from all sorts of different storytellers in her travels, Nyla once again found herself piecing together the tale in her mind while she remained idle. This time, it wasn't merely different versions of the legend she'd heard, but rather the truth that she tried to fill the gaps of the legend in with.

The world outside their compartment faded away, just as the scarlet-splotched plum leaves and honey-gold trees of the Godberd Woods began to mix with the Harvum-kissed sapphire leaves and crackled ashen bark of the Shadow Forest. Nyla replaced the ambiguous figure of the sorceress detailed in the legends the people of her country told of the Shadow Forest with the all-too-real woman that she was.

Dinora.

Dinora was absolutely the sorceress immortalized in the legends of the Shadow Forest. And the souls of those who fell victim to her and her loss of control over the magic she'd stolen from the land were definitely alive and well, just as the legends claimed they were. After all, hadn't one such spirit led Nyla and Xander to the pathway to Fortune Falls?

Nyla bit her lip.

If Dinora was the sorceress, and the tendrils of smoke were representatives of her victims—if not the *souls* of her victims—then… what were those creatures?

The scene replayed once more in her mind. Nyla latched on to the memory of the feeling she'd gotten when her magic and intuition had sensed the creatures. They had a writhing and miserable energy. A restlessness in the hum of their essence, like they were agitated. More than that, though, Nyla had felt a hopeless desperation weave its way into the air.

There were those that believed the souls of those the evil sorceress had damned in her quest for power and blood were trapped in the

Shadow Forest. And there were stories told of people who had tried to free these restless souls from their damnation and right the wrong committed against them by the evil sorceress—by Dinora.

Nyla's brows furrowed, her thoughts darkening with each inch the train progressed down the tracks.

The world outside fully morphed into the Shadow Forest. Eventually, the *chugga-chugga-chooms* of the wheels slowly broke into her stream of consciousness. The short blasts of the train's whistles called her back into full awareness as they approached where the tracks intercepted with a country road. Nyla blinked. Her eyes finally focused on the world she'd long forgotten since they'd pulled away from the station back in Covington. The backdrop of a town and then the rippling waters of the Union River passed outside her window.

Across from her, Edwin was oblivious to anything that wasn't his book. The brush of the pages turning was like a metronome, keeping time for their ride. Xander's leg bounced beside her. From what she could see in the reflection of him from the window, he was also oblivious to the world around him. His eyes were worried and withdrawn. It was a forlorn look she'd rarely seen in Xander's eyes.

Nyla shifted in her seat and stretched her legs out across the compartment floor, knocking her feet up against the solid base of Edwin's bench seat before straightening in her seat. Glimpsing out the window, she caught the sight of thinning trees. Her lips quirked as she watched the Shadow Forest transform into a sparse landscape with markers of civilization cropping up as the train passed by.

A sigh caught her attention. Edwin tucked his bookmark between his current pages and shut his book firmly, tucking it against his chest. He glanced out the window, almost smiling.

"Ah, we're almost there," he said, breaking the long-held silence of their compartment.

Nyla peeked over at Xander, drawing her attention away from the window. He met her gaze with pursed lips and stormy eyes.

"About how much longer from here?" she asked.

"Not long at all. Maybe about ten minutes." Xander surprised her by answering. She didn't think he had it in him to reply, but here he was, slowly breaking through whatever anxious thoughts were haunting his mind. Nyla reached over, grabbed his hand, and gave it a squeeze as a silent reminder that they didn't have to do this, but that she would be right beside him no matter what. Xander squeezed back, and they stayed like that as Huntington blossomed right outside their window.

Buildings as tall, if not taller, than the tallest trees Nyla had ever seen sprouted up from the cityscape, becoming denser the farther into Huntington the train traveled. Beyond the track, Nyla could see people milling about on the sidewalks and carriages *clacking* along the wide cobblestone roads.

No one that she could see was smiling. Everyone seemed so brisk, so focused, as if the world around them didn't exist but to serve them and their own purpose.

Nothing Xander could've ever told her would've prepared her for just how different Huntington was from other parts of the Shadow Forest. Here, the constant reminder of the sapphire leaves and crackled bark of a perilous world didn't exist. The edge of the Forest couldn't be seen from the ground, and Nyla doubted very much that even the occupants of the tallest building could see the Shadow Forest looming at the city's edge like an invading force.

The train began to slow. Three short bursts of the whistle signaled that they were about to pull into the station, and the dread that Nyla hadn't felt since they'd first arrived at the Woodlane Manor returned to her like an old friend. It was probably only a fraction of the emotions whirling around in the pit of Xander's stomach. She didn't think he realized the strong grip he had on her hand.

"Well, here we are. Welcome to Huntington, Nyla." Edwin set his book down in his lap and glanced out the window with a thoughtful frown. "I much preferred the sight of Covington and Gossamer over this."

"I think anything is better than the sight of a city this big with this many people under the circumstances we've come here for," she replied, her voice tight.

Edwin laughed, but Xander seemed to be in a state of paralysis. As Edwin packed away his book and glanced around their compartment for anything that could get left behind, Nyla studied Xander. He'd fallen quiet again, his lips quirked downward in a grim frown. His gaze was fixed firmly on the window, staring out into the city she wondered if he'd ever wanted to return to.

She tugged on his hand to get his attention. "We really don't have to do this. We could find another way. I'm not opposed to finding Dinora and ending this now without involving anyone else."

Xander shook his head. "No. I think I have to do this."

"Then I'm right here with you," Nyla promised. "You don't have to face any of this on your own."

Xander's grip on her hand loosened. The train shuddered to a stop, and Nyla peeked outside their window. The train station at Covington was practically abandoned compared to the dense hustle and bustle of Huntington's. Already, people were crowding the platform to board the train. Nyla could see the shadows of people passing their compartment toward the rear exit of the train car so people could begin boarding.

Edwin stood and stretched. Wordlessly, he grabbed his bag and exited the compartment, leaving just the two of them to gather their things—and their courage.

"I guess it's now or never." Xander stood, oddly unsteady on his feet.

"Look at it this way—your grandfather's already helped us by sending Edwin to the Woodlane Manor and by arranging travel for us from Gossamer to Huntington. He wouldn't have done that if he didn't want to see you or help you or, dare I say, love you."

Xander sighed, shouldering his pack. "I know. It's just…I expected a major confrontation, and now I don't know what to expect, and I don't know what's worse: the fact that I was expecting a shouting match or that I'm more nervous that that isn't going to happen."

"It's a little strange, but at the same time completely normal. At least your family knows you're alive. I suppose one day I'll have to tell my mother's family that I'm alive and would…well, I haven't thought that far ahead yet."

Xander laughed, sliding the door of their compartment open and stepping out.

"Yeah…maybe you should write to them while we're here."

"Mm…maybe," she considered. Maybe she'd wait until she survived the oncoming war with Dinora.

Then, once she'd survived all of her trials and tribulations, she would reach out to her surviving family and rebuild her roots.

But she had to survive first.

18. THE NAMESAKE

Edwin waited for them on the platform. A few other stragglers remained, some surrounded by excited family happy to see their relative returned from their travels, while others were alone, clearly waiting for a means of transportation to their destination.

They wouldn't be like those people, those with family around them or tapping their foot impatiently with pursed lips. Even though Xander hadn't seen it in three years, he could still pick out his grandfather's unassuming carriage. It looked like the hundreds of others that bustled around the city at the behest of their occupants, but there was one thing that set his grandfather's personal carriage apart from the hordes of others: their family crest emblazoned on the side above the front wheels.

A tiny detail most people overlooked, Xander never failed to be on guard for it. It was a habit, one that he would probably never be rid of.

"I see my grandfather sent his personal carriage," Xander stated, still staring at it as he and Nyla came to a stop beside Edwin.

"I've already been over to let them know we're just waiting on you two." Edwin's eyes followed Xander's gaze. "He isn't here, if that's what you're frowning about. Stephen said that he was still at Pemberly Hall."

Xander let out a sigh of relief. Beside him, Nyla shifted impatiently on her feet.

"All right, then I guess we shouldn't keep him waiting. Unless…is there anywhere you want to stop and see first?"

He glanced at her then, finding her wide, worried eyes on him already. The tension in his chest eased only the slightest bit. With a decisive shake of his head, Xander answered, "No."

Gathering his courage, Xander straightened his shoulders and took a step toward where the carriage was waiting. "I need to do this," he said more to himself than to Nyla. "This is probably a long overdue reunion anyway."

As they approached the carriage, Xander found himself acting as if he were a spectator in his own body. Already, he could feel old habits and posture taking hold over him, his thoughts. He didn't like it. He didn't want to fall back into being the young lord who'd pushed himself into exile and let his tempered pride estrange him from his home.

He handed his pack off to the footman, Timothy, with a word of thanks and joined his fellow companions inside the carriage.

At some point, in the two years he'd been away, his grandfather had had the interior reupholstered. Instead of the dark maroon Xander remembered it being, the cushioned seats were now a dark shade of teal not unlike the teal the Shadow Forest's leaves turned in Harvum.

As Nyla laid a hand over his for a heartbeat too short before pulling away to watch out the window, Xander found himself swallowing thickly. It was only upholstery. Upholstery needed to be updated, especially since the maroon had needed to be replaced years before Xander had even left home. It didn't stop him from considering what else had changed—for better or worse. Xander contemplated what other changes had taken place while he'd been gone as the carriage ambled down the city streets to his ancestral home.

With any hope, the amount of family overstaying their welcome at Pemberly would've thinned out since he'd been gone. At any given time, nearly half of the Huntington family was "visiting" Pemberly.

More often than not, half of the Huntington family was actually living under Pemberly's roof, rather than their own respective roofs.

He rested his elbow against the windowsill and rested his head in his hand. His worries manifested in the slight bounce of his leg or the way he was constantly moving his feet, fidgeting in a way that was definitely unbecoming of his family's status. But he wasn't his family. He was Xander. He took a deep breath through his nose and let the sensation of air filling his lungs consume him. He forced his mind to focus on the expansion of his lungs, the shift of his diaphragm, the swell of his chest as he breathed deeper and deeper until he couldn't possibly hold any more air in his lungs. He exhaled slowly, repeating the process a few more times to steady himself and expel the nervous energy flitting around his bloodstream like the flap of a bird's wings.

It didn't matter how long or short the carriage ride was, or how interested Nyla seemed in their surroundings as she asked Edwin about this or that regarding the city. Xander realized that he would rather be walking. That would prolong the inevitable long enough for him to fully digest the prospect of his homecoming.

But all too soon, Stephen led the team of sagittarii off of the main streets and onto the old cobblestone roads of the original city.

Before Huntington had grown to the size and status that it was today, it was a city much like Covington or Caselle, where merchants stored their wares and the farmers of surrounding towns came to sell their harvests.

Then H&R Trading was born and steadily grew in size and importance, becoming the economic giant that the city was built around. Or at least, that was the gist of the city's history. Lots of things happened over the centuries, but the one thing that remained constant was the presence of the Huntington family in Pemberly Hall.

Xander knew his family roots went back almost as far as the country's history, if not further. He'd seen the tapestries growing up but had never paid much mind to them. They were simply there. It was stranger to see the bare spot on the wall when they were taken down to be cleaned, and Issie would say that it was more interesting to see the mortar lines in the old stone walls of the Hall's exterior walls than it was to see the embroidered faces of people long since dead.

He supposed she was right, but it was important that they knew their family history too. After all, they were still a part of the nobility as much as they were entrepreneurs—not that the distinction mattered much anymore as the monarchy had dissolved, though the titles remained.

It was something his grandfather had used to grumble about a lot. Xander's parents were the only ones capable of balancing and carrying on the duties of both respects in his grandfather's eyes. He'd often heard his grandfather dismiss his aunts and uncles or cousins for one reason or another. Too greedy, too idealistic, too selfish, too narrow-minded, too kind, too troublesome.

Xander suspected that it was because of all of his critiques and pressure over the years that there was so much fighting and protest over his announcement that Xander's mother and father would take over the company upon his retirement. His grandfather had announced this over the Harvum celebrations, and by the time Pagmas had come, the family was at war. And then the following year, just after his parents' first Pagmas as head of the Huntington half of H&R Trading, they'd died in an accident while traveling to oversee a new shipment coming into port.

It was shortly thereafter that his relationship with his grandfather had begun to deteriorate. And Issie's passing hardly a season later had completely destroyed whatever shred of familial ties remained between them.

They'd said some truly awful things to each other in that time. *He'd* said some truly awful things in that time, the echoes of which had haunted him since. But even so, his pride and then his fear of rejection had kept him from the apology he desperately wanted to convey.

"Are we here?" Nyla's voice forced him out of his contemplation.

He glanced out of the window to get a look at where they were.

"Almost," he said, eyes lingering on the long driveway that had since been laid with pavers, effectively cutting in before Edwin could reply. "This is the mile road to Pemberly, also known as the unnecessarily long driveway."

Nyla laughed, sitting back against the cushioned wall of the carriage. "At least it's not a creepy gate that opens on its own."

"This is true." Xander went to touch the ring hidden under his shirt, but stopped himself. "Did Stephen happen to mention if anyone else was here?"

"No, but he didn't have to," Edwin said matter-of-factly. "Your grandfather arranged a little family gathering in the main dining hall for your arrival."

Xander's blood went cold, then stopped flowing altogether. "No!"

In his panic, Nyla's sharp intake of breath had almost gone unnoticed. A quick glance at her revealed she was just as panicked as he felt.

Edwin sniggered. "No, he didn't, but the look on your face was well worth it."

Beside him, Nyla tried in vain to stifle her giggles. "That was awfully cruel!"

"Sure it was." Edwin smirked. "No worse than using magic in a water fight."

Nyla's giggling cut off outright, her mouth stunned open. "How did—you know what? Yes, much worse!"

Xander chuckled, "Says the woman who sent a wall of water at me like she intended to drown the whole beach."

"Says the man who tackled me *after* I'd reached the safety of the shallows."

"Okay, so we're all guilty of being awful. At least we're allies in that."

"Don't count me in on that. I'll have both of you know that I'm an upstanding, mor—why are you laughing? I'm right!" Edwin argued.

"You have no moral high ground here, Eddie, and you know it," Xander teased.

"Ooooh, does that mean there's stories about Eddie that he doesn't want me to hear about from when he used to be less stuffy?" Nyla added.

"Scores," he assured her, knowing that Edwin hadn't missed the veiled threat to spill all of his secrets to Nyla if he were so inclined.

Nyla hummed in speculation, checking their progress outside the window again.

Xander's eyes followed, and he found that they'd reached the end of the long driveway. They were now rounding the turnaround cut around the fountain of the front courtyard and would be stopping at any second right in front of Pemberly Hall.

He almost wished they were being dropped off at the rear entrance, if only to have a few more moments before he'd be forced to exit the carriage.

Luck wasn't on his side. The carriage rolled to a gentle stop. The *plock* of boots on the driveway's pavers signaled that Timothy had descended from his perch beside Stephen and was making his way to grab the stool for them to step onto as they exited the carriage.

"Your grandfather asked the rest of your family, or rather the ones that weren't 'necessary to the function of Pemberly or to that of H&R' to return to their empty homes and not return until Pagmas before he even sent me to the Woodlane," Edwin said softly.

Xander blinked, dazedly searching for a reply. Not a second later, the door was being opened for them by Timothy. The time to respond had passed. Instead, he nodded curtly and exited the carriage. Turning, he offered his hand to Nyla and stepped away from the carriage to get a good look at Pemberly Hall, squinting against the late evening sun.

Pemberly was still as large and daunting as it always was. The stacked slate-colored stone loomed up into the shadows of the afternoon light. The carved granite of the entry's wide archway showed the weathered face of a raverin swooping down with open talons. The hedges were neatly trimmed, and unlike the Woodlane Manor, not a single vine of ivy was out of place or obstructing the arched windows of any level of the house.

His eyes followed the wide steps up to the towering arched doors. Well-manicured pots of plants he knew to be his late grandmother's favorite still sat proudly on each step near the banister that was seldom used.

Guards stood at attention at the doors, dressed in the Caradels' colors. That was the only difference Xander could see. Usually, it was their own guards who stood sentry, wearing their family crest of a swooping raverin with a single forget-me-not in its clutches.

Xander raised his eyebrow in question, but didn't want to bring attention to it. He wondered if Edwin would know why the Royal Guards would be stationed here rather than his family's own security force. Instead, he cast the question aside for when they had a moment of privacy.

"Wow," Nyla breathed. "And I used to think the Woodlane Manor was a castle, and then as an adult it was just massive, and now, looking at this…wow."

"It'll be less impressive once you meet whatever family *didn't* adhere to my grandfather's wishes, trust me." Xander found himself smiling fondly as he watched Nyla take in the looming estate, her eyes wide with wonder as she tilted her head back to see the whole of the hall.

"I sincerely doubt that."

"Are we just going to stand here looking at it, or can we get something to eat?" Edwin started up the stone steps of the estate, not waiting for an answer. If Edwin was perturbed by the sight of the King's men, he didn't show it.

Xander just glanced at Nyla in time to see her roll her eyes, muttering under her breath, "Oh, you know, only the biggest building I've ever stood in front of, but yeah, no big deal, Edwin!"

Xander toed the paver beneath his boot, chuckling. "Something to eat doesn't sound bad," he said, starting toward the stairs. "Besides, you still haven't seen inside yet."

Nyla shook her head, laughing. He offered her his arm, and together, they walked up the front steps of Pemberly Hall. As they crossed into the shade of the front porch, Nyla whispered, "Please tell me I'm not going to meet a lot of people whose names I'll be expected to remember."

"I can't promise that, but I can promise that I probably won't know all of their names either." He scrunched his nose. He definitely hoped it didn't come to that.

Eyeing the pair of Royal Guards as they passed by, Xander led Nyla into the grand foyer. She let out a quiet gasp as he watched her eyes rove the foyer with its lavish, magicitric crystal chandelier and suits of Huntington armor and old family portraits dating back longer than historical memory cared to remember.

"Xander!" A bright voice bounced through the foyer, making both himself and Nyla flinch at the sudden burst of energy in the still entry.

Before Xander had the time to truly recognize the blur racing toward him, Nyla had pulled back just in time for his younger cousin to pounce on him.

"You're home! I didn't believe Grandfather when he told us over breakfast!" The girl squeezed him even tighter, if that were possible.

Sucking in a breath, Xander found Nyla almost crying with the effort to hold back her laughter over the top of Meredith's head. He hugged Meredith back almost as tightly as she'd embraced him.

"I'm only here for a little while, but I'm glad you're here too, Merry."

Prying himself out of the enthusiastic ten-year-old's grip, he motioned to Nyla. "Merry, I'd like you to meet Nyla. Nyla, this is my cousin Meredith."

"Hello," Merry said, eyeing Nyla from head to toe intently. "It's nice to meet you. Are you why Xander's come home?"

To her part, Nyla smiled. "It's nice to meet you too, Meredith." Her eyes met his over the top of Merry's head questioningly, but only for a heartbeat before she answered Merry's question. "I suppose I am. We need your grandfather's help, but I promise we won't be too occupied by it."

"Good." Meredith nodded, apparently satisfied that their visit wasn't strictly business. "I want to hear about everything you've been doing since you've been away, and I have *so* much to tell you—"

As Meredith chattered away, she took him by the hand and started to tug him down the hall. Xander looked over at Nyla apologetically. She only shook her head, beaming. With a wave of her hand, Nyla silently assured him that Merry's intervention didn't bother her, though he couldn't say the same. Xander tried to tell Merry to slow down or let him get Nyla settled first, but he couldn't get a word in edgewise. All too soon, Merry had led him around the corner and had left Nyla standing in the entryway alone.

"Merry, I should really—"

"It's okay. I saw Eddie. He said to distra—oops." She cringed with a crooked smile. "I wasn't supposed to tell you that."

Xander pulled her to a stop and turned her to face him by the shoulders. Crouching down to be eye level with her, he asked, "Why does Edwin want you to distract me?"

"Grandfather wants to meet with Nyla alone. I don't know why, though." She frowned, pouting at him in speculation. "Why did you bring her here? She doesn't seem like…well, like us? You're not going to marry her, are you?"

"Meredith!" he scolded. "Who I marry isn't your concern, and no, I am not going to marry Nyla, and that's definitely not why we're here. I promise we'll talk later, but right now I have to go."

Merry caught him by the arm as he tried to push past her. "You're not going to leave so soon, are you?"

Swallowing the bitter panic thrumming in his chest, Xander's pinched expression softened as he faced Merry again. "As soon as I know how Grandfather intends to help Nyla and that she's okay, I promise we'll do something just the two of us every day I'm here, just like we used to."

"But are you going to leave again?" Merry dropped her hand, recoiling like she'd been burned. "You didn't even say goodbye last time, and you never wrote to me like you always would. Is it because of her?"

"No, it's just—I…" Xander found himself at a loss for words. Instead, he opted to explain Nyla's presence in his life. "I only met Nyla several weeks ago, okay? She really needs help, and Grandfather might be the only person who can help her."

Merry nodded, considering his words. "You've only known her for several weeks? Xander, how could you be so naïve? She's taking advantage of you!"

"Meredith, listen to me: Nyla isn't taking advantage of us. She didn't even know who I was until last week."

"So…she's really your friend?" Merry asked as if the concept was so outlandish. Xander supposed it was, given how many people they'd known were only friendly for their own gain in status or wealth or favoritism.

"Exactly."

"And you'll tell me everything before you leave again?"

"Promise."

She rolled her eyes. "Then you'd better go and save her from Grandfather. He hasn't been much company lately."

"Was he ever?" Xander grinned, starting to turn away.

Merry sighed in a way that sounded much too weary for someone so young. Xander froze as he took her in. Grave seriousness darkened her usually bright eyes.

"More so than usual."

"How so?" he found himself asking, his brows arching as Merry's words had him turning his back on the way they'd come, the way that would return him to Nyla.

***

Nyla watched, laughing as Xander tried to keep up with Meredith. This definitely wasn't the homecoming Xander had expected, and she certainly hadn't expected someone to throw themselves at Xander like an attack either, but it was nice to see. She hoped it put him at ease, even if Meredith's excitement had left her stranded in the middle of the foyer.

A prickle of energy washed over her senses. Her laughter died in her chest as she recognized a magic signature, having opened her awareness up to the massive home as a means of gauging just what she'd gotten herself into by coming here. Edwin's magic was like a subtle whisper carried on the breeze. Nyla turned on her heel as he came around the corner and into the foyer.

With a grim nod, Edwin motioned for her to follow him down the hall. "I know you probably want to get settled, but Lord Huntington would like to meet with you first."

Nyla took a deep breath. "I figured there wouldn't be any rest for the weary. Meredith was your doing then?"

"Couldn't be helped. Xander probably won't be long. Merry can't keep a secret when she's excited," Edwin replied as he led her down the warmly lit hallway.

The family portraits continued through the hallway, though the beautiful hardwood floors were mostly covered by a carpet that ran the length of the corridor. For an old estate, it was welcoming, so unlike the Woodlane Manor with its drafty hallways and cold demeanor. She didn't know if it was the warm paint or cozy wallpapering adorning the walls, or if the home of one of Tenebris's most powerful families was just that…inviting.

She hadn't known what to expect based on what Xander told her about Pemberly Hall or his grandfather. No picture had come to mind, only vague impressions of stuffiness and civil pretenses. While she did sense a certain air of stiffness, she couldn't help but see something cozy and old in a way that whispered familiarity. It was the sort of feeling you got when you visited someplace sacred, like an ancient place of worship or the sight of a miracle. It was the sort of comfort she got when she'd first seen the Godberd Woods after being away for so long.

But even that cozy atmosphere couldn't hide the air of deceit and jealousy in the undercurrent of the energies tickling her senses. Silently thanking Shamira for teaching her how to sense things while she'd been imprisoned at the Woodlane Manor, Nyla focused her attention on Edwin, breaking the silence between them.

As Edwin led her around a corner and down another cream-colored hallway, Nyla stopped.

"Is everything so underhanded here? Should I be expecting that?"

Edwin paused, taking a breath before he answered. "If I were you, I would expect anything, even the simplest level of deceit, no matter how trivial it might seem."

"Then I suppose the real question is where does your friendship lie, if not your loyalty?" She didn't mean it maliciously, but she did wonder how much had changed in the years that Xander was gone. Her curiosity poked at how the bond between Xander and Edwin might have changed in that time, especially if Edwin had remained under Lord Huntington's influence all this time. What's to say their friendship hadn't faded? Xander had also warned her about how deceptive people's intentions could be here, but she couldn't understand why Edwin would be warning her of that as well, especially if he was truly acting as Lord Huntington's agent.

Edwin shifted uncomfortably, not meeting her eyes. In his moment of hesitation, Nyla's heart clenched.

"It's a simple question, Edwin. Are you Xander's friend or not?" she pushed.

His eyes flicked up to hers with venom in the piercing blue hue. "I've been his friend longer than anyone else, but friendship and loyalty are different things."

"No, they aren't," Nyla insisted, studying his face. Why was it so important for Xander's grandfather to meet her alone? Why separate her from Xander through a slight deception? Why couldn't his grandfather simply ask, or was this his way of showing his influence over people, by ordering Edwin to separate them by any means necessary? She didn't find any answers written on his nearly unchanged features.

He opened his mouth to reply, but Nyla cut him off with a dismissive wave of her hand. "Never mind," she said. "It's none of my business, though I hope whatever the answer may be, it doesn't become a burden to Xander."

She turned her back on Edwin and strutted down the hall, already seeking out his lordship's presence with her magic. It was probably something similar to Xander's but older, stiffer maybe, and most definitely bitter.

Just as her magic found it, Edwin called out to her from where she'd left him standing alone. "The double doors on your left."

Nyla bit her lip to keep the sarcastic quip begging to leap from her tongue at bay. Instead, she ignored Edwin and focused her eyes on the double doors that would lead her to the man who wished to see her, and had set so much in motion already.

As Edwin's presence receded, Nyla slowed her pace. She tugged the hem of her blouse down, biting her lip.

Why wouldn't Xander's grandfather want to see Xander first?

Did he not want to see Xander at all?

So many questions flew through Nyla's mind as she approached the double doors with her head held high. Resolutely, she knocked on the door and entered when a calm voice acknowledged her. Through the door, the voice sounded old but strong, nothing like the preconceived notion in her head.

With a final glance down the hall, Nyla turned the knob. The metal was smooth and cool beneath her fingers as she slipped through the door. The knob dug into her back as she pulled the heavy door closed behind her, barely stepping inside the dimly lit room.

One long wall was dedicated to a row of built-in bookcases. The shelves were lined with knickknacks and oddities as well as the odd scroll or cluster of neatly perched books. The air in the room was still, and somewhat stale, proof that Edwin had told them the truth of Lord Huntington's habits as of late. According to what Edwin had told Xander back at the Woodlane Manor, his grandfather was spending much of his time alone in his study.

Nyla's eyes fell on the lone figure silhouetted by the firelight. Taking in the tall man, Nyla could understand why. While his voice was even and confident, the state of his person said otherwise. Beneath the rich suit, she saw a pained old man whose spine couldn't bear the weight of standing so proud after all the years he'd spent doing so. Maybe his affliction wasn't from a physical ailment, but it was pain all the same. He hadn't even turned to look at her or address her when she'd entered beyond allowing her entry. He only stood with his hands in his pockets, staring into the dancing flames.

Swallowing, Nyla took cautious steps across the carpeted study. She stopped at the other end of the mantel, keeping Lord Huntington in the corner of her vision.

"You're the girl that managed to get my grandson to speak to me," Lord Huntington drawled quietly, speaking more to the flames than to her. Nyla couldn't tell if it was a question or a fact, but she nodded her head anyway. "I do not make a habit of helping everyone my family should wish to help."

"Is that why there are Royal Guards at your front door, because you *do* intend to help us?"

Lord Huntington finally turned and looked her over with more scrutiny than even Meredith had. Nyla squared her shoulders and held his gaze. He and Xander had similar eyes, she noted. The only difference, and it was a rather stark contrast in her opinion, was that Lord Huntington's eyes were dull, nearly void of any emotion or flicker thereof.

"I do, but not because my grandson asked me to," Lord Huntington affirmed. "It is my duty as an Heir of Tenebris."

Nyla's eyebrows rose. Even if she ignored the pang in her heart from the fact that Lord Huntington hadn't decided to help them simply because Xander had asked him to, an icy prickle trailed down her spine as the second half of his statement settled on her mind.

Nyla swallowed her skepticism, asking instead, "An Heir of Tenebris?"

"I'm sure you are well aware of the grave complexities of your problem, Miss…Forgive me. My grandson's note never mentioned your surname."

She shuffled backward as the intensity of Lord Huntington's eyes drowned her. The heat of the flames was an unwelcome breath against her skin. "Nyla is fine. My lord?"

"Alexander is fine." He smiled thinly. Nyla doubted that it was an expression his face was all that accustomed to. With a little more genuine happiness in his life, she'd wager that his smile would be nice and maybe even endearing, especially since she could see so much of Xander in his features. "Tell me, Nyla, what sort of man has my grandson become?"

"Maybe you should ask him yourself. After all, he did come all this way, and I doubt it was solely because of my situation that you brought him here," she sniffed. A trickle of anger flooded her bloodstream. How dare he question her about his own flesh and blood? If he was so curious, why go through all of this instead of just meeting with Xander himself?

And moreover, why had he wanted to meet her alone at all? Shouldn't his top priority be reuniting with Xander?

Nyla's blood simmered.

As Alexander stared at her with a wide-eyed gaze, Nyla closed in on him. "Tell me, Alexander, what exactly is an Heir of Tenebris? How do you intend to help me? Why would the King's men be on your estate? What sort of man are *you*, exactly?"

At this, the old lord ruffled.

Before he could say a word, Nyla extinguished the flames and replaced them with her magic. She let the lilac-colored energy flood the room, expanding around her as an extension of herself. The gentle static was like an airy breeze that swept through her hair. It was reminiscent of the way her magic had moved around her that day on the front steps of the Woodlane Manor, except she felt stronger. Rage and desperation had fueled her then, but today, it was her own strength and cool mental clarity that she wielded her powers with, summoning them in this quiet display of her capabilities. She stood before the Lord of Huntington calm and collected, and she wanted him to know it.

She didn't know the sort of man he was, only that he was in the unique position of stifling her efforts to stop Dinora or actually giving her aid. If she could be certain of anything, it was that Lord Alexander Huntington was a man who exuded power.

Nyla didn't know if she wanted his help after all, not if it came at the cost she was beginning to fear. Not if it put Xander in a position he had no desire to be in.

She let her power recede, leaving them in the dark.

Light tried to break through the heavy curtains pulled across the windows of the back wall of the room, but to no avail. It was but a grim reminder of the way Nyla perceived her own plight against Dinora. Nyla relit the fire. Lord Huntington stared at her a moment longer in the darkness before his gaze flicked to the cold fireplace. She let the fire build slowly from the dimmest flicker to the dancing flames she'd extinguished.

"I should hope that my grandson is a better man than I have been," he said quietly, staring into the roaring flames. Nyla watched as his brows furrowed in contemplation and he shifted his stance so his hands were clasped loosely behind his back. Glancing at her, he asked, "Has Alexander told you about the circumstances in which he left home?"

A solemn expression lined his face. Nyla decided that self-pity was the only genuine expression he was capable of. Everything else was a calculation, a façade meant to guard himself from the hungry eyes of those who would use his status. She couldn't help but see the loneliness hovering over his shoulders and imagined the chasm it formed in his heart.

Just what had this family been put through?

"No, but if he wanted me to know, Xander would have told me." Nyla's magic fluttered. She could sense Xander stalking closer. By the way his energy writhed and frenzied, she knew he was angry.

She sent a silent prayer up to Helpet that he wouldn't do something that would jeopardize why they'd come. This was just as much about his relationship with his grandfather as it was about Dinora.

"Then I'll let him tell you in his own time." Lord Huntington turned toward the fire once more. Nyla tried to quell the hostile tension from her bones. "You must be weary from your travels. Forgive me. I'm usually a better host, but times are difficult—"

The door to the study burst open. Xander came flying in, grim-faced and fuming.

"Ah, Alexander," Lord Huntington began, "you're just in time. Would you care to show Nyla to the Lavender Room? It must have been wearisome to travel all this way. You should both get some rest before dinner, which I expect we'll have much to discuss then."

Nyla's eyes bounced between the two men as if lightning would spark between them. To her surprise, the snarl of Xander's lip relaxed, and the tension in his features eased, as if he'd had to turn his emotional state off at the release of an arrow a million times before.

"Of course, Grandfather. It would be my pleasure." Xander's eyes met hers for the first time since he'd stormed into the room. Nyla didn't know what would've happened or what had happened between the two, but she was certain she would much rather not be caught in the middle of it.

At the slight tilt of Xander's head toward the door, she nodded, drawing closer to him. Realizing Xander wasn't ready to get reacquainted with his grandfather quite yet, she mustered up the barest of polite smiles, too tense to care at how insincere it might seem. "It was nice to meet you, Alexander." She took Xander by the arm and began to steer him out of the room as if everything was completely normal. "Thank you for welcoming me into your home."

Lord Huntington bowed his head. "It is my pleasure, Nyla."

As she and Xander stepped through the study door and she closed it behind them, Nyla let out a slow breath. The tension in the room had been palpable, more so than the stale air of when she'd first entered.

"'Alexander?' You're on a first-name basis with my grandfather?" Xander sputtered under his breath.

"I think that's the least of what I've done in the few moments we were alone," Nyla whispered, her voice barely above a murmur.

Xander drew closer to her, if that were even possible, ducking his head as if he could physically hide the conversation they were about to have. "What do you mean?"

"I mean…I may have extinguished his fire and showed off what my powers are capable of…" She bit her lip. Maybe it didn't sound as bad as she thought it was. "I just wanted to…"

"You what?" Xander whispered, shocked. "Wait, did you *threaten* my grandfather?"

"No! I mean, not really," she explained hurriedly. "I only meant that I wanted to…to show him that we—*I*—was capable of handling Dinora without his help…"

Xander laughed, a true, full-body laugh, breaking any conspiring pretense they'd had. "I wish I had been there."

She let out a sigh of relief as she let Xander lead her through the halls and up a flight of stairs. She was almost disappointed that they hadn't passed a single stained-glass window, though she supposed that there was still plenty of the estate she hadn't seen yet. Every so often, Xander pointed out a room or portrait of note to her, though the words were lost on her.

Nyla bit her lip. How would she ever navigate this place by herself? Already her head was spinning, and her sense of navigation was turned around. Just from the fraction of Pemberly Hall that she *had* already seen, she was overwhelmed. It didn't help that many of the hallways looked the same, right down to the paint color.

When Xander finally slowed to a stop before a pair of cherrywood doors, Nyla marveled at the flower-shaped sconces on either side. The wrought-iron handles on the door were curved and made to look like leaves on a vine. While the metal was unmoving and without a life of its own, the blacksmith that had forged them had given a vibrancy to the design. The vine had movement, and the leaves were delicate enough that Nyla could almost see the veining the forger had tried to capture.

"I'm just down the hall if you need me. Meredith has the room between us," Xander assured her. "I think she's jealous that I didn't come home alone and that I won't be able to spend as much time with her."

"What makes you think that?" Nyla pulled away and faced him.

"She told me as much." Xander stuffed his hands in his pockets and looked down at the soft carpet runner beneath their feet. "I was her favorite cousin growing up, so we're pretty close."

"Then by all means, I can handle things with your grandfather. You should catch up with your family," Nyla smiled warmly, reaching out to squeeze his shoulder.

Xander took a staggering breath. He reached up and gripped her hand. "We're going to be here a while, aren't we?"

"Probably." Nyla nodded, withdrawing into her own thoughts for a moment as she mulled over her interaction with Lord Alexander. "Hopefully, Alexander is more forthcoming with honest information than anyone else we've dealt with thus far."

Xander chuckled, taking a step back but not quite dropping her hand. "If it's one thing my grandfather is, it's honestly blunt." With a gleam in his eye, Xander bowed like the young lord Nyla now knew him to be and placed a gentle kiss to her knuckles that made her pulse flutter in her throat. "Until we meet again…which will probably be soon because it's almost dinnertime."

Nyla tried in vain to keep the fit of giggles she could feel buzzing in her chest threatening to overtake her at bay. Hiding her grin as she curtsied, she said, "Until then, my lord."

"You're not going to let this go, are you?"

"Never." Nyla smiled wickedly. Her eyes glinted with humor as she reached for the door handle behind her. She smirked a little as she found the slightly rough metal and leaned into the door to open it. As she stepped into the Lavender Room, she couldn't resist teasing Xander just a little more. "If you don't want me to address you as a lord, then don't act all gentlemanly and lord-like."

Xander stared at her, caught between a rueful smile and mock offense. "If you don't want me to act like a lord, then you shouldn't be so worthy of a title yourself."

"Me? A title?" Nyla scrunched her nose. "Sounds rather trouble-some if you ask me."

Xander chuckled, "Having a title definitely has its perks…though I can't think of many at the moment."

"Well, if you think of any, you'll know where I'll be." Nyla stifled a giggle as she shut the door and left Xander standing in the hallway. Sagging against the door, she waited for his footsteps to pass down the hall before she turned and took in the Lavender Room.

Now she understood why it was called so. The room was painted a dusty lavender with delicate lacy valances and parted soft gray curtains. Late afternoon sunlight streamed in through the arched windows of the south-facing wall. A canopy bed called to her from the right side of the room. It sat in the center of the raised platform that divided the room into two areas, a seating area arranged by the fire and the bedroom area.

At the sight of the dancing flames inside her fireplace, Nyla frowned. She moved over to the fireplace and extinguished it without so much as a blink. Magic caressed her bloodstream. A magic fire replaced the wood-burning, smokey flames with vigor. Warmth spread throughout the room just as quickly.

She closed her eyes against the world around her. Nyla didn't know how long she would have alone, or how often she would even be, so now was as good a time as any to ground herself. There was no telling what would come next now that they were here, but she hoped it would start with an explanation of what an 'Heir of Tenebris' was.

She crossed her arms, loosely hugging herself. As she concentrated, her brow furrowed. Her heartbeat quickened and fluttered in her chest. *Shamira?*

Rooted to the spot, Nyla flung her magic as far as her mind's eye could see. She pictured it rolling over a map of Tenebris, searching for the slightest hint of her friend or the path she might have taken.

I'm here, Nyla. Have you made it to Huntington? Shamira's voice broke through the static in Nyla's ears.

Her lips pulled into a smile. *We have, though Dinora sent these creatures to attack our carriage on the way here. I don't know what they were, though. They were some kind of stone, but they had this…this energy about them that I thought was familiar.* She paused. *I still can't place it.*

Can you describe it? Shamira asked.

Nyla's brows furrowed. *It's old, maybe even ancient. And there's this undercurrent of anger or something like that. It's like the energy itself is agitated, but I don't even know if that makes sense.*

Are you three all right?

We're fine, Nyla sighed, hugging herself tighter as her mind replayed their harrowing fight all over again. *It took nearly everything Edwin and I had to destroy them. We had to tear them apart with our magic from the inside out. And then they just faded. Chunks and fragments of rock, just gone. Disappeared…like smoke.*

Shamira didn't answer immediately. Nyla nibbled on her lip in the momentary silence.

That explains the shift in magic I felt, she said. *I should've reached out to you sooner, but I couldn't.*

Nyla bobbed her head, reluctant to ask why. *Have you made it back to your clan? Is everything okay?*

There was a long lapse in which the staticky cotton in Nyla's ears increased. Sweat beaded between her brows as her face twisted further in concentration. Her ears strained as if waiting for a physical noise to pick up on when there was nothing she could do but wait until Shamira's voice flitted across her mind again.

I did, yes. Shamira sounded hesitant, like she was anxious. *I'm awaiting the Elders' decision. They are to judge me for my crimes and the situation which I have presented to them.*

Nyla forced herself to remain still even though her body's instinct was to reel back in shock. Her temper wanted to flare. The hot prickle of anger trailed down her spine.

Calmly, she asked Shamira, *What crime?*

Leaving the clan without permission, forsaking my vows and duties, Shamira explained automatically. Nyla suspected that the pumpkie was trying to distance herself and her emotions from the trial she faced. *The High Elders from the other two clans are here as well. I think they've realized the gravity of current events and may be inclined to aid your cause against Dinora.*

That's…that's great, but what will happen to you? Nyla's stomach flopped. She wasn't sure she truly wanted an answer.

As if she could sense her trepidation, Shamira laughed. It was a gruff sound and humorless, but Nyla understood that Shamira was trying to defuse the weight of her words. *You needn't worry about me, Nyla. I'll be fine. We should focus our energy on Dinora and look toward the future. Have you been practicing your magic more to help build up your endurance?*

Nyla's temples began to pound. *Yes. I've been keeping a magic fire going as often as I can to stay consistent and have been doing little things like sensing my surroundings and things like that. I even displayed my magic to Xander's grandfather.*

As a threat? Shamira asked, a teasing lilt in her tone. *That might not have been wise, Nyla.*

You know, Xander asked me the same thing, about whether it was a threat or not. She laughed, heat creeping along her cheekbones. *But*

I suppose it wasn't the best decision I've made, though I don't think Lord Huntington took it as anything more than a display. I don't think there's much that that man would consider a threat. He's…

Nyla paused, searching for the right word as her stomach grumbled with hunger. She was certainly burning a lot of energy today. *I'm sorry. I don't know how much longer I can keep this up. He's just a lot like Xander, but…different. From what Xander's told me and just the impression he left me with, it's like skepticism reigns over his approach to life and people. It's like he doesn't expect…genuine connections or situations or actual truth anymore, and is guarded against the world.*

Shamira waited a beat before responding. *Perhaps life has soured him into expecting the worst of even the light.* Nyla considered that for a moment, but Shamira didn't give her the time to tack onto her hypothesis. *You should rest, Nyla. We'll speak again before long.*

Nyla nodded grimly. She wondered if Shamira could sense how solemn her words had made her. *I know. We miss you!*

I miss you too. I even miss Xander too.

Nyla laughed aloud as she reeled her magic back in. Stumbling a bit, she found her footing as her mind stopped tilting. She plopped herself down on the nearby couch and lazily pulled the curtains shut to block out the bright light with her waning magic stores. All she wanted right this very moment was to lay on this cozy couch and rest her eyes.

She certainly had a lot to think about. At some point, she supposed, she'd have to get up and make herself presentable for the most curious dinner she'd probably ever take part of, but she had a few moments. And in those few precious moments, she attempted to prepare herself for a chess match in which she didn't know the rules of combat.

19. THE VERDICT

Shamira opened her eyes. Relief slammed into her, nearly knocking the breath from her lungs. Not only did she have an explanation for the shift in magic, but she knew beyond a shadow of a doubt that Nyla and Xander were unharmed. And they hadn't forgotten her. She wasn't alone.

In more ways than one, it seemed, she wasn't alone.

You seem at peace. Kasand crested the gentle slope of the terrain and settled next to her.

Shamira straightened her posture, sitting proudly. *I am. I've just heard from the human girl, the Royal Mage's heir. She's growing stronger with each day that passes.*

Kasand bobbed his head in a nod. *That's good. She'll need the stamina and the strength if she truly must face the Kashars.*

You don't believe that Cedric Kashar is dead? she pried.

I fear not. Kasand frowned grimly as if soured by the sunlight dancing over the slopes and valleys in the distance below their clan's mountaintop home. *I have not felt a shift in magic that would indicate his death.*

Then we must find him, Shamira declared thoughtlessly.

Beside her, Kasand howled with laughter. *Your fate has not yet been decided, and already you would forsake your vows? Was your testimony truthful?*

Shamira began to sputter an apology, or an explanation, but Kasand cut her off with a jesting hiss. *As your friend, I believe this has gone on long enough. The Elders do not intend to punish you to the extent of the law. Your future has been decided for the better.*

She glanced at him with narrowed eyes. Her tail flicked curiously. *If that is so, then why put on this charade? What are they deliberating now?*

The future, Kasand said ominously. His eyes glinted with laughter.

Then as the High Seer, shouldn't you be there? Shamira knew he really should've been. Seers were the only pumpkies who had the magical skill and aptitude to call upon the far distant past, recalling it from the land's memory or from the reflective pool. Seers might not have been able to "see" the future, but they could interpret the past and present to see the possibilities of what might come to pass. The most powerful of Seers were said to see glimpses, potential visions of the future, though that gift was rarer still than even her talent for empathy.

I have done my part already, Kasand said in quiet resignation. *Based on what you have divulged and what our past tells us, the future is an uncertain path…more so than usual, anyway. But I do not see a full-scale war as it was 647 years ago. I think there will be unspeakable horrors, but not to the scale that it was. It will be a horrific battle to get to the brighter side of Moerae's grace.*

Shamira hesitated. Did she really want to know what Kasand's thoughts and predictions were for the future? Her throat tightened, but still she asked, *And Nyla? Do you think…do you think she and Xander will survive to see that grace?*

Do you have faith in them and their capabilities? Kasand countered. Shamira wished he'd granted her an answer instead.

I do.

Then time will tell, Kasand answered.

Shamira's mind whirled with new speculations and concerns. The tranquil view soothed her soul almost as much as the crisp, pure mountain air invigorated her. Shamira didn't know what she would do or what the Elders had decided for her punishment, even if Kasand believed they had chosen leniency. There wasn't any point in asking Kasand. He wouldn't give her a straightforward answer, and Shamira wasn't certain she wanted to hear it. She wanted to help Nyla, but she wanted to stay true to her clan as well.

Could she do both? Shamira pondered over the question. Possibilities flooded her mind, some easily dismissible, some not. But she couldn't voice them. If Kasand didn't know what law or vow she was breaking, then there was a certain degree of plausible deniability for the actions she was contemplating that could save him from being seen as an accomplice.

But Shamira knew exactly what she would do. Her decision, though difficult, had come to an easy conclusion. A conclusion, she realized, her heart had known all along.

No matter what the Elders decided, she would fight for Tenebris. She would fight with the humans, or for them, if Kasand was correct in his interpretations of the future.

She would fight for Nyla.

She would die to save her.

No matter the cost, Shamira would not let what had happened 647 years ago happen again. She would save her clan and her kind. But most importantly, she would save her friends. For the future—*their* future—she would fight so that the world could remain as it was and continue to grow in what relative peace it had enjoyed until Dinora's threat had risen anew.

I see you've made your decision, Kasand said with a huff of air, the pumpkie equivalent of a human's sigh. Shamira blinked. *Your energy is restless. You're ready to face what's to come. And whatever that decision is, I support you in it. The Elders cannot wholly forgive your actions, but passing a harsh judgement on you would only reflect poorly on them. The Reyhart and Zeldher High Elders were most displeased with High Elder Florence after your testimony and the truths you laid bare before them of our Council's 'incompetence to communicate matters that would implicate more than just the Brewardt Clan.' I suspect that the Elders' verdict is a reflection of trying to project their integrity and awareness of the matter. I would not be surprised to find a warmer reception from the Elders when they call upon you next.*

Kasand stood and glanced back at her. Shamira shifted under his gaze, seeing a friend and mentor, but most of all, the only sense of belonging she'd ever had in the clan. Kasand left with a bow of his head and not another word.

It was highly possible that Kasand suspected she was going to leave again, whether the Elders permitted her to do so or not. Shamira wondered if he was upset with her for having left the clan. She wasn't sure if he were more upset because she'd left without asking him to come with her or that he couldn't have gone with her even if he'd wanted to. Or perhaps it was because she'd never once tried to contact him, and now she was communicating with Nyla. While Nyla was an important figure because of her relation to Astrid and the Corvid Uprising, Nyla was only human—a girl—whom Shamira had only known for a short time.

Nyla shouldn't have to face this alone, especially not when Dinora's wrath had been simmering for six long centuries. And even more so because there were other powers meant to protect the sanctity of magic—and the kingdom.

That was the pumpkies' most sacred vow. To guard and protect magic and, to an extent, Tenebris. The frivolous vows of her clan and of the other clans were of a lesser importance to her, no matter how much she'd meant every word of her testimony. She was a guardian of Tenebris, as all pumpkies were. That was the only vow she wouldn't ever break. All the others were a construct, but their ancestral duty to protect Tenebris and all of magic was a sacred pact she had no intention of dishonoring.

With a final glance over her homeland, Shamira stood on strong legs and held her head high as she descended into her village.

The Elders would have her wait for them, but she had reached her own verdict.

If what Kasand could interpret of the future was correct, then one pumpkie could make a difference. If it was not a war they faced but the vengeful wrath of one human, then the clans needn't rally together for the first time in centuries.

It was with a renewed hope that Shamira faced the future rather than the grim pessimism of someone surely doomed. And it was with that hope that she strode into the meeting hall and met the startled eyes of High Elder Florence.

Forgive me, High Elders, but I have something I should like to say. Shamira waited as the discussion amongst the three High Elders and the Brewardt Elders halted at her interruption. With the concealment magic masking their emotions lifted in her brief absence, Shamira now felt everything. The stiffness of irritation, the fizzing of nervousness, the steady beat of anger, and the shadowed breeze of smug respect assaulted her as she came to a stop in the middle of the meeting hall.

High Elder Florence turned reproachful eyes on her. *You dare enter a private meeting amongst a joint session of clan leaders, and have the audacity to speak out of turn?*

Yes. Shamira's lips curled into a snarl. A growl vibrated in her chest, but she managed to stop it in its tracks before it could escape. *I would like to fight with the humans against the Kashar threat.*

A few of the Elders shook their heads slowly. A couple outright glared at her, though their ire didn't surprise her. What did were the four who showed a curious interest in her display. Her fur prickled as she found Elder Hecates's eyes fixed on her. An impassive expression graced his features, with the hint of acute concentration in his eyes. Shamira's courage wavered at the weight of his gaze. Perhaps she should've stopped to consider her actions before blindly giving into this wily impulsiveness. She swallowed as High Elder Florence's lips curled into a snarl that matched her own.

You have shown your disregard for your vows to the clan, as well as a cavalier attitude toward the safety of your kin, and yet you still have the audacity to make demands of us? High Elder Florence hissed. *Shamira Rhi—*

It is because of my 'audacity,' as you call it, that you are even aware of the danger threatening not just the humans of our country, but its threat against all of magic as well, Shamira interrupted. A few of the Elders shifted where they sat. One openly growled at her, though she wasn't certain if it was in warning to temper her mood or in reprimand for her display. *I am prepared to fight this threat and fulfill my most sacred duties demanded of me by our laws and vows, without risking my kin.*

High Elder Florence's tail flicked with the streak of irritation that flashed across her eyes. But before she—or any of the Elders—could speak, Shamira finished, *Consider my compliance with your request to return a formality and nothing more. I will fulfill my duty as a guardian of Tenebris with or without your permission, and I am wholly prepared to face Moerae's judgement when my time comes, knowing I have done all I could to follow my conscience.*

Silence met her declaration. Shamira leveled her stare with each and every pumpkie present. The only one who could hold her gaze was Elder Hecates. Him, and the trio of High Elders.

Her heart thundered against her chest, keeping count of the seconds that passed. The obvious signs of telepathic conversations—the twitch of a whisker, the swivel of an ear, the curl of a lip in response to something disagreeable—were the only indication that the world continued to revolve and that time had not frozen.

As she surveyed the Council of Elders one last time, the High Elder from the Zeldher Clan—marked by his thick coat of fur and rugged appearance—offered her a solemn nod. Stunned by the gesture of respect, Shamira nearly collapsed onto her haunches.

A wicked gleam shone in High Elder Florence's eyes. *Then we are in agreement. You will fight with the humans, and if you survive, you may do as you wish. You may return to the clan or live amongst the humans, whichever pleases you. But you must honor your vow to act as a protector of Tenebris and survive in order to bask in the grace bestowed upon you.* Her sharp eyes slid to Kasand, who must have returned after he'd spoken with her on the outlying hilltop. *I believe you wished to add something to our verdict, High Seer? Does that stand true?*

As he stood, the weight of Kasand's crystal-blue eyes landed heavily on Shamira's shoulders. Her mind reeled from the High Elder's words, uncertain if she could comprehend much more tonight. *As many of you here on the council know, I have sought to name my successor for many seasons now in order to begin their training. I and the other High Seers have often discussed the future of the clans at length, and for the reasons of how difficult it can be to predict tragedy or any aspect of the future with accuracy, we have decided to name our successors so as to prepare them for what could happen as we were not.*

He paused here, his eyes boring into her with a sharp intensity that made Shamira's stomach quiver. *I am naming Shamira Rhinuun of Clan Brewardt as my successor should she return to the clan and wish to take her place as Seer-to-be.*

Shamira stood, stunned. Most pumpkies would have been honored, elated, and maybe a bit prideful to have such a gift bestowed upon them. Kasand's announcement filled her only with dread. It sank into her bones and rendered her speechless. Her mind went blank, waiting for a spark to restart the whirring that had consumed her for most of the day.

An Elder near the center of the dais let out a noise of indignation, reminding her of a human scoff. A quick glance from the High Seer had them shrinking back where they sat. Shamira gulped, uncertain of how to respond, or if she was even capable of doing so at the moment.

I am honored, Shamira found herself saying. *Truly, I am, High Seer, but I know not where my journeys will take me or if I am to survive them. I don't believe this honor was meant to be mine.*

Should you choose not to return to the clan, Kasand began, not relinquishing his gaze even when the piercing intensity had softened, *or should Mordimere claim you to join the ranks of Her realm, then I shall name another successor, but I believe there are none as competent as you.*

Shamira bowed her head, hoping her doubt didn't show. *Thank you, High Seer.*

It was Elder Hecates that dismissed her from the meeting hall with the curt explanation that the clan would meet tonight, though her presence was not required should she wish not to attend. Shamira took her leave gratefully.

Tomorrow, she would leave again, but this time with the blessing of the Elders and any members from the three clans that should wish to join her cause. The announcement would be made at the gathering tonight.

She needed to tell Nyla, but first, she needed to find a place to rest. She could only hope that Nyla had done the same after they'd spoken this afternoon.

Shamira walked through the village in a daze that numbed every fiber of her being. As she wound her way between the earthen homes, she searched her mind for something that proved her wakefulness, her life.

All she could hear was how her own heartbeat echoed Kasand's announcement, and his jest from earlier when he'd called her a Seer. She supposed he was right in that respect, but to be his successor? To become the High Seer?

She would never be able to leave the clan again. Shamira couldn't even comprehend what she wanted for tomorrow, and she certainly couldn't determine what would happen over the course of the coming weeks, let alone what she would want when Dinora was at last defeated.

At the edge of the village, in the last row of dome-like homes, Shamira saw her own. The roof had caved in, probably because of the snow, but it was still standing. She hadn't expected it to be. After all these long seasons searching for Nyla, she would've thought that the clan would've let it return to the earth it was once a part of.

Continually stunned by the afternoon's events, Shamira focused her magic and made the necessary repairs to her home. Without a moment's hesitation, she ducked her head and dragged herself inside.

No one had ever told her how exhausting good tidings could be. Or how dejected relief would make her feel. Curling up, Shamira wrapped her tail tightly around herself. Magic thrummed in her bloodstream, warming herself and her home. No matter how comfortable she forced herself to be, rest would not come.

All at once, the numbness of her shock wore off, and Shamira's mind leapt into a fray of jumbled thoughts.

Kasand didn't believe Cedric was dead. Nyla would probably hunt him down herself if they found any truth to the speculation and she learned of it—which Shamira knew would have to be her burden. Nyla deserved to know the truth, no matter how difficult it may be.

Then there was the fact that the Elders of all three clans were going to ask the pumpkies to volunteer to fight alongside the humans. For centuries, not a single pumpkie had left the realm they'd claimed for themselves in the mountains of northwestern Tenebris. Would they be able to adjust to life outside of their isolation? Would they be willing to volunteer to defend a world that had wholly forgotten them—that they'd wholly ignored?

Shamira shook her head. She couldn't say for certain how that would play out, but of all her wonderings and of all the shocks her mind fought to process, there was one she couldn't digest.

Kasand's startling announcement that he wanted her to be his successor, and that the choice was hers, plagued her anxious mind.

The suggestion—the appointment—was almost too much for her to consider in a single night, or even a single lifetime.

Now she understood the weight in Nyla's eyes and the constant moodiness the girl was recently predisposed to. Shamira had centuries more ahead of her to consider her future, but Nyla only had decades—and even then, they both had to survive and decide their paths quickly if they wanted to enjoy the rest of their lives.

Shamira grumbled and pushed herself to standing. She paced the tight length of her home. Back and forth, back and forth, just like her thoughts.

Her first duty would be to locate Cedric. Even if only two other pumpkies joined her cause, their combined magics might be able to circumvent any cloaking spell he was using to mask his whereabouts. Then, she would regroup with Nyla and whatever human forces she and Xander had gathered.

It was a vague plan, but since Dinora hadn't done much and Shamira had only sensed one instance of unusual magic since Dinora had been freed from the Woodlane Manor's bond, there was still time to strategize.

Especially when she considered the fact that the humans and the pumpkies would have to learn to cooperate and fight with each other, just as they had six and a half centuries ago. Shamira realized that responsibility and leadership would fall on herself and Nyla more so than any leaders the two factions might appoint. She and Nyla were the only ones in recent centuries to have worked with their particular magics.

Shamira's whiskers twisted, her stomach knotting.

Maybe the other pumpkies wouldn't accept the call to aid the humans, so keeping the harmony between humans and pumpkies wouldn't fall on them.

That was the best worst-case scenario Shamira could hope for. The absolute worst scenario she could envision was that Kasand's assessment was incorrect and Dinora could garner the forces to wage a full-scale attack against Tenebris.

Shamira would gladly force peace between the pumpkies and their human counterparts if it meant not having to face a war of lasting impact. The world had seen enough of those, especially ones that involved the Kashar family.

With the shadows of the setting sun darkening her doorstep, Shamira was restless and weary at the same time. There was no use in hiding in the shadows of her home. She would be present at the public meeting tonight, even if her fellow Brewardts shunned her. This was her home, and the grave news they were to be presented with had come on her tail. It was only just that she be present there tonight.

With a final glance around the bare hut, Shamira ducked her head and joined the straggling pumpkies walking toward the village center. If the other pumpkies had noticed her trailing behind them, they didn't acknowledge her. Shamira decided to be grateful for that. She didn't know what sort of reaction the clan would have once the rumors had been dispelled by the truth the Elder Council would bestow upon them all.

An impressive bonfire had been lit in the center of the village. The flames leapt and licked at the wind coming off of the taller mountain peaks around their village. Sparks trailed in the wind before they died out in the chilled air. Already, the majority of the Brewardt Clan had gathered. All of the Elders and Kasand were already seated on the dais set before the bonfire. The High Elders of the Reyhart and Zeldher Clans were nowhere to be seen. They must've returned to their clans to make their own announcements.

Shamira took a seat near the edge of the crowd. Some pumpkies eyed her and huddled closer to those beside them until a quiet ripple had seemingly traveled through the whole crowd.

Telepathy was quickly becoming the bane of Shamira's existence. She now understood why Xander hated it so. With verbal communication, there was the risk of the subject of conversation overhearing it, and while Shamira could clue into the private telepathic communications around her, she didn't dare try for the simple reason that it could shatter the minds of those she forced herself into. Or, on a lesser scale, it would only cause more strife if others realized what she'd done.

The risk was too great. She would endure their judgement—and their outrage should the announcement not go over well.

Who knew? Maybe her fellow Brewardts would banish her on behalf of the Elders. It wouldn't be the first time in all of creation's history that the public acted on the sly impulses of the ruling class.

A single roar pierced through the air. The obvious conversations amongst the assembly came to a halt as all eyes turned toward the dais.

Pumpkies of Clan Brewardt, High Elder Florence called out, *as I am sure you are all aware, a wayward pumpkie has returned home. Shamira Rhinuun has spent the last several seasons on an errand of great importance on behalf of the clans.*

Shamira's mind wavered. So that's the story they would weave? She studied the gathered pumpkies with a worried eye. Some glanced her way while others tensed where they sat. She caught the eye of Caitil, a pumpkie that had hissed at her earlier. Her face was unreadable and her expression more guarded than Shamira could ever remember the amber-furred cat being. At least that was one pumpkie's emotions that wouldn't drown her any longer once she'd returned to Nyla and Xander.

Upon her return, she has brought devastating news that concerns not only our clan, but the Reyhart Clan and Zeldher Clan as well. The High Elder paused once more. Shamira's fur prickled. She was nervous. The steely-eyed pumpkie that had trained more than half of the clan in magic and warfare was nervous.

In her hesitation, Kasand stood and went to stand beside her. *Many of you know or have heard of the Corvid Uprising. It is a grievous tale we all know and have been instilled with since birth. Though none of us are old enough to have lived through the Corvid Uprising, we know it in our hearts.* Kasand paused, allowing his words to settle their weight over the crowd. *Shamira Rhinuun was tasked with investigating a strong disturbance in the flow of magic we sensed some twenty years ago. Then once more, about two years ago, another disturbance ruptured the harmony of magic followed by a third, and Shamira was sent into the kingdom to track down the source of these disturbances. In doing so, she has found the Royal Mage's heir and also discovered the Kashars. Dinora Kashar has escaped her centuries-long imprisonment, a feat that should not have been possible for any human.*

Some pumpkies glanced at each other; others let out low mewls like a murmur. Kasand continued on.

The Kashar queen is still a threat to this world and the balance of magic. Her son, Cedric Kashar, is unaccounted for, though hopefully presumed dead thanks to the heir's burdensome act of courage.

A low whisper rippled through the crowd. The murmur of their primitive language was as foreign to Shamira as most of the humans' expressions once were. So rarely did they communicate with each other verbally anymore, she'd almost thought her kin had forgotten how to, or what the *chitters* or guttural noises even meant.

High Seer Kasand silenced them all with a hiss.

As members of the Elder Council, we stand before you and ask for support to join the human cause in a war against this destructive force. Our histories tell us that Dinora has once changed the balance of magic and therefore the properties of the lands within Tenebris. The potential destruction she can cause today is untold, and it is with this knowledge that we solemnly ask for volunteers to join Shamira in fighting alongside the humans as we have done before.

As Kasand finished, Hecates stood and joined the High Elder and High Seer at the forefront of the dais.

In the silence, his eyes scanned the crowd and landed on hers. Shamira felt the awareness of every pumpkie shift to her presence. As Shamira stared back at the deep green eyes searing into her, Elder Hecates spoke. *I will join the human cause, of my own free will and with the understanding that I may never again see the sun rise on this mountaintop. These are trying times, but as Shamira has so reminded this council today, we are guardians of Tenebris, and it is not only our ancestral duty to answer this call—it is our most sacred duty to stand against forces that would seek to destroy not only our allies, but the balance of magic. This is our home, and if war is to be fought around us, then I should like to see it end before it seeps into our realm.*

Uneasiness swept over the gathered pumpkies. Elder Hecates resumed his place in front of the fire and gazed expectantly at the crowd before the dais.

Shamira's heart pounded in her chest. She hadn't expected any of the Elders, least of all Hecates, to commit to fighting Dinora, especially alongside the humans. Her tongue went dry. It was obvious that pumpkies were having conversations amongst themselves, checking in with friends and relatives, weighing their options, biding their time. She tried to see their perspective. Would she volunteer if things were different, if she were more like them?

Without hesitation, Shamira knew the answer. Even though she was more sensitive to the world around them, more disposed to being a Seer in the way that Kasand was, she'd already volunteered to follow Nyla into battle, even if she hadn't known it when she'd left the village under the cloak of the night sky and all its stars.

And she would continue to do so, even if it were only herself and Hecates to uphold the alliance between their kind and the humans of Tenebris.

I will join this cause, a cocky voice said.

Shamira's heart stopped. Her eyes searched helplessly over the crowd. In the dark and shadows cast by the glow of the flames, she couldn't find the splotch of orange fur she sought. She couldn't find nose nor tail of her brother. Very few pumpkies in their clan bore the burnt orange mixed into their fur, but her mother and father had. All of her siblings had some type of orange in them, but it just so happened that her brother and herself had a patch of orange fur splashed on their foreheads. It was nearly the only disruption to their otherwise dark fur. Shamira's coat was more varied in color, with rippled stripes of gray, black, and a hint of brown, while Talmec was mostly gray and black.

Talmec? she sputtered once she'd found where he was.

He pushed his way through the crowd as more pumpkies voiced their assent to join the human cause. *All this time and not a word, sister? Lynx'll have your head when she finds you.*

Lynx can try. Shamira bared her teeth. Talmec was a hulking pumpkie. Well-muscled and suited for non-magical combat as well as offensive magic, Shamira almost couldn't bear the idea of him on the battlefield.

I don't know if I would be so confident, sister. A hiss sounded behind her, and Shamira turned just in time for the youngest of her siblings to lunge at her.

Knocked onto her side, Shamira grappled for the upper hand, attempting to throw Lynx off of her. *You've gotten stronger in my absence, but not strong enough, dear sister.*

Panting, Shamira managed to force Lynx off. The crowd of pumpkies was beginning to disperse. Some watched the reunion amongst siblings; others idly chatted amongst themselves. Shamira gazed reverently at the dispersing assembly. More pumpkies than she'd expected had volunteered to fight with her alongside the humans.

Lynx got to her feet and shook herself off. *There was no one here to protect me anymore, so I had to.*

You were perfectly capable of protecting yourself before, Shamira pointed out.

I wouldn't have known it since you were always so eager to come to my aid. Lynx rolled her eyes.

Shamira growled playfully. *What can I say? It comes with the territory of being firstborn.*

Talmec howled with laughter. Shamira shifted on her paws. Not only had she led the clans to opt into a potentially devastating war, but now she was responsible for leading her own sibling toward the fiery gates of Mordimere's realm.

Noticing her somber expression, Talmec leaned forward and nuzzled her neck. She nuzzled him back before they broke apart, and Talmec's matching sage-colored eyes bore into her with a rare moment of seriousness. *You didn't bring us to war. Rumors were spreading well before you came home. We've all had a lot of time to consider the possibility.*

Truly? She blinked.

Let's just say you made quite a dramatic exit from the clan, Lynx started. *Pumpkies demanded answers, and Kasand gave them readily. Most of the Brewardts pressured the Elder Council into admitting the truth. It was the first time in history that the Elders didn't garner the respect their position demanded.*

Shamira hummed. *I never thought my actions would inspire such a revolution.*

I think it inspired more jealousy than it did a revolution, Lynx countered. *That's why most pumpkies are so upset: you left the clan and returned, unpunished. So, what stopped them from following after you before? Or what had stopped others from leaving before you?*

Well, I didn't leave because I wanted to. I left because I had to, to find the source of the disruptions throughout the balance of magic, Shamira reminded her.

Yes, so you left for a noble and righteous purpose, Talmec interrupted. *That's dandy! But the real thing pumpkies want to hear about is the world beyond the boundary.*

At his admission, the lingering pumpkies drew closer to their tightly knit circle. He'd obviously broadcasted his statement to all those in their vicinity.

What's it like, Tenebris? a hazel-eyed cub asked.

Others chimed in with exclamations of agreement and wonder. Shamira glanced at the group that had gathered around her. Most were pumpkies around their age, a few about a century older, maybe a century and a half, and a couple of cubs not much older than a few decades.

It's…much different than our village and the realm between the boundary, she started slowly. *There are places with tens of thousands of humans located in small areas, cities with great, towering buildings.* She paused, gathering her thoughts for a moment. *Admittedly, I spent little time in areas like that because of…my sensitive disposition, but I saw them from a distance. More commonly, there are hundreds of humans scattered over swaths of land and cultivated fields.* Shamira lost sight of the darkened village around her until even the crackle of the dying bonfire faded from her awareness.

Tenebris was truly beautiful, even though the magic of the land was off balance. Shamira had particularly enjoyed the change of scenery in the Shadow Forest. The Godberd Woods was familiar to her in a way that her own heartbeat was. She looked over the Godberd Woods every day of her life for four centuries now. She knew every dip in the surrounding valleys, every peak of the higher mountains in the distance, and each shift of the sun's rays as the day yielded to the night.

But the Shadow Forest was dim with an eerie glow caused by the excess of magic rooted in the land. The sapphire leaves shaded the rusty, amber dirt from even the smallest speck of the sun's golden light. The crackled bark of the ashen-colored trees was precisely like the cinders of a fire. It was uncanny and striking at the same time.

Nyla and Xander had told her that the Forest turned darker the farther into the heart one traveled. They'd told her that the soft dirt became pebbly, only to be replaced by a sheet of the blackest rock. Nyla had said that it was slippery, like ice. She'd had a difficult time keeping her balance on the sheet of rock in part because of her worn boots, though that's how Xander described them. Knowing Nyla, he probably wasn't wrong about the wear of her boots, but Shamira could picture the heart of the forestland in her head as they'd described it to her.

One day, she wanted to see it for herself.

It would be like a testament to herself, of her strength and growth. She knew the perils of the Shadow Forest, but she was a pumpkie. They weren't to be trifled with either.

Then there are the Plains, she found herself saying. *They have a little more magic than the Amber Dunelands of southern Tenebris and the eastern extremity of the country, though not much more. On the outskirts of the Godberd Woods and Shadow Forest, the Barrier Plains are an endless field of grasslands or fields of golden grain as far as the eye can see. The grain whispers in the constant breeze. It's like a gentle caress, and I found myself most at peace there. It was almost like home in that sense. The tranquility of its simplistic wonder almost made me forget that magic dwindled the farther south I traveled.*

And of the Amber Dunelands? a starry-eyed pumpkie with all gray fur asked. A cub.

Shamira smiled. *I only pawed at the Dunelands, as the humans call the southern Amber Dunelands.* Her whiskers twitched in her hesitation. *The Dunelands are not a happy place. The air is suffocating, and the lack of magic there was like a constant scratching in my skull. Thankfully, I did not dwell there long at all, for the heir's trail was not strong there either, not like it was in the Shadow Forest.*

You've met them? The heir? Lynx asked her.

I have. Shamira tensed. She didn't want to talk about her human friends; she didn't want to tell them about Nyla quite yet. Shamira feared that by speaking of them, her concern would grow greater, and also that their absence would only fester.

Talmec yawned, exaggerating the gesture and drawing the attention of everyone present. *Well, Shamira, I can only imagine how exhausted you must be after all of this excitement.* He glanced at each pumpkie in turn with a withering gaze. They shifted and began to disperse. *Perhaps it's time we all get some rest. We have a busy day ahead of us for sure.*

Between herself and Talmec, Shamira thanked him. *You really didn't have to do that, but I appreciate it.*

What are brothers for? He pounced at her, in a gesture that was oddly reminiscent of a human hug as his front paws nearly wrapped around her neck before they broke apart and Talmec was back on all fours.

Besides annoying their siblings? she teased, grinning at him. He hissed at her in response. *You're right. Brothers can be helpful when they're so inclined to be.*

Talmec let out a low howl, a laugh. *There's the sister we've so missed!*

Shamira didn't respond. Tomorrow promised to be a long day, and she'd yet to figure out what role the Elders would like for her to fill, if any. She had no choice in fighting alongside the humans to stop Dinora, even though there hadn't been a choice for her to make. She did, however, know for certain that she hadn't wanted her own siblings to volunteer for what could be certain death. At least Lynx had had the good sense not to. But Talmec…Shamira truly wondered if he understood just what he'd volunteered to fight for, and had then persuaded others to join in the effort.

We should rest, she said at last. Silently, she turned and slunk away down the winding paths of the village until she reached her hut. Talmec and Lynx called after her with their well wishes for a peaceful night's sleep, making Shamira's heart twang with guilt.

Could she leave this all behind if she survived the war? The Elders *had* said she could do what she wished once she'd served her sentence. She hadn't even begun to fully consider what Kasand had announced after she'd burst into the closed meeting of the Elder Council earlier this evening. He'd named her as his successor, and the position could be hers if she only returned to the clan after Dinora's defeat.

If she accepted, she could never leave the clan—if leaving became an option for all pumpkies after the war. The idea of being able to come and go as she pleased, as they all pleased, rather than being bound by archaic laws to remain within their realm's boundary was enticing. But if she accepted Kasand's proposition to become his successor, she would have to remain here, or wherever the clan was, to perform her duties when called upon.

Shamira nearly banged her head into the low entry of her hut, too consumed by her thoughts to realize how far her paws had brought her. Grumbling to herself, she ducked her head and continued her pacing from earlier.

She could only hope that Nyla and Xander were having an easier time with Xander's grandfather than she was with the clans.

20. ECHOES OF THE PAST

Nyla was absolutely going to be the death of him, though Xander was beginning to realize it was more of a metaphorical death.

His grandfather, on the other hand, quite literally might be the death of him. Where was the lecture? The scolding? Surely, his grandfather had *something* to say about Xander's three-year absence from the family, so why hadn't he? Or was he more concerned about why they'd come, about Nyla?

Xander's heart stopped. None of it made any sense to him.

Why had he wanted to see Nyla alone? What had he said to her that made her want to show off just how much she didn't need his help if she didn't like the conditions his help would probably come with?

Even though they'd seldom discussed it, Xander knew that Nyla ultimately had reservations about accepting help from his grandfather, and if the way he imagined their meeting had gone…it didn't seem likely to him that Nyla was willing to play the games his grandfather was prone to. He didn't know what boundaries Nyla had decided on before they'd even come to Pemberly, but if he knew anything about her, she'd probably added a few more stipulations before she'd ever accept his grandfather's help. She could be stubborn when she was so inclined. And his grandfather could be difficult and lofty in his beliefs. The head of the Huntington family always thought he was more knowledgeable, more powerful, and overall superior to everyone around him.

How could he have ever thought asking his grandfather for help was a good idea? Or even a halfway decent idea?

Xander ran his hand through his hair roughly, pacing up and down the length of his room. He was surprised he even still had a room here, or that it'd been kept exactly as he'd left it. The ornate and bulky armoire still held his clothes, even though he'd outgrown them now. The dresser too still held his things, and the few trinkets displayed there were left untouched, but cared for. Everything was exactly as he'd remembered it.

Except for one addition.

A new portrait hung over the fireplace. It was a portrait he'd never seen before and couldn't for the life of him remember posing for.

Even in the time that Xander had lived at Pemberly after the death of his parents, there had never been a family portrait of the four of them. But in his absence, a portrait of himself, his parents, and his sister, Issie, had appeared over the mantel. Xander didn't know what to make of its appearance.

Had it been hung after he'd left? Was it only hung when it was evident that he was coming home? He knew it shouldn't really matter *when* the picture was hung, but it did. Xander was hoping that if he figured out the 'when' of the matter, it would give him some insight into how to approach his grandfather. If it was hung after his departure, Xander could take it as a sign that his grandfather came to the same regrets that he had. If it was hung recently…then Xander could only guess it was done so out of appearance, or in an effort to make him feel guilty.

Or maybe it was to instill some sense of belonging, of family? Like a reminder of sorts, of who he was—and *should* be.

Then there was the question of *why* it was hung. Why was it hung in his room? Why was it hung at all?

Xander never considered his grandfather to be a sentimental man, not in the traditional sense of the word at least. He was a forward-thinking man with a blasé attitude toward sentimentality. He didn't covet symbols of the past. He didn't hold on to the fraying threads of trinkets that could clutter his home.

But, Xander supposed, he was sentimental in his own way. His grandfather kept his family. Yes, he was difficult and expectant, but he'd always kept Pemberly Hall open to the family that often descended upon their ancestral home.

A slow smile drew itself upon Xander's face. This portrait held the key to his grandfather, and the way in which Xander was to connect with him.

Perhaps the past was just that: the past. Dropping his gaze from the portrait that had captivated him, Xander stared into the laughing flames of the fireplace. He could feel the gazes of the portrait looking down on him. They weren't judgmental, but the weight pressed over him.

Studying the faces of his family once more, Xander wondered what advice his family could offer. Issie would probably say something sassy and that he was treating this like a caged pyrosa. She wouldn't be wrong.

Xander imagined that if their roles were reversed, Issie would march right up to their grandfather and say exactly what burdened her heart, no matter how much it might hurt, just so she could lessen the chokehold of her fear. *That* was what Issie would do. She was fearless like that, and Xander envied her for it. She never let something bother her for long, and because of her blunt nature, people never stayed too bothered by her for long either because once she'd said her piece, she was usually on her next warpath.

Their mother could be like that, except she had more tact than Issie. He supposed that came with maturity. If she were here right now, his mother would say something to make him laugh and make it seem as though there was nothing to be nervous about. She would assure him that no matter how difficult his grandfather seemed, there was no limit on his love for his family. Pemberly would always be open to him, no matter what had happened.

And his father would echo that statement. He would remind him that the first step was always the hardest step of all. Pride, he would say, only led to more difficulties. Walking away from it became easier with each step because the weight of it dissipated with each step forward.

He'd heard his father say that every now and again, and could hear his voice saying it now.

He'd usually say it in response to the most recent Huntington family debacle and Mother's irritation at whatever deceit or sleight of hand had tried to disrupt the business or pit family against family. She didn't understand how Grandfather allowed so many chances to people who habitually proved they would cut the throats of every other Huntington if given the chance.

Xander hadn't understood what she'd meant, but now that he was older and in the wake of their passing, he knew now. Their family was plagued by competition, and by greed. The family business was a great and terrible responsibility, one his grandfather had meant to bequeath to them.

The clock ticking away on the mantel drew his attention. Glancing at its face, Xander's eyes bulged. How had it gotten so late?

Hastily, Xander set about getting ready for dinner, his first dinner at home in over three long years. Crossing the room into the en-suite bathroom, he washed his face. A quick peek in the shower confirmed that his favorite shampoo and conditioner were still half-empty, exactly as he'd left them when he'd walked out of Pemberly Hall for what he swore would be the last time.

He shook his head, huffing a laugh at the sight. Who would've known all these reminders would still be here? Not giving himself the time to linger, Xander went to his backpack and pulled every article of clothing he had out of it and laid them on the bed. It was the best he could do, and given that this dinner wasn't a Pemberly Hall social event, he figured no one would chastise him for the state of his wardrobe.

Quickly dressing in the finest, cleanest clothes he could find in his travel pack, he took a hard look at himself in the mirror. He needed a trim. His hair had gotten longer than he usually liked it, but it wasn't too shabby yet. There were worry lines permanently etched around his eyes just like the crease between his brows and the slight frown of his lips.

Xander reeled back, bouncing on his heels. He was becoming his grandfather.

As soon as this dinner was over, he was going to have to do something to rectify that. He didn't know what, but he wasn't ready to become the man that his grandfather was. Shrewd and willingly detached from those around him.

But first, Xander needed to meet with his grandfather.

Alone.

And maybe, if Corruptio were willing to ease the barriers between them, heart to heart.

Solemnly, Xander strode toward the double doors of his room. With every tick of the clock on his mantel echoing throughout the room, Xander knew it was getting closer to dinner, but he wanted to see his grandfather first—and this time, he was ready.

Based on what Edwin had told him before they'd left the Woodlane Manor, Xander gambled that his grandfather would be found in his study. With a slight tremble tingling in his fingers, he yanked the solid door open a little more roughly than he'd intended to, but Xander wouldn't be deterred.

He would see his grandfather, and they would talk.

It might be difficult, and it might be awkward, but Xander needed to speak with him and hopefully forgive the past before it was too late—and before it impacted more than just their relationship.

As he padded past Nyla's room, he strained his ears. There wasn't a sound to be heard from inside the Lavender Room. He supposed the silence was good, that she might actually be resting before dinner and after all the magic she'd so cavalierly used since Shamira had parted ways with them. He'd noticed that she'd even used magic for the simplest of tasks, like setting the table and making the ponanchkas this morning.

He never would have thought he'd see the day when Nyla wholly embraced her magic. He certainly never would've guessed that that day would come mere weeks after her horror-struck discovery of said magic. It made him wonder if there was a part of her that was cognizant of her magic throughout her whole life, and had just never realized it.

But if so, then where did Dinora fit into all of this? If she was bound to the Woodlane Manor and her powers were restricted by a curse Astrid had placed on her before she'd been killed, what did she have to do with the deaths of Nyla's family and Astrid's magic? For over six centuries, Dinora was trapped in the Woodlane Manor. Why hadn't Cedric freed her before now? What stopped him? Was he unable to break the bond?

Xander had a difficult time convincing himself that Cedric had failed to break it in all the time they'd had to try. He'd seen what the ballroom had looked like in the aftermath of Cedric and Nyla's battle on the astral plane. He could still feel the sympathetic ache in his back—and his immediate wrath toward the red-eyed man—at the sight of the cracked stone pillars, the chunks of material strewn throughout the room amid shattered glass from the chandelier, and the damaged plaster of the walls.

If Cedric had tried to free Dinora, then he simply hadn't been able to. There probably wasn't enough magic between the two of them to break the bond. Dinora had to have transferred it to Nyla if what Shamira and Edwin had said about the impossibility of breaking the bond to be true. There wasn't any other way Nyla could've ended up bonded to the manor while Dinora went free.

But why wouldn't Astrid's magic reappear in an earlier generation, especially with Dinora still alive in the Woodlane Manor? Why had it taken 647 years for Astrid's spell and the bequeathment of her magic to take effect?

Hurrying down the back staircase, Xander shook the jumbled thoughts from his mind. If he was truly going to face his grandfather, he wanted a clear head. He couldn't be distracted by theories or anxieties.

And unlike any other time reconciliation had crossed his mind, this time, he wouldn't cower from it. He was going to see this inclination through for the first time in three years. There had been other times over the course of his estrangement, through the cold nights and dark loneliness, when he'd considered crawling back to Pemberly, to ending his chosen exile, but never had. The impulse always ended up with a sleepless night spent in the tavern of whatever inn he'd picked up work at in exchange for money and shelter. He'd drown his cowardice, his pride, whatever it was that kept him in that darkness of self-pity.

And then, when he'd decided to seek out the mystical Fortune Falls, he couldn't pluck up the courage to drink from its waters. Even faced with the prospect of being granted his deepest desires, Xander hadn't been brave enough to see the consequences.

But now? He still wasn't certain he wanted to know what consequences would soon be revealed to him, but he had to face them. The prospect of *not* facing them now seemed like a worse fate, especially as he grew older.

And as Xander came to stand before the double doors of his grandfather's study, he realized Fortune Falls wouldn't have been able to give him what he wanted. These doors couldn't give him what he wanted.

Only the man within this room could give him what he wanted. Everything else only offered empty assurances or the temptation of what could be.

Swallowing, Xander reached his hand up to knock. Shifting on his feet, he waited for an answer that didn't come. Taking a deep breath, Xander knocked again, this time louder.

"Enter." The muffled voice of his grandfather sounded through the solid wood doors. At the creak of their hinges, Xander's blood froze, and his spine stiffened.

From across the room, his grandfather looked over and simply stared at him. In the dancing shadows of the flames, Xander saw a solemn expression complete with passive eyes beneath brows on the verge of furrowing and the slight downturn of his grandfather's lips.

"Alexander." Neither a question nor an exclamation, only a neutral means of greeting.

"Grandfather," Xander returned just as evenly. Closing the door behind him, Xander crossed the room to stand beside the fireplace with his grandfather.

This was going rather well, and not at all like his worst fears. Xander knew he should've basked in the mercy of it all, but he found himself at a loss for words, for sense, for *anything*.

"It's funny," his grandfather said without any humor at all, "after three years, one season, and fourteen weeks, I would have thought we would have more to say to each other."

Xander's head snapped in his grandfather's direction. "You've kept track?"

Xander's grandfather chortled, clasping his hands behind his back and turning to face him straight on. "Of course I have. My oldest grandson sends himself into exile without so much as a word to anyone in the family, and then after three years and nearly a season more, I receive a letter from a family friend, from *George* of all people, confirming to me that he is alive and well and traveling with some girl who had had a magical episode before they'd left town again. And then I receive two consecutive notes from my grandson with the worst penmanship I have ever seen asking for help on behalf of this stranger. Of course I kept track. I had to if I expected any news of you."

Xander was struck speechless. The quiet crackle of the burning logs filled the lapse in conversation.

"She made quite the impression on me." His grandfather spoke after a moment, apparently content with his lack of response. "Nyla and Isabelle would have gotten along well."

Xander licked his lips and forced the dryness from his parched throat. "They would have, though sometimes I think I would've rather torn the world apart myself just so they'd never meet."

His grandfather laughed this time. "I suppose that's true. They would've wreaked havoc together if given the opportunity."

Somberly, both men cast their gaze back to the licking tongues of the fireplace. "I still miss them. Sometimes, I expect Isadora and Rupert to come bursting through that door. They always had that sort of energy, the kind that swept everyone up into the fold. Half whirlwind, half genuine enthusiasm, your mother and father were the best people suited to take the company over. You and Isabelle would have been perfect successors should they have passed it down to you both." He paused, taking a deep breath as the tension from his shoulders loosened.

"Business is about balance. George is friendly and good at navigating relationships, whereas I am not. I see numbers and calculations, schedules, things that have to be managed. I am a difficult man, and sometimes a horrible man, even to the people I care about most.

"I forget that life is about balance too, and it's cost me a lot of time with the people I love." His grandfather spoke softly as if the weight of his confession was too much to bear. "Don't ever forget that, Alexander. Balance is the key to life, and the people in our lives deserve more of the scale than anything else."

The words fell heavily between them. They turned around and around in Xander's head as he sifted through them, dissecting any unspoken intentions behind them. Nyla was right: everyone spoke in riddles, but he understood what his grandfather was saying. He was set in his ways, but Xander wasn't. There was still time for Xander to grow into a better man, unlike his grandfather, who saw himself as a 'horrible man,' unable to adapt to a world that was ever changing or the needs of a family who needed him. But Xander had his whole life ahead of him and could benefit from the triumphs and mistakes of his grandfather, and from the lesson he sought to impart on him.

"You aren't a horrible person," Xander said at last. "I do agree that you can be difficult, but I can be too. We both said things we never would have said if…I think the things I said were directed more at myself than at you.

"Sometimes I still hear them, echoes of them, when I look in the mirror, and I have never regretted anything more." Xander stepped toward his grandfather and placed a hand on his shoulder. His grandfather straightened. "I would've come home sooner, but I'm glad I didn't because I would've never met Nyla, and I would've never grown into the person I am today. Huntington would've drowned me as it did you."

"Then perhaps the rest of the family could benefit from exile." His grandfather smiled. "I should like to see Marilynn deal with paving her own path through life without our family name."

Xander snorted. "She wouldn't fare well. The sun very much so sets in the west with her."

"Welcome home, Al—Xander." His grandfather drew him into a rare embrace that Xander returned.

"I'm glad to be home, Grandfather."

Before long, the two broke apart, and his grandfather motioned to the couches. "We have a bit of time before dinner is served. Let's talk about Nyla. Tell me about her."

Xander sat on the couch across from his grandfather's favorite armchair and fixed his gaze on the ornamental carpet beneath his feet. His heart pounded against his chest. A rock seemed to lodge itself in his throat as he searched for something to say. If his grandfather wanted to know who Nyla was, he'd sit down with her personally, so he must've meant as it related to why they'd asked for his help.

"She's…well, she's completely on her own now. Her family was killed in a fire a couple of years ago by Cedric, the son of the woman recently freed from the Woodlane Manor."

"So I've gathered," his grandfather sighed. Xander raised his eyebrows questioningly. How would his grandfather know anything about

Nyla's past? "I was asking about the nature of your friendship. How did you two meet? How long have you known each other?"

Xander hesitated.

Sensing his reluctance, his grandfather explained, "I've already decided to aid in her efforts to stop Dinora, and we'll all discuss that over dinner. I just want to get to know the girl my grandson has been traveling the country with."

"There isn't really much to tell," Xander started, considering his words. "We met in Halberry only several weeks ago. Well, technically, we met somewhere *outside* of Halberry because of this storm that forced us both to take refuge in a cave."

His grandfather prompted him to continue with the raise of an eyebrow. Xander took a breath and carried on with his narrative. "We'd both set off through the Shadow Forest, unbeknownst to each other because we hadn't even met at that point, though I did see her in Halberry trying to barter for a map and compass. Unfortunately, though, we both got caught in a terrible thunderstorm, and by the time I found any shelter, Nyla was already there—"

"What were you both doing in the Shadow Forest outside of Halberry?" his grandfather interjected.

"Oh." Xander scratched the back of his neck sheepishly. "It just so happened that we were both heading to Fortune Falls."

"Fortune Falls?" his grandfather echoed in disbelief. "Did you find it?"

Xander grinned. "We did. There was this wisp of smoke, and Nyla decided to follow it, and at that point I had to follow her, and the whole thing was so absurd, but we found it. We found Fortune Falls. I probably wouldn't have if it weren't for Nyla and her reckless intuition."

"Then I hope you achieved what you sought," his grandfather replied earnestly.

"I think I did." Xander nodded, not bothering to mention that he hadn't drunk from the Falls. Crossing one leg over the other, Xander continued, "Then Nyla discovered her magic before we left, and that led us to Caselle where we visited Nan and George."

"And from there you went to the Woodlane Manor and got yourself into a meddlesome snicket?"

"Unintentionally. Nyla thought the Woodlane Manor might've been able to help her find answers about her magic, though I'm sure she would rather tell you about everything over dinner if she hasn't already," Xander summed up.

"And you continued to travel with her…" His grandfather trailed off, gazing at him expectantly.

"I don't know why, exactly," Xander admitted, refusing to let his gaze wander for the fear that looking away would admit something he hadn't yet confirmed for himself. "I guess I liked the idea of an adventure, and Nyla seemed like she needed help, and…I don't know. I guess there were a lot of reasons why I went along with her."

The clock *cooed* from beside the door where it had always resided. As the seven *chirps* receded, Lord Alexander rose from his seat. Xander mirrored his grandfather and forced himself to his unsteady feet.

"I didn't realize the time." His grandfather motioned for Xander to lead the way to the door. "I'm sure you both must be hungry after your travels. Moretta offered to make your favorite in honor your homecoming."

At this, Xander perked up. "Roast jik with wildflower rice and chocolate-blackberry torte for dessert?"

"Precisely."

As he and his grandfather walked side by side to the breakfast room, Xander all but floated through the halls. He couldn't remember the last time he'd felt this whole. The day at the beach had come close, but there was still this piece of him that wouldn't allow himself to forget his sins. But today, walking down the halls of his ancestral home with his grandfather, and knowing that there *was* a place for him still at his family's table, finally put that part of him at peace. For all his fears and doubts, Xander had come home to welcoming arms.

The breakfast room was a small, intimate room used for dining when there were only a handful of people sharing a meal. It was also one of the rooms his grandmother and mother had loved dearly. They said there was nothing like sitting at the table and watching the sunlight stream through the windows as it rose over the dewy gardens in the morning.

The open doors revealed that Edwin had already arrived. They exchanged a curt nod in lieu of any sort of greeting. Xander hadn't forgotten his friend's earlier deception. Xander's grandfather offered a greeting to Edwin as he took his seat at the head of the table, though the three of them were soon enveloped in a thick silence. Xander chose to sit at his grandfather's elbow, facing the door. The clock behind his grandfather ticked quietly, filling the void between the trio. Soft candle-light flickered from the candleholders in the center of the table. Xander's lips pulled into a tiny grin. He wondered if Nyla would replace them with a magic flame as he'd noticed she was doing at every opportunity.

Stifled giggles interrupted the quiet sanctuary of the breakfast room. Seconds later, Nyla and Meredith walked in, arm in arm. Their heads bowed close together, the pair were obviously in the midst of a deep conversation. A million possibilities raced through Xander's mind. Whatever it was that they were talking about, they stopped as soon as they'd fully stepped foot into the breakfast room. Merry turned her head away from his curious eyes and took her seat across from him. Nyla stifled her smirk, schooling her face into a polite smile before he could even guess what it was they'd been discussing. He could only hope it wasn't something he would be embarrassed by.

"Alexander," Nyla greeted, "Xander, Edwin."

"Nyla," his grandfather returned with an equally polite smile as she slid into the seat next to Xander. "Good evening, Meredith."

"It is, Grandfather," Merry said, placing her napkin on her lap. Edwin was forced to take the seat beside Merry, the one directly across from Nyla. Xander's gaze fixed on the lone chair without an occupant.

The seat at the other end of the table had remained empty for many years now. Xander couldn't remember the last time it had been filled. He supposed it was one of the last times his parents, grandparents, Issie, and himself had shared a meal. After his grandmother's passing, the breakfast room was seldom used, or at least by his grandfather. He didn't know if any of the other Huntingtons would've used the room for themselves. He barely had time to consider it before servants appeared from the adjacent kitchen and settled trays piled with food along the center of the table.

A round of thanks went around as each of their glasses was filled in turn before the last of the kitchen staff exited the breakfast room. Xander inhaled deeply. He'd missed this. Not necessarily the excessive amount of food, but the setting, being around other people, specifically people he cared about. Under the table, Nyla's foot accidentally nudged his leg. When he'd glanced over, she had a slightly amused look on her face shadowed by the smallest hint of bewilderment. He nudged her foot back.

"I trust your travel here was untroubled?" his grandfather asked, glancing at them as he reached for the dish closest to him.

Xander hesitated, stealing a glance at Nyla and then at Edwin. "Well…" he started, "our carriage was attacked on the way to Covington."

"By whom?" his grandfather asked, passing the dish to Merry.

"By *what*," Nyla muttered. Xander glanced at her in time to see her take a breath. "It wasn't really *who*, but more like some*thing* Dinora summoned to attack us. We aren't really sure what they were, but I have a small guess."

"Me too," Edwin added, filling his plate as the dishes made their way around the table.

"Well, someone might as well tell me."

Xander watched as a silent conversation passed between Edwin and Nyla. Nyla ultimately shrugged and said, "We know Dinora is the evil sorceress from the legends of the Shadow Forest, and it made me wonder what other truths were hidden behind the guise of mythology. I think the rock-creatures were somehow manifestations of the souls she took 647 years ago."

"But why are they rocks?" Edwin asked. "Why do they have to be the souls of those she killed?"

Merry whined, her eyes wide as she passed a dish to Edwin. "This is just wonderful dinner conversation."

Xander smiled at her. "I'm sure they're just stories."

"But that doesn't change what attacked you!" she pointed out, glancing around the table.

Xander wracked his brain for something to soothe her, but nothing came to him. Merry was old enough to know these things, even if she didn't feel prepared to handle them. He supposed it was better to ease her into these things than to let something burst that youthful innocence as had happened to him and his sister Issie.

His grandfather called the attention of the table with his steady words. "I guess now is as good a time as any to discuss why you've come to ask for help?"

Beside him, Nyla shifted in her seat and reached for her glass of water. Edwin sat back in his seat, his utensils crossed over his plate.

"It can't wait until after dessert?" Xander chanced. He knew they'd have to address why they'd come sooner rather than later, and ask why there were Royal Guards stationed around Pemberly, but he wasn't quite ready to tumble down the crest of his recent triumphs, of his homecoming.

"Afraid it'll ruin the chocolate-blackberry torte?" Nyla snickered.

"How did you—who told you?" Xander's brows raised.

"The walls."

Xander turned his eyes on his dearest cousin. Merry shrank in her seat, her shoulders drawing up around her ears as she avoided his gaze.

His lips curled slightly in amusement, caught between a smirk and a smile. "I'm sure the walls have a lot to say."

"I'm sure they do," their grandfather said. "Though I'm sure there will be time for all of that later. We are here, so we might as well use what time we have in privacy to discuss the matter now."

"Is there a reason we have a limited amount of privacy?" Nyla asked.

Xander snuck a glance at her from the corner of his eye. She didn't seem to be bothered by the realization. In fact, she was still occupied by her plate, cutting into another piece of jik and stabbing it with her fork.

"Yes," his grandfather said. "I've dispatched messages to many of my contacts, most of which have already assembled here to discuss Dinora's threat beginning tomorrow. Until then, I'd like to learn more about what's happening before we have to address the masses."

Xander stiffened. He hadn't known what to expect when he'd reached out to his grandfather for help. He certainly hadn't realized his grandfather would put things into motion before even meeting Nyla, let alone hearing what they had to say.

Just what was going on?

He didn't have time to ask as Edwin debriefed Alexander and Merry on what had happened at the Woodlane Manor from the moment he'd arrived to how Nyla had transferred the bond. They'd all long since finished their meals by the time Edwin was done, only occasionally interrupted by himself or Nyla to clarify something Edwin had overlooked.

His grandfather said nothing, his lips pursed in the silence. After a moment, he rang the bell to summon the kitchen staff, and there was a reprieve as the table was cleared. Edwin excused himself and promptly left the room, saying he needed to see to a task.

Nyla and Xander stood by the windows of the back wall overlooking the gardens. Cast in twilight, the sapphire and gray willow trees cast long shadows over the shaded pathways of his grandmother's garden. The gardens were kept just as she had left them, right down to the gazebo with climbing ivy along its pillars and the flowers that only bloomed under the full moon and the arching flower trellis that marked his grandmother's favorite spot for tea. Xander found himself smiling as he drank in the sight. Nyla didn't speak as she studied the gardens, though when he glanced at her, a soft smile graced her face even as her eyes had grown withdrawn.

Just as he was about to point out his grandmother's favorite place to her, the kitchen door swung open and stole his attention. Moretta came bustling into the dining room. His eyes lit up at the friendly face—and the decadent dessert on his grandmother's favorite cake plate.

His smile slipped as Moretta scowled at him. "Three years! Over three years and no sight of you!"

Clucking reproachfully, she set the platter down on the table as Merry and his grandfather reclaimed their seats. Hands on her hips, she bore down on him. "Well, what do you have to say for yourself, *Lord Alexander the Third?*"

"The third?" Nyla stifled a giggle and gravitated toward her chair at the table.

"And you." Moretta's tone softened as her attention shifted toward Nyla. "Welcome to Pemberly Hall. If you need anything, anything at all, come and find me."

"Oh, thank you," Nyla blinked, taken aback at Moretta's complete change in demeanor.

"Nyla, this is Moretta, Moretta, this is Nyla." Xander's breath hitched as Moretta's attention swung back to him.

Just as her fiery gaze pinned Xander to the spot, Nyla spoke again with the slight lilt of a laugh in her tone. "It's very nice to meet you, Moretta! Were you the one who taught Xander how to cook?"

Stunned out of her attempt to scold Xander, the fire in Moretta's eyes extinguished. "I was, yes, I was! Has he been treating you well?"

"Not like the roast jik tonight, but in all fairness, I'm not much of a cook in *good* conditions, and traveling is anything but!" Nyla laughed. "But no, Xander has been the best chef any traveling companion could want, even while we were without a kitchen."

"Good," Moretta sniffed, "it almost makes up for the fact that he never wrote or visited."

Nyla laughed, a sound that infected everyone in the room. Xander laughed despite himself, rubbing the back of his neck. "In my defense… okay, I don't have a defense, only a truly heartfelt apology."

Moretta smiled warmly, bringing him into a bone-crushing hug. "I accept your apology, but only because you've been good to Nyla."

"I missed you too, Moretta." Xander broke away from Moretta so the woman could head back into the kitchen and glanced over at Nyla. Raising an eyebrow, he said to her, "If Moretta knew how much of a mess you made this morning with your ponanchkas, she would faint."

Nyla glided to her chair, thanking him as he pulled it away from the table for her. "No one has to know about that."

"What are ponanchkas?" Merry asked, eyeing the torte with eager eyes.

"They're a breakfast dish my mother made a lot. It's an old family recipe she brought with her from Eurland," Nyla explained. "You serve them with a fruit compote, and it's the perfect blend of sweet and buttery and savory. It's like home on your tongue."

Xander's grandfather stood and began to cut the torte, passing a plate first to Merry and then to Nyla. He even served himself before serving Xander. "Your grandmother loved ponanchkas. She used to have them once a week or any time it was damp outside. She used to say that they warmed the soul."

Xander paused in his assault of the rich torte. He vaguely remembered a rainy morning spent in this very room with his grandmother, but didn't remember anything else, only the vague feeling of the memory.

Beside him, Nyla hummed. "Wow. This is *really* good."

"How have you been all over Tenebris, and *this* is good to you?" Merry asked. Xander remembered she wasn't a particular fan of chocolate, especially when it was so densely rich.

"Because I have never tasted something so delicious in my life," Nyla answered, taking another forkful and swiping it through the puddle of blackberry confit on her plate.

"Then you and Xander can fight over the last slice if you're so inclined to eat it for breakfast tomorrow morning," his grandfather said, finished with the small slice he'd given himself.

Nyla turned to him and batted her lashes. "This *is* the first time I've ever had a chocolate-blackberry torte."

Xander gave her a crooked smile, pushing his clean plate away. "I'll be nice and say whoever gets to the kitchen first tomorrow morning can have the last slice."

Nyla smirked wickedly, her eyes sparkling. "May the best person win."

"Well, now that the truly important matters have been settled," his grandfather started, drawing the table's attention, "perhaps now we had better discuss the business of why you've come."

Xander swallowed thickly. Maybe he should've forced Nyla into a full-fledged debate over the last slice of torte.

"Meredith," his grandfather continued, "why don't you go and torment Edwin for a while. I'm sure he has plenty more stories to tell you about their journey here."

Merry pouted, but slid out of her seat. Offering them all a solemn farewell, Merry said, "Goodnight then."

Xander felt a pang in his heart at the disappointment in her eyes, and found himself offering her a sympathetic lie. "Trust me, Merry, you aren't missing anything of interest. This is going to be long and boring, and Grandfather is probably going to give one of his long-winded lectures. I'd go with you, but I have to stay and listen."

At this, their grandfather cocked an eyebrow, but Xander's words had the desired effect on Merry. The ten-year-old bobbed her head and sped out of the room in search of something more interesting than the laborious conversation Xander had described.

With her departure, the gravity of the conversation ahead fell over the room and cast it into shadow. Xander's gaze fell to the table, his brows furrowed. Beside him, Nyla slumped back in her chair. Any sense of relief he'd found in finally being home deflated.

"Let me start with this: there are Royal Guards patrolling the estate, something I'm sure you've both noticed. They aren't exactly the stealth force the situation calls for, but their royal majesties insisted when they heard about Dinora." His grandfather paused, ensuring the weight of his words could settle on the stifling air in the breakfast room. "Secondly, the Heirs of Tenebris are an old society of people like myself who have been sworn to secrecy. We are the only ones to know and keep the full history of what happened 647 years ago. One day, that task will most likely be yours, Xander, as it is mine and was my father's and his mother's before, and so on through our family tree. I would have mentioned it sooner, though I didn't want to mention it in front of Merry. I fear she may not understand why this burden would likely fall to you and nag at some fault in herself, which is a disservice to the young lady she is becoming."

Xander blew out a breath. "How…how did our family become inducted into the Heirs of Tenebris? Who—"

"We are one of the founding houses of Tenebris. Ourselves, the Remington family, the Thornraven family, the royal family, of course, and the handful of others whose bannermen fought in the Ten Years' War." His grandfather waved his hand, as if that answer was sufficient enough. "As for the Heirs of Tenebris, Astrid Thornraven left rather explicit instructions for her most trusted allies, and those were the families who became the trusted keepers of this history."

Nyla lurched in her seat, sitting bolt upright as if in a panic. "Astrid formed the Heirs of Tenebris?"

"After her death, her instructions were revealed to a chosen few through a vision she'd created for them by way of some intricate spellwork and followed as willed, yes."

Nyla's wild eyes met Xander's. He nodded, encouraging her to tell his grandfather what he probably already knew.

"I—" She took a forced breath through her nose. "Somehow, Astrid and I are related. I'm not sure how, but we are. And I'm sure you already know this, being an Heir and all, but before Astrid was killed, she cast a spell that 'bequeathed' her magic to someone in her bloodline should there ever be a need for it. I inherited that magic like someone would a trinket."

His grandfather nodded contemplatively. "Yes, we were wondering about that. Tell me, how do you know you inherited Astrid's magic?"

"Look at me!" Nyla burst, more exasperated than angry. "I have her *silver* hair and *lilac*-colored eyes. Have you *seen* a portrait of Astrid? We're the spitting image of each other!"

His grandfather smiled kindly. "Yes, you are, but that could be genetics."

Nyla shook her head firmly. "It's not. My hair and eyes changed after…I used to have brown hair and eyes."

"You say they changed? How?"

Nyla's desperate eyes landed on Xander's. Nodding at the pleading gleam in her eyes, Xander took it upon himself to explain what Nyla didn't want to—or couldn't—explain.

"Nyla said that they slowly changed into the silver and then the lilac that they are now over a short period," he answered. But this didn't satisfy his grandfather.

"But *why?* Why did these changes happen?" he pressed.

"I don't know," Nyla said quietly, averting her eyes away from either of them. "All I know is that it happened after…after my family died, and that's all I'd like to say right now."

Xander's grandfather leaned back in his chair. Xander could see it in his eyes that he wanted to force Nyla to answer him. His hand found hers under the table, offering what little support he could, mentally preparing himself to discourage his grandfather from asking again. He was stunned as the tension eased from his grandfather's prim posture. The lord inclined his head like a bow. "I'll respect that. Maybe this conversation would be better had in the morning when we've all had some sleep."

"And the other Casters? When will we be speaking with them?" Nyla asked wearily.

Xander raised his eyebrow, glancing between the two. His grandfather met his eyes, just as stunned as he was.

Glancing back at Nyla, his grandfather's lips thinned. "And pray tell, how did you know that there were other Casters on the premises?"

"I can sense them." Nyla slowly raised from her seat. "But if that's all for tonight…I think I'd like to turn in for the evening. Thank you again for welcoming me into your home, Alexander. Dinner was amazing. Goodnight!"

"Goodnight," Xander and his grandfather echoed in tandem.

Once Nyla had left, his grandfather stopped him from following suit. Holding up his hand, his grandfather tilted his head, evidently waiting. Once he was certain of what he was waiting for had come to pass, his keen eyes drifted to Xander's.

"She's a very powerful Caster, isn't she?" he asked curiously.

Xander nodded. "She once obliterated an ogre, and that was *before* she knew she had magic." At his grandfather's questioning gaze, Xander added, "It's a long story, one that I think Nyla should really tell."

His grandfather's eyebrow raised in surprise. "Extraordinary…"

With a hard blink and the slight shake of his head, his grandfather's words pinned him in place before he could even attempt to excuse himself.

"It's time you learned about your legacy, Xander."

"My legacy?" Xander echoed. Sagging in his seat, Xander didn't know if it was the exhaustion of travel bearing down on his body or the resignation of yet another complication added to an already puzzling predicament.

"As I was saying earlier," his grandfather started, "our family and a handful of others are considered to be the founding families of Tenebris.

More than that, a select few of these families, ours included, founded the Heirs of Tenebris in the wake of the Corvid Uprising in honor of Astrid Genevieve Thornraven.

"I'm sure this will be difficult for you to understand, and I hadn't made any plans to pass this burden on to anyone anytime soon, but it seems that the powers that be have chosen for me," his grandfather continued. "And it just so happens that I choose you to succeed me should there be an Heirs of Tenebris to join once Dinora is defeated."

"Why?" It was all Xander could think to ask, for there was too much clouding his mind and tugging on his attention to truly focus on what mattered most.

His grandfather's eyes twinkled in a way he hadn't seen for a very long time, if ever in his whole life. "Because I'm proud of who you've shaped up to be, and couldn't think of someone worthier to protect our history and country than the only member of this family to have actually seen the country and its people from beyond the walls of our family name."

Xander's breath stuttered. He couldn't form a coherent thought, let alone the syllables needed to form a single word. Thankfully, his grandfather carried on, as if he didn't expect any response in the slightest.

"The Heirs of Tenebris was formed almost immediately after Lady Thornraven's death. Our records say that her image presented itself to the original members of the Heirs, urging them to form this society and protect Tenebris against the evils within and to ensure it did not rise again.

"And as the story goes, they had discovered her passing and answered her call. The Woodlane Manor had been abandoned during the war, and so the founding members took care to ward it against those who might seek it, effectively shielding it from the world and any prying eyes so as to prevent the magic, history, and threat that allegedly lurked within from destroying the country. The Corvid Uprising had left our country in tatters, as I'm sure you remember from your history lessons. It was then that the monarchy was dissolved, though the Caradels managed to keep their title and with it their lands, which was of grave importance to the Heirs of Tenebris, as they remain the wealthiest family in Tenebris and our primary source of funding.

"For all these years, we've relied on our own funds and influence to maintain the proper channels of knowledge and power so that if a threat like the Corvid Uprising ever rose against Tenebris again, we would be prepared." His grandfather paused, his brows drawn. "I suppose that after 647 years, none of us ever considered the legends to hold any truth."

Xander waited a beat before speaking, not wanting to interrupt his grandfather and what might be the only truth he and Nyla had discovered since her powers emerged. "So what you're trying to tell me is that even the Heirs of Tenebris began to believe that the Corvid Uprising, or rather the 'evil sorceress,' was just a myth?"

"It's been centuries." His grandfather bristled. "Of course we'd all begun to consider the possibility that this secret society was obsolete, and that our families had spent generations working in the shadows and keeping our positions in society, in politics, in the public sphere for no reason at all except for our own greed or ambition."

"Who else knows about the Heirs?"

"Not the Chamber of Commons or the Chamber of Justice," his grandfather replied with a wry smile, "though several Heirs have held positions through all levels of government throughout the centuries, just as our family and the Remingtons have remained in the public sphere through our business ventures."

Xander nearly fell off his seat. "Are you saying that you and George started the company for the sole purpose of the Heirs of Tenebris remaining relevant?"

His grandfather shrugged. "Not especially, no. We started it because it was a good business opportunity, but it's certainly proven helpful for the Heirs too in passing and gathering information through our shipments."

Xander clenched his jaw. His blood stilled in his veins. "Is this why my parents are dead?"

His grandfather sputtered. "Of course not!" His wide eyes shone earnestly. "Your parents' death was an accident. I've had three investigators look into it, and they've all come to the same conclusion. If it were anything different, I promise you I would've sought more than justice."

Xander studied his grandfather and his loss of composure. Sighing, he said, "I'm sorry for asking." He glanced away. "It's just always bothered me."

"Me too." His grandfather's hand landed on his shoulder. Xander's eyes flicked up. His grandfather offered him a forlorn smile. "There isn't a day that goes by that I don't feel some form of regret for what's happened. But now, I can see that the only way through it is to hope I can do better than before."

Xander nodded. "That's all we can ever do, isn't it?"

"I'm glad to have you home again, Xander."

"I'm happy to be home." Xander smiled.

Greed

Dinora paced the length of the cottage and back again. Her brows were drawn sharply over her eyes. No matter how hard she tried to think, the dark shadows swirling over her mind would not yield. Grinding her teeth, she ignored the ache in her jaw.

Nyla had defeated her creatures. But she'd had help, and if the images shown to her in the crystal ball were accurate, then the girl was on her way to receiving an army—a real, tangible force to defeat her while she was utterly defenseless.

Rounding on the cottage room at her back, Dinora's eyes landed on the raverin that had finally answered her call. All the beast was good for was perching itself on the darkened mantel. The beast watched her through half-lidded eyes. She clicked her tongue.

"Like you've ever been of any help to me," she muttered under her breath. If the beast even heard her, it showed no signs of the insult, though Dinora doubted it even understood her words anyway. It was a beast, nothing more. And if she were being completely honest with herself, it had served its purpose.

Dinora drew upon her power. Thrusting her hand out, a bolt of scarlet magic erupted from her fingertips. Its feathers rustled as it flapped its wings. Having narrowly avoided her magic, it *snapped* its long, scaly tail. The beast hissed at her. The plaster behind it smoldered. Delicate cracks laced the wall from where her magic had struck. Hovering over its perch, the raverin's eyes gleamed with a matched ferocity.

"You're lucky to be alive at all," she said, sending another wave at the beast.

The raverin dodged her attack, flapping its great wings once more. As it ascended higher, the beast nearly slammed into the ceiling from its swift efforts to avoid her attacks. The mantel fell with a great crash. Wood splintered off from where the underside slammed into the hard slate hearth. The beast *cawed* at her. With a flap of its large wings, Dinora held her breath, ready to strike again, but at the last moment, the raverin swooped over her.

Whirling around, Dinora just managed to see the beast fly through the open window, snapping its tail one last time before soaring into the sky.

She had no need of a messenger or a reminder of her son's failures.

What she needed was an army, something to overwhelm her adversaries. Three stone creatures hadn't been enough to stop or slow Nyla and that other Mage, but a whole army of them would prove most useful. The damned souls and rocks weren't an issue, but her waning magic was. Where was she to get the magic needed to raise such an army?

Dinora's lips curled into a wicked smile.

If memory served, there was one place in all of Tenebris where the overabundance of magic was ripe for the taking. And how poetic would it be to claim victory in the very place where she'd lost control of the war prior?

Without a moment's hesitation, Dinora darted to the workbench. Sweeping away the clutter from the wooden bench, she sought the quartz point her son had left behind. Without a wand, the crystal point was the best she could do to help contain and control the magic she intended to mine from the land.

If anything, Dinora grimaced, she'd learned from the mistakes of her past. All her life she'd trusted only herself, and the moment she'd dared to stray from that principle, she'd lost everything. Her empire, her status, her power.

Marveling at the smooth panes of the crystal point, Dinora's eyes dotted with hot tears. After so long, she'd nearly forgotten what it was like to stand on the precipice of conviction. It was empowering, but dangerous. Exciting, yet troublesome.

Fate was a fickle thing. She'd never dared to give it much of her faith before, and aside from that one blunder, she'd gotten everything she had ever dreamt of and aspired to have. She'd lost it all, of course, but this time…

This time, she would win it back, even if there was no one left to revel in her victory and the empire she sought to rebuild or the crown she planned to reclaim.

Let Fate be fickle, she resolved. Dinora knew who and what she was. A queen, a force to be reckoned with, a woman who'd triumphed and who would succeed once more.

21. THE LEADER WITH LILAC-COLORED EYES

Nyla replayed the conversation—or rather, the lecture—Lord Alexander had given them over breakfast about the day's itinerary and who would be attending what he'd called a "war council."

He'd explained who the Heirs of Tenebris were, and how the society was formed by Astrid in a vision that had appeared to the original members upon her passing. She didn't bother to correct him and mention that it was upon her murder that the founding members had received that vision, but the thought had crossed her mind.

In truth, her head was still spinning from his explanation of how the Heirs continued to ensure their families' relevancy all these centuries by holding positions of power or societal prominence. But it certainly explained why noble titles still existed and why the Caradel family had retained their lands, their palace, and their status as the royal family for most of Tenebris's history. It explained why their personal guard hadn't been dissolved, as the King's men were the unofficial militia of the Heirs of Tenebris, even as many of the society's members believed their role as Heirs to be antiquated or unnecessary as they too began to write the history off as nothing more than legend.

"That's Representative Wesson; she's the head of the security council in the Commons," Xander whispered. He'd been pointing various people out to her as they entered the great hall. Select politicians, members of the Tenebrese military, the Caster Corps, and the Royal Guard would be joining them. If Xander knew who they were, he hadn't pointed them out to her, though she doubted he did.

Nyla studied everyone as discreetly as she could. They seemed to form small groups or pairs around the room. The different classes of people were marked only by their robes and magic wands or, in the knights' case, their weapons, but otherwise, whatever Xander had told her of them was already lost in the fog of her mind. Her eyes flitted to the royals, King Albert and Queen Clarice of Tenebris, who were regally stoic in their expression, but Nyla noticed the pained fear in the corners of their eyes. Everyone knew the precipice on which the country stood, and that they were faced with the detrimental task of deciding its course in spite of what Fate and all the gods humanity believed in had already written.

She should've been nervous. A few weeks ago, Nyla would have run out the front doors of Pemberly Hall and never looked back. She would've run straight back through the Shadow Forest and up into the mountains that loomed in the distance of the Godberd Woods, a place she'd never been to before. But oddly enough, her nerves were quiet. They weren't quite calm, but they weren't writhing with uncertain terror either. While slightly malleable, her composure held firm enough to give her the illusion of being able to stand tall amongst the room of trained soldiers, decorative nobles, cunning politicians, and seasoned Casters.

Beside her, Xander shifted his weight from one foot to the other. "If I'd known about any of *this*," he murmured, "I probably would've cut ties with my grandfather forever. I mean, this is *crazy!*"

"As crazy as inheriting magic from an ancestor that was murdered over 600 years ago, and also a war?"

"Well, when you put it like *that*, I kind of inherited this war too."

She laughed, flashing him a grin. "Think it's too late to run?"

"Might be worth a try." Xander's eyes focused on something else, and Nyla followed his gaze, watching as Lord Alexander strode to the center of the room.

The quiet hum of conversations ceased. Nyla sobered as she watched Lord Alexander command the room's attention, even as he bowed to the Caradels seated at the front of the room. A few other people sat in the cushy armchairs along the perimeter, but most people stood, leaving the center of the room empty save for the man about to address them all.

"I am sure you are all aware why I have asked you here today." A few eyes shifted to Nyla. She pointedly ignored them. "For over 600 years, many of us in this room have been tasked with the sacred duty of keeping the darkest parts of the country's history in memory, even as it has faded from public recollection and devolved into fairytales and legends. I am also certain that as the centuries have passed, we have allowed ourselves to believe that this past is just that: the past, a myth, a legend that cannot harm us. But I stand before you today as a man of reason and skepticism. It is with the deepest regret that I must inform you all that this history is real, and the Corvid Uprising has survived for the last 647 years."

A low ripple of whispers circled the room. Nyla noticed the queen's hand subtly clench around the arm of her chair where it had previously been lax. Aside from the twitch of his brows, the king remained impassive. Her mind still digested their role as Heirs of Tenebris and how they'd stayed in power all this time, just so the Heirs would be able to operate if the legends came back to haunt Tenebris.

"By what evidence can you make this claim?" King Albert asked.

Nyla's gaze shifted to the monarch to find that his eyes were already fixed on her. She held his stare even as the hair on the back of her neck stood on end. Was she supposed to bow? Look away?

It didn't matter as Lord Alexander began to explain himself. "This young woman and my grandson visited the Woodlane Manor, unaware that Dinora Kashar was imprisoned there."

"Dinora Kashar?" a woman interrupted. "She would be nearly 700 years old if she were truly alive today."

Nyla stepped forward, joining Lord Alexander in the center of the room. "She survived. Even though her magic was limited and she was bound to the manor, she and her son both found a way to prolong their lives."

"And who are you in all of this?" the woman asked. She couldn't be older than thirty, but the steel in her eyes told everyone in the room that her soul was far more weathered than she appeared.

"I inherited Astrid's magic." Nyla's lip curled. "Before she was killed, the Royal Mage cast a spell that bequeathed her magic to another in her bloodline, and somehow I'm that person."

"Then why now?" Queen Clarice asked, peering curiously down her nose at Nyla.

"I know you're not one for formalities, but you should at least bow your head," Lord Alexander told Nyla under his breath.

Ignoring him, Nyla approached the royals with a polite smile. "Your grace," she started, "I am Nyla of Hart. I grew up there with my family and discovered the Woodlane Manor with my siblings. We went there often to play and explore, like our own little secret, but never once did Dinora show herself while we were there. Xander and I returned there last week after I'd discovered my magic and began seeking answers as to why my magic suddenly appeared. This was when Dinora showed herself and later attacked us with the help of her son, Cedric."

"And what of her son if she has escaped?" King Albert countered measuredly.

Nyla hesitated. "We believe he's gravely injured or dead."

"What led you to return to the Woodlane Manor? You said that you sought answers about your magic there, but what led you to believe the manor could provide them?" Queen Clarice's voice was soft and dainty, a complete contrast to the feminine armor beneath her regal cloak Nyla hadn't noticed before.

"It's a long story, your majesty," Nyla offered with a slight frown, "but I'd astral traveled there and spoken with Astrid briefly. At the time, I didn't realize what astral projection was and thought it was a dream, but I recognized that we had stood in the Woodlane Manor."

"Why not ask your family?" Queen Clarice asked. At her hushed tone, Nyla knew this was meant to be solely between themselves with only the king as their witness.

"They passed away." Nyla swallowed hard. Bowing her head, she turned to address the room. There was no sense in trying to avoid her family's deaths. She realized its significance in the chain of events that had since transpired and could transpire. She briefly caught Xander's eye. His lips were pursed, his eyes stern as if he too, realized what she was about to explain at the mercy of all of these strangers.

"Two years ago, my family died in a fire. I was the only survivor because I hadn't been in the house when the fire was set." She struggled through the statement and forced herself to push on. "I ran away a few days after the fire because my hair started to turn silver, and…I believed I saw someone that I'd never seen before and that they were still there and that they were somehow still watching me."

People began to avoid her gaze as she addressed the room. Lord Alexander and Xander watched her solemnly, becoming anchors for her when her words faltered or she found that she didn't want to go on.

"After two years of trying to outrun my instincts and the fear they brewed, I traveled to Fortune Falls, where I not only discovered my powers, but learned the truth about the fire that had killed my family. The Falls showed me three visions, the first of which confirmed my deepest fears that someone was there the day of the fire who shouldn't have been, the second was a battle scene that I believe to be the one from the legends of the Shadow Forest, and the final showed that Cedric had in fact been watching me all this time. It's my belief that Cedric set the fire, and that Dinora has likely been communicating with him from within the manor throughout these past six centuries."

Nyla took a breath, glancing at Lord Alexander for a moment, but in her hesitation, another man spoke.

"I remember that investigation," he said. Nyla turned her eyes on him as he stepped forward. One of the Royal Guard, marked by his sword and indigo cloak. As her gaze fell on him, he bowed his head. Brief recognition scratched at her mind. Xander had pointed him out to her earlier as Sir Hubert, the Commander of the Royal Guard. A long, puckered scar adorned one half of his face, but there was an overall gentleness to his demeanor that made Nyla instantly want to trust him. "I'm truly sorry for your loss. We never could figure out how the fire was set, but now…it's all beginning to make sense."

Nyla nodded her head, her mouth dry. Had this man harbored guilt for being unable to provide answers for all these seasons? Had the fire scarred more than just her own life?

Taking in the scores of people gathered around the room once more, Nyla found her answer. The fire and loss of her family had only been the beginning of a new era of Dinora's vengeance, a continuation of the war previously lost to history. Her eyes landed on Xander, his dark eyes flooding with concern as worry creased his brow. She offered him a small smile, finding her voice and heart again.

"Dinora and Cedric have been plotting for centuries, and now that Dinora is freed from the bond that prevented her from leaving the Woodlane Manor before, *she will not stop*," she said. "Dinora wants all of us dead and our country destroyed. She's willing to do *anything* to get what she wants, a fact she's proven during the Corvid Uprising. All those legends about the Shadow Forest being haunted by the souls of those she betrayed or took, I think they've manifested in the rock points. I think she's managed to bring them to life, as we were attacked on our way here by stone creatures. I can't be certain, but I think they were the stone points of the Shadow Forest."

"That's ridiculous," one of the Royal Guards scoffed. "Rocks were never alive to begin with, so they can't be brought to life."

"They could be animated and manipulated by magic," one of the Casters countered. The man was average-sized, but his posture told Nyla that he was someone of importance, and he knew it too. Even his richly made robe was embroidered with an iridescent silver thread that gave the black material life and status.

"I think the *stone points* are representations of the souls she took in her quest for power 600 years ago, or maybe their physical presence, given that there's the wisps of smoke to account for too." Nyla's statement was met with hushed conversation and blatant disagreement. Sensing the pungency of their disbelief, Nyla asked, "Have any of you actually studied the rock points? Felt the energy they give off? Have any of you actually *been* to the heart of the Shadow Forest, or are you too busy guarding the world from the comforts of your own homes?"

"Nyla," Lord Alexander said sharply.

"Oh, I like her," a voice nearly purred from behind them. Nyla's blood stilled. Whoever had spoken had a low, smooth voice with a little rasp in it. Nyla slowly turned to face the speaker. From the corner of her eye, she could see the Casters stand just a little straighter and the soldiers go the slightest bit tense. "You have potential."

Nyla lightly tilted her head. This woman reminded her of Astrid in the vision the Falls had shown her. Tall, lithe, commanding.

"Nyla, meet the Mage General and Royal Mage, Ingrid Ravencroft. Ingrid, this is Nyla, Astrid's heir," Lord Alexander introduced with a gentle bow.

"Ah. So you're the one Frederick will be training. My condolences to Frederick." She smirked, a twinkle in her eyes. "I do hope you won't be too hard on my second-in-command."

At this, the man in the black robe with silver embroidery came forward. "General."

"I'm glad you could join us, Ingrid. I almost believed we would have to defeat this evil without you." Queen Clarice's soft voice echoed through the room with enough bite that Nyla reconsidered the woman's friendliness and calm.

"Your majesties," Ingrid started, "forgive my lateness, but I was involved. Evil can only be fought if you've found it first."

"And have you found her?"

Ingrid's lips pulled into a thin line. "I'm afraid not yet." The queen huffed impatiently, but before she could reprimand the Mage General, the woman whistled and addressed the room again. "I did, however, find *him*."

Nyla turned just in time to watch as two Casters hauled a man into the room. Hardly held upright between the two Casters on either side of him, Nyla took in the bloodstained clothes, the ragged appearance, and the fear beginning to brim in her blood. She stared, her body completely rigid now. Even without having seen his face, she knew it was him, the red-eyed man that had terrorized her for two years, the man she blamed for the murder of her family, and the man she'd *almost* hoped she'd killed.

Her eyes flicked to Xander. If she thought her blood boiled, it was nothing compared to the loathing that had etched itself on Xander's face, his jaw clenched tightly.

"This is Cedric Kashar, former crown prince of the old Empire of Corvus."

Ingrid's words were met with cold silence. Nyla forced her hands to still, for the anger and fear simmering in her blood to stay. There was no telling what it would have her do if she didn't focus on taking one breath at a time. A tiny part of her said that she would kill him, and make certain of it this time. Another part of her wanted to wrap herself in her magic, a shield in which she could hide away if only to keep the others from seeing the emotional onslaught wreaking havoc on her mind.

At the sound of his name, Cedric forced his head up. He was paler than usual. Grogginess clung to his features like the darkness Nyla imagined lurked in his aura. She didn't dare focus her sight long enough to see it. His scarlet-colored eyes could barely focus, let alone keep themselves open.

"Get him out of my sight *now*," she gritted through her teeth.

The weight of Ingrid's gaze further rooted her to the spot. "Lord Huntington, it's my understanding that you have a secured dungeon from the old days?"

"I do. The warding may need to be updated, but the structure is usable," he answered with a certain shortness to his words.

"You heard the heir—get him out of here," Ingrid ordered.

"Edwin, show them the way."

Nyla watched as Cedric was hauled from the room with Edwin in the lead. A handful of soldiers and Casters followed on their heels. She had half a mind to follow after them, but knew no good would come of it.

"Xander," Lord Alexander started quietly, "perhaps you should take Nyla back to her room while we—"

"No." Nyla snapped out of the haze Cedric's appearance had put her in. "I'd like to stay."

"It is your future we're discussing anyway," Ingrid said, drawing the room's attention back to herself.

As Ingrid began to tell the tale of how and where she'd found Cedric, Nyla stalked back to stand in the shadows of the room beside Xander. She crossed her arms over her chest. Her eyes tracked Ingrid as she paced the length of the room, only half listening through the cotton in her ears as her mind remained fixed on Cedric.

"Are you okay?" Xander had shuffled closer to whisper in her ear.

"No," Nyla muttered under her breath, fighting off the itch in her hand to reach for his. She didn't know if that would actually offer her the stability she sought, but if she didn't find something to ground herself soon, she wasn't certain what would happen. All she knew was a pounding headache in her temples. "I'd gotten used to the idea of him being dead. I'd even come to terms with his death being my fault."

From across the room, Frederick watched her interaction with Xander. She leveled her scowl on him until he glanced away. At this point, Ingrid's story registered with her.

She'd managed to track Cedric's essence to the Amber Dunelands in eastern Tenebris, near the sea. It'd taken a huge amount of magic for him to wisp from the Woodlane Manor, a feat Ingrid admitted she didn't think him capable of. By the time she and her team had found him, he'd healed himself enough to survive. A previously cast spell and enchanted talisman aided in his ability to mask his signature and presence.

His weakened state and the lack of magic available in the Dunes wasn't enough to hide nor heal him. Ingrid admitted that his capture was as much chance as it was their efforts to find him.

"Can he be of any use to us in defeating Dinora?" King Albert asked after a brief conversation with the queen.

Ingrid hesitated, evidently contemplating Cedric's merits. "Perhaps, perhaps not. I am not of the belief that Cedric was anything more than a pawn to his mother, only a means to an end."

"It's true," Nyla said, more surprised by herself than anyone in the room. She glanced uncertainly at Xander. He offered her a small smile. "When Cedric showed up at the Woodlane Manor before Dinora was freed, she…she's not the loving mother type. I don't think there is much of a relationship binding them together aside from their blood."

She'd essentially called him worthless. It was a fact that Dinora had probably made known to him all 600 and however many years of his life.

Why would he have helped her when she gave him nothing? Why betray Astrid when the alternative was a cold, ruthless woman incapable of loving him at all?

Nyla couldn't fathom it. Not just all that Cedric had done for a mother who wouldn't ever love him, but also the fact that there were people like Dinora who only ever took, leaving empty shells and broken pieces of people in their wake.

The king sat back in his chair, crestfallen. Queen Clarice laid a hand over his, and they shared a rather hopeless look before she addressed the room.

"Then what are we to do? We can't have an all-out war," she stated firmly. The handful of representatives present nodded or offered vague utterances of agreement. Queen Clarice continued, "It will only panic the country, disrupt our way of life, and dredge up old resentments. As a country, it is our understanding that we cannot afford a war if we want to maintain the quality of life our people have, and it is not wise to be at the mercy of others' charity and interest in our affairs."

"Your majesty, if I may," Sir Hubert started, "Mage General Raven-croft and I have discussed the matter at length and believe that the best strategy is to mount a limited offense of both Casters and the Royal Guard in a joint effort led by Mage General Ravencroft."

King Albert's eyebrow raised. Before he or the queen could say a word, Lord Alexander cleared his throat, bringing the room's attention back to him.

"History tells us," Lord Alexander began, "that when Astrid Thorn-raven was the Royal Mage, she assumed the role of leading the king-dom's forces after the horrendous Battle of Endpoint, where now stands Fortune Falls and the heart of the Shadow Forest, thus becom—"

A clock chimed the hour. It was nearly lunch time, and as the *gongs* rang clear through the room, everyone glanced toward the bright light of day streaming in through the windows. Nyla had almost forgotten the daylight smiling outside this room, and probably would have if not for the clock.

"We should reconvene after we've all had some time to digest recent developments and mull over the circumstances," Lord Alex-ander suggested.

"I agree." The Royal Mage leveled her gaze with each person in turn as if challenging them to disagree. Even the most divisive politicians Xander had pointed out to Nyla now averted their eyes as if they feared Ingrid would turn *them* to stone. She glanced toward the king and queen. "Does this suit your majesties?"

King Albert inclined his head. "We all have much to think about. A brief reprieve to clear our heads might do us some good."

Nyla found herself leaning into Xander with relief. He wrapped an arm around her hip and whispered. "Last I checked, that torte was still in the kitchen…"

"Split it with me?" She'd forgotten all about the leftover slice from last night's dessert when she'd realized the war council was meeting today, and that Lord Alexander had already set an offensive in motion in the time between receiving Xander's note and their arrival.

"It's a deal," he promised, guiding her from the room. A few others had already broken away from the gathering and could be seen a few idle steps ahead, their heads bowed together and whispering with the person beside them.

"Nyla," Ingrid called.

She groaned and forced herself to turn around as Xander's arm fell from around her waist. Meeting the eyes of both the Mage General and Frederick, Nyla found herself wishing she'd ignored the woman's call. "Yes, Ingrid?"

"You will begin training with Frederick this afternoon."

"And what, exactly, am I training for?" Nyla asked with irritation in her voice. She knew there was still a lot about how to wield magic that she didn't know, though she hadn't realized others would've noticed that too. Or rather, that they would feel the need to train her themselves. It didn't seem like she had any choice in the matter, a theme she hoped wouldn't continue.

"To begin with, I will be assessing your magical ability," Frederick explained. "Then I'll begin training you in the best magic practices to help build and maintain strength."

"And Dinora?" Nyla again looked to Ingrid.

"What about her?" The woman countered with a dismissive shrug.

"If it's already been decided that Frederick will be training me, what else has been decided on my behalf?" Nyla's features twisted into a scowl as her anger grew to a crescendo.

Frederick frowned at her reproachfully, opening his mouth to say something, but Ingrid cut him off. "Nothing has been decided. I want you to train so that when decisions need to be made regarding Dinora and whatever part you want to play in this conflict, they can be made soundly."

Nyla arched her brow. "Is that so?"

"It is." Ingrid nodded. She sighed breezily, watching the people streaming around them for a second before speaking again. "Enjoy the recess. They never last long enough." With that, she began to walk away with a glowering Frederick at her heels.

Nyla and Xander watched them walk down the hall. Stragglers filtered out of the meeting room. Nyla shot him a simmering look. He met her eyes with a placating gesture and a quirked smile.

"I knew nothing, I swear."

"I know," she said, taking a step down the hall. Shrugging off her irritation as best as she could, she added, "Now, I believe you promised me there was still a slice of that torte left?"

"And you," Xander said, putting his arm around her shoulders, a gesture she returned by wrapping an arm around his waist and tucking herself into his side as if he could shield her from the impending storm of people and decision-making and a literal battle for Tenebris's survival, "promised you'd share?"

"I remember no such thing," she teased, intertwining her free hand with Xander's dangling over her shoulder.

"We—well, *you*, could always ask Shamira to come back. It wouldn't hurt to have an ally fighting for *you*," he suggested.

Nyla silently agreed, already withdrawn into the chaos of her mind. Fragments swirled around in a flurry of anger surrounding Cedric's appearance. Other thoughts worried at the idea of strangers making decisions about *her* life without ever considering her and her thoughts or feelings.

Even though she didn't quite know what she wanted, she knew she didn't want to concede her stake in the matter. Dinora was free because of *her*. *She'd* inherited Astrid's magic. Cedric and Dinora had killed *her* family. So why shouldn't she decide what part she wanted to play in defeating Dinora? Didn't she have that right?

And suppose she was the only one who *could* defeat Dinora? Wasn't that what Fate had seemingly set up? Astrid's spell had made it so her magic would only be bequeathed to someone in her bloodline if and when Dinora became a threat again. With that in mind, it did seem like Fate had chosen her for this task.

Nyla knew the only way to stop Dinora was to kill her. She didn't know if that was a burden she wanted, or if it would even be her burden to bear. And like the royals, war wasn't something Nyla wanted to see, and perhaps Fate didn't either. She wanted to stop Dinora, but… at what cost to herself or to Tenebris?

Maybe she should let the adults and Heirs of Tenebris decide their course of action. Maybe she didn't want any accountability at all. She had every right to hide in the safety she was certain Xander and his grandfather would grant her at Pemberly if she wanted no part in having to kill Dinora.

Fate had given her this choice. Now she only had to make it.

22. TO BECOME A WARRIOR

Nyla wished she and Xander hadn't split the remainder of the chocolate torte. Its density sat in the pit of her stomach as she followed Frederick down the winding garden paths of Pemberly's court-yard. The remnants of its rich flavor burned like acid on her tongue now. It didn't help that when they'd finally reached their destination, Frederick had hardly said two words to her before he'd begun to circle her in a way that made her feel like prey—a feeling she'd managed to overcome for too short a time.

"Your stance is weak, like that of a beginning Caster who has little to no education on wielding magic," he said. His voice was smooth like the velvet robe he wore. She wondered how he could manage to wear such a thing with the sun blazing down upon them and the humidity in the air that made even her cotton sleeves hug her skin. "You'll never be able to produce or deflect a strong attack. Square your shoulders, widen your stance, and bend your knees slightly. In doing so, you can put your whole body into your magic."

"What about intention?" she asked, following him with her eyes until he came to a stop in front of her. She matched the slight tilt of his head, staying her hands at her sides. Frederick pursed his lips, and she couldn't help but imagine what Cedric must've been like six and a half centuries ago. Did he have the same sort of authority and ego that Frederick possessed? If he was tasked with teaching magic, would he use the same methods of instruction?

Nyla had always assumed teachers were warm and encouraging. Her mother certainly had been, and so were her other teachers growing up. Even when they were correcting a mistake, they managed to do so with a gentle guidance that led to a new discovery or wisdom in the end—a lesson she'd never forgotten.

"What about it?" Frederick shrugged dismissively, nearly leering at her.

Nyla pressed her lips together. A prickle of irritation grew and rippled through her like lightning. Slowly, so as to control her rising temper, she said, "Shamira told me that magic is about imagery and intent. If I know my intention, why would I need a particular stance?"

Frederick let out a long-suffering sigh. Turning to the side, he began to pace before her again. Nyla rolled her eyes. As his voice rolled over her, she found herself crossing her arms and shifting her weight, slouching to one side. "What good is intention and imagery when an opponent's magic is physically more powerful than your mind, when it cuts you down because you have not braced for it? By all means, rudimentary skills are a foundation, but they are not the end. You may know a little, but it's what you *don't* know that will put you and others in danger. If you refuse to acknowledge the limitations of the mind, then you will cease to grow as a magic user. That is why we are training today. Now stand straight."

Nyla narrowed her eyes. While his words hadn't been overly offensive, she couldn't help but feel as though they masked an insult behind his instruction.

Still, she forced herself to adjust her posture, willing to at least *try.* Ingrid, one of the most powerful Casters in Tenebris based on her station as the Royal Mage and Mage General, had wanted Frederick to train her in magic, so she'd do her best.

Nyla assumed that this was a test and that failing it wasn't an option she could afford. Her mind provided her with the memory of Edwin's warning.

He'd told her to expect anything. He'd specifically mentioned that she should expect even the smallest acts of deception, but how was she being deceived in this moment? Was that the goal of this training session? To trick her in some way?

Or was it something different?

If this was a test, an evaluation of her skills in wielding magic, what did it mean? Why were they testing her? What outcome did they hope for, and which outcome would allow her the freedom to be as she was?

The question lingered in her mind as she adjusted herself, trying desperately not to squirm under Frederick's intent stare.

As Frederick circled her one last time, nudging her foot so she widened her stance just the slightest bit, Nyla couldn't stop the anger she felt in her blood from darkening her features.

The thought that foundations were meant to be built upon instead of abandoned for a new house crossed her mind just as Frederick had come to stand in front of her once more.

"Good," Frederick started, taking a step back from her. Taking in her glare and the tight twist of her lips, Frederick arched his brow, frowning mockingly at her. "I'm sorry if formal instruction is disagreeable to you, but you need to learn how to wield your magic properly, if not for your participation in defeating Dinora, then to at least understand the relationship between magic and Casters, *not* wielders. Shamira was a pumpkie. Our magics are different, and in truth, I believe our methods are more refined."

Nyla gritted her teeth.

Frederick stared at her, a gleam in his eyes that she could only assume was amusement. By the suspicion crawling over her skin like the phantom webkers of the Woodlane Manor once had, she knew that twinkle was at her expense.

"I won't pretend to know how difficult this all must be for you, what with your upbringing—"

"My upbringing was *perfect*," Nyla seethed. Her hands clenched into fists at her sides. A spark of magic flooded her veins, frothing like seafoam on the tip of a rolling wave in her bloodstream. "Though I can't imagine you were raised to be so cruel."

"You think I'm cruel?" he laughed. Sobering, he leveled her with an authoritative stare that didn't quite suit him. "You know nothing of the world if you think this is cruelty. I don't know what it was like in Hart, but here, you can't just run amok and expect to be given what you want. Here, you earn your rewards and your station. You earn your respect, and when you fail, you lose it, and you face the consequences of your actions. *This* is how the world works. The world doesn't wait for you to mature with it. It moves on, and if you must insist on fighting me through every step of this process, this war effort will move on without you as well."

Nyla lifted her chin. "You can't earn the respect of someone who's already decided against you, as you have to me."

Frederick scoffed. "It's not my duty to like or respect you. I don't need to in order to teach you the proper way to wield magic."

"There's more than one way to wield magic," Nyla said smoothly, a dangerous edge to her voice. "Just because this is the way you know and have taught others doesn't make it the proper way."

"Since you know so much," Frederick sneered, "perhaps we'd better begin." He clasped his hands behind his back. His eyes bore into her. "When facing an opponent, you cannot rely on the idea that you will have time to gather your magic. *That* is why stance is so important. Sir Maffis will assist us in this portion of the lesson."

Nyla's eyes flicked toward the movement of a lone figure approaching them over Frederick's shoulder.

"I believe you two have already been acquainted, so we shall skip the introductions," he continued as Edwin came to a stop beside him. She wanted to ask him what he was doing here, but hadn't the time to utter a single syllable before Frederick was speaking again, explaining how Edwin would demonstrate the proper technique as he went on instructing.

Nyla spared a pleading glance toward the sky. This was truly going to be a long afternoon spent with Edwin serving as a model pupil and Frederick admonishing her every time she got something wrong.

But she wouldn't give him the satisfaction of giving up. She wanted to learn, even if her teacher had no interest in encouraging her or guiding her.

By the time she was finally allowed to summon her magic, Nyla's heart knew a weariness she hadn't felt in days. Trying to remember the different forms and stances Edwin had demonstrated was impossible. Frederick didn't miss a single opportunity to correct her, even if her stance was only a fraction off from the "proper" form. And with each correction he made, Nyla began to wish that Edwin was the one teaching her.

For all their differences in character, for all the reservations she held against him, he at least was kind and patient. He at least respected her, or so she assumed.

But Frederick, for whatever reason, didn't.

As the afternoon surrendered to early evening, and Nyla was forced to call upon her magic over and over again without ever actually expelling it, she couldn't help but wonder what would happen if she let some of it loose on Frederick, as a training accident.

Surely, Corruptio would understand her reasoning for doing so. After all, it couldn't possibly be healthy to summon her magic this much, stoking it from scarce embers to an instantaneous wildfire, only to never expel it. As it was, she could feel it lingering beneath the surface of her skin, buzzing in her blood, and licking at her bones like icy waters.

Her magic wanted freedom, to be released, nearly as much as she wanted to slap the self-satisfied smile from Frederick's face.

"I think that's enough for today, Sir de Chante. It's getting late, and I'm sure the Huntingtons will expect Miss Delhart at dinner," Edwin said.

Long shadows stretched across the cobblestone square hidden amongst the courtyard's winding paths. The waning sun glared in the sky above, as if it too were irritated by his entire person for simply existing.

Nyla sagged with relief at Edwin's words, even as she doubted she'd make it to dinner.

With a long sigh, Frederick waved his hand dismissively. "Of course. Please offer my apologies to our hosts for keeping you so long. I expect tomorrow should prove to be successful now that you know what to expect from these sessions, Miss Delhart."

Nyla opened her mouth to offer one final barb, but Edwin cut her off. Her eyes slid to him as she pressed her lips together.

Edwin didn't acknowledge her. "I'm sure it will, Commander." Turning to her, Edwin offered a civil smile. His eyes flashed pleadingly, as if he knew exactly what was going through her mind. And he probably did, given how she was certain her sour mood was written plainly on her face. "Care to accompany me to dinner, miss?"

She narrowed her eyes. Exhaustion clung to her mind like cobwebs. Finding that she couldn't bother to care about Edwin's motivations, Nyla shrugged and silently took his offered arm. She didn't offer a single glance toward Frederick, or a word of parting. While Edwin had probably saved her from her own tongue, Nyla still wanted the slight satisfaction of being petty. It seemed about the only bit of enjoyment she could get from these training sessions, however long she was expected to undergo them.

Once she was certain Frederick was out of earshot, she whispered to Edwin, "So it's 'Miss Delhart' now?"

"Only when Frederick's concerned," he muttered.

Nyla furrowed her brow. "Why?"

Edwin sucked in a breath and seemed to hold it as they finally rounded the corner of the hedge-lined path, leaving Frederick far behind them and yet not far enough away for her taste, Nyla found herself grateful toward the man beside her.

Not only had he stopped Frederick from continuing, but she now realized there was no way she could've gotten this far on her own two feet as she leaned more of her weight on him for support.

"Frederick is…well, adept at the art of political relationships…" Edwin hesitated. "His family isn't very prominent, but you wouldn't know it with the way they act, or how many people they've managed to ensnare in their bid to elevate themselves. It's all because of their ability to manipulate relationships in their favor or trap people into owing them favors that they've managed to rise through society."

"So it's nothing against me personally," Nyla mused. "He's just ambitious and feels training me is a waste of his efforts?"

"I'm sorry he was so abrasive," Edwin said quietly. "He's a difficult teacher."

Nyla snorted, too exhausted to care whether or not Edwin was acting as the friend he was to Xander or as the subordinate he apparently was to both Lord Huntington *and* the Royal Mage. A man of many masters, she wondered when he found the time to listen to his own head and heart.

"He's a jerk, you mean."

Edwin's laugh was like a puff of air, as if he didn't want to allow himself to fully realize his own amusement. "Your words, though I don't disagree."

They'd hardly made it a few more steps up the garden path before Edwin came to a stop, stepping in front of her to face her. "You should get some rest. I know what you just went through was different from how you're used to conjuring magic, and I can't imagine your magic liked it very much. I know I had a difficult time after facing those creatures with you. I'd never wielded my magic quite like that before."

Nyla's lips fluttered, on the verge of offering a smile through her exhaustion. "How did you manage, then?"

Edwin smirked. "As I recall, we both took naps immediately

afterwards. That seemed to help my headache a great deal and the buzzing in my veins."

"You feel that too?" she asked. Edwin glanced at her peculiarly. Swallowing uncertainly, she pushed for an answer. "Does magic feel the same to every Caster?"

"I…I've never thought about it," he admitted. "I suppose it must," he added, turning slowly on his heel and resuming their hike back to Pemberly. Nyla slowly ambled down the path, falling a step behind him until he matched her pace once more. "I don't think anyone's ever spoken about it, not at the university anyway. By that point, most Casters are already aware of how to summon and wield their magic because of their informal training with other Casters related to them or through the university's outreach programs for young Casters. Either way, no one ever really talks about what magic feels like when you wield it."

Nyla hummed, too tired to respond as she trudged along beside him.

She wondered if her training with Shamira diminished her abilities in the eyes of most human magic users, or if it didn't matter how she was taught or what she believed in when it came to wielding magic.

Perhaps all that mattered was her intent. And she had no intention of betraying what she felt was right, no matter who or what tried to convince her otherwise.

As they reached the stairs leading into Pemberly Hall, Edwin pulled away from her. His smooth voice broke through her thoughts. "You wield magic differently than the way most of us have been taught," he said. At his words, her irritation flared once more. As if he could sense it, he gave her a pacifying smile, his eyes twinkling humorously. "I didn't mean that in the way Frederick would. I just meant…it's a different style. The way you wield magic isn't any less than the way we've been taught—don't ever let anyone lead you to believe it is. If you do, then they'll sweep you up in the undertow, and you'll lose yourself to their whims. Don't let that happen, Nyla."

Nyla blinked, surprised. "Thank you, Edwin. That means a lot to me."

23. HOWLS OF WAR

She'd only had an evening, but already Shamira found herself staring at the magical boundary between the human lands and their shielded domain. All around her, scores of pumpkies from the three clans had gathered. For the first time in six centuries, the pumpkies were leaving the home they'd carved for themselves in the midst of humanity.

Shamira had never thought she'd see the day when the three clans would come together again, let alone for the purpose of leaving their realm to help the humans of Tenebris.

I've never been this close to the veil before, Talmec said, breaking the anxious silence amongst the pumpkies.

No one has except for Shamira and the High Seer, Elder Hecates answered. *Sometimes the Elder Councils visit the veil to strengthen the wards, but aside from that, no one comes near enough to the veil to consider leaving.*

And how would you know that? Shamira asked.

Elder Hecates smirked at her. *The Councils have their ways.*

Of course they do, Shamira muttered before she could stop herself.

Beside her, Talmec snickered, but Elder Hecates remained silent. The pumpkie was almost pensive. A few other Elders from the Reyhart and Zeldher clans had joined their ranks, but the majority of the Elders—and the pumpkies as a whole—had chosen to remain within the safety of the realm. Shamira knew it was for the better. The more pumpkies that stayed behind, the more magic they could rely on as a reserve.

Unlike humans, pumpkies often shared magic with each other. They also borrowed magic from the land around them, but not like the way Dinora had stolen it. The magic they borrowed was easily replenished.

The land absorbed magic just as much as the world emitted it. From the sun's rays to the wind blowing off of the oceans, the world was full of magical energy. Anyone could harness it—for a price. Oftentimes, that price could be paid upon their passing.

But sometimes, Casters took too much, and it destroyed not only the source they'd stolen it from, but also themselves.

It was uncanny and impossible that Dinora had managed to steal so much from the land and hadn't died from the consumption. It wasn't possible—or at least, it shouldn't have been possible.

One day, Shamira would learn how she'd done it. She had no inclination to replicate Dinora's methods, but her curiosity wouldn't be sated until she'd learned *how* Dinora and Cedric had accomplished such a feat. To have harnessed and contained so much magic within herself…Dinora didn't seem strong enough to do so. Shamira couldn't recall any spells that would've allowed Dinora and Cedric to exceed their physical capabilities, but she knew Cedric to be a clever Caster. He would've mastered or contrived some way for them to do so.

I truly hope you aren't waiting for me to lead the way, Shamira, Elder Hecates said. *You are the only pumpkie to have left the realm in centuries. You are leading our kind into battle.*

I— Shamira blinked, whipping her head around in his direction. *Thank you, Elder Hecates.*

High Seer Kasand thought it for the best, he admitted. *Now, we'd best be off…* Elder Hecates paused. *Going through the veil isn't painful, is it?*

No, she assured him, *going through the veil is painless,* she broadcasted to the assembled pumpkies. *We have many miles before we reach the heir, but before we descend on the humans, I will contact her to ensure all of*

Tenebris knows we come as allies. We all know the risks of our decision to aid our human allies against this threat, but I have no doubt that Moerae's hand will guide us and grant us victory against an old and feeble, though no less dangerous, threat, just as She has in centuries past.

Her speech was met with howls and roars of approval. Baring her teeth as if the enemy stood before her, Shamira stepped through the shimmering veil. Stepping out onto the other side, the Elders and Talmec were close behind her with the scores of pumpkies from across the three clans filing through after.

Without a glance back toward her home, for the fear that she wouldn't have the strength to carry on, Shamira led the way down the steep mountain path.

***

By the time the company had descended from the mountaintop realm and into the lower-lying Godberd Woods, Shamira was on edge. Sniffing the air, she recognized the Shadow Forest's scent. It wasn't the spicy Harvum tang of the Godberd Woods, but the musky scent of the Shadow Forest in the undercurrent that set her fur on edge. Taking in the honey-golden trees and Harvum-kissed leaves of the Godberd Woods, Shamira searched for what she couldn't see, hoping she could trace Dinora's essence back to her.

As the other pumpkies made camp and hunted for their dinners, Shamira wandered off, leaving the Elders with a few words of caution before she found a secluded spot amongst a copse of trees.

Nyla? Shamira prayed the girl had enough energy to converse with her, or was in a place where she could do so.

Yeah? She sounded exhausted, as if she'd used a lot of magic recently. No, that wasn't quite it. She was tired, but not physically. Something had taxed her emotionally.

You've earned yourself a company of sixty-three allies.

Shamira could almost picture the way Nyla sagged in relief. *That's amazing! I take it everything went well with your clan?*

It went…we have a bargain, but all three clans have agreed to be at your service. This is monumental, Nyla. Shamira tried to sound proud, but couldn't muster the temperament to do so. *Is everything all right with you and Xander?*

Yeah, everything's fine between us. Wait—where are you? Are you coming to Huntington? Nyla asked anxiously.

No, Shamira laughed, noticing Nyla's choice of words in response to her question. *That's part of what I wanted to speak to you about. We have a few days before we reach Huntington, but I very much doubt that we want to be seen by humans just yet. It would cause too much of a stir. But I meant are you and Xander making out well in Huntington? Have you managed to wrangle any help or come up with a plan to defeat Dinora?*

Nyla sighed, pinched. *There's…all kinds of politics involved and secret societies and…* She could sense Nyla's apprehension and realized the girl was about to tell her what had caused her such emotional turmoil. *Cedric is alive. The Royal Mage-General woman, Ingrid, found him. He's alive, Shamira, and I—I'd hoped he was dead. And now it's like none of our problems have been resolved, and it all just got way more complicated and—* Her words choked off as Nyla hiccupped with a sob.

Shh, shh, shh, Shamira tried to soothe. How did Xander do it? More importantly, where was he that he couldn't comfort Nyla? *It'll be okay, Nyla. If the humans can't figure things out, we are more than prepared to. We will defeat Dinora, whether you're able to fight with us or not. I promise you.*

I know. Her voice wavered. *I have to go. I have…Ingrid wants her second-in-command to train me in magic. He's…I don't understand why it matters to them how I wield my magic.*

Did he train you today? Shamira didn't like the way this sounded.

Yeah.

And?

He says that magic is about technique more than raw emotion, and he tried to teach me all these stances to help focus power, and—he's an awful teacher. It's like training someone like me is a burden to him, but from where I stand, he's no great Caster either.

How so?

He never once demonstrated his magic. He let Edwin do all of that for him. He's utterly loathsome. I can't even begin to tell you how badly I wanted to snap at him today. All he did was insult me!

Nyla, Shamira tried, wanting to ask her the specifics of how he'd tried to train her, but she couldn't get a word in as Nyla ranted, explaining to her the comments he'd made about her upbringing and her foundation of magic-wielding.

When Nyla's energy tempered wickedly, Shamira could picture the devious glint that had surely flashed across her lilac-colored eyes. *I think I'll challenge him to a magic duel.*

Shamira's blood ran cold. Magic duels were dangerous. *Nyla, I don't think that's such a good idea. Who even—Xander said something sarcastically, didn't he?*

No...his grandfather did.

Shamira growled. *Nyla, under no circumstance are you to fight a magic duel against a Caster far more experienced than you.*

I'm—so-sor-sor-can't-he-oo.

NYLA!

The connection broke. Nyla had willingly ignored her warning. If that girl was still alive by the time Shamira found a safe path into Huntington, she'd reprimand her herself.

Readjusting herself and forcing the stiffness from her posture, Shamira took a deep breath. *Xander?*

The boy startled. No response came, though she didn't expect one. Xander had barely a trace of magical ability in his bones, the sort of trace that most humans had and never cultivated because they were unaware of it.

I know you can't respond, but I need you to please make sure that there is a way into Huntington for a company of sixty-three pumpkies. We've just arrived in the Godberd Woods. We should be arriving in Huntington by the end of the week if we stick to the wooded paths and away from civilization, she explained and then added, *You should check on Nyla. She's just told me about Cedric.*

She waited a beat before letting the connection between herself and Xander fade. Any shock from her initial contact had faded, and so had the irritation at being bothered telepathically. She knew he hated it, but it was the only way, unless he could suddenly speak the limited language of the pumpkies. Even then, she wouldn't have been able to convey *half* of what she'd said to him. Pumpkarian was a primitive language that had never evolved with the needs of the pumpkies. Instead, they'd just learned the languages of the humans who had settled in the lands around them.

It certainly avoided the horrific bloodshed and had led to alliances that lasted through the ages, so much so that pumpkies had originally taught the human Casters how to use their magic. But it seemed their minute lifespan and historical memory had twisted the origins of magic. Shamira doubted whatever it was Nyla's trainer was going to teach her would do her any good.

Technique was nothing without intent. The only technique that mattered was building endurance and feeding strength; the rest would come with time and practice.

Shamira knew Nyla was talented and powerful, but it was concerning that she would challenge someone she'd only seen perform a minimal amount of magic to a duel. It could be disastrous.

Nyla? There was no answer, but Shamira noticed Nyla's attention. *If you do challenge this trainer of yours to a duel, don't be afraid to borrow magic from your surroundings. Magic is everywhere. Harness it if you find yourself in trouble. There will be a price to pay, but you can easily give your energy to where you borrowed it from. Don't be afraid to deflect his magic back at him either.*

Shamira's heart beat in time with the symphony of the niphonies around her.

Thank you.

Get some rest, Nyla.

You too.

***

Xander flinched harshly, nearly dropping the book he was reading. Shamira's voice flitted unwelcomingly across his mind. He didn't even know that was possible. Even though she'd often told them that she was 'communicating with the Elders,' he'd never really understood what that had meant. Were they communicating telepathically across a great distance? Was that possible? Were they astral projecting? Maybe they were sending raverins to each other? Did pumpkies eat raverins?

Wait. Sixty-three pumpkies were marching to Huntington?

This time, Xander did drop his book and sprang upright in bed.

Shamira was leading a company of sixty-three pumpkies to Huntington. They would be here by the end of the week, maybe sooner, and somehow, they had to figure out a way to get them to Pemberly without raising an alarm through the countryside.

Where was his grandfather?

You should check on Nyla. His heart plummeted. Immediate panic flooded his veins. How did Shamira know there was something wrong with Nyla? *Was* something wrong with Nyla? *She's just told me about Cedric.*

Xander cursed, throwing back the covers and sliding out of bed. Hopefully, Meredith was fast asleep and dreaming of whatever it was that his ten-year-old cousin would dream about most soundly so she wouldn't be able to hold it over his head that he'd gone to Nyla's room in the middle of the night.

As he crept from the bed, Xander tried to remember where the squeakiest floorboards lay in wait. It was a painstaking task given how his heart raced, but he made it to the door without raising any alarm from the old wooden floors.

The door opened soundlessly. He poked his head out of the door and glanced down both ways of the hallway. Every other lantern was dimmed, giving off just enough light to guide anyone who might need to traverse Pemberly's halls at night. Certain that no one was around to witness him, Xander slipped through the doorway and painstakingly closed it behind him.

Tiptoeing passed Merry's bedroom, Xander wondered what he'd say to Nyla. Shamira sent him to check on her, and he'd listened? He made a habit of checking on her, as friends do? *He* couldn't sleep and wanted to see if she were awake? With each excuse that crossed his mind, the more ridiculous they became.

All too soon, Xander was met with the double doors of the Lavender Room. Before he could even knock, one of the doors slowly cracked open. Through the opening, Xander caught sight of Nyla. Her head hung, and she sniffled. Xander saw the moment she stiffened upon realizing that someone was already at her door. Whipping her head up, Nyla's red-rimmed eyes met his.

"Hi," he whispered, giving her a broad, lopsided smile and a slow wave.

"Hi," she responded quietly, her voice crackly. Stepping aside, she opened the door a little wider, motioning for him to come in. "What are you doing here?"

"Shamira told me to check on you." He eased past her, taking in the tear tracks on her face and the sad slope of her shoulders. Nyla closed the door as soon as they were both inside and leaned her back against it, sagging against the hardwood. "She also said that there were sixty-three pumpkies marching to Huntington?"

Nyla pressed the heel of her palms against her eyes before pushing her hair back. "Yeah, she told me that too."

Xander nodded, wiggling his toes against the cool floors of Nyla's room. He glanced at the fireplace, knowing Nyla's magical fires were usually enough to keep even the farthest corner of a room this size warm. "No magic fire?"

"Not tonight," Nyla sighed, peeling herself away from the door and walking toward the seating area. "I'm trying to save energy."

Xander followed her and sat beside her on the couch. "Any particular reason?"

"I'm challenging Frederick to a duel tomorrow."

"You're *what?*" Xander shot to his feet and whirled on her, ready to list all the reasons why that was a horrible idea, and that she could get seriously hurt.

"Don't start with me, Xander," she hissed through her teeth. Closing her eyes, she leaned her head back against the edge of the sofa and hugged herself. "We don't have time for Lord Frederick—"

"He's not technically a lord," he interjected, dropping down beside her again. She was impossible—and inconceivable. Every time he thought he knew Nyla and could anticipate her every move, she did something like this. Her reckless streak was unpredictable, and would likely be the death of him.

Or at least the death of his sanity.

"Whatever. Frederick is an annoying, narcissistic, know-it-all who doesn't have the kindness in his heart Helpet demands for respect. He deserves to be publicly humiliated by a 'beginner Caster' with 'little to no education' and 'no proper upbringing.' It's *truly* a wonder how I've *managed* all seventeen years of my life without good Lord Frederick to teach me how to say my own name."

Xander stiffened, watching Nyla's face and taking in the hollowness of her features, the worry of her brow and the grim line of her lips. The war council had aged them both, but Xander saw now the full extent seeing Cedric again had taxed Nyla—and the adverse effect training with a Caster like Frederick could have on someone he unfairly deemed beneath him.

His fist clenched against his knee. Nyla was twice the Caster—the *person*—Frederick was. Sitting up straight to his full height, the anger slipping into his blood demanded that he stand and drag Frederick out of his bed here at Pemberly and ban him from the estate. Clenching his jaw, Xander forced the tension from his limbs and focused on Nyla. Taking a breath, he let his shoulders sag and tried his best to keep his anger at Frederick from overwhelming the concern he now held for Nyla in his voice.

"He said that to you?" At Nyla's nod, Xander considered dueling Frederick himself. "I'm guessing Shamira tried to talk you out of it and you ignored her, despite her literally being in your head?"

"Yup," she sighed, lifting her head off of the back of the couch and looking him dead in the eye.

"And there's no use in trying to talk you out of it?"

"None."

"I mean this in the least insensitive way possible—"

"Then don't say it."

"Just don't kill him." Xander laid his hand over hers.

Nyla pouted at him. "There's only two people in this world I've considered actually killing. His *lordship* isn't all that deserving of that designation."

He snorted. "Don't hold back tomorrow."

"Wasn't planning on it." She leaned her head on his shoulder. Letting her eyes flutter shut, Nyla leaned more of her weight against Xander and gripped the hand he'd rested over hers. Xander couldn't help but chuckle quietly, though he bit his tongue. Nothing he could say would change her mind, and he certainly couldn't tell her anything she didn't already know herself.

The gentle crackling of the fire soothed the quiet static flooding his mind, until Nyla slowly muttered, "I can't sleep."

"Me either," he admitted absently, stroking his thumb over her knuckles in time with his thoughts. There was too much to overwhelm him. From the revelation of who and what the Heirs of Tenebris were to the events of the informal war council today, Xander had found that as mentally taxed as he was, rest just wouldn't come.

"Stay with me?" As Xander's breath faltered, she picked her head up to watch him. His eyes studied her intently, his brows raised in question.

"You need to rest," he reminded her.

At this, Nyla frowned and threw her arm across him. She even turned herself in her seat to drape her legs over his lap, placing their joined hands against her chest. "You being here isn't going to stop me from the rest I'm already not getting. If anything, restlessness likes company…and warmth."

"You spoiled yourself with magic fires, and now wood-burning fires aren't good enough for you?" he laughed, freeing his other arm from under her legs and resting it on top of them.

"Pretty much, yeah." She nodded weakly, tucking herself further against him. Xander shook his head in slight bewilderment. He didn't quite understand why she was doing all of this, though he couldn't help but think of that night in the study. They'd both been alone for so long. Maybe she just wanted to be close to someone, to feel safe.

Squeezing her hand in quiet assurance, Xander found himself offering a silent promise he wasn't certain was possible to keep. Forever was quite a long time to be there for someone, in any capacity, but still, he promised himself he'd stay by Nyla as long as she'd let him. "If we're gonna stay up and refuse to sleep, we should get more comfortable."

Nyla groaned. "Fiiiiiinnnne. I'll grab the pillows. You grab the blankets."

Reluctantly, she clambered off of the couch—and his lap—with a yawn. Xander trailed after her, shaking his head, and stepped onto the raised platform. As Nyla reached for the pillows, he went to untuck the blankets from the foot of the bed.

"Oof." Xander shook his head. Looking from Nyla, to the pillow she'd thrown at him, he forced a scowl to his face. "Seriously?"

"Whoops." She yawned again. "Guess it slipped."

"Mm-hmm, I'm sure," he said, yanking the blankets from the bed as Nyla tucked two pillows up against herself. Starting back toward the seating area, he added teasingly, "Maybe a magic duel isn't the best idea if you're already so weak."

"I am not!" she whined, placing a pillow on either end of the couch. "I'm just tired. It's been a long day."

"Still don't want to talk about it?"

Nyla settled against the pillow she'd set on the couch and shook her head, bringing her knees to her chest. He sat on the opposite end and spread the blanket over them both, stretching out his legs.

"We could run," he teased, hoping to make her laugh and ease the tension settled like a fine dust over the room.

"I'm done running," Nyla said. Her stare was blank. Xander was taken aback by her assertion. This wasn't how it normally went, but before he could say so, she said, "If I run now, I will never be able to stop, and I *want* to stop. I want to stop being afraid or anxious or lonely. I'm tired, Xander. I am so tired of running away from my life. That's what I want. I want to live."

"Then let's do it. Let's live," he said decisively. "We owe it to ourselves."

She smiled through the exhaustion taking hold over her features. Leaning her side against the back of the couch, she sagged into the niche she'd carved for herself in the corner of the couch, closing her eyes. Xander smiled, watching the tension ease from her features as she echoed his words. "Let's live."

24. HER OWN SAVIOR

Morning came early. When Nyla awoke, she was warm and well rested. The troubles that plagued her mind had all seemed to flee. Turning over, she blinked slowly as the memories of the night before came back to her. A small giggle fell from her lips at how ridiculous her actions seemed now. She hadn't even noticed Xander had left at all, or had apparently carried her to the bed and fixed the blankets back over her. He'd even untied the canopy drapes and drew them shut around the sides of the frame, leaving the curtains tied back at the foot of the bed. And it was a good thing he had, or else she wouldn't have woken in time for breakfast.

Nyla sprang from the mattress, crawling over the foot of the bed so she wouldn't have to deal with the curtains or untangling herself from the blankets. With a hurried glance at the clock on the mantel, she darted into the washroom to make herself presentable. Everyone would be at the breakfast in the main dining room, and if she dressed quickly, she'd arrive just after everyone else. She wouldn't say dramatics was something she enjoyed, but she *wanted* to make a spectacle of her duel with Frederick.

These people didn't know her or her strengths. They didn't know what she was capable of or the lengths she was willing to go to defeat Dinora. She might have bared her heart to them by divulging the details of how she'd come to inherit Astrid's magic after the fire, but that didn't mean anything to them. In their eyes—the eyes of some of Tenebris's most powerful people—she was only a girl, nowhere near their equal. Not in magic, not status, and certainly not a part of their circles.

And Frederick was the perfect person to help her demonstrate to them that she was worthy of being in their trust and capable of defeating Dinora no matter what conclusion they might reach in their councils.

It didn't take long to brush her hair and teeth and dress in fresh clothes. Pulling the door open and stepping out into the hall, Nyla fixed the sheath of her knife to her waistband. Extending her powers outward from her body, she sought out a trace of Xander or Lord Alexander, hoping that they were already in the dining hall and she could use their signatures to find her way.

As Nyla wove her way through the brightly lit halls of Pemberly, she gathered her courage. It wasn't that she was afraid or even anxious. She was uncertain. She'd never seen Frederick use much magic before. She'd never seen any of the Casters here use magic before, with the exception of Edwin.

There was a stiffness to his magic, like he was overthinking every aspect of his intent. And from the rare instance he *had* used magic while "training" her yesterday afternoon, Frederick's magic was just as calculated. She'd even say it was *over*-calculated. She might just have a chance against him.

Taking a deep breath, Nyla straightened. She squared her shoulders and took measured steps into the dining hall. Her eyes swept over the faces and tables until they reached the table set in front of the massive fireplace. Its mouth was easily as tall as Alexander was. A good portion of the wall was consumed by its width. Someone, or multiple someones, had lit a magic fire that kept the room at a comfortable temperature despite all the people crowded at the three long tables.

Nyla reached the front table where a seat had been saved for her between Merry and Xander. She bowed her head and greeted the king and queen before she excused herself from the conversation she could see in their eyes and turned toward Ingrid on their right, but more importantly, to Frederick who sat beside her.

"I challenge you to a duel," she said calmly. Her voice carried throughout the room, just as she'd planned.

All conversation ceased. Out of the corner of her eye, she could see Alexander's utensils still and the sharpness in which he'd turned to stare at her from his seat beside the king. She knew he'd only been jesting when he'd suggested over dinner last night that she should challenge Frederick, but now he was facing the harsh reality that she'd decided to do just that.

Frederick set down his utensils and narrowed his eyes in scrutiny. Beside him, Ingrid hid a smirk behind her goblet, unfazed by the turn of events.

"No."

"So, you forfeit then?" Nyla smiled dangerously, goading him.

"I don't think you understand what you're doing. It wouldn't be a fair duel," he claimed. A low ripple of whispers erupted throughout the room, but not at the front table. All eyes were fixed on the two of them.

"I suppose you're right," Nyla sighed. "I inherited the magic from a Royal Mage and the first Mage General. It wouldn't be fair to you."

Slowly, Frederick stood, placing his fists on the table and leaned forward. "Withdraw your challenge."

"No. Either accept it, or forfeit."

He glowered at her, his lips pursed.

"What's the harm, Frederick?" Ingrid asked, tilting her head as she looked at him. "You either prove your methods to your student, or your student proves herself and her skill. I really don't see an issue in this challenge."

Frederick glanced at his superior. His fist tensed against the tabletop. Nyla arched her brow impatiently.

After a moment, he addressed her for all to hear. "I accept your challenge, however misguided."

"After breakfast then." Nyla smirked and made to walk away with her head held high.

"Afraid you'll lose your nerve?" Frederick taunted at her back.

"Never." Nyla glanced over her shoulder at him as she strode toward her seat. After all she'd been through, dueling Frederick didn't seem like a challenge, however uncertain she felt about her chosen task. But in truth, Nyla had faced much worse.

If she could face both Dinora and Cedric, she could handle dueling a man like Frederick. She'd faced her darkest nightmares and had conquered many of them despite her fear. And through it, she'd found that she wasn't afraid of them anymore, not for herself anyway. She didn't think there was much more in this life that *could* scare her anymore.

"That was bold," Alexander murmured as she took her seat. He'd had to lean over Xander to make certain she'd heard him. "And ill-advised, even for someone with your power."

"Time will tell." She smiled politely at the mixed group of Casters and Royal Guards looking her way.

"Did you encourage her to do this?" he reprimanded his grandson.

"Not especially, but I couldn't discourage her either," Xander replied defeatedly.

"I think it's about time," Merry added, leaning over Nyla's empty plate to come face to face with her grandfather. "You're always saying how slimy Frederick is and how someone ought to put him in his place, and who better than Nyla?"

"Can we eat?" Xander said. "If Nyla is going to duel after breakfast, she'll actually need to have *had* breakfast to beat Frederick."

"Xander's right." Nyla nodded. "Someone pass the cinnegals and crème please?"

It was Edwin who passed the basket of round bread. He said nothing about her challenge with Frederick, but Nyla could see in his eyes that he wanted to. She ignored it and thanked him for the cinnegals. Taking two from the basket, Nyla sought the eggs and fruit next. All were handed to her in turn as the whispers shared between those sitting beside each other receded.

Nyla focused intently on the breakfast laid before her. She didn't think she would manage to eat with the duel looming over her, but looking at the sugary comfort promised by the cinnegals that she'd gone so long without, her stomach clenched with eager hunger.

Quickly, she sliced the round bread in half and spread crème on the inside. She ate it half by half, beginning with the top. The cinnamon brought a warm, earthy hint to the smooth, sour-sweetness of the crème spread. Savoring every bite, Nyla's eggs had gone cold by the time she'd gotten to them. With a little extra salt and pepper, they were salvageable—though she would've much rather hunted down another cinnegal.

As people finished their breakfasts, they filtered out of the dining hall or remained seated to entertain the conversations of their table. Nyla only hoped the impending duel wasn't the only topic being picked apart by the gossip weavers that filled the room.

She'd only just finished her plate when Alexander leaned over Xander again and drew her attention. "I hope you've thought this through, Nyla."

"I have," she assured him with a confident smile. "And Shamira gave me some pointers last night. Has Xander mentioned that there's sixty-three Pumpkies on their way to Huntington and that they've dedicated themselves to fighting Dinora no matter what the Heirs or the joint-military coalition decide to do?"

Xander choked on his water.

"No, he hasn't mentioned it." Alexander eyed him.

"Sorry, it just didn't seem like a good time." Xander replaced his cup beside his plate and pushed his chair away from the table.

"You *knew* Nyla was going to challenge Frederick publicly?"

"I wish I had. I would have come down earlier and gotten a better start on my breakfast," Xander grumbled, staring at his half-finished plate.

"We will all discuss this after Nyla duels Frederick. Now, where's Sir Ian?" Alexander made a show of searching the room for Sir Ian before he stood and bid farewell to his breakfast companions.

"Who's Sir Ian?" Nyla asked, watching Alexander clap his hand on the shoulder of a sharp-jawed Royal Guard.

"He's one of the King's Guard and second-in-command to Sir Hubert—the one who mentioned the investigation into…well, the fire," Xander responded. "He's also a known bookmaker."

"Is your grandfather *betting* on my duel?" Nyla scoffed, her lips nearly curling into a snarl.

"Probably." Xander reached for the basket of cinnegals and took the last one. "So, I guess I shouldn't make a wager?"

"You better!" she shot back under her breath, sliding out of her chair. "And it'd better be in my favor!"

"As if I'd *ever* bet against you," he laughed.

Nyla rolled her eyes as she stalked around the end of the table, willing her heart to stop beating like a war drum at Xander's comment. Or was it the impending duel that caused it to beat furiously against her chest? Nyla shook the thought from her mind as quickly as it came. She was *meant* to do this. She had to. She looked over at her future opponent one last time before heading toward the hall's door. Frederick hadn't yet finished his breakfast, still conversing with whoever it was that sat on his other side. From his left, Nyla could feel Ingrid's gaze on her. Catching her eyes on her, the woman subtly raised her goblet to her, offering her a secretive smirk before engaging Queen Clarice in a deep conversation.

Irritation prickled in her blood. Passive energy rippled over her senses alongside a cool whisper of obligation. She picked up her pace in an effort to heed her instinctual reaction to a certain blue-eyed man.

"Nyla, wait, please," Edwin called from behind her. She glanced pleadingly up at the ceiling. Even though she'd made it clear to him that she had no intention of stopping or conversing with him, Edwin caught up to her and matched her pace. "Please just listen to me. Frederick is a skilled Caster. He'll do anything to win a duel and protect his ego. Nearly everyone's bet against you, though that doesn't really matter much."

"No, it really doesn't, so what did you *actually* want to tell me?" Nyla prompted, still uncertain of what Edwin had meant by his last conversation with her and unwilling to have her mind occupied by yet another of his vague but meaningful discussions before her duel. She'd hoped to make it to the courtyard to look over the landscape Xander had told her would serve as the dueling grounds.

"You should tie your hair back. Frederick likes to use wind magic a lot. He's also one of the toughest professors I ever had." Edwin licked his lips, stopping her in her tracks with his straightforwardness. "He's critical and full of himself, but a good Caster for the way most of us perform magic. But you're different. Shamira taught you an ancient form of wielding magic, one that I know Frederick doesn't understand nor appreciate. It's raw and pure instinct. You can win this."

"Have you placed a wager yet, Eddie?"

"I'm not a gambling man."

"I'm not much of a gambler either, but I don't have much of a choice." Nyla glanced away, focusing on the end of the hallway where the proud garden doors stood waiting for her. "Do you think I'll win?"

"I hope you do. I'd love to see the look on his face when you do."

"Tell me more about Frederick and how he uses magic," Nyla said. She started to walk again, forcing Edwin to come with her.

"Gladly."

***

By the time she and Edwin wove their way to the designated dueling grounds, Frederick had already arrived, and so had everyone in Pemberly. She even saw Moretta amongst the crowd of Casters, soldiers, politicians, and the Hall's staff. As Edwin left her standing at the end of the aisle, her eyes sought out Xander and his grandfather before landing on her supposed trainer.

"I was beginning to think you'd withdrawn your challenge," Frederick called from across the strip of courtyard. "There's still time if you want to."

"There's still time to forfeit," Nyla offered with a wry smile.

Ingrid stepped between them, standing in the center of the aisle. "Seeing as you're both here, I'm assuming neither one of you has chosen to forfeit," she said clearly for all to hear. "The rules are as follows: no harmful magics are permitted, intentionally deadly attacks will be met with severe punishment, no matter the outcome, and, finally, only the basic elements of magic may be used. As a reminder, the elements of magic are Energy, Fire, Earth, Water, and Air. The goal is to incapacitate, not kill or maim." The Mage General looked toward Nyla. "Do you agree to these terms?"

Nyla nodded. Xander had explained them all to her the night before, and Edwin had clarified what counted as harmful magics and intentionally deadly attacks. They couldn't manipulate their physical surroundings, but they could conjure the elements—though Nyla didn't really see how one could conjure Earth from nothing, especially without manipulating the physical environment. Harmful magics included manipulating the air inside someone's lungs, and deadly magic was much the same. He hadn't explained if the term "deadly magic" had any connotation to a specific practice or element, but for the purpose of a duel, he'd said, deadly magic was *any* magic used with the intent to kill, such as a direct attack aimed at someone's heart.

He'd also confirmed that redirecting magic would be allowed, but borrowing magic from outside sources was an ambiguous area that might disqualify her, so she'd just have to do without. In Edwin's opinion, the best way to win was to render Frederick unconscious by either exhausting him or attacking him head-on. Her lips set into a grim line.

Ingrid looked to Frederick at the opposite end of the aisle. "Do you accept these terms?"

"I do." Even from the marginal distance, Nyla could see the wickedness in his grin.

Stepping back into the crowd, Ingrid clapped her hands and spread her arms wide. A protective barrier shielded the crowd from whatever magic Nyla and Frederick were about to sling at each other.

Everything—her freedom to make decisions, her reputation, her skill—was at stake here. She would win.

She *had* to win.

This duel wasn't just about her dislike for Frederick or the things he'd said about her magical abilities yesterday, but because she had to prove herself to all of these strangers. Casters, soldiers, politicians, all of them. They all knew each other or of each other, but no one knew her. They didn't know where she came from or how she grew up. They didn't know her family or their reputation. All any of them knew of her was that she claimed to be Astrid's descendent, and that she'd inherited the Royal Mage's magic 647 years later.

"Begin."

Nyla took a deep breath to steady herself. Gathering her magic, she held it at the very tips of her fingers. Frederick had to make the first move. She needed to show patience and restraint, a level head. Xander had said that if she attacked as soon as the duel began, people would find her impulsive and ill-tempered, especially since she'd challenged the Mage Apprentice and not the other way around.

Frederick sent a bolt of forest green energy at her. She split the magic down the center like Dinora had to Xander's arrows that day on the Manor's courtyard, and redirected the halves away from her. The magic hit the barrier with a sparkling *sizzle*.

She knew she should counter, but something in her told her to wait, to stay her hand. Instead, she licked her lips and flashed a grin at Frederick. "Is that all you've got? What a pity."

His nostrils flared. She saw him draw in a deep breath through his nose. Nyla smirked as a wave of green magic barreled toward her. She stomped one foot down in front of her and brought her hands up like she was going to shove the magic away. The magic splashed and splayed as she maneuvered it, arcing it over and around her. Pushing it to the side, she brought it back around her and redirected it back at Frederick. He barely managed to fortify a shield before the tidal wave of his own magic assaulted him.

Nyla used his surprise to her advantage and launched a barrage of her own lilac magic against his shield. The green shield splintered into a million shards. Her magic hit him square in the stomach, knocking him back a few steps.

Wind kicked up the dust of the gravel pathway. A cyclone formed in front of Frederick as he recovered, swirling the sand and gravel around. It raced toward her, her braided hair pulling toward it. Nyla squinted against the debris. She shut her eyes as the whirlwind snagged at her clothes. In her head, she saw the whirlwind disappear.

The wind slowed. Nyla opened her eyes and watched as the whirlwind shrank and dissipated in a gentle swirl of plum leaves settling against the gravel. A harsh wind slammed into her without a second for her to breathe in the clean air.

It pushed against her, forcing her back a step and then another until she could hardly stand. Nyla braced her arms in front of herself. Prying against the bone-crushing force with her magic, she separated the gust and redirected it toward the barrier Ingrid had created on either side. The veil *crackled* as Frederick's magic met with Ingrid's.

One small step at a time, Nyla regained the ground she'd lost. No matter how much she tried to stop the onslaught by making it disappear like she had with the whirlwind, the gale-force wind didn't stop. Frederick had tested her with his earlier attacks. Desperately, Nyla wracked her brain for any idea that wasn't shielding herself and hoping Frederick tired before she did.

She could try freezing the wind, but then what? She might be able to throw her magic at him, but it could recoil against the wind, effectively backfiring at her instead.

There was only one thing she could do. She had to absorb the energy of his attack, even if it might disqualify her. It might cost her the duel, but the strategy might be the key to gaining the respect of not only the rest of the sworn Heirs, but also the other members of the war council.

Bracing herself, Nyla let her shield fall. Frederick let out a triumphant huff that quickly turned into a curse of disbelief. Nyla inhaled the energy of his attack. New energy flooded her veins. The hum flooded every extremity until she feared the lively buzz would tear her apart from the inside out.

She had to redirect the energy, or it would ruin her.

Frederick doubled down on his attack. As the intensity of the wind grew, Nyla had no choice but to allow the energy to flood her. All she could do was lightly spread her arms to either side and let the energy transfer to the ground beneath her. Twisting through the gravel, she pictured twin seeds blooming, its sapling and roots spreading through the earth.

Out of the corner of her eyes, she saw a delicate twig on either side of the aisle. As she continued to serve as a conduit for the energy flooding her and into the earth, the twigs grew into young trees. Buds bloomed on the ends of their branches as the trees grew taller and stronger.

Slowly, the wind began to weaken. The buds unfurled, revealing leaves of the most delicate lilac, just like the color of her magic. The bark took on the hue of her hair, of Astrid's hair. And as the magic energy coursing through her slowed, the trees stopped growing. Nyla absorbed the rest of the magic for herself, staring Frederick down.

His chest heaved.

Without so much as a second's hesitation, Nyla sent a steady stream of magic in his direction. It was the most power she had ever felt run through her.

It was too much magic. She could kill him.

Quickly, she shot her hand out near her side and simultaneously released the excess magic into the land. Her eyes sparked. Her assault died, and Frederick fell to his knees. Nyla watched as he slumped and doubled over.

Her blood still thrummed with too much magic. Casting a nervous glance at Ingrid, the Royal Mage nodded at her.

"You had better expel the rest of that energy unless you want to be sick," she called over to her.

Nyla nodded shakily. Exhaling a slow breath, she let the magic flow into the breeze. Her heart calmed. Swaying a bit on her feet, Nyla tempered the magic within her. The rest was her own, only her own magic now—or, she supposed, only Astrid's magic and whatever drop she'd been born with.

Ingrid allowed the barrier to fall. A couple of people rushed to Frederick and turned him onto his back. Grim-faced, Ingrid approached her. Wordlessly, she came to stand beside Nyla and watched as the two Casters assessed Frederick.

"That was bold," she said quietly.

"I didn't know what else to do," Nyla admitted.

"If he's not dead, you've just won your first duel." Ingrid's lip twitched as if she wanted to smile. "That was an impressive display of combat magic. I take it you've been in a magical confrontation before?"

"Twice."

As Nyla said this, one of the Casters stood and signaled to Ingrid. Relief flooded Nyla. Frederick was alive, just unconscious either from her attack or his own vapid use of magic. She didn't know and didn't care.

Ingrid took hold of her wrist and raised her arm. "Nyla, heir of Astrid Genevieve Thornraven, has defeated Frederick de Chante!"

Nyla locked eyes with Xander. Cheers and applause echoed in her ears. There were a few leers and unfriendly faces, but Nyla ignored them, too consumed by the reality of having defeated Frederick.

As Ingrid released her wrist, Nyla found herself at a loss for feeling.

"Congratulations, Nyla." Ingrid smiled warmly. "I look forward to aiding you in whatever way life takes you, even if you should choose not to fight Dinora. This fight doesn't have to include you just because you feel like you've inherited it like you did Astrid's magic. You don't have to choose this, though the choice is yours to make."

"I know," Nyla said, "but I never considered any other option. There has only ever been one path in my mind."

Ingrid nodded solemnly. "Then I will support you in it."

Nyla's mouth ran dry. She nodded her thanks as Ingrid drifted away. Across the aisle, the two Casters had lifted Frederick between them and were aiding him up the path back to the Hall. She wondered if he'd needed to be healed, or if he was still unconscious.

Someone slammed into her, knocking the wind from her. Merry squealed, wrapping her arms around her in a fierce hug. The girl's embrace was probably the only reason she hadn't fallen over as her excited words gushed over Nyla.

"I'm so happy you beat him!"

Nyla patted the girl's back, laughing. "Me too."

Merry pulled away and squeaked a few more exclamations before Xander pushed through the crowd that had flooded the aisle. Nyla's head spun from the excitable din of conversation and occasional yelling or boisterous laughter from the assembled crowd. At the center of it all was Sir Ian. She could just barely see the top of his blonde head amongst the crowd. She supposed he was collecting the money people had lost and was dispersing it to anyone who had bet on her.

"That was amazing!" Xander breathed once he'd reached her. Already he had a leather pouch in his hand. "You wouldn't believe how much money people put on this duel. I think Grandfather put a couple thousand libacs on it."

"*What?*" Nyla balked. "A *couple thousand?*"

"Yeah, he's an astute gambler when there's great reward to be had." Xander made a show of weighing the leather pouch in his hands, before he tossed it to her. "Congratulations, Nyla."

Nyla's jaw dropped as she nearly fell forward upon catching the pouch. "Helpet's heart, how much did *you* wager?"

She went to hand the pouch back to Xander, but he shook his head and curled her fingers around it with his own. "It's yours."

"Xander, I can't just—"

"You're not," he assured her with a gentle smile, his touch lingering for just a moment longer than necessary before he pulled away. "I'm giving it to you."

Nyla pursed her lips. Edwin's arrival at their little circle stopped her from arguing with Xander any further about the pouch full of jangling coins.

"Those are some beautiful trees," he commented. "You'll have to teach me how you did that."

"Thanks," she grumbled. Her head pounded. The sunlight was like a dagger slicing across her vision. She couldn't wait to go inside and get something more to eat.

"Here." Edwin handed her a shimmering potion in a squat bottle. "I figured you might need this when it was all said and done."

Nyla accepted the bottle with a quirked brow.

"It's an energy potion. It should help get you through the rest of the day until you can rest properly," he explained.

"Thank you, Edwin. I appreciate it." She uncorked the bottle and chugged its contents. Shuddering, her face pinched in disgust. "Of all the magic in the world, why hasn't anyone figured out how to make these taste better?"

Edwin laughed. "No idea. Potions rarely change. I've actually been working on some of my own, though they haven't really been that successful yet."

"You really went into potions at university?" Xander asked.

Edwin smirked. "What can I say? It's always been my calling."

Nyla's eyes floated over the crowd, lost to the conversation between her friends. People were glancing over at her. Some tried to catch and hold her attention; others looked as if they were going to approach her. Still dizzy, Nyla interrupted the conversation amongst her companions. "Maybe we'd better head inside."

"Not ready to meet your adoring fans?" Xander teased.

"Not in the slightest," Nyla said grimly. Nyla flushed. If she wasn't already exhausted and left feeling empty in the wake of her faded adrenaline, she might've sprinted back inside.

"Go," Edwin ordered, "I'll handle this while you three make your escape."

Faltering a step toward the much-too-distant steps, Nyla said, "Thank you."

Xander wrapped his arm around her shoulders, helping her keep her balance. Merry led the way through the assembled crowd with ease. Nyla marveled at how she managed to walk so proudly in spite of being so young and shorter than nearly everyone else.

As the three of them passed, people turned to glance at them, at her, but Nyla paid them no mind, shrinking into Xander's side as if he could hide her. Every now and again, someone would take a step toward them, but Merry would immediately step in and thwart their attempt to block Nyla from getting inside by way of a tedious introduction or maybe a congratulations.

"How is she so good at this?" Nyla asked as Merry skirted passed them again and took up the lead just as they stepped over the threshold and into the cool hallway.

"It comes with the title." Xander smirked. "It doesn't matter what you want or who you are. If you grew up like this, you just have to accept that this is no place for people who'd rather withdraw. It helps though that Merry is a natural conversationalist, if you haven't noticed."

Nyla laughed, stepping away from Xander as Merry led the way into an empty room. "Oh, no, not at all."

"'Not at all' what?" Merry blinked, closing the door behind them after glancing either way as if to make sure they hadn't been seen.

"Thank you, Merry," Nyla smiled, "for protecting me from all those people."

Merry beamed. "Well, someone's got to do it! You didn't grow up here with all these people, and it's really hard to talk to strangers, especially people like this." Merry paused, glancing toward the door. "They really only ever care to know you if they feel you're someone important to their own success."

Nyla arched her eyebrow. "That's a horrible way to go through life."

Merry shrugged. "It's nothing personal. You get kind of used to it. My parents are never around, and Grandfather's been distant, so I just… occupy myself because there's no one else around my age anymore, and everyone else is just so serious all the time." Merry frowned at her feet. "That and *someone* hasn't been home in an awfully long time."

"Well, I'm home now," Xander reminded her.

"Until the war starts. Then you'll both be off again."

Nyla pulled the girl to a stop and turned her so that they could face each other. "Even if we do go off to fight Dinora, we'll be back. Whatever happens, it won't be forever."

Xander crouched down beside Merry and touched her shoulder. "Promise."

"Good!" Merry threw herself at them, wrapping an arm around each of their necks. The force of her hug nearly knocked Nyla off balance. When she pulled back, she blinked away a few tears.

Xander smiled, standing straight again. "We'll come find you for lunch, okay?"

Merry nodded and offered them a small smile, even though it faltered slightly at the corners. "Okay."

As Nyla watched her slip carefully through the door and shut it behind her again, her heart cleaved in half. How were they going to avoid war with Dinora? If she brought all the rock points in the Shadow Forest to life, Nyla didn't know what would happen. It'd taken nearly everything she and Edwin had in them to defeat the three she'd sent to attack their carriage. Would they be able to stop an army of the warped souls trapped in the Shadow Forest?

"Don't look that grim. Someone might think we can't defeat Dinora," Xander said almost teasingly, closing the gap between them to wrap her in a gentle hug.

"That's exactly what I was wondering." She returned his embrace slowly, letting herself melt into the comfort he offered just for a moment, knowing it was all she could afford with all that they still had to do to prepare. "We'd better find your grandfather and talk about the pumpkies before they get here."

"Maybe you should rest first?"

Nyla nodded her head against his chest, not bothering to pull away from him. "Rest sounds like a better plan."

"I know just the place." He pulled away from her slowly, reaching for her hand. Nyla laced her fingers with his and let Xander lead her from the room through a secret passageway hidden behind an inconspicuous bookcase. "Follow me?"

25. VALIANT-HEARTED

About an hour later, a steward came rushing into the hidden gardens. Xander had told her that they were his grandmother's most prized gardens and how she'd tended to them herself for the sole purpose of hiding away from society when it all became too much.

She'd almost believed his words were true, but the breathless words of the steward shattered the illusion that they could hide there forever.

"Lor—Mister Xander, Miss Nyla, your presence has been requested in his lordship's study," the steward informed them.

Glancing over at Xander, she sighed as dramatically as her weary heart could manage, "I suppose there's no chance at peace then."

Xander laughed, but the poor steward just glanced between them in confusion.

Wordlessly, they followed him back to Alexander's study and entered without a moment's hesitation. As the door closed behind them, several people turned to look their way.

"Ah, so nice of you two to join us," Alexander drawled, looking up from the large oval table he'd been bent over.

Xander cleared his throat. "We would've been here sooner, but I wanted to show Nyla the gardens after the duel."

His grandfather waved a dismissive hand, as if an explanation for their tardiness didn't matter. "Please, sit."

Ingrid, Sir Hubert, and a handful of other Casters and soldiers were sat around the table along with the king and queen. Nyla even recognized a few other members of the Heirs of Tenebris, but couldn't quite match their names to their person yet.

Frederick was nowhere to be seen. Nyla briefly found it in herself to wonder how he was faring after their duel, but refrained from asking.

"You made quite an impression on everyone, Nyla," Ingrid said. "Many of us would love to learn your techniques, if you'd care to share them."

Nyla swallowed, approaching the table slowly with Xander right beside her. "It's not technique so much as instinct, I guess. Shamira, the leader of the host of pumpkies, taught me everything I know about magic. I suspect that if we work alongside them, we'll have to learn and adapt to each other's way of casting or fighting if we hope to defeat Dinora and the army I hope she isn't animating."

"Yes, you did mention that," Sir Ian said. "By the way, a great deal of people might be just as angry with you as they are impressed."

Nyla bit her tongue. She didn't know who'd placed bets and lost money because of her winning the duel, or which of them could be sitting at this very table.

"Then perhaps they shouldn't make wagers on their limited knowledge," Alexander said. "But back to the matter at hand—you said the rock points in the Shadow Forest are the 'souls' Dinora took during the Corvid Uprising? How do you know this?"

"I don't. I only suspect it based on what I've sensed and by piecing the legends together. There's something about the rock points that's alive, but not in the way that we're alive or the Shadow Forest is alive," she explained. "When I was near the rocks, I thought I was just anxious because I was in the Shadow Forest, alone, vulnerable, but after being attacked by Dinora's 'creatures,' I think the points and her rock-creatures are one and the same."

"She could have just animated them," a Caster with fiery hair suggested.

"How do you defeat them?" one soldier asked.

Nyla looked over at him, meeting his determinedly focused eyes. "I don't know. It took nearly everything Edwin and I had to defeat them. Surface wounds won't kill them. You have to kill them from the inside out." Glancing around the table, she held the gaze of everyone she could in turn. "I shredded them apart with my magic when Edwin and I realized that fire and pointed attacks wouldn't work. It was a feral, raw magic. Magic that isn't sustainable if Dinora manages to animate all of the rock points throughout the Shadow Forest."

The table was silent. A hefty weight settled in the downturned eyes of the experienced adults sat around the table. Nyla stole a glance at Xander. His lips were pressed into a somber line, but when he met her eyes, the worried crease between his brows eased.

"We have to find Dinora before she can raise an army, or there will be war," she said resolutely. Her gaze drifted over the table's occupants. Ingrid met her eyes with a shadowed determination. "If you found Cedric, we can find Dinora, right?"

"It's possible, yes," she said with reservation halting in her voice.

"And what about Cedric? Is he useful?" Hubert asked.

"According to himself, no. All he wants is to die," Ingrid sighed. "I've sent a doctor to him. Maybe they'll have better luck than the Healers."

"Can we find Dinora without Cedric's help?" Nyla kept the venom from her voice. She hoped their entire plan didn't hinge on the ambitions of a traitor like Cedric.

"It will be difficult…" a representative from the Chamber of Commons started, "but not impossible, especially if we have the help of the pumpkies."

Nyla remembered Xander saying that she was the head of the security council, though according to his grandfather, Representative Wesson wasn't an Heir of Tenebris.

"That's our other point of discussion," Alexander mumbled. "How are we to get the pumpkies here without raising alarm through the countryside?"

"It's rather simple." Ingrid rolled her eyes. "All we have to do is meet them and cast a concealment charm. They'll be practically invisible, just like Dinora is to us."

"Simple, but taxing, Mage General," another Caster with hair so blonde she thought it was white pointed out. Nyla remembered that he was one of the ones who'd helped Frederick inside earlier. "It might use too much energy and leave us all vulnerable to Dinora and whatever army she can muster."

"I think we're all forgetting something rather important," Xander interrupted. "Dinora is trying to continue a 600-year-old war, a war that nearly no one remembers outside of myths and legends. She might be able to raise an army of rocks, but she won't be able to inspire any human allies. Corvus won't go to war with us on the word or ambition of a woman history forgot."

"Corvids never forget," Sir Ian countered.

"It's been *600* years," Xander insisted. "Tenebris and Corvus have too much to lose going to war with each other, even if Corvids never forget."

"She was once their queen and Cedric their rightful heir before the Ten Years' War," Alexander said, rubbing his temple with a hand. "But I believe my grandson has an excellent point. Neither Tenebris nor Corvus can go to war with each other. Between trade and treaties, as well as finances, it isn't feasible. Neither country would benefit from it, and as far as any of us know, Dinora hasn't returned to Corvus. How could she?"

"If Cedric can wisp, couldn't Dinora? He made it as far as the Dunes. What's to stop Dinora from wisping to Corvus and garnering support to destroy us?"

"She couldn't. Her magic was bound for over 600 years. I doubt she has the strength," Nyla muttered. She picked through her memory. What was the most amount of magic Dinora had used while they were all at the Manor? "She can wisp because we've seen her do it at the manor, but I don't know how far she could potentially travel because she was bound to the Woodlane at the time. Once the bond was broken…she disappeared. We don't know the extent of her injuries, if any, but I know we threw *a lot* of magic at each other, so given all of that, I can't imagine she would've gotten very far with her magic alone."

"And, what, exactly is 'a lot' of magic to you?" a hard-faced Caster asked. She was the other one who had helped Frederick inside.

"I take it you lost a lot of money on my duel?" Nyla smiled. The woman flushed with anger, further irritated by the quiet chuckles Nyla's quip had earned from around the table. Bracing herself for her next words, Nyla peeked at Xander before holding the eyes of the woman unflinchingly. "To answer your question, it was enough magic that I almost died from the backlash of our magics colliding, and the only reason I'm alive right now is because Shamira healed me."

The woman's mouth gaped open and then closed. Under her gaze and the startled tension blanketing the table, the woman shrank back in her chair.

"You…" Alexander began, drawing her attention. Immediate concern flooded his shocked features. She didn't know if it was the result of hearing about her near-death or because her recount of the battle gave them some barometer of Dinora's power. "You almost died?"

Nyla nodded, nibbling on her lip as she suddenly regretted her words.

"Shamira had to heal Nyla twice before she could fully recover," Xander added. "I didn't think that much magic from a single person was possible."

She reached for his hand under the table and squeezed it, uncertain if she was comforting herself or him. "Dinora has an immense amount of power too, but I doubt she has the stamina to do much of anything right now. We need to find her before she has the time to get stronger and possibly find allies to join her cause."

"Then it's worth casting a concealment charm to bring the pumpkies here," the blonde Caster from before said at last.

"Time might be our enemy as much as Dinora right now," Queen Clarice said.

King Albert nodded in agreement. "The sooner our forces are together, the better. We cannot risk war, and we cannot panic the people. We need to control the situation before it becomes impossible, and before Dinora gains the upper hand."

Nods and murmurs of agreement met the royals' words. With the consent of everyone present, the council moved forward with planning the arrival of the pumpkies and what would come next.

Nyla settled back in her chair as the conversation, thankfully, steered away from her. She still held Xander's hand under the table. Neither of them had let go, and she wasn't certain if he were waiting for her to pull away because she no longer needed the assurance that someone here was actually her friend and could be trusted, or if he just didn't mind. Either way, the Master of Finance, and consequently a member of the Heirs of Tenebris, droned on and on about the expenses of their endeavor.

He'd already gone on about the amount of food and supplies they should expect to need for not only the Casters, Royal Guard, and the limited military force the Chamber of Commons had given to their cause, but was now discussing the added expense of the pumpkies.

All eyes turned to her and Xander. Under the table, Xander's hand tightened around hers the slightest bit.

"You've met a pumpkie, correct?" Representative Abacus asked them.

"Yes," Xander answered.

Unspoken questions lingered in the air between themselves and the other members of the war council. Nyla's lips pulled into a small smile, nearly laughing at the clear confusion written across the faces of those sat around the table.

"I think they're rather self-sufficient, though it may be difficult for them to hunt and gather resources if they're forced to remain on the estate like we intend," Nyla started. "I'll speak with Shamira to coordinate what to expect of the pumpkies in the meantime so we can get a better idea of their needs and what sort of costs might be associated with their arrival and stay here."

"That sounds—"

A knock sounded at the study door. Alexander stood from his chair and went to see who it was. He'd barely opened the door a crack and exchanged a few words with whomever stood out in the hallway.

Nyla strained her ears to catch any fragment of the conversation she could, but to no avail. She did know who was on the other side of the door, though. It was Moretta. Even if food sounded delightful at the moment, she hoped they wouldn't break for a long lunch. As the queen said, time simply wasn't on their side. Any amount of time spent on anything other than defeating Dinora was something she could use to her advantage. And she *would* use their laziness to grow stronger, to seek allies she didn't have to animate or awaken or whatever it was that she did to the rock points of the Shadow Forest.

At length, Alexander closed the door and returned to the table. "I do hope that no one here was looking forward to a full luncheon. Moretta has just come to see what my plans were, and I informed her that we would take lunch here and that there wasn't time for a big to-do. The others can do as they please."

"The Casters Corps have their own provisions, but breakfast was certainly appreciated, Lord Huntington," Ingrid said.

Hubert nodded his head in agreement. "The Guard also has our own provisions, and would again like to thank you for your hospitality."

"Good, then it's all taken care of. The only thing left to decide is what Nyla's part will be in all of this." At Alexander's words, all eyes turned expectantly on her. "Given recent events, I think I can speak for everyone here when I say that you are a great addition to our forces. Upon reflection, it's been recognized that the technique with which you wield magic is akin to how Casters used magic 600 years ago. You are the only one who may be able to match Dinora's style and teach the rest of our numbers how to combat it—you and the pumpkies. What would you like to do, Nyla? The choice is yours."

Nyla didn't expect that she could grip Xander's hand any tighter. Reluctantly, she let go and folded both of her hands in her lap.

"I want to do whatever it will take to defeat Dinora. I want to fight."

26. THE MAN WHO MADE A PROMISE

Xander's mouth went dry. He'd always known that it would come to this. Nyla wouldn't want to walk away from the possibility that she could defeat the woman responsible for killing her family.

But that didn't stop the stutter in his chest when the words had left her lips.

"Are you certain, Nyla?" his grandfather asked her, leaning forward with his hands clasped tightly on the smooth tabletop. "You don't have to fight this war. None of us expect you to, and certainly no one would judge you if you wanted to remain safe and hidden until—"

"Thank you, Alexander, but I'm certain." Nyla nodded solemnly. "I have to do this—I *want* to do this. Dinora has taken so much from not just me and my family, but from magic and all those people in years past. I was prepared to fight her alone, but I'm glad to have all of you to help me."

"Astrid was much older than you when the Corvid Uprising began," Ingrid said. She folded her arms over her chest, leveling Nyla with a contemplative stare as if she was examining every facet of the woman beside him.

"Astrid was a lot of things. She was the Royal Mage, she had training, she became the first Mage General," Nyla listed, "but she was alone. She chose not to share the burden and tried to defeat Dinora single-handedly. I don't intend on doing that. I know I can't defeat her alone."

"Your duel with Frederick says otherwise," someone muttered from the opposite end of the table. A couple of snickers and agitated looks met the remark, but Nyla only smiled softly.

"Dinora is much more ruthless than Frederick. I'd like to think his last effort wasn't meant to kill me."

Xander wasn't certain about that. It had looked like Frederick wanted to smother her with that torrent of wind. He'd like to ask Nyla how she'd done it, and where the trees had come from. Edwin hadn't been able to explain anything in his excitement, though Xander wasn't certain if that was because Nyla had won or if he'd placed a large wager on the duel and wanted to collect it. He supposed he'd have to find out later, when he had a spare moment—if he survived long enough to have a free moment.

"Then I guess all there is to do is wait for the arrival of the pumpkies," his grandfather said.

"Not quite," Ingrid started. "In the meantime, Nyla and I will try to find Dinora."

Nyla sat straighter in her seat. The corners of her lips turned up in a pleased smile. Xander swallowed. This was her choice, just as he'd always known it would be.

"Sounds like a plan to me," Nyla said, just as there was another knock on the door.

"Ah, that must be Moretta with lunch," his grandfather said as he stood and made for the door.

Moretta wheeled a cart full of sandwiches and stoppered drinks into the study. Delicate cakes and china were stacked on the second tier should they need to take an afternoon snack at some point during their deliberations.

As she left, some people made themselves plates, but Xander couldn't stomach the idea of eating as the discussion turned toward potential battlefields and strategy.

Sir Hubert and General Edwards of the Tenebrese Army were presenting different scenarios they could hope for. It all hinged on Nyla's theory that Dinora was raising the rock points of the Shadow Forest—a theory apparently being tested by members of Ingrid's Circle.

"In theory, we could force Dinora to fight a war on two fronts with the pumpkies and a limited force of troops joining us here," General Edwards pointed to a spot on the map outside of Huntington, in the thick of the Shadow Forest, "from the northwest and our troops from the east."

"Do you think that would work if Dinora is raising an immortal army?" a blonde Caster—Alastair, he remembered—asked.

"I wouldn't say they're immortal," Ingrid said, her first words in nearly thirty minutes, "just inanimate."

Xander arched his brow. They hadn't seemed inanimate to him as they were attacking their carriage. As the table's attention turned to Ingrid, a wry smirk came to her face.

"Nyla said that she and Edwin Maffis defeated three of them," Ingrid explained slowly, "which means calling them immortal sets an inaccurate precedent that sounds more daunting than it is. Calling them inanimate and difficult to defeat at least sets an expectation, but doesn't instill trepidation in our forces."

Xander blinked. He supposed when it was put like that, Ingrid raised a valid point.

Sir Hubert broke the brief silence that'd met the Mage General's words. "Then we'll call them inanimate and hope that blasting them with cannon fire can destroy them if the Casters become fatigued."

"We won't," Ingrid ensured him. "I've already had the Healers prepare tonics and instructed every Caster to keep a few on their person from now until the time that Dinora is defeated. Nyla." Ingrid paused. Beside him, he heard Nyla take a sharp breath. "You'll want to grab a few tonics for yourself from Edwin."

"I will." She nodded.

Xander caught her eyes. She only offered him a thin smile before turning her attention back to the table as the conversation steered toward fortifying the country and managing public information.

Soon, battle plans had been made with the hopes that Dinora could be found before she could raise an army, and plans to fortify the country and its infrastructure were made in the meantime—just in case.

With their dismissal, a few people took their leave, some taking a pastry on their way out now that lunch had come and gone. The so-called Heirs of Tenebris all remained behind, conversing quietly amongst themselves. Nyla and Ingrid chatted near the door, and Xander found himself suspended between states of being.

He had no idea what he wanted to do, and hadn't really put much thought into it now that he had time to let it all sink in. Before now, they'd been consumed with breaking the curse that bound Nyla to the Manor, and then they were off to Huntington, and he was left to his own worries about his homecoming. But now, sitting here, the full weight settled on Xander as it was all that he could focus on. There were no more distractions to delay his decision.

He didn't want to fight in a war and possibly die, but he also didn't want to abandon Nyla. She was right, though. Even though she wouldn't be fighting this war alone, he had to wonder if these people would keep her in check, or if they trusted her to own her actions and intentions.

"Xander, a word?" His grandfather's hand fell on his shoulder.

He nodded and let his grandfather steer him toward the study's balcony. Shutting the curtained door behind them, his grandfather came to stand beside him. They looked over the courtyard in silence. Xander's eyes focused intently on the two new trees of lilac blooms and silver bark.

"With so much focus on Nyla and Dinora, you must be feeling lost." His grandfather's voice was soft, but not quite questioning either.

"They aren't going to let her die, right?"

"No. Ingrid might be many things, maybe even callous, but she does truly care about the people under her charge," his grandfather assured him. "It's difficult to lead, Xander." A pause. His grandfather took a deep breath and seemed to hold it, making Xander tense up at the question he knew was coming, even as the weight of his grandfather's previous sentiment settled on him. "What do you want to do in all of this, if anything?"

"I don't know." He shook his head, pushing off of the banister where his forearms had rested. "I thought I would know by the time we got here and by the time Nyla had definitively decided to fight, but the truth is…I have no idea what I want. The only thing I know is that I might love her."

His grandfather chuckled.

"It's not funny," Xander protested, before ultimately letting out a small chuckle himself. "Okay, maybe it is, but this is still serious. I don't want her to die, and I'd really like to stay alive myself."

"Sometimes it's harder to stay behind because all you can see is what was and what could've been. You never move forward or backward your-self. You only live to see the other side and what's left, if anything is left at all." His grandfather's voice grew distant, as if his words had brought to mind Issie and Xander's parents. Shaking his head, his grandfather patted his shoulder. "It sounds like your choice is Nyla, and if I have any understanding of people at all, I think Nyla would choose you too."

Xander stared at his grandfather, bewildered. How could he say something so certainly when he hadn't even known Nyla for that long?

Before Xander could ask, his grandfather had moved inside, and the woman in question had taken his place beside him. Xander tried to calm his heartbeat, hoping Nyla wouldn't notice how stricken he was by the flutter of panic in his veins. Had she overheard any of what he'd told his grandfather, or what his grandfather had told him?

She didn't give any indication of having overheard them as she gravitated toward the banister as though she floated on a breeze.

"Wow, Pemberly is beautiful," she breathed, taking in the view. The slanted rays of the sun crowned her in a golden light. Snapping out of her wonderment, she offered him one of the plates in her hands. "Hungry?"

"Sure," he said, shoving all memory of his grandfather's conversation out of his mind with a slight shake of his head in an attempt to hide any evidence of his feelings for her from his features. Taking the plate she'd brought for him, he turned his back on the garden view and leaned against the banister. "What are you doing after lunch?"

Nyla tilted her head from side to side, swallowing the bite she'd taken. "Ingrid wants to get started on finding Dinora right away, so I guess that's what I'm doing. Tell Merry I'm sorry."

He nodded, taking a bite of his own sandwich.

"Are you all right?" she asked, leaning against the banister beside him.

"Fine." He offered her a smile.

Nyla only rolled her eyes. "You are such a liar."

"All right, you really want to know?" He set his plate aside, wiping his hands on the napkin she'd brought and trying to avoid the fact that he'd have to look her in the eye at some point.

"Obviously, I wouldn't have asked if I didn't care," Nyla frowned.

"I'm scared. I'm scared for you, for me, for Shamira, for everyone," he explained, turning to her. He itched to reach out to her, if only to help himself realize that she was real in this very moment, and that he was awake. Forcing himself to take a breath, Xander ran a hand through his hair, his eyes flicking toward the two trees and back again. His hand grazed the simple ring hidden beneath his shirt. The slight brush of his hand against the dainty metal transformed it into an anchor that sat on his chest, becoming a weight he didn't think he could bear. "I'm scared that you'll die, that Dinora *won't* die, and that life as we all know it will end."

Nyla's eyes searched his, but for what he didn't know. She set her plate on the shadowed table in the balcony's corner, wrapping her arms around herself as her face twisted in what could only be distress. "Please don't be afraid. We can't both be afraid of what's coming."

"Maybe being fearless can be Shamira's job then."

"No," Nyla said with a tight shake of her head. She made to step forward, but something stopped her. Xander watched, his chest caving in on itself as Nyla drew in a deep breath, closing her eyes for a moment as if what she wanted to say pained her. And when their eyes met next, that was all he saw. Her lilac eyes were marred by pain. His stomach twisted at the sight, fearing what she might say and knowing that the possibilities were near endless. "I can't do this if I'm worried that you're worried about *me*. I'll be too busy trying not to die because I know you're afraid, that I just might die because I can't focus. And Shamira can't be the only one to face Dinora. It wouldn't feel right to me."

"So, what then?" The tension in his chest eased somewhat with her words, but not quite enough to quell his nerves. He stepped forward, gently closing the gap between them. "You don't want me to be afraid, and I don't want you to fight at all, but I can't stop you. It sounds like the only thing either of us can do is to stop caring, and that's not happening."

"No," Nyla agreed softly. "I guess not."

Staring at each other, silence filled the space between them and threatened to push them apart. Nyla glanced away, staring down at her shoes. "She killed my family. I have to fight. I *want* to be the one to…to—"

"I know." Xander wrapped his arms around her. "It's why I wasn't going to say anything."

"But you'll be here?" Her voice was muffled against his chest as she all but melted against him. It made him wonder about all that might be plaguing her mind at the very moment, or if there was any burden he could alleviate for her so she could focus on what mattered, on living.

"I guess you just have to accept the fact that you're stuck with me," he sighed dramatically, shrugging.

Nyla laughed, pulling back but not away as she tilted her head up to look him in the eye. "Am I? I thought you were stuck with me?"

"You know," he chuckled, "that doesn't seem like such a bad thing."

"I don't mind being stuck with you one bit," she said, her eyes dancing. Xander smiled at her grin, finding the insecure whispers that'd crawled to the forefront of his mind banished for the time being. Something *thumped* within the study, causing him to flinch as he'd all but forgotten the room full of people mere steps away from them. Nyla's eyes glanced toward the door as his own eyes flicked in its direction before going back to her. Nyla groaned, all light in her face gone. "I guess I should see if Ingrid is ready to get started."

Staring back at her, Xander wondered if she was going to say something more. Realizing their closeness and how fragile this single moment was compared to the weight of everything they were about to face, he found himself committing each and every flicker of Nyla's eyes to memory. And alongside this moment, Xander saw the way she'd stared back at him when he'd dipped her during their waltz.

Thinking of that moment, he almost wanted to ask her what she wanted, after Dinora was defeated, but found that he couldn't speak. Instead, the silence bloomed between them as they stayed just as they were, gently holding each other as if they were the only two people in the world.

Nyla dropped her gaze. "I should go."

"Yeah," Xander said. "I should really check in on Merry or see if my grandfather requires my presence."

"You'll tell Merry that I'll see her later?"

"Of course," Xander said with a small smile. "I'm sure she'll understand. She's really grown up since I left home."

Nyla hummed, pulling away slowly. "When this is all over, you know, with Dinora dead or however we end up defeating her, do you…"

As Nyla trailed off, her eyes flitted to the door again. She bit her lip. Shaking her head slightly, she gave a half-hearted laugh as she met his eyes once more. "I'm sorry. I don't know what I was going to ask. I'm just thinking about Cedric and finding Dinora, and all I want when this is all over is a long nap."

Casting his skepticism aside at Nyla's sudden bout of forgetfulness, Xander attempted a smile. "Then maybe you could stay here, at Pemberly? You know, until you're ready to decide what you want to do next."

"Yeah." Nyla nodded slowly, a soft smile spreading across her face. "I think that sounds nice. I'll think about it."

Xander nodded as she took a step away. "Nyla," he said, reaching out to her before he could stop himself. His fingers barely grazed her shoulder. When she stopped and glanced over her shoulder at him, he dropped his hand and said, "Whatever you and Ingrid are about to do to find Dinora, please just be careful."

"I will be," she said quietly with the ghost of a smile.

As Xander watched her return inside, he cast another long glance down at the garden. Lilacs were a funny thing. First love, old love, remembrance.

He wondered about Astrid and the things she'd done. Why hadn't she killed Dinora? Was she unable to? Or was it that she couldn't? If so, why couldn't she?

Xander didn't know, and doubted he ever would. It seemed unfair to him that Dinora was able to cheat death for over six centuries. And it was just as unfair that she was allowed to continue her rampage after so long. He didn't care what god could claim responsibility for that blunder, if any did at all, or for the parts Cedric had played in all of this as well.

Any faith he'd held in Balmae or Corruptio—even Helpet—dimmed.

It was left up to the Heirs of Tenebris and the assembled force gathered inside his ancestral home, to Nyla.

And he was expendable.

Try as he might to tell himself otherwise, Xander couldn't help but feel as though any part he chose in the matter was insignificant compared to the people within Pemberly Hall. From trained Casters to the Royal Guard to the Heirs of Tenebris, there weren't many opportunities for him to prove his worth or to help Nyla. He was just here.

Maybe that would be enough. Maybe simply being here to support Nyla was the best part for him to play. After all, who else could truly be there for her when they all had their own interests in defeating Dinora at any cost?

Xander grabbed their plates and went back into the study, determination swelling in his heart.

He would fight. Not for revenge, not for honor, and not for duty. None of that mattered. He would fight for Nyla because, as it turned out, he did love her, and he wanted to be there for her, even if the prospect of going to war terrified him more than death.

27. THE MAN IN THE PAST

Nyla followed Ingrid through the halls of Pemberly, replaying her conversation with Xander along the way. She'd wanted to say something, to tell him how much his help had meant to her, and how she'd miss this—miss *him*—but the words hadn't come. She also didn't know how to tell him all he'd come to mean to her and how grateful she was that he was with her through all of this in a way that didn't make it sound as if she expected to die fighting Dinora, but the truth was, she did. Even if she didn't lose her life, she knew she would always bear some scar of this war, especially as her mind turned toward Cedric's reappearance.

"Ingrid," she started hesitantly, "could I…would it be possible to see Cedric?"

The woman glanced sharply at her before coming to a complete stop in the middle of the hallway. Her face was nearly unreadable, though her eyes betrayed how much Nyla's request shocked her. "Why do you want to see him?"

Nyla licked her lips. "I don't really know."

Ingrid inclined her head, studying Nyla in a way that made her feel as though she was being dissected. Her eyes sparkled with something Nyla could only assume was amusement as the dim light of concern finally faded from them. "Do you think he would give you any information that he wouldn't give to us otherwise?"

"We could try?" Nyla offered her a shaky smile. Uncertainty flooded her veins, the sort that she hadn't known for days.

"I suppose." Ingrid clicked her tongue. "We should ask Lord Huntington, as an Heir of Tenebris and...our host, before you see him."

Nyla wondered about Ingrid's hesitation, lingering on it for a moment longer than was probably necessary. Had Ingrid intended to say something else? Or was it just that Ingrid didn't like Alexander, or the body he represented? Nyla wondered if there was some strife between the Heirs and the Mage General, but couldn't figure out why. Astrid had started the Heirs of Tenebris, in a roundabout way. And she was the first Mage General in Tenebrese history, so why would Ingrid bear some animosity toward the Heirs?

"I didn't realize the Heirs wielded so much power throughout Tenebris," Nyla said carefully, "though I guess that's how secret societies work."

"You could say that," Ingrid grumbled, beginning to walk away. "The Heirs were a myth, just like Dinora. They were supposed to be a piece of history that had faded all the same, and yet, as we're all finding out now, it's all very real and rather present."

Nyla nodded slowly, following along with Ingrid's brisk pace. "Well at least you knew *of* them. I didn't think any of this was real, that they were only myths to tell around the fire."

"If only they were."

Nyla swallowed, realizing Ingrid wouldn't say anything more about the Heirs or divulge the reason behind her mistrust of them.

"We'll see Cedric first," Ingrid said, taking a sharp turn down the hallway Nyla recognized as the way to the back gardens of Pemberly. "Then we'll find Dinora."

"What about asking Lord Huntington?"

"He'll just have to understand that this was your choice," Ingrid said dismissively. "Cedric is as much a prisoner of the Caster Corps as he is of the Heirs. Besides," Ingrid smiled softly at her, "you are more than capable at making your own decisions. I will respect your judgement of the situation, and am admittedly curious about the response you may receive from him."

Nyla scrunched her nose. Whether or not Ingrid truly meant what she said, she understood now that the woman merely hoped her physical similarity to Astrid could be used to their advantage. Nyla wouldn't pretend to be offended by it, not when her mind knew this turn of Fate might just lead them to discovering an advantage.

Cedric had loved Astrid, or vice versa. Maybe there was a truth to that love, one that would prove useful to them even if it came at her expense.

After all, weren't they all just trying to save as many people as possible? Weren't they all working toward a singular goal for the benefit of their neighbors, their friends, their families, for the idea of life itself?

Nyla shook the thought away, unwilling to contemplate the gravity of that last realization in this moment. She needed to focus on what she would do when she faced Cedric. Minding their surroundings as Ingrid pushed open the courtyard door and stepped out into the dazzling sunlight, Nyla found herself biting the inside of her cheek as she considered her options.

A pair of Royal Guards flanked the doors, standing the slightest bit straighter as Nyla and Ingrid stepped over the threshold. Hurrying down the stairs, Nyla made every effort to keep up with the dark-haired woman. The well-tended plants and garden paths melted away as Nyla followed Ingrid down weaving paths and toward the tree line of the Shadow Forest at the edge of Pemberly Hall's sprawling courtyards. Sometime after their arrival, Xander had given her a tour of the estate and when she'd asked about it, he'd told her that Pemberly held a vast 127 acres. She couldn't picture how an estate this big could reside in a city like Huntington, but then she'd remembered that the city had expanded and built around the founding family and the empire that was their trading company.

Reaching the end of a hedge-lined path, Ingrid glanced both ways down the aisle and back over her shoulder. Nyla frowned at the leafy bush with its prickly amber leaves.

"What I'm about to do stays between us, understood?" Ingrid's voice had taken on an edge of authority.

"Yeah." Nyla bobbed her head, glancing over at the woman curiously. There was still so much about magic that she didn't know, but no matter how hard she tried, she couldn't sense anything. There was only the plant life around them, but if she pushed harder, Nyla could vaguely sense an intricate layer of spellwork and magic beyond the well-kept hedges.

Ingrid's blush-colored magic burst from her hand. Nyla blinked against the brightness, stumbling on her feet as the hedges trembled and the pavers began to part with a grinding grumble. Her mouth dropped open as the hedge before them slid backward, pavers and all, exposing a magicitric-lit stairwell leading down into what Nyla could only assume was the heavily warded prison Alexander had spoken of yesterday.

"Follow me," Ingrid started, gesturing toward the stairs, "and remember, I'll be with you every step if you want me to be. You will never have to face either of them alone again."

Nyla nodded, her mouth going dry at the sentiment. "Thank you."

Ingrid offered her a comforting smile before taking the first step down into the dungeons of Pemberly Hall. Steeling herself with a deep breath, Nyla followed after her. Planting a hand on the rough stone wall, Nyla worried her bottom lip between her teeth. Maybe asking to see Cedric was the worst idea she'd ever had, but there was a part of her that needed to. She didn't know why, and she couldn't even begin to understand the vague feeling that this was somehow the right decision, only that her bones knew it was.

A few steps after Nyla's head had cleared the opening, a low rumble filled her ears. Ingrid didn't pay the noise any mind, though Nyla flinched and cast a glance over her shoulder in time to see the dangling roots of the hedge and the garden pavers slide back into place as if they'd never moved in the first place.

"You'll get used to these things in time. It's all still pretty new to you, isn't it?" Ingrid asked, chuckling a little.

"If you say so," Nyla muttered, trying not to shiver as they traveled farther away from the earth's surface. "I've gone all my life thinking I didn't have magic, only to inherit a long-dead relative's and a war that's over 600 years old."

"There's still time to turn back," Ingrid offered, though her footsteps didn't falter. "And I don't just mean about this little visit to Pemberly's dungeons."

Nyla shook her head, not that Ingrid saw it. "I can't. I would never forgive myself for passing this problem onto someone else when I'm the reason Dinora's free." Nyla paused, her words settling on her own mind. She rubbed at the goosebumps on her arms. "Besides, I would love nothing more than to see her fall and to know it was because of me."

"Ah," Ingrid said philosophically, "I see. It's about revenge for you and not so much a noble duty."

"It is and it isn't," Nyla clarified, trying to sound convincing. But there wasn't time for that as they reached the bottom of the near endless staircase.

They were met by four guards, two bearing the indigo cloaks of the Royal Guard and the other two distinctly under Ingrid's command as the former visibly relaxed as she and Ingrid stepped into the light.

"Mage General," one of the Casters, a broad-shouldered man with a trim beard and mustache, said with a bow of his head, "Miss Delhart."

"We've come to pay a visit to Kashar."

The four guards shared a grim look, seeming to collectively glance back at Nyla before quickly averting their gazes back to the Mage General.

"That won't be a problem, will it?" Ingrid asked almost sweetly.

"No, ma'am," a portly Royal Guard said. "Please, follow me."

Nyla swallowed, passing by the remaining three guards and the uneasiness in which they regarded her. Was it because of the duel? Her age? Or the magic she'd inherited from Astrid? She didn't want to know. Nyla understood the concern in their eyes, but she'd hoped by now the majority of them would've accepted her choice to fight Dinora.

All too soon, the Royal Guard stopped before a thick metal door. In the dancing light of the magicitric torches, Nyla's eyes roved over the etched sigils carved into the metal. She remembered seeing some of the sigils on the wands and daggers—athames, she knew now—in George's shop back in Caselle, but she still didn't know what they meant or why they were used. She'd have to remember to ask Ingrid once they were done.

"If you two need anything at all, or are ready to come out, knock *twice*," he said, eyeing Nyla particularly hard before slotting the key in the lock.

Ingrid smirked. "Thank you, Abraham, but I'm sure we'll be fine."

Abraham pursed his lips, but didn't dare contradict Ingrid as he finished unlocking the thick bolts and yet another padlock before easing the door open and motioning them inside.

Nyla took a deep breath of the stale air wafting from the cell before crossing the threshold. Ingrid stepped in after her, though as Nyla stood waiting anxiously for her eyes to adjust, she realized any plan she'd scraped together in her mind had gone. Nyla blinked into the dimly lit cell, staying her hands as she listened to Abraham click the locks back into place.

"Hello again, Cedric," Ingrid drawled, filling the silence as she took a step closer to the figure huddled in the corner farthest from the door.

Nyla successfully blinked away the rest of the light spots blurring her vision. Her stomach coiled tighter as her eyes landed on Cedric curled up in the corner, his knees drawn up to his chest and his head buried in his arms.

"Please," he rasped without moving, his voice thick with grogginess and hoarse from either disuse or dehydration, Nyla couldn't say for certain. "Leave me be."

Against her will, Nyla's heart clenched.

This was the man who'd come striding into the foyer of the Woodlane Manor, his cloak billowing behind him and exuding power? *This* was the man who'd tried to murder her in cold blood on the manor's astral plane?

"Why would we do that when there's so much to talk about?" Ingrid countered.

At this, Cedric shifted his head just enough to peek one eye out at them. All at once, Cedric shot to his feet, swaying unsteadily. "Ast—"

Just as quickly as he'd stood, he sagged against the wall with his head hanging limply. Nyla watched, her lips quirked in a deep frown as his knees wobbled and gave out. Sliding down the wall, Cedric's chest heaved. Even in the dim light, Nyla could see the twinge of gray marking his already pale skin. He shook, shivering, but Nyla didn't think it was from the absent chill of the dungeon. By all means, it was rather cozier down here than she'd expected it to be, given that it was after all, a dungeon. But the comfortable temperature hadn't kept away the goosebumps she could see plaguing his arms or the slight chatter of his teeth.

"Astrid," he breathed, pain lacing his voice.

"He's been refusing medical treatment, but as you can see, he needs it if he is to survive," Ingrid whispered to her.

Dazed, Cedric's hazy eyes blinked longingly up at Nyla. Staring down at him, she didn't know what to do or say.

"Why are you refusing treatment?" she asked, finally finding her voice again. She didn't bother to correct the fact that he thought she was Astrid, hoping the trick would work in their favor.

He frowned, blinking as if it could give him some clarity. "Don't deserve it."

"Because you said so, or because you have no intention of helping us?"

Her heart thudded in the beat of silence that followed her question. Cedric seemed stunned by it, blinking through his daze. His face crumpled as the misty glaze over his eyes cleared somewhat and for a moment, Nyla didn't think he was going to answer her.

"I…" Cedric trailed off. "I can't help. But I want to."

Nyla arched her brow, glancing at Ingrid. The woman only shrugged, encouraging her to continue with a gentle wave of her hand.

"Then tell us something, anything," Nyla encouraged. "Maybe it's more helpful to us than you think it is."

Cedric took a shuddering breath, as if it physically pained him to do so. Maybe it did, but Nyla couldn't worry about that. All she cared about anymore was how he was even still alive or if there was some secret way to defeat Dinora without a huge confrontation.

"She…she'll cross any line to win, no matter who it hurts," he said, his face crumpling with confusion. "Don't show her any mercy."

"We've gathered that, yes," Ingrid said. "What else can you tell us? Does she have any allies, any special skillset, magic cache—"

"No." Cedric shook his head adamantly. "Dinora is many things, but she isn't a skilled Mage. All power and no skill."

"Then why help her all these years?" Nyla couldn't help but ask.

Cedric paused, opening and closing his mouth. Drawing his knees up to his chest again, Nyla cursed herself. Yes, she desperately wanted to know why, but if he stopped talking to them again, it would be all her fault.

When Cedric finally answered, his voice was no more than an utterance. "I thought maybe…" He shook his head. "It doesn't matter."

His eyes grew vacant.

She opened her mouth to ask why, but thought better of it. Cedric had curled in on himself again, a certain dismissal if she ever saw one. Her eyes cut to Ingrid. The woman's lips were pursed as she stared at Cedric. As though she could feel Nyla's gaze on her, Ingrid turned her head.

Unspoken questions passed between them, each wanting to ask more of the captive man.

What should we do now? she asked Ingrid.

That's the most he's spoken to anyone, she said. Her voice skirted over Nyla's mind with as much confidence as the woman spoke with. *Maybe it will be enough.*

What about his injuries?

We can't treat him if he keeps fighting us.

Nyla nodded, glancing uncertainly at Cedric once more. *Then I guess that's all there is to do. I'm ready if you are.*

Ingrid hummed. "You've been most helpful this time, Cedric. Enjoy your solitude."

He didn't respond. Nyla eyed him as Ingrid knocked on the door as Abraham had instructed. As the silence of Cedric's cell was broken by the sound of the metal bolts sliding back and the locks *clicking* on the other side of the door, Nyla turned what they'd learned over in her head.

Just as she'd moved to step out into the hallway, Cedric's voice clawed down her spine.

"I'm sorry, for all of it." She glanced back at him only to find him staring at her with that same hazy look in his eyes that told her he was still living in the past, of a time long since gone. "I know I'll never make up for all I've done, but I needed to tell you how sorry I am."

"For what part?" Nyla prompted. "For hurting me, my family, or for helping Dinora all these years and never once stopping to think what you were doing was wrong?"

"All of it," he repeated. "I'll never forgive myself for any of it."

Nyla hesitated, glancing at both Ingrid and Abraham pleading with her to move so they could shut Cedric in his cell, injured and alone.

"Let them tend to your injuries," she said, licking her lips. "You're no good to anyone dead."

She didn't wait to take in Cedric's face at her words, or how Ingrid's brows raised in question. Gliding past her, Nyla walked a few paces down the hallway before coming to a stop, thankful for the grate of metal against metal filling her ears as Abraham locked Cedric's cell.

"Feel any better?" Ingrid asked, clasping a hand on Nyla's shoulder.

"I think I'm going to be sick," she breathed.

"You did just fine in there," Ingrid ducked her head to catch Nyla's eye, making certain that she was staring back at her before continuing. "I think you got some very important information for us."

Nyla nodded her head absently. It wasn't the information that had scarred her. It was the hollow gaze and the gaunt features that had disturbed her. She'd been too stunned to truly look at Cedric when they'd hauled him into the great hall two days ago. She didn't know if the wrenching of her heart was warranted, but Nyla couldn't say that she had ever seen someone look so…broken.

But it was Cedric. A murderer, a traitor, an accomplice.

It definitely said more about her humanity than anything that her heart could feel a twinge of pity or sympathy for someone like that, but her mind didn't want to acknowledge it. Her mind said he was undeserving of her mercy even as the morality in her blood told her that this was what made her different than them, than Dinora.

Even after all the terrible things and horrible crimes they'd committed, the things they'd taken as well as the lives taken by their hand, her heart could scrounge together the tiniest bit of mercy even as her mind knew they—that *he*—didn't deserve it.

"We should probably work on finding Dinora," Nyla said, pushing herself away from the wall. "Even if what Cedric said is true about her having no allies, there's still the possibility of her raising the rock points of the Shadow Forest to become her army."

"But he also said she lacked skill." Ingrid took a step down the hall, back the way they had come earlier. Nyla followed beside her, using the residual adrenaline she hadn't realized had flooded her veins back in Cedric's cell to keep up with her. "She might have the power necessary to do so, but if she doesn't have the proper technique or stamina to raise the rock points, we'll still be facing a limited force, if any at all."

Nyla considered Ingrid's assessment. "Her magic was bound until recently too, but…"

Ingrid turned to her, a question flashing in her eyes. "But what?"

"She's known to steal magic from the land," Nyla reminded her just as they'd entered the guard station at the base of the hidden entrance. "What's to say she won't steal the magic necessary to animate or resurrect enough of the rock points to become a force too difficult to defeat?"

Ingrid fell silent, her face pinched and her lips pursed. Nodding curtly to the guards scrambling to their feet as they passed by, Nyla waited anxiously for a response.

Just as they'd mounted the staircase, Ingrid muttered, "We'll find Dinora, and then we'll depart immediately to face her."

Nyla swallowed around the tension in her throat. "What about the pumpkies?"

"Tell Shamira of our plan, and that there is a set of Casters who will wisp to their location immediately in order to help them travel swiftly to meet us at Dinora's chosen battlefield."

Wrath

The heart of the dense woodland they'd so aptly named the "Shadow Forest" was exactly the place Dinora had been searching for. The overabundance of magic here tickled her senses. She inhaled the warm scent of the forestland, relishing the power in even that single breath.

The navy and indigo leaves whispered in the breeze overhead. She watched, transfixed by the colorful essences swirling all around her. There was magic in the swaying leaves and the long, spindly branches as dark as coal. Sparks of red and orange magic flitted through the currents like popping embers. Even the sheet of onyx-colored rock beneath her feet held an immense power.

And it was all because of her.

When she'd expelled the magic she'd mined from the land, she'd created all of this. But more than that, she'd obliterated the enemies and traitors in her path.

Dinora smiled almost fondly. Surely consuming the magic once again and wielding it against Nyla and whatever army she'd managed to muster would result in as sweet a victory as killing Astrid had.

Drawing the crystal point from the pocket of her long skirt, Dinora grounded her stance. Closing her eyes, she set her jaw. She clenched her teeth in the immense effort to clear her mind of even the worthiest of her victorious imaginings.

Slowly opening her eyes, Dinora unraveled her magic. Letting it prowl over the landscape, she urged it to pluck at the magical essences around her just as she had 647 years ago. Her scarlet-colored magic guided the land's emerald and mossy green magic back to her, trapping it within the crystal point. The faintest of blues, the color of the wind, swept toward the crystal next, joining the steady stream of the land's colors of coal and green and sapphire.

Dinora watched, savoring each layer she mined from the land. The softest golds of the light's essence added a delicate beauty to the radiant crystal point in her hands.

If only she'd had a crystal point all those centuries ago. She could've mined and controlled so much more energy. She thought she'd known and wielded power then, but it was nothing compared to the power clasped between her hands.

Gasping, Dinora tilted her head back. The few leaves left on the shrinking trees were plucked from their fragile branches. They faded into a wisp of sapphire energy that flowed straight into her crystal, joining the myriad of magical essences there.

The trees withered around her, exposing the dulling sky to her wide eyes. The ground beneath her feet cracked and splintered before it too, joined the energies contained within her crystal, leaving her standing on a short pedestal of onyx.

Ash-colored sand swirled in the breeze created by the flying magic racing to join her cache. Through the magic, she could just make out the clusters of onyx stones jutting up from the earth. Blinking slowly, Dinora stoppered the flow of magic to her crystal.

Wanting to save the magic stored there for the battle to come, Dinora redirected her mining efforts to the stone points. As the magic flowed there, the earth began to tremble beneath her pedestal. Cracks opened in the earth. Rays of cosmic light shot from the fissures, the rawest energy of the land's magic she'd ever seen.

As she watched the wavering light, the world groaned. The grating of stone against stone clawed at her ears. A low moan swept through the air, morphing into a whine that became a piercing shriek.

Her army.

It was awakening.

28. RISE OF THE EVIL SORCERESS

The walk back to Ingrid's room was tense with silence. Her mind whirled with what Cedric had told them—and wondered about what their efforts to find Dinora would actually entail, as Ingrid hadn't been very forthcoming about her plan. A part of Nyla had hoped that someone would stop them and delay the inevitable if only for a few more seconds, but as luck would have it, Pemberly Hall was oddly empty. She didn't know it was possible for such a large host of people to disappear, though she supposed the Royal Guard was off preparing to face Dinora alongside the Casters and that the few representatives in attendance had returned to Mageffery to make their report.

She didn't have any time to sift through any of that now as Ingrid hardly stopped before a door and opened it with a wave of her hand. Nyla extended her magic, meeting with the wards Ingrid had used to protect her room before she recalled her powers back. Was the Royal Mage always so cautious? Was that how she became the Royal Mage, and then the Mage General?

Glancing around Ingrid's sitting room, Nyla imagined it was just as tidy as when the room was assigned to the Royal Mage.

"Wait here for just a moment," Ingrid told her, not waiting for a response as she walked toward an adjoining door on the opposite side of the room.

Nervously, Nyla watched as Ingrid removed her overcoat and cast it aside carelessly, revealing a short-sleeved blouse that complimented her rich skin tone before disappearing into the next room. Nyla reached out with her senses. Ingrid's room was devoid of any trace. It was like the woman wasn't present in any sense of the word. It unnerved Nyla that there were people in this estate that she couldn't get a read on. After all, Shamira had spent hours teaching her how to tune into the magic signatures around her for this very purpose.

How was she supposed to trust people whose intentions she couldn't discern?

Body language, actions, words, it was all meaningless because people could train themselves to act a certain way or believe in what they say or do, but auras and magical signatures couldn't lie. They were like peering into a looking glass, an unbiased filter of someone's very essence.

Maybe she should've asked Shamira how to shield herself from others instead of learning to sense the world and people around her.

Ingrid came back with a scroll and a square box in her hands. "Have you ever scried before, Nyla?"

"No…" She watched as Ingrid spread the scroll over the coffee table, gesturing for her to join her as she weighed down the ends with rugged crystals she pulled from the box beside her. Ingrid unwrapped each in turn as Nyla held the map of the world in place.

"Then this can be a learning experience for you as well," Ingrid said lightly, placing the final crystal on the corner of the map. "Scrying is an ancient art, a form of divination. It can be done in many ways and often without any equipment. In our case, though, we need to find someone, so we'll be using a map and this."

She pulled a slim jewelry box from the larger box and lifted the lid. From a layer of tissue, she pulled out a crystal point on a chain. "As we focus our energy, the crystal will point to Dinora—if we manage to find her. I have a feeling we will though, regardless of what charms she's cast to hide herself, because you've actually seen her and know what to look for. Before, my Circle and I could only search for concealment magic, but that isn't sustainable because a great deal of people use concealment charms for whatever reason they deem them necessary."

"Do you think it would be easier if this was only a map of Tenebris?" Nyla asked.

"Dinora could be anywhere, even if we don't believe her to be." Ingrid went to sit on the floor in front of the coffee table, gesturing for Nyla to take a seat on the floor opposite her, against the couch. "Could you hand me that pillow, please?"

Nyla twisted herself around and passed the pillow to Ingrid over the coffee table, careful not to disturb the map or any of the crystals.

"Don't worry, Nyla. I'll focus on searching the map. You focus on seeing Dinora." Ingrid reached out her hands. Nyla took them skeptically. "Ready?"

Nyla nodded. Ingrid's soft, dusty rose magic lifted the pendulum. As Ingrid closed her eyes, she encouragingly offered two final words to her. "Just focus."

Closing her eyes, Nyla cleared her mind. She kept her breaths even and conjured up any image of Dinora that wouldn't make her blood boil. At first, she thought about the way she'd initially presented herself as a caring old lady, the keeper of the Woodlane Manor. But as she thought about her in that state and the story she'd told her and Xander in the library, Nyla's anger awakened. Quickly, Nyla recalled the image of Dinora pulling the hunting knife from her back. She'd seemed shocked that Nyla was even alive.

Unfortunately, Nyla had had something to fight for. Whatever that strange potion had been be damned. And the things Nyla had to fight for hadn't gone away. She still had plenty left to fight for. Her family, her friends, Xander, Tenebris.

Life.

She was fighting for life. Not just her own life or the lives of those she cared about, but the broader spectrum of life. Nyla felt compelled to fight for life just as much as she wanted vengeance for what Dinora had taken from her.

Most of all, Nyla realized, she was fighting for the idea of life, not the preservation of it or to avenge the lives lost 647 years ago or two years ago or even the lives to be lost when they found Dinora, but the idea of what life should be.

The idea of time spent with loved ones. Of time spent laughing and smiling and dancing, of crying and screaming, and, yes, even seeking revenge.

Nyla would fight for it all. It was the promise she'd made after all. She'd promised her family and Astrid that she would live, and not just live, but that she would build a life for herself with the time she had left. She wouldn't wander aimlessly anymore, running from a shadow of her own fears and anxieties.

Nyla wanted all of it. For better or worse, she wanted everything she could ever dream of. And if not for herself, then at least for those she cared about.

She would stand against Dinora until her dying breath if it meant that life could go on. If the rock points littering the Shadow Forest were truly the souls she'd taken in her hungry attempt for power during the Corvid Uprising, Nyla hoped that Dinora's death would free them and bring light to the Forest.

All those legends, all those tales of the haunted Shadow Forest, and no one had realized just how much truth was in them. The history of Tenebris was laid bare before the country's memory, and no one had even realized it. She wondered if it was an invention of the Heirs, or if people had just passed the stories down through the generations until they became nothing more than a way to pass the time during the cold Serenmae days.

Thunk.

Nyla's brow furrowed. She couldn't let the noise distract her; she had to keep focusing on Dinora so they could find the old hag.

"Nyla!" Ingrid whispered in astonishment, her voice resonating with pride.

She peeked her eyes open and saw that the pendulum had landed on the map. It pointed to Tenebris, but, more specifically, to the heart of the Shadow Forest.

They'd found her.

And it was just as Nyla had feared.

"She must be building an army!" Nyla shot to her feet, pulling her hands free from Ingrid's. "She—"

"Nyla, calm down," Ingrid placated, getting to her feet. "Even if she is building an army from the rock points, we know where she is now! We can get through her magical defenses and stop her."

Nyla's chest heaved. She wanted nothing more than to hunt Dinora down where she stood. There was hardly any distance between them, and with all of these Casters, one of them—*Ingrid*—should be able to wisp right in front of Dinora and—

"What's that?" Nyla asked, her inner balance tilted and swayed. She and Ingrid collapsed into each other, gripping each other for stability.

"I-I don't know!" Ingrid shouted as the shaking of the earth became physical. The clock on the mantelpiece rattled and fell off the shelf. Portraits crashed to the floor. "Stay close to me."

Ingrid grabbed onto Nyla and hauled her around the coffee table as Nyla stumbled from the trembling of the earth and her own memories of the giant that had passed her by. Huddled together, Ingrid instantly formed a protective shield around them, not unlike the dome Astrid had created on that battlefield Nyla had observed when she'd drank from Fortune Falls. Nyla jumped as the crystal light fixture crashed into the coffee table, sending wood and glass splinters in every direction.

"Please tell me this is just an earthquake," she pleaded with no one in particular.

"I wish I could," Ingrid said, shifting to wrap her arms around

Nyla as if to offer her comfort or a more apparent idea of protection. Nyla wasn't certain.

Nyla shut her eyes and tried to steady her breathing. Whatever Dinora was doing, it was having a more physical effect on the world than just in the balance of magic, and Nyla didn't like it one bit.

The quaking ceased.

Cautiously, Nyla and Ingrid pulled apart and surveyed the destruction around them.

Goosebumps erupted along Nyla's skin. Her gut dropped into a bottomless chasm. Ingrid let out a curse under her breath. Outside of the window opposite them, the world plunged into shadow. It was the same oppressive shadow Nyla and Xander had traveled through in the heart of the Shadow Forest to get to Fortune Falls.

Dinora.

She'd done something horrible, and in doing so, she'd possibly just declared war on them. Time had run out. And now, there was no way to know what she had planned or how long they had to prepare a counter initiative.

Coming back to herself, Nyla started, flinging her magic out into Pemberly. She scrambled out of Ingrid's embrace. "Xander! I have to find Xander!"

"Nyla, wait!"

But it was too late, Nyla had already found him and Merry. She didn't hesitate as she shoved open the door, its frame cracked.

Xander, I'm coming, she thought desperately, letting out a relieved sigh as she noticed the immediate flinch and relief flooding his essence at her words.

Racing down the cracked or crumbling hallways of Pemberly Hall, two things begged for Nyla's attention as she jumped over or swerved around debris: she had to get to Xander, and she needed to stop Dinora.

Shamira! she called out, casting her magic out as far as she could manage. *Shamira, where are you?*

We're just outside the Shadow Forest, she panted. *Are you all right?*

Fine, but Dinora, she—

We know. She's created her army. I'm sorry, Nyla, but we cannot wait for you or the Casters.

I know. I'll meet you there. Nyla nearly faltered, remembering what it had taken for her and Edwin to finally stop the three stone creatures Dinora had sent after their carriage. *If she's summoned the same creatures as before, you need to use the most primal magic to stop them, tearing them apart from the inside out. It'll exhaust you, but that's the only way I know of how to stop them.*

I'll let the others know.

Crunching over broken glass, Nyla launched herself through a broken doorway to the private gardens off of the season room.

Edwin, she called out desperately, *if you're still alive, promise me you'll keep them safe? I need to know someone will be here for Merry and Xander, someone I trust.*

I will, he promised, his voice sounding strained. *And for what it's worth, I'm not so easy to kill either.*

"You're okay!" she breathed, her heart swelling at the sight of Merry and Xander up ahead. She nearly laughed from both her relief and Edwin's final words to her, coming to a stuttering halt as Xander met her halfway up the path.

"We're fine. We're both fine," he said hurriedly, reaching out to her. "Are you—"

"Fine." She nodded, still catching her breath as Merry crashed into her. She hugged the girl back just as fiercely, staring at Xander over her head. A sad smile crossed her face, realizing that this was it. Xander nodded solemnly, his eyes mournful, as if he knew how she felt in this moment. Her throat tightened as she blinked away the tears forming in her eyes.

"Nyla!" Ingrid called, not far behind and just as winded as Nyla was. She hadn't realized the woman had sprinted after her, too desperate to see Xander and Merry with her own eyes and make certain that they were all right.

At the sound of Ingrid's voice, Merry pulled away. For the first time, Nyla saw the tears streaking down her face and bent down so she could look her in the eyes as Ingrid's footsteps crunched over the fallen leaves, debris, and gravel pathway.

"Everything will be fine, Merry," she said, hoping she sounded reassuring. "You're safe, and we're going to do everything we can to make this better."

She nodded weakly, taking a deep shuddering breath. "Be safe, Nyla."

Nyla offered her a small smile, holding back her own tears. She couldn't muster the words to assure her she would be and instead straightened, looking over at Xander.

He drew closer as Merry stepped away to wipe at her eyes. Nyla didn't know what to say or do, only that she didn't want this to be the last time they ever saw each other. Her heart thundered in her ears, desperately trying to convey a message her addled mind was too preoccupied to wholly understand. Silently, Xander brushed the stray hairs away from her face, but didn't drop his hand. She turned into it, seeking out what little comfort the soft gesture could bring her. The touch was like a phantom, distinctly there but so gentle and careful she wasn't all that certain it was real. Nyla steeled herself, stopping the grim pout she could feel twisting her lips even as her chest fluttered from nerves and the urge to break down and cry all at the same time. All of Pemberly, it seemed, was full of shouts of those preparing for battle, of Casters and soldiers alike clamoring to follow whatever orders she couldn't wholly hear and discern.

There was a commotion behind her, but she didn't dare look. Ingrid barked orders to whomever had joined them out in the courtyard, but her words were lost over the roar of blood in Nyla's ears as she reached for Xander's hand before she could stop herself.

It was time.

Nyla needed to take her place, but she wasn't ready. She just wanted one more second. She yearned for time to freeze, if only for this second with Xander's hand lightly wrapped around hers, their pinky fingers the only real link they had.

"Do you remember that favor you owe me? From Caselle?" Xander murmured, his eyes slowly canvassing her face like he'd never see her again, just like she studied him under the assumption *she'd* never see *him* again. She took note of the light dusting of freckles on his face, and the subtle golden flecks of his eyes she'd only ever seen one other time. How she wished they hadn't wasted that moment, how they could go back to that moment and just keep dancing forever and ever with the rest of the world forgotten around them.

Nyla nodded, even though she hadn't the slightest idea what he was talking about, her throat too dry to speak.

"I think you should pay that back now," Xander started.

"What? Right now?" Nyla stuttered. The illusion of her mind cracked in spite of the softness in his voice. Xander nodded, about to speak again, but she cut him off. "Xander, I'm going off to defeat Dinora! I can't just—"

"I need you to do me a favor and come back," he said earnestly. His desperate eyes held hers, and if Nyla didn't know any better, she'd think she were already dead and that Fate had already spoken—and not in her favor. Her lip wobbled, realizing his words for what they were: the desperate plea of a loved one. "I need you to promise me that you'll come back, no matter what."

Nyla's heart ached. The words she wanted to say caught in her throat. Someone called her name. They were out of time. "I can't promise that, but I don't intend to die…if I can help it anyway."

"Then promise me you won't do anything reckless." His hand grasped hers now, the other cupping her face as though she would turn away from him.

Nyla gave his hand a squeeze. A rueful smile blossomed on her lips. It seemed like that was all she could muster at the moment. She had all she ever wanted, right now. A friend, family, almost safety, a chance at happiness again. But yet it was slipping through her grasp. She hadn't quite gotten it yet, her home.

"Since when have you ever known me to be reckless?"

Xander brushed his thumb over her cheek. A slight smirk quirked his grave features. "Do you really want me to answer that?"

"Miss Delhart!" a gruff voice called behind her. Determined boot steps stomped closer to where they stood, intent on ripping them apart and settling this war once and for all no doubt.

The pair ignored Sir Hubert as he joined Ingrid behind them. Nyla would've been surprised at Ingrid's silence had she been unaware of the hesitation in her energy. It read like a silent permission for Nyla to take this moment, as if Ingrid knew what it was like to have to leave someone behind and fight until a bitter end to come back to them. Even with an urgent wind fueling the soldiers of the combined Caster Corps, Royal Guard, and scant military presence, Ingrid was allowing Nyla to have this moment with Xander, just so she wouldn't have to regret not having it if things turned grim and Dinora stood a chance at victory.

"No," Nyla shook her head, her voice cracking, "you definitely don't need to answer that."

"Nyla." The Mage General grasped her shoulder. "It's time."

Nyla shook her off and kept Xander's intense gaze. "I'll be careful. I promise."

Xander gave her hand a final squeeze. "I'll be right here, waiting. I promise."

Nyla kept Xander's gaze, allowing Ingrid to steer her away. Her hand slipped from Xander's.

No matter how desperately she wished she could hold tight to him and drag him and Merry both somewhere far away from all of this, she knew she had to face this, and that there was the possibility she wouldn't come back. It should've terrified her, but the thought of running away terrified her more.

Nyla knew she needed to see Dinora defeated, or else her mind would never let her find peace or safety, surrounded by people she loved and who loved her.

It didn't stop her from imagining what things would've been like if she'd accepted Xander's offer to run away. They could've run all those weeks ago. This all could've been someone else's quest, and she and Xander, and maybe even Shamira, could've been far, far away from here.

Happy, safe, and home.

If they'd run all those weeks ago, Dinora would've never gotten free, and they could all be off, living their lives in peace.

But where would that have brought them?

Nyla didn't know.

All she knew was the final breath she took as Ingrid clasped her hand. Squeezing her eyes shut against the flash of blush-colored magic, Nyla's lips pressed into a grim line as Ingrid's magic enveloped them both. Nyla's insides flopped as her skin prickled. Not unlike the first time she'd astral traveled, her body was consumed by an unbearable heat and the sensation that her bones and sinew and even her flesh were torn apart by a savage beast. Her breath hitched as she was fused together again only seconds later.

Inhaling deeply, Nyla's mind caught up with her body as if waking for the first time. The sturdiness of the cobblestone pathway was gone. Beneath her feet was a soft cushion that Nyla couldn't name. As the ringing in her ears from having wisped for the first time faded, terrible screeches filled her ears. Her insides knotted together at the inhuman wails. Her muscles coiled tightly. The furious clash of magic grinding against stone and the harsh blasts of gunfire and cannons joined the overwhelming symphony.

At last, Nyla forced her eyes open.

ACKNOWLEDGEMENTS

It's crazy to think that a year ago, I was preparing not only the first novel in the *Heirs of Tenebris* trilogy for publication, but getting ready to make my author debut, and now I'm doing it all over again with *Embers of Eternity*.

I cannot even begin to thank everyone who has supported me through this new chapter, from my readers to the friends I made along the way and of course my family and amazing team at Paper Raven Books. I'd hoped that the more I wrote, the easier my acknowledgements would come, but the truth is they've only gotten harder as my heart has filled with more gratitude.

To my readers, I thank you for journeying into Tenebris alongside Nyla, Xander, and Shamira. Your time is invaluable to me, and I am so incredibly thankful to you for embarking on this adventure, not just beside my characters, but with me as well. I cannot wait to share the conclusion to this story with you, but most of all, I hope you've found a home here in Tenebris and know that you are always welcome back.

To my family, who is just insanely awesome. For bearing with me when I'm being dramatic and dropping publishing bombs in the middle of Thanksgiving dinner or forgetting to tell everyone only to blast it all over social media (SORRY IF THAT'S HOW YOU FOUND OUT!). Y'all have seen my greatest triumphs and my most stressful "I have a deadline next week and I've been procrastinating" moments. Thank you for not only loving me as I am, for supporting me even when my brain short-circuits and my communication skills throw up a "404 error code," but most of all, thank you for taking this journey with me in stride. <3

No matter how often I tell my cover designer and chief graphic artist "thank you," I still feel like it's not enough. From the bottom of my heart, thank you, Marcella! Your designs flawlessly capture what my thousands of words try to emulate, and I couldn't be more honored to work with you on bringing this world to life. Thank you a million and one times (and probably a million and one times more!) for all of your artwork and enthusiasm throughout this adventure. I'm so excited to see where the next chapter takes us both!

The hardest part of my self-publishing journey was facing the prospect of doing this without my amazing, talented, delightful, and encouraging team at Paper Raven Books. I LOVED working with y'all to publish *Fire & Flight,* from our banter to the establishment of #TeamXander in the editing notes, but also because you took my novel and helped me to polish it in a way I couldn't on my own. I knew fairly soon after release week that I wanted to work with y'all again on *Embers of Eternity* and *Winds of War,* and the only thing holding me back from getting the ball rolling was the fact that I was still editing *EoE* at the time! Thank you, thank you, thank you for taking me through this process again with *Embers of Eternity* and sharing with me your expertise, your constructive feedback, but most of all, for your friendship. None of this would've been possible without y'all.

And now for my writeblr friends: For the memes, the amazing snippets we share amongst each other, to the messages we pass back and forth, THANK YOU for creating such a wonderful writing community. I love reading through my dash and look forward to seeing what y'all create next, but most of all for being able to keep tabs on my next great reads. May this be the year we all publish something, big or small, a book or a snippet, traditionally or otherwise.

No matter where in the world you are, I'm so glad you took the time to visit Tenebris. Thank you for taking part in Nyla, Xander, and Shamira's story. I hope you enjoyed your time here!

JOIN THE JOURNEY

Want more from the world of Tenebris? Visit brswrites.com to sign up for my newsletter to receive *Tenebris: An Introduction to the World of Fire & Flight* for FREE as well as access to the archives where additional monthly bonuses crafted just for you will be waiting to be read!

Let's Connect!

Follow me on social media for insights into my life as a writer, fun behind-the-scenes tidbits, and the latest updates on my author journey!

Facebook: @BRSWritesOfficial

Instagram: @brs_writes/

Tumblr: @world-of-fire-and-flight

TikTok: @brswrites

ABOUT THE AUTHOR

Brianna R. Shaffery is a speculative fiction author known for her award-winning young adult fantasy trilogy, the *Heirs of Tenebris*. Always looking toward her next project, Brianna has also written several novellas that can be read on her website, BRSwrites.com.

Aside from her love of literature, Brianna can often be found listening to music while engaged in some kind of craft or whipping up one of her favorite desserts.

DID YOU KNOW THAT READER REVIEWS ARE LIKE GOLD TO INDIE AUTHORS?

For authors, reviews not only give our books some social clout, but they also help readers just like you discover their next read!

Leaving the star rating of your choice and even a line or two about what you honestly thought of the book is a huge boost to indie authors and our book's long-term success. And who knows how many readers like yourself you'll be helping along the way by posting what you thought of the book on retail platforms, your social media, book sites like Goodreads, or on your own blog?

I would be forever grateful if you could leave a review and help me grow as an author.

Happy reading!

BRIANNA R. SHAFFERY